A Perfect Pledge

A Perfect Pledge

RABINDRANATH MAHARAJ

Farrar, Straus and Giroux   New York

Farrar, Straus and Giroux
19 Union Square West, New York 10003

Copyright © 2005 by Rabindranath Maharaj
Printed in the United States of America
Originally published in 2005 by Alfred A. Knopf Canada
Published in the United States by Farrar, Straus and Giroux
First U.S. edition, 2005

Library of Congress Cataloging-in-Publication Data
Maharaj, Rabindranath, 1955–
    A perfect pledge / Rabindranath Maharaj. —1st American ed.
      p. cm.
    ISBN-13: 978-0-374-23070-8 (hardcover : alk. paper)
    ISBN-10: 0-374-23070-6 (hardcover : alk. paper)
    1. Boys—Fiction.   2. Trinidad and Tobago—Fiction.   I. Title.

PR9199.3.M344P47 2005
813'.54—dc22

                                                    2005007070

Designed by Jonathan D. Lippincott

www.fsgbooks.com

1 2 3 4 5 6 7 8 9 10

FOR MY GRANDPARENTS

Part One

On the evening the baby was delivered by Mullai, the village midwife, a chain-smoking dwarf who smelled of roasted almonds, cumin, and cucumber stems, Narpat, who was fifty-five years old and had given up the idea of fathering a son, was sitting cross-legged in the kitchen methodically compiling one of his lists: ginger, saffron, sapodilla, pineapple, avocado, coconut jelly, and *sikya* fig, a small banana found in all the birdcages in the village. Narpat had pored over his list for more than an hour, adding new ingredients and crossing out others. Finally, satisfied that he had achieved a balance between restorative and purgative items, he untwisted a long piece of copper wire from a nail on the wall and stabbed the sheet so that it lay atop a jumble of yellow dietary clippings he had pinched out of newspapers and magazines. Over the years the nail had accumulated scores of lists, most detailing dietary stipulations, but others an odd blend of injunctions and affirmations, and in miniature scribbles, baffling classifications: *Small men with cracked skin who eat quickly and suffer from sleeplessness, accumulate and waste money quickly. Fat men with oily skin and a bad body odour are slow in decisions but fast in temper. Men with a medium body and small, light eyes are enterprising but faultfinding.*

The groceries and fruits were for Narpat, who had calculated, typically, that neither mother nor baby would have much appetite for the next few days. He strung the wire on the nail and returned to the wooden bench, the Pavilion, drawing up both his feet and tracing the veins that ran along his calves to his ankles. When he heard the midwife alternately berating his wife in Hindi and encouraging her in English, he got up, walked to the small wooden porch, and leaned over the railing.

He had single-handedly built the house when he moved from Piarco to Lengua in 1926, thirty years ago, and it had been constructed in the simple style of that time: a boxy, threadbare structure with a roof of corrugated aluminum and walls of unpainted cedar and toporite. "People who live in painted houses," he would tell his daughters, "just playing with fire. The toxic fumes that outgassing bit by bit, will breed bloating and brain fog. Then they will blame these complaints on *obeah* or *maljeau* or *jadoo*. People in this country have a thousand different reasons for every simple thing. It make them smarter, they believe. Like little children trying to understand how a toy operate."

There were other unmistakable traces of Narpat's hand in the design. The front of the building was elevated about three feet from the ground with thick, stubby *mora* logs, but the posts at the back were shorter, or had sunk, so there was a slope all the way to the kitchen. Occasionally Narpat grumbled about the water from the kitchen sink—in reality, a ledge projecting from the back window—spilling over and softening the posts' foundation, but at other times he maintained that the decline would strengthen the calf muscles, enhance balance, and tone up circulation. He told his daughters stories of loggers in Canada balancing on massive trees in the rivers and of sailors from around the world swordfighting on tilting vessels. Transforming the house's defect into a romantic fancy, he sang, "Our own little ship sailing to the Azores, laden with pepper and spice."

The inside of the house was as bare as a ship's deck too. The small front porch, enclosed by shaky wooden bars knocked into a split railing, led to the dining room, its floor built with uneven mora planks so the children could peep through the gaps at the rusted tools and aluminum sheets their father had, over the years, lodged beneath the house. There were spaces on the walls too, which his wife, Dulari, had tried to cover with the calendars she got every Christmas from the Chinese grocer. Whenever she complained that the cedar, hollowed by termites, was paper thin in some spots, Narpat would grin at his three daughters hunched over the low table and weave the almanac pictures of hollies and watchful deities and kittens into implausible stories. When he was finished, he would call one of his three daughters, Chandra, Kala, or Sushilla, to his knees and say, "Crazy story, crazy story."

It was only with his children that his playful side surfaced; for them he had named the bench in the living room the Pavilion; and to its side, the bookcase crammed with manuals on agriculture, diseases, and construction, Carnegie. On its top shelf, enclosed by two dusty glass windows pimpled with mud dauber nests, were old Hindi texts and mysterious yellow folders. One end of the bookcase was elevated with a wedge of *poui* to accommodate the floor's slant. On the other side of the wall was the children's bedroom, with two beds jammed together and taking up half the room's space. Sometimes late at night the girls would be awakened by their father knocking back books in the bookcase, or by conversations, usually in Hindi, from their parents' bedroom. In that room was the only piece of furniture of any significance: a dresser with three oval mirrors and brass-knuckled handles on the wooden drawers. The dresser was a wedding present from Dulari's brother, Bhola, and over the years the wood had warped and the varnish had risen in concentric circles, which had grown so familiar to the children, they seemed to be decorations rather than blemishes. The kitchen, the last room in the house, was a little cubicle with a *chulha*, a clay fireplace set at the corner and surrounded by pots and pans hanging from nails on the wall. The ceiling and the walls were powdered with soot that sometimes dropped on the floor in soft gray clumps, like dead bats. In the nights the smoldering coals in the chulha cast a dull pall on the pots and pans and on the dusty almanacs. The entire house smelled of ashes and woodsmoke, which, Narpat maintained, cleared the lungs of congestion. Just before the chulha was the door leading to Dulari's backyard garden, with small beds of tomatoes, pepper and *melongene*, and *machans*, bamboo trellises with *carailli* and cucumber vines. In the center of the garden a narrow trail of tiny white *melau* pebbles that glinted like scattered shillings in the night led to the latrine.

The beds of marigolds, periwinkles, zinnias, and daisies, and the poinsettia tree and the thorny bougainvillea on both sides of the porch, were also Dulari's. The front yard was paved with asphalt, which had sunk and fragmented into irregular slabs, exposing muddy boulders beneath. To the left of the house, the asphalt had completely succumbed to knot grass, which flourished around the short Julie mango tree and the copper, a huge water basin bought from the sugar factory in St. Madeline.

Narpat heard his wife's groans, loud and dragging, and walked to the copper, partially covered with an aluminum sheet slanted to collect rainwater from the roof. He opened the tap at its base, allowing the water to slide over his open palm, and watched for tadpoles and *keewees*, mosquito larvae. In the backyard garden a wild carailli vine curled up a bamboo stake toward a blue bottle inverted at the top—his wife's defense against maljeau. He removed the bottle and threw it in the air, watching it arc above a clump of wild bananas—*mataboro*, the fruit long and purple. It was shunned by the villagers because of its suggestive appearance, but he knew it was rich in iron and potassium.

If Narpat had been a superstitious man, he would have noticed that his child's birth was not propitious; in a village where parents proudly recounted the peculiar events that heralded their children's arrival, his wife's pregnancy had been singularly ordinary. No favorite pet had turned suddenly vicious; no idler had suddenly disclosed a cure for cancer or diabetes; no new case of madness had been discovered in Lengua.

Lengua, a small, impoverished cane-farming village with a population of about four hundred, was linked to the neighboring villages of Monkeytown, Petite Café, and Barrackpore through a network of crumbling asphalt roads and muddy agricultural traces interrupted by broken bridges, pockets of paragrass, and intervening *lathro*, untamed bushes. The access traces were used mainly by tractors and bull carts, but a few car owners had worked out a risky and complicated tangle of shortcuts. Frequently their vehicles had to be dragged out of the mud by bisons. The roads sank and warped with each rainy season, and the loads of sand and boulders hauled in by government contractors were usually coopted by the villagers for repairs to their yards and houses. The contractors, mostly from San Fernando and Princes Town, complained that entering Lengua was like descending into a swamp. But the land was softened by hills with *immortelle* and *palmiste* and, on their gently rolling slopes, miles of vibrant sugarcane.

The older villagers, mostly Indians with a sprinkle of blacks, Portuguese, and mixed-race *coco panyols*, complained noisily in the rumshops of the village's neglect, but familiarity with their problems—they had known no other life—and a comforting fatalism had dulled the edges of these complaints, and when they returned to their wooden houses and their straggle of bare-bottomed children, they thought only of their crops.

Narpat scorned this backward approach. He was proud of his inventiveness, his knowledge of minutiae, and his determination. He glanced across the road at an abandoned wooden house, its doors and windows removed, thick vines creeping up its sides and disappearing into its decaying cedar walls. Vines grew in the yard too, competing with bristling razor grass and several withered sour orange trees that hosted a family of noisy bananaquits. The tumbledown house had belonged to Samsoonder, who, like almost everyone in Lengua village, was a cane farmer. Four years ago he had packed his seven children and his wife in his pickup van and left for Princes Town. Weak stock, Narpat had thought then. Water in his blood. He had observed Samsoonder and his sons struggling with tables, chairs, chests, and cardboard boxes. Only when they were weaving a network of cables and ropes around furniture piled dangerously on the top did he cross the road and offer instructions on the proper method of anchoring and securing it. "Put all the heavy stuff on the top so it wouldn't fly off when you hit a pothole. And loop the rope a good few times before you strap it to the bumper. Is not a goat allyou tying up here." Narpat had walked back immediately to his house, not bothering to watch the stuttering, lurching van pull off.

Now he returned to the porch and called his children. Kala, who was almost five, came immediately. He took her hands and swung her down the steps. She giggled and asked, "Where we going?"

"Away, away."

"Not Chandra too?"

From the road he called his eldest daughter's name, and she emerged reluctantly, not wanting to leave her mother. "Come, girl. Mammy have to be alone with the midwife."

"Why Sushilla could remain?" Chandra asked.

"Because she is a baby herself. Just three years old. A whole four years younger than you."

They walked along the gravelly road until they came to a cluster of small wooden houses that seemed to be tilting on the sloping land. From one of the houses a mangy pothound bounded out. Chandra drew behind her father, but Kala picked up a pebble and tried to fling it at the dog. "Don't bother with it," Narpat said. "If you don't show fear, it will leave you alone." Some of the neighbors gazing from their porches shouted greetings to the girls. As the family approached the *couteyah*, the temple enclosed by colorfully decorated walls, the children expected to hear one of their father's fables on idolatry, but he was unusually subdued. Dimly recalling an earlier trip, Kala asked, "We going to the sale?"

"Scale." He spelled the word. "The weighing scale shut down now. No bull cart and bison and train there until the end of the crop season in July, when all the cane finish cut."

When they came to the Lengua government school at the intersection of Kanhai road and First Scale road, Chandra pointed to a whitewashed L-shaped building on the hill and whispered to Kala, "My school."

But Kala was transfixed by a lagoon across the road with gently undulating rice. "Pretty grass."

"Rice." Narpat bent and scooped her up. "The land too flat and swampy here to plant cane. And in the rainy season the lagoon does overflow on the road, and hundreds of fishes, *cascadoo* and *guabeen*, does be jumping all over the place."

Narpat recalled a time when Lengua had been a bustling agricultural district, but diseases like witchbroom and the annual floods had decimated the cocoa and coffee plantations, and most of the farmers, broken and bankrupt, had left for the nearby towns of Siparia and Princes Town. Many of these farmers had blanched at the idea of turning to cane because they still linked its cultivation with slavery and bonded labor. The few who remained worked from morning to night during the crop season and barely managed to survive off their small fields.

In his fifty-five years, Narpat had known no other occupation, and though his own father had been swindled out of his field by his brother, he had transferred to his son a reverence for the land. The sequence of events that, he believed, had made him a man had been recalled so often, they were fixed in his mind: the swift transfer of property from his ailing father, his uneducated mother's helplessness in the face of his uncle's treachery, the family's ouster to an abandoned shack, slaving and scrimping as a laborer until, at the age of nineteen, he was able to purchase his first half-acre plot, surveying his little field with pride and anger and each crop season repeating his promise: *Even if I have to die in this field, no one will take it from me.*

They walked in silence now, Chandra struggling to keep up with her father.

Following the birth of each of his daughters, Narpat had listened to the young workers from the adjoining fields bold enough to suggest local remedies for the conception of a son. "Is stupidness like this which pulling this country down," he would say to them before he launched into a general defense of girls. So these workers never suspected that Narpat secretly wished for a son who would grow up strong and confident, and who would follow him to the field to renew the promise he had first made thirty-six years ago in Piarco.

"Mammy goods store," Chandra said as they approached Lumchee's grocery. Though the grocery was closed, the doors of the adjoining rum-shop were open. A group of young men were dancing around a table.

"Tonic for the liver. And half of them don't even hold deeds for their land."

Just past the rumshop, a tiny, bald man in loose cotton clothing and oversize wooden shoes, *sapats*, was pushing a Humber bicycle. He slowed as Narpat approached. His ears were so hairy, it seemed as if a little animal had roosted inside. "Pretty baby," he said, and when Chandra emerged from behind her father, he added graciously, "Another pretty girl." Huzaifa was one of the few villagers not put off by Narpat's brusque manner. From his bicycle handlebar was slung a khaki bag with books pil-fered from YesRead, where he worked. "All my children big already so I does spend the whole night reading. These nights I reading about the Indian Independence and the Congress." He moistened his thumb as if he were about to turn a page. "Thick, thick book. Two, sometimes three inch. They talking about independence down here now. Have some book-let in the store too, but I don't think anything will come of it. Communist fellas. Booklet barely half-inch thick."

"Little children arguing about a playground. What you think this inde-pendence will accomplish here? It will suddenly make everybody smarter?"

Huzaifa dug into an ear and played with its hair. "We could make our own clothes. Spinning jenny. Sell it right here."

"We doing that already. And it does last a month, if so long." Huzaifa was warming to the topic, but Narpat walked away, adding, "People here want independence because they think is a big pappyshow with fete and holiday and plenty rum." About five minutes later he told his daughters, "It getting late. Better we hurry back to see if your mammy make another girl or a little boy."

"I want a girl." Chandra, suddenly excited, tugged at her father's hand.

"Boy." Kala raised her head from Narpat's shoulder.

———

At that exact moment, Dulari took one look at her thin, knobby-looking son and remembered a bloodied *carite* head she had seen at the Princes Town fish market, the mouth slightly open, the eyes bulging from its soft, dark-gray face. "Hold him," the midwife croaked. "Plenty baby does resemble monkey and fish," though this was, by far, the least attractive baby she had ever delivered. "Hold him!" She toppled the baby into his mother's stiff arms. Jeevan opened his tiny fish mouth and wailed.

$\mathscr{J}$eevan was sickly right from the beginning. Some of the neighbors whispered about Dulari's age, and others mentioned Narpat's well-known dietary eccentricities. The boy developed sores on his knees from creeping about on the hard floor, and Dulari nightly applied a balm of aloes to his feet. Occasionally his mother placed him on the step leading to her garden while she picked at the weeds. Once he rolled off the step and crept beneath the house. She dropped her cutlass, pulled him out, and dusted his knees and palms. "Don't ever go there again, Jeeves. You understand?" As was the habit with Trinidadian Indians, she had shortened and anglicized his name. The new name stuck.

Every evening Jeeves squatted with Chandra, Kala, and Sushilla on the Pavilion and listened to lengthy lectures on ethics, religion, and nutrition. His sisters sat attentively, chins on cupped palms, but Jeeves struggled to stay awake. Occasionally he recalled the straggle of little boys he had spotted earlier in the day, running along the road dragging sardine cans fashioned into cars and trucks or returning from the rivers with strings of guabeen and cascadoo, and at other times he focused on a cockroach crawling on the wooden floor planks. He frequently dozed off, awakened by the moths banging against the gas lamp set atop Carnegie.

Interwoven into the lectures were snippets of information on cane farming, the island's politics, and fables that Narpat called "Nancy stories." One of these fables terrified Jeeves, and he would cover his ears whenever his father was midway, though he had heard its conclusion many times. The story was of a warrior besieged in battle and, in desperation, promising his god the first person he saw when he returned to his homeland. "This master fighter, tired like a dog, finally reach home. And

the first person he spot was his last little child running out to greet him."
Narpat would pluck Jeeves from the bench and hoist his squirming son
before him. "But the warrior had already made a promise so he had no
choice."

Jeeves would look in confusion at his father's face, stricken with the
clench of too many frowns, and then hear his mother from the kitchen,
her voice seeming to float on a long sigh, "Leave the boy alone. Don't
frighten him for nothing."

As the evening progressed, Narpat grew more serious. He constantly
criticized the neighbors, who were busily wiring their houses ever since
electricity had come to Lengua a year ago. "What you see happening
around here," he told his children one night, "is nothing more than follow
fashioness. Monkey see, monkey do. What is the point of this electricity
nonsense when you could get the brightest light from any gas lamp? No
outage, no blackout, no monthly bill." Jeeves gazed at a moth trapped inside the lampshade, scraping the soot with its frantic fluttering. "And why
you want a big, fancy concrete house when a small, humble, two-bedroom
hut with no unnecessary furniture is so comfortable? A hammock? That
is the prime cause of laziness and hunchback. A rocking chair? The shakes.
Malkadee. A couch? Stoop shoulder and lumbago. I could spot these
couch people from a mile walking like if they dragging a tail." Jeeves tried
to imagine these strange people. After each lecture, his mother fed him a
bowl of soup made from pumpkin vines, fever grass, and vervine brought
in the evenings from the canefield by Narpat. Occasionally this grim diet
was enlivened by slices of mangoes or squishy pawpaws or wedges of fragrant soursop.

The nighttime arrangements were disastrous both for Jeeves and for
his sisters—who drew turns to nap next to him—not only because he was
a boy but also because the diet administered by his father left him suffering frequent bouts of diarrhea. "The system getting rid of all the slush and
sledge," his father said. "I have to strengthen you up so you could help me
in the canefield." This was the only intimation to the boy that he was different from his sisters, and it managed to transform his tasteless meals
into a manageable ritual. Each morning, while his sisters were dressing
for school with their white blouses and green skirts, plaiting and oiling
their hair, dusting their faces with Johnson's Baby Powder, his mother re-

moved the old plastic tablecloth she had placed beneath the sheet the night before, examined it for stains, flipped it a few times, then draped it over the railing on the porch. Jeeves would stand next to the bed, his thumb in his mouth, and stare at this early morning activity. One evening Chandra, the eldest sister, complained about Jeeves's "bulgy eye watching me all the time" and received a stern reprimand from their father who had named the bedroom the Barracks because in it sleeping arrangements were fluid and everyone was treated equally. "Our own little commune," he had said. "The way all proper family suppose to operate."

The sisters, particularly Chandra and Kala, were irritated by Jeeves's constant clapping at the mosquitoes trapped inside the bed's netting, the wet, lapping sound he made sucking his thumb, and the way he would follow them to the porch when they were leaving for school, wearing a nightie they had outgrown. Occasionally he was massaged with a yellow *hardi* and turmeric paste to deter sandflies and mosquitoes. His sisters bolted down the road, praying that none of their schoolmates would notice Jeeves glowing like a weak bulb and peeping through the wooden balusters, the nightie skimming the ground.

Jeeves would remain in the porch for a while, watching the little boys shouting and laughing on their way to school, until his mother shooed him inside with her *cocoyea* broom for his orange juice and his small bowl of soup. This special diet didn't agree with him; each month he grew knobbier, and his knees, his eyes, and his shoulder blades more protuberant. His mother usually started the day in a good mood, but after she had cooked, swept the entire house with her cocoyea broom, and washed the wares on the wooden ledge projecting from the kitchen and the clothes on the ribbed concrete tub outside, she was flustered and short-tempered. By then the light-colored cotton dresses she favored would be damp and smudged with ashes and vegetable stains. Only when her three daughters returned from school, their khaki bookbags crammed with loose paper and pencils, would she soften a bit and inquire about their day while she set the food on the table.

Jeeves was frequently annoyed by Chandra's tendency to follow him around circumspectly and by Kala's habit of interrupting and correcting his manner of speaking. Most of all, though, he was peeved that they were allowed to go to Hakim's parlor, about ten minutes away, to fetch butter and cheese and tins of sardine. In her own way Sushilla was just as insufferable because she would cry for inexplicable slights and hide beneath the table until she was coaxed out by her mother.

Once he had followed Chandra halfway to the parlor, hiding in the roadside ditch until a neighbor, One-foot Satoo, spotted him. Chandra ran back screaming, and Jeeves, fished out by his mother and dragged to the porch, received a serious flogging. When his father returned from the canefield at six-thirty, he told Jeeves, "Right now you have more than one hundred germs crawling all over you and inside your body like *bachac*, eating up everything on the way. Hookworm and tapeworm already climbing up to find a nice nest next to your kidneys. You ever hear about this little boy who used to play in these nasty drains?" Narpat gazed at his son's sickly body. "He end up looking like a crappo fish that not even his own mother could recognize. A black, nasty, slimy tadpole." He glanced once more at his son and conjured a pet name. "You understand, Carea?" Jeeves, imagining the queasiness in his stomach to be the hookworm and tapeworm establishing a beachhead, shook his head. "The only cure is the cornhocks."

Kala ran immediately into the kitchen and returned with a corn husk, ribbed like a frayed, elongated grenade. Narpat hauled Jeeves outside to the copper, dipped in an aluminum bucket, and heaved the water over his son's naked body. Jeeves pressed his palms against his eyes and spluttered. While Narpat was lathering him with a blue, foul-smelling laundry soap, he explained that the drain was overflowing with dead animals, water snakes, and leeches that could hide between his toes and live there for years. Jeeves raised a leg and tried to spread his toes. The rainwater from the barrel mingled with the soap to form a soft oily solution that was difficult to wash off, so Jeeves had several buckets of water dashed against him before he was led into the house, abraded and thoroughly cleansed. That night he received an especially strong dose of the laxative senna, and Chandra, whose turn it was to sleep next to him, remained awake for half the night, sniffing and murmuring.

Two weeks later, a month after Jeeves's fourth birthday, Narpat hired Janak, a stiff, morose man who owned the only taxi in the village, an Austin Cambridge with a cracked windshield and its shocks shot through, to carry the family to the Ramleela celebrations at St. Julien's village, about half an hour from Lengua. Janak had also decided to bring along his four sons, who sat in the back with Chandra, Kala, and Sushilla. The boys were as stiff and grim-looking as their father, and while Jeeves's three sisters frowned in displeasure, their neatly ironed dresses threatened by this intrusion, Jeeves, sitting atop his mother, shifting each time the car landed in one of the potholes, took in the view.

They passed Hakim's parlor, its front steps almost running into the road, then a few wooden houses built on awkward slopes and, as the car grated on, a pond with ducks swimming in the muddy water. Beyond the pond, a bison was dragging a log while its owner swished his whip on the animal's back. After about ten minutes they came to a road curving down a hill and narrowed by a jagged landslide. Exposed boulders and gravel dredged and beaten by the rain were scattered all along the slope, which, Jeeves saw, led to a ravine shadowed by tangled bamboo. A few etiolated pawpaw trees with sickly yellow leaves clung to the eroding soil.

Janak drove slowly, making no attempt to evade the potholes, and Jeeves peered out of the car to gauge the distance between the tires and the landslide. Occasionally, to save on gas, Janak switched off the engine and allowed the car to coast before he kick-started it with a jerk that pitched the children forward. His eldest son, lanky and bony, pursed his lips and made a strange droning sound. Chandra, sitting next to him, tossed her hair angrily and squeezed forward.

"This road is killing my vehicle. Just now the whole place will cave away. But my understanding is the government don't care—"

"All these homeowners have to do is build some good soakaway at the back and retaining walls at the side. One weekend work."

Jeeves pushed his head out of the window to look at a narrow wooden bridge that groaned and shook as the car passed over the loose planks. Farther along he spotted men and women, some on bicycles, with cutlasses slung from their waists. A few of the women glanced at Janak's vehicle, and one of them said, "Where you going with that sardine can, Janak?"

His eldest son stopped droning. "Daddoes! I tell you that would happen." He tried to stamp his feet, and Chandra tugged her skirt away.

"Don't worry, Bankey. Dog have mouth. Let them bark." And after a while, "Let them try to go to the Ramleela in they tractor." Bankey rattled out a high-pitched chortle. "See how long it will take." Bankey's brothers joined in his mirth. "Pok-pok-pok-splut-splut." Janak imitated a tractor stalling. His children giggled.

But Narpat put an end to this frivolity. "I travel once on a tractor straight from Lengua to Port of Spain. Take me the whole day. August the eighteenth, nineteen forty-seven. It was during the war, when these Americans had set up their base in Chaguaramas. Everybody was rushing to work there because of the nice American dollars. Half the sugar mills shut down during that time." As he recounted his trip, Janak's children sank into a fretful gloominess.

A few minutes later Janak pulled up alongside a parlor, a huge wooden box balanced on two planks atop a drain. He got out of the car and asked solemnly, "Penny sweet drink and sugar cake? Anybody want?" His children snorted and raised their hands. "One hand, two, three, four. That make it four penny sweet drink in all."

"*And* four sugar cake," Bankey rasped.

"*And* four," Janak repeated. "Children nowadays," he gushed. "They too smart." He peered into the car. "Any more hands? Only four?"

"These children don't drink sugar water," Narpat said. "Poison does taste nice sometimes." When Janak returned, Narpat added, "You know how these sellers does make sugar cake? Grind up the coconut with their teeth and spit it out in a bowl with sugar and water. Careful you don't find any teeth in it." For the rest of the trip, Janak's children turned their sugar cakes, biting cautiously.

Narpat remained silent until they approached the crowded town with the wares of small shops advertised on elaborate Plexiglas signs and gaudy banners strung above the doorways. As the car inched forward in the traffic, he pushed his head out of the window and shouted to a listless policeman hovering outside Maggie's bar, "Why you don't lock up all them idlers instead of looking for a free drink?"

The policeman glanced up angrily, but Janak, grinding his gears, overtook two slow-moving cars and moved out of view. "That Pangay is a bad man to cross. He don't make joke."

"He just looking for bribe. Like everybody else in this country. Trinidad. Tricki-dad. Everybody with some scheme in their back pocket." He turned to the children in the back. "Learn it when they still small. While children in other country learning to read and write, here they mastering trickery and thiefing." As they approached the recreation ground where the Ramleela was being enacted, the children came to life. They spotted a huge cardboard cutout of Ravana, the twelve-headed demon-god, swaying in the air. Jeeves had never been to this festival before. He was impatient to get out of the car, and while Janak searched for a parking spot alongside the road, shaking his head at the erratically parked vehicles, Jeeves gazed at the *rakshas*, the demons, their bodies glistening with black oil, and the *rishis*, wise old sages with beards made from loosened ropes. Skipping monkey-men with rigid, erect tails and animals with papier-mâché faces and cardboard torsos scampered about.

Finally Janak squeezed in between two cars, slightly bumping the vehicle behind him. Jeeves wanted to rush into the ruckus, but his mother's firm grasp restrained him. Vendors were standing over boxes filled with *doubles*, oily chickpea sandwiches, and pickled mangoes and *pomme-cythere*. Janak and his children disappeared into the crowd, and a few minutes later Jeeves's sisters wandered off with their mother.

Standing by his father, Jeeves was exhilarated by the aroma of sweetmeats, the chatter coursing though the crowd, the actors dancing and jousting with one another, and the pulsating rat-a-tat of *tassa* drums. But his father, who started walking ahead, said, "Primitive nonsense. People hopping about and making a mockery of their religion." When he passed the vendors, he said, "Toxins. Look at how much bloat-up people it have in this crowd. Diabetes and stroke just waiting to happen. The poison shoot straight up to their brains. Eating up everything on the way."

A mournful Hindi film song grated out from two loudspeakers fastened to the branches of a *samaan* tree. A group of young men danced tipsily to the music, wriggling their fingers above their heads while executing complicated twirls. When they moved on, he told his son, "In ancient times, these festivals wasn't just a pappyshow with drunken, sickly people parading about in their fancy clothes. They were like training camps." He gestured dismissively to the dancing men. "Look at them. Look at how far the Aryans fall. They take all these great ideas and make it in a big game. What you think all these *munis* and rishis would say if they know that these things that they take centuries to write, end up as a big pappyshow?" He didn't wait for a response. "How much people around here really understand the meaning of this performance? Not one! Not a single one." Jeeves stared at an actor with antlers fashioned from a guava branch pretending to butt a group of excited young boys who had strayed into the rectangular area reserved for the performance. "And that family over there." He gestured to a chubby teenaged boy plodding along with his fat, sweating parents. "A perfect example of a couch family. Couch father, couch mother, and couch son. They not going to last too long because the spine already damage. Liver and kidneys cramp up and twist out of shape. Mucus leaking from every vent. The organs have only thirty percent cranking potential again, if so much."

A few men greeted Narpat but then hurried away. Jeeves was given a brief commentary on each of them. "Goolcharan. Suppose to be a *sadhu* taking care of the Craignish temple, but every night he in the cinema. Cinema Sadhu, they call him. And Malik. The most popular doubles vendor in Princes Town. You notice how dirty his fingers was? Salmonella and gastro. Kill more people than World War One and Two combine."

Finally one couple stood their ground: Dulari's brother, Bhola, his wife, Babsy, and their daughter. "Ay-ay. How you and the boy land up alone so?" Bhola, a stocky man whose paunch was neatly outlined in his tight banlon jersey, glanced at his wife, a tall, straight woman with thin, impatient lips. "You didn't see little Mr. Dubay here?" He chortled and tugged the hair above Jeeves's ear roughly. His wife ignored Jeeves, pulling her little girl—who had already developed the mother's rigid features—closer.

"I didn't cut out to be a duck with fourteen children quacking behind me. Women have their own matters to discuss, and that is none of my business."

The wife moved away. "Come on, Bhola. We missing all the drama. Come on, Prutti."

"Yes, go. Go and see the pappyshow. It good for little children. Plenty jokes and thing. Real interesting and educational."

"Okay, little Dubay." Bhola pinched Jeeves's arm, almost wringing out a gob of flesh. "We will leave you two to enjoy the pappyshow." He shot out a clattering laugh. The mother spun around angrily, and the daughter, almost in the same fashion, pirouetted and strode off.

"Take a good look at that family. That spread-out walk of Bhola mean that he have a serious case of *godi*. Hernia. Weak abdominal muscles. Stones tie up in a knot. Everything slipping down. Mother and daughter no better either. Not out in the sun long enough. Living in the dark like cockroach. That is why they was perspiring so much and blocking the sun with their hand." Bhola, some distance away, clapped a man on his shoulder. "A very bad influence."

"Who?" Jeeves asked.

"Your uncle Bhola. He have a mistress."

"What is that?"

"Another wife."

Jeeves tried to make sense of this, then gave up. They passed a vendor scooping out shaved ice from a bucket, slapping it into a glass, lathering the cone with syrup, topping it with a dribble of condensed milk, then whacking out the compressed ice from the glass.

"Snowball. You want one?"

Jeeves knew he should refuse, but the sight of the excited children clustered around the vendor, and others walking away licking their cones and dipping their fingers in the condensed milk, was too much. "I could have one?"

"Wait right here."

Narpat returned, holding the snowball before his face as if it were a glowing light. Jeeves took the snowball, punched a hole at the tip, and slurped some of the icy syrup. He crumbled away thimbles of ice and sucked joyfully. Throughout his father was silent, but when Jeeves was licking the red dye that had rolled down his elbow, he asked, "How it taste?"

"Sweet. It taste sweet and nice."

"So you happy now?"

Jeeves looked up at his father and smiled.

"Now tell me how long you think this happiness will last?"

Jeeves puzzled over the question.

"Where the snowball now?"

"It finish."

"Good. Very good. And that is exactly what happen to the happiness too. It finish. But you know what remain? The paint and the sugar. In a hour or two they will start working on you. Plastering the stomach. Coating the vessels. Slowing down the system. Now tell me what lesson you learn?"

Jeeves thought for a while. "That snowball will make you sick?"

"Good. Very good. People who only interested in a few minutes of happiness without bothering to think about what going to happen later don't last too long. Instant gratification. Say gratification."

He looked at the red trickle on his wrist. "Gra-fi-ashan."

"Remember that word good. Bhola look like he forget it. Now let us go and look for the women and them."

Holding Jeeves's hand, Narpat steered him to a shirtless man squatting and turning a tassa drum against a coalpot. "They have to heat up the goatskin for it to make a good sound. Heat it up good, brother," he told the squatting man. When they walked away, he said, "You notice how muscular his hands was compare with the rest of his body? Is hard work beating that drum."

"He tired then?" Jeeves glanced back.

"Too drunk to be tired. He operating on automatic." He told Jeeves that alcohol released gas bubbles in the brain, the bubbles merging until it was big enough to take over the body like a copilot, but his son had stopped listening; a few yards away a very dark man with his long hair tied in a ponytail and with a thin, slippery-looking moustache that ran straight down his chin, was brandishing a wand, dipping the flaming tip into his mouth, puffing out his cheeks, then withdrawing the still-glowing tip. A group of children watched in fascination.

"Fire-eater." Narpat chuckled.

"How he could do that?"

"Easy. Is not real fire. Only crappo could eat fire."

"It look real."

Narpat smiled. "Everything look real if you not paying proper attention." He walked up to the fire-eater. "I could borrow that for a minute?"

The fire-eater looked confused, but he gave Narpat the wand, thinking perhaps that this impudent spectator wished to test the heat of the fire, but as he watched in astonishment, Narpat opened his mouth wide and plunged the burning tip inside.

Jeeves uttered a stifled cry. He saw his father's mouth with a trace of a smile closing around the fire, the look of surprise and pain in his eyes, his cheeks swelling, spitting out the wand, and coughing out little drops of fire.

For the rest of the afternoon, Narpat remained silent. He said nothing when the crowd gathered excitedly for the ceremonial burning of the Ravana effigy; he held his peace when, on the way back, Janak commented on the Ramleela; he made no comment when the children gushed about the club fights and the funny cardboard animals. But when Janak dropped them off, he leaned over and whispered to Jeeves, "I have the cleanest mouth in the whole village now. Properly sterilize. Burn out all the germs and parasites. Get rid of them for good." He smiled painfully.

THREE

The week after the Ramleela in September, rain fell continuously, darkening the sky and sending Jeeves scurrying to the kitchen each time he heard the rumbling of thunder. Water filled the drains and spilled over into the roads, filling the potholes and submerging parts of the village, so that entire areas were cut off. Huge chunks of mud caved away from Crappo Patch, a landslide-prone section of Lengua. Wooden huts on the slopes lost their mooring and tilted like frozen dancers. A small house collapsed one morning, the frightened children rescued by a neighbor who lined them up, counting and recounting laboriously to make sure his rescue effort was not in vain. Bisons with humps of mud struggled in the brown water, dragging logs that sometimes stuck in the sludge.

Lettuce, cabbage, and pakchoi floated in the water, filling the air with the smell of rotting vegetation. The water rose and receded, then rose again with each new thunderstorm. Sadhus from the neighboring villages stood before the couteyahs they oversaw and invoked their favorite deities; when these entreaties failed, the Brahmin pundits, armed with Sanskrit books, were summoned. Schools closed early and parents grew short-tempered with their children. Jeeves spent the mornings gazing at his mother standing on the table and patching the holes on the roof with putty and tar. When he grew bored of catching errant drops in his open mouth, he wandered to the kitchen step and stared at the carailli vines swishing like snakes in the muddy water. A young, nondescript journalist known only as Partap's son descended on the villages and filed dramatic stories, many beginning with, "On a day blight with black, quarreling clouds . . ."

One night Narpat came home later than usual, when it was already dark, slushing in his tall tops and leaving muddy trails on the wooden floor. Jeeves eyed the tall tops hungrily but knew he would be rebuked if he attempted to slip his feet into them. During those evenings Narpat did not lecture his children on ethics or nutrition, but with his head propped against the wall and his palms flat on his knees, he spoke about the desperate attempts of farmers to haul their cane to higher ground. He explained that most of the crop was now useless because of the rain's intensity, and that the flood had been caused by a hurricane called Flora that had destroyed most of the coastal villages in Tobago, the sister isle. Trinidad had escaped the eye of the hurricane, but houses in Debe and Penal were almost buried in water. He pulled a foot up and showed his toes, swollen from tramping in his drenched tall tops. While Jeeves stared at his father's dilated toes, noting how much they looked like cherries and briefly wondering if they had the same taste as his thumb, Chandra said that her teacher had spoken to the class about the destruction in Tobago and had asked the students to donate unused clothes and toys. She stood up expectantly, wringing her hands until Narpat asked her to fetch the old clothing. Both she and Kala ran into their bedroom and returned with Jeeves's nightie. Jeeves removed his thumb from his mouth and glanced at his father.

"You getting too big for this now, Carea," he said, using his pet name for the boy. "Time you get a proper outfit. Something decent and comfortable. A nice flour bag shirt. The solid material will toughen your skin just like a shell. You hear that, Mammy," he shouted to his wife in the kitchen. Then his mood lightened, and he told his children that he was drawing up plans for the village council, which met at the end of each month, to build a web of drains, aqueducts, and dikes to prevent flooding, and he was also thinking of constructing a moat around the house. Kala asked if he would fill the moat with alligators and water snakes, and he smiled and changed the topic. Some nights their mother pulled a stool and listened silently, but later the children heard her worried voice percolating from their parents' bedroom.

Then as suddenly as it had descended, the rain stopped. Children on their way to school dipped their feet in the potholes and kicked up the watery mud. A few pothounds ventured out and sniffed the drains. Ducks wandering about like drunken midgets were chased back to their ponds.

Walls were hurriedly repainted and posts strengthened by pounding boulders around their bases. The sun baked the mud on the road and congealed the silt that had been washed beneath the houses into crumbly wafers. Waves of heat, thick and smelly, rose from the road. The humidity was so strong that everything seemed weighted with lead. Dulari banished her son to the bedroom with one of Narpat's *National Geographics*, while she shoveled away the mud from the front yard and pulled out the soggy tomatoes and the carailli vines from the back. When she saw Jeeves peeping from the gallery, she warned him about water snakes and lizards just waiting to climb up his new flour bag pants. He rushed back to his bedroom and flipped through the *National Geographic*, staring at men and women naked but for straw skirts, and monkeys hanging by their tails from trees.

Dulari grew increasingly short-tempered. Her irritation was directed not only toward Jeeves; when Sushilla returned home with carbuncles on her knees, she was reprimanded for scratching and set in the corner, smelling of camphor, aloes, and saffron paste. Once Jeeves noticed her tasting the mixture and reported this to their mother. For the remainder of the afternoon, Sushilla glared at Jeeves from beneath the table, grumbling, "Little news carrier."

By contrast, Narpat grew increasingly mellow. He scratched outlines of his proposed aqueducts and dikes on the ends of cardboard boxes. The children sitting around him peered at the detailed illustrations while the gas lamp choked and threw a flickering light on the cardboard, making the drawings seem like small dismembered animals.

He became more expansive as the night drew on. The flood, he told them, was not the result of divine punishment, as some of the villagers were claiming, but was a natural occurrence that, if harnessed, could lead to surprising benefits. He thrust out his hands and said that the world was constantly balancing itself. The silt that had been swept beneath the houses and into the backyard gardens was rich in nutrients. The houses buffeted by the water were little reminders to the owners about repairs postponed. His own house—he stamped his feet on the sloping floor—had survived because it was built with precision and foresight. Anything that was defective or weak must be swept away: this was how the earth cleansed itself. Countries like Trinidad were in particular danger because nothing was ever attempted with planning and foresight.

In the kitchen, Dulari tapped her broom loudly, the way she did when she was exasperated, but the children, fascinated by Narpat's commentaries, forgot the discomfort of the last few weeks and listened attentively. Narpat brought out his old Hindi texts from Carnegie and said that the world was always changing, and those who were not prepared were swept away. "Right this very minute, each of you changing." He looked at his children circumspectly, as if he could detect these changes. Jeeves glanced at his arms and legs. At night, while they lay in bed, the images of ancient, engulfed cities drowned the sound of displeasure from their parents' bedroom.

One Friday night Narpat showed them one of his more detailed drawings, which looked like an ascending submarine. He explained that they would soon have hot water with which to bathe. "Is the flood that give me this idea. All this water that cause so much damage could be very useful with the right planning. But you have to be a futurist to see this. Take all that heat that coming up from the chulha, for instance. What happening to it? It escaping, just escaping. Yet is the same heat that does power train from city to city, and ship from country to country."

The next morning a hammering on the aluminum roof awakened them. They ran outside and saw Narpat on a ladder balanced against the eaves, hauling up a bucket of water. Two lengths of pipe had been removed from beneath the house and now stood at the side of the ladder.

"Allyou move out from there quick sharp before that water contraption fall on somebody head." The children rushed back to the porch to their mother, who was shaking her head in dismay. For most of that morning, she glanced up apprehensively at her husband hammering away. At night she and Narpat could be heard quarreling from their bedroom.

"All right, the hot-water system complete now." The children bounded out and saw Narpat on the topmost rung of the ladder, gazing at a network of pipes running from a barrel perched on two scantlings on the roof, down to the side of the house, where they were tied together with bicycle tubing. "It still have a little work here and there. Have to get a proper valve and some unions and a lock joint to stabilize the apparatus good and proper. Get it to balance. It still rocking a little bit." He glanced at the barrel. "But it should hold."

The next day Jeeves was dragged by his ear from the yard. "What happen, you looking for gold and silver?" His mother kicked the mound of mud Jeeves had been exploring. "I wonder if any pile up here?" She scanned the roof. "Or maybe you come outside for a nice hot bath. That blasted, blasted man." For the rest of the afternoon Jeeves puzzled over that statement.

Then unexpectedly, the quarreling stopped. Two entire days passed without any major flogging. Tasty fruits were served with dinner, Julie mangoes, pawpaw and slices of pineapple. In the middle of the week stew chicken and pigeon peas and wedges of sweet potato, a meal usually reserved for Sundays, were placed on the table. The children, intrigued by this pleasant development, pressed their ears against the wall, straining to hear the conversation from their parents' room, glancing at one another when they caught bits of laughter and strange, purring sounds.

Chandra and Kala both offered differing interpretations over the mix of Hindi and English their parents used in private conversations. One night Chandra, who had been lying awake in bed, bolted up. "Baby!"

"A baby going to happen tonight?" Jeeves asked.

Sushilla glanced dismissively at Jeeves. "Stupidee. It take"—she paused. "It take one year."

Chandra pressed a finger against her lips. "Shh. Go turn down the wick and sleep." After half an hour Jeeves fell asleep, dreaming of squirming babies stacked on the Pavilion.

The next morning he followed his mother around, flicking swift glances at her belly, but Chandra had cautioned him not to ask any questions. His mother smiled wryly and patted him on his head. Later, while she was poking the firewood in the chulha, she said, "Let me see what Bhola will say now. Let me see what Babsy will say when we buy it."

Buy it?

In the afternoon Jeeves reported this snippet to Chandra. She snapped the rubber band holding her plaits, chewed her lip, and frowned. But she could make no sense of it.

A few hours later the mystery was laid to rest. Their mother barged excitedly into the children's bedroom. "Come quick. You hearing it?" Jeeves listened for a baby's cry but could hear only a faint grumbling in the distance. "Come in front." They had never seen her so agitated.

The rumbling grew louder.

Dulari wiped her hands in her apron and held Jeeves before her on the porch. The growling grew into a clatter as if something far away were crashing to the ground. Dulari held Jeeves tighter. He looked up at her face. The house vibrated and wobbled. The pipe hanging from the roof swung like a pendulum. The barrel rocked on the scantlings. A slight frown appeared on her face. Jeeves glanced at his sisters and then stared in the direction of the commotion.

"Daddy!" Sushilla ran to the yard. "On a tractor."

"Get back here now."

Jeeves freed himself from his mother's clasp and climbed the railing. From around the corner an old rusty tractor seemed headed straight for the house.

"Get back here now, I say. Look how old it is. You don't know if it have brakes." Dulari sighed, and in that sigh Jeeves felt that all her enthusiasm had bled away.

The tractor headed for the drain, spluttering and coughing up slabs of mud. It stalled briefly, then seemed to leap into the air with a roar and charge into the yard. Jeeves screamed and fell off the railing. Miraculously, it stopped right before the front step. Narpat stood on the axle, his legs on either side of the seat, surveying his astonished family and waving his hat like a cowboy. "You like it, Mammy? Top of the line."

Dulari gazed at the rusty tractor and thought of a skeletal beetle and then of a dead crab. The tractor shuddered and belched up a spurt of smoke through its upright exhaust. She smelled the gas and glanced at the dented fuel tank and the line leaking gas onto her crushed zinnias, daisies, and marigolds. "It nice."

"Just nice? Is a top-of-the-line tractor. A Farmall H. Nineteen forty-one model." He tapped the long rusty pipe onto which the steering wheel was attached. "Four-cylinder incline overhead valve. Idle speed of sixteen hundred. Firing order of one, three, four, and two." The tractor, as if understanding, bucked violently, spitting sparks above Narpat's head. He grinned. "You see the power? Is like a wild horse." He patted the steering wheel and ran his fingers along the pipe. "I think I might have to tame him a little bit. Break him in. All right, who want to go for a ride?" Jeeves's sisters glanced at their father and at the old smoke-belching tractor, but when their mother walked silently inside, they followed her. "The last train to Bangalore pulling out now," Narpat said jovially. "Hop aboard, hop aboard before it full up." Jeeves walked down the step to the tractor and Narpat bent down and hoisted him up. "Women and machinery don't mix much." He ground into reverse, and the tractor jerked back sharply. Jeeves almost tumbled off his father's lap. They pulled off in a cloud of smoke, bouncing over the drain.

"You smelling that smoke? Is the best thing for some of these stubborn bacteria and them. Wipe them clean out. Take a deep breath." Jeeves inhaled and felt dizzy, but Narpat shouted, "You just kill out half the hookworm in your belly." And a few minutes later, "You notice them loosening up with all this bouncing up and down?"

Jeeves felt a soreness in his body each time he landed on his father. "Yes. I feeling them."

They passed Crappo Patch, a stretch of narrow, dilapidated roads dotted with mostly abandoned houses. A dog, startled into motion by the tractor, ran yapping after them. Soon other dogs joined. "Royal escort." Narpat chuckled. He shifted gears, and soon the dogs were left behind. "Hold tight. We pulling into Toolia trace to survey the canefield." Jeeves held tightly to the steering wheel, twisting with its rotation.

Narpat drove more slowly now, explaining to Jeeves that the squealing, flapping sound was caused by a loose belt. He suspected that the fuel line was too close to the exhaust manifold, causing vapor lock and misfiring. He would have to wrap some aluminum around the line and, when he was finished, check the radiator for lime buildup and core leakage. Jeeves strained to hear what his father was saying, fascinated by his knowledge of so many things. "Every single pound of pressure raise the boiling point by three degrees. Might have to change the pressure cap, or that hose right below there will blow straight out." He swelled his cheeks and made a popping sound. Jeeves laughed.

They passed a few tired-looking men returning from the fields, and Narpat shouted to a young man seated on a bison, "Time to trade in that *bhisa*, Jairam, for a newer model." He came to a creaking stop beneath a mango tree with the branches spreading over the road. He stood on the seat and raised Jeeves onto his shoulders. "Pick the reddish one." Jeeves reached for a plump purple fruit and twisted it off its stem. "Calabash mango. The sweetest variety you could find anywhere. Full of vitamins and iron." He allowed Jeeves to climb down from his shoulder and retrieved a penknife from his pocket.

While Jeeves was eating the sweet, spicy mango, Narpat pointed to his field. "Your legacy. Hard work but honest. You don't have to outsmart anybody or depend on anyone when you own one small plot of land. 'Cause it always there." He jumped down from the tractor and spread his arms, but Jeeves clutched the seat and dismounted carefully. "When you depend on the land for your livelihood, you grow close to it. Like a part of the family." The dusty track leading to the field was shadowed by a towering hogplum tree with perpetually yellow leaves. "Careful you slip on these." His father pointed to the carpet of spotted hogplums on the track. Kiskidees and semps were flitting from fruit to fruit.

Jeeves inhaled the sweet, decaying fragrance. "It good to eat?"

"Only if you suffering from constipation."

As they walked alongside the narrow drains separating the cane into rectangular plots, Narpat explained that unlike most of the other farms, his field had escaped the brunt of the flood because it was on slightly higher ground. He held Jeeves's arms lightly and swung him over a drain. The trickling water was transparent enough for Jeeves to notice tiny black conches fastened to mossy pebbles. While they were walking in the field, Narpat spoke about his early days in the canefield, like his father and grandfather before him. He mentioned the negligible price paid for cane, the early death of his father, and the times when he, his mother, and his younger sister had been close to starvation. "Some days all we had to eat was boil plantain and *bhaji*. Bush that I collect from the ground."

"How that taste?"

Narpat opened his mouth and fanned his tongue. Jeeves grinned. "From morning to night, I was working, working, working," Narpat said. "No time for play, no time for school. And by the time I meet your mammy, I already had my own little field."

"Mammy family had their field too?"

"No, Carea. They was business people. They thought cane farming was a backward profession. You believe that? Look at how interesting this field is. Just me and two other workers maintaining it. Two youngboys I hire during the crop season." Jeeves followed his father's gaze and was transfixed by the ringed stalks, the waving arrows, the ravines with multicolored guppies and conches, the aroma of cane, and his father's hand on his shoulder. Narpat broke off a stalk and twisted it, allowing the juice to fall into Jeeves's mouth. "Okay, is time to go back now." Jeeves didn't want to leave; he wished this trip could last forever.

He gazed at the fishes in the ravine. The mud in the field, from yearly plowing, was hard and grainy, and the ravine was not as muddy as the roadside drains. "This water looking good to drink."

"Too much chemicals. But it good to bathe in." After a while he added, "You don't need to drink the ravine water when you have cane all around. Is a perfect meal. A man could survive on that for a month, at least."

"It might have somebody hiding here then?"

"Just a few animals."

"Like in a zoo?"

"A sanctuary. Or a sort of burial ground. Some of these animals like to die in a peaceful place."

On the way back the boy held tightly to the steering wheel and watched the branches, some of which he could almost touch, streaming by. By the time they came to a stop on the flattened flowers, he had already decided that it was the happiest day of his life.

His mother though was not so thrilled. She grew moody and touchy; the conversations in the bedroom stopped entirely. Jeeves received some of his most memorable beatings during this period. He began spending more time in the bedroom, sitting on the floor with the *National Geographic* magazines and gazing at the wondrous pictures of animals and huge rivers and strangely dressed people. One morning Dulari saw him staring at a photograph of women wearing nothing but skirts and head-dresses. She scooped up the magazine and rolled it into a cylinder. The first whack rocked Jeeves against the wall, the second sent him spinning to the floor, and the third loosened his throat.

"Yes bawl. Bawl hard so everybody will know that I is a useless old mother." He blocked a blow with his feet. "A useless woman with a son who like to spend his time watching shameless naked women."

Jeeves rolled over, knowing from experience that his back was more tolerant to pain. "His father training him good. Nasty magazine! Hot water! Tractor! Mash up flowers!" Jeeves, scrunched up in a ball, contemplated the connection among the four. "Useless, *obzokee* tractor. I can't wait for Bhola and Babsy to see it. I just can't wait." Finally, overcome by exhaustion, she gave up.

For the rest of the morning she blew into the chulha, rearranged pieces of wood, stirred the pots, and grumbled. Jeeves lay on the bed with his eyes on the doorway, and when he heard her approaching footsteps, he shut his eyes tightly and pretended he was sleeping. He smelled the aroma of porridge, opened his eyes, and saw his mother with a bowl of Quaker Oats in her hand. Her eyes were red, and a streak of hair fell over her forehead. While Jeeves sipped the porridge, she straightened the sheets and thumped the pillows, and when he was finished, she sat on the bed next to him singing an Indian movie song and passing her hand through his hair.

Jeeves basked in this unexpected softening and imagined it was a sign of better days. In the afternoon, when his sisters returned from school, they saw Jeeves on his mother's lap. Sushilla folded her arms, sank her chin into her chest, and began to sniff. "How was school, Popo?" Dulari asked, using Sushilla's pet name.

Miraculously the arms loosened and the sniffing stopped. "It was okay."

When their mother went into the kitchen with Chandra and Kala, Sushilla unlatched the clasps on her khaki bag and held it upside down, spilling three dog-eared copy books, a *West Indian Reader* with a varnished cover, two pencils, a chewed-down eraser, a bowclip, five tamarind seeds, and some loose sheets held with a rubber band. She reached for the sheets, snapped the band, and looked at Jeeves. She cracked it once more, irritating Jeeves with the buzzing sound and with her mysteriousness. Then she rolled away the band and arranged the pages on the bed. Pictures of deer with twisted, intersecting horns. Trees covered with ice. In the middle of these strange trees, a white cottage with light shining through one of its windows. Three frightful-looking men gazing at the sky. A chunky man smiling as if he had remembered a joke.

"Who is that?" Jeeves took the sheet with the smiling man.

Sushilla snatched it away. "Pappy."

"Pappy?"

She bit her lips, thinking. "Pappy Christmas."

"What he does do?"

"Drop toys on the house."

"Why?"

"Stop asking all these stupid question. Is his job."

"How?"

She rolled her eyes, a habit she had picked up from Chandra. "He could do these things. That is all."

"From a plane?"

She thought for a while, clicking her nails. "From a tractor." She retrieved another picture. "These deer does pull it."

Jeeves pushed his thumb into his mouth and sucked. After a while he began to laugh, but that night he dreamed of a rusty tractor plowing through the clouds while a fat, cheery man unloaded his toys onto the houses. In the morning his memory of the dream shifted, and he remembered only his father flying through the air in his tractor.

FOUR

Sushilla had always considered Jeeves an interloper. Soon after his birth she'd begun complaining of random, unexplained aches that struck without warning. She had also developed the habit of peeping from the corners of her eyelids to see whether any parental affection was being transferred away from her. Taking her cue from Chandra and Kala, she had feigned irritation at all his annoying habits: his way of trailing after them in his dirty nightie, the slurp of his thumbsucking, and the way he would coil up like a *chinney*, a foul-smelling caterpillar, when he was being whipped. Now, suddenly, she developed a quiet friendliness with him.

Each day she returned with some new picture or postcard. She and Jeeves waited like conspirators for Chandra and Kala to leave the bedroom before they sifted through the contents of Sushilla's bookbag. Disclosure, they knew, would lead to a severe reprimand, but this just increased the thrill.

During the mornings, while his mother was cleaning the front yard, Jeeves grabbed the opportunity to rummage through the *National Geographic* magazines, looking for pictures of the plump man with his twinkling piggy-eyes and his red cheeks almost covered with beard. He saw photographs of men huddled in a small circle around a squirming animal, but they were all sleek, thin, and clean-shaven. Next, he turned to the *Farmer's Almanac* and saw tables and charts and diagrams, and when he scanned his father's Hindi books, he noticed strange flourishing letters joined at the top.

One morning a photograph fell from beneath the jacket cover of a Hindi book, and when Jeeves reached for it from the floor, he saw a young man, the top button of his shirt undone, one hand at his waist, the other resting on a chair upon which a woman sat. The woman, who was wearing an *orhni* pulled slightly across her forehead and three thick bracelets on her left hand, was staring solemnly at the photographer. The photograph was creased at the center, bisecting the couple, as if it had been folded to fit into an envelope. Jeeves sat flat on the floor and gazed at the waterfall behind the couple. When he looked closer, he saw that the waterfall was drawn on a cloth that, twilled at one end, looked like parts of Crappo Patch during the flood.

He was so engaged with the photograph that he didn't hear his mother tapping her cocoyea broom on the step to dislodge the dirt.

"Jeeves!" She was by the front door and, more ominously, had the broom in her hand. He pushed the photograph beneath his leg and tried unsuccessfully to think up some excuse. "What you hiding there?" She advanced toward him, and he slid backward, resigning himself. "Move your foot." She bent down and retrieved the photograph. After a while she asked in a surprisingly soft voice, "Where you get this?"

"From a book." As she was still staring at the couple, he asked, "Who is these people?"

At first he thought she had not heard. Then she said, "Your pappy."

"Pappy?"

"Yes. When he was much younger."

"And the lady next to him?"

"That ugly woman?" He was about say that the woman, though serious with her lips pressed together, was still pretty, when she said, "Me."

"You? You and Pappy?"

"Mm-hmm. A long time now. When we were younger. It get shoot in a studio in Princes Town."

"How you meet Pappy?"

"My father arrange everything, boy."

"So he did like Pappy?"

"Like had nothing to do with it. I was at the age to get married, and your father was the right caste. A Brahmin."

"But he don't like them."

"Your father don't like a lot of things."

"And you?"

"And me what?"

"You like him?"

"What nonsense you asking, child?" In the weeks preceding her marriage, she had pleaded endlessly with her mother about being sent off with a cane farmer. She had imagined a dirty, illiterate man who spoke halting country English and was drunk all the time. But on his first visit to their house in Charlieville, she had peeped from her bedroom door and had seen a handsome, well-dressed man speaking confidently to her father in the living room.

"So you did like him?"

She passed her fingers along the picture's crease as if trying to smooth it; then her face went blank. "You shouldn't be interfering with his books. Look at all the mess you make." Now she glared at him suspiciously. "What you was looking for?"

"For a picture of Father Christmas."

She patted his head, but soon her voice reverted to its tired, annoyed tone. "Clean up this mess right now. Quick sharp." He bent forward on his knees, piling and replacing. "You know your father don't like anybody digging up with his books and things."

Narpat arrived late every night now, smelling of gas and burnt oil, his hands smudged with grease. "You must always have a backup plan," he told them one night. "For every emergency you could think about. Even this body here." He tapped a knee and lightly grasped the muscle on his thigh. "One day all of this could suddenly go bad. Strike down with some disease." But his eyes were bright, and he was smiling as if he believed none of it. He told them that the brain was the last to go. While it was healthy, there was no cause for worry.

After his stories he would uncover the food left on the kitchen table and eat slowly, as if he were exhausted or, as Jeeves suspected, contemplating some far-fetched plan that he would soon spring on his family. Occasionally Dulari, cleaning her pots and pans, would gaze at him chewing lethargically. Sometimes she came to the table and dusted away small crumbs and picked at others that had lodged in the nail dents and reminded the girls, sitting on the Pavilion, of school the next day.

Occasionally, Chandra would catch one of the little glances exchanged between Jeeves and Sushilla. One afternoon she sneaked up on them. She placed her hands on her waist like her mother. "What the two of allyou looking at?"

"Nothing." Sushilla buckled her canvas bookbag.

Jeeves pushed his thumb into his mouth and fell back on the thick cotton pillow. Chandra gazed at Jeeves's knobby knees poking upward and at Sushilla's now-blank face and said, "Hmm," in a rather adult voice. Jeeves pulled out his thumb with a plop and examined the wet skin. Chandra said, "Hmm," once more, narrowed her eyelids, and strode out.

The next afternoon she sprang on them from behind the bedroom door where she had been hiding. Jeeves almost choked on his thumb. Sushilla tried unsuccessfully to push the pictures and drawings into her bag. Chandra took two long steps forward. "What is all this?" she inquired in a loud voice. "What is all this *pakpakkawing* about?"

Jeeves pondered the word he had heard so many times from his mother, but Sushilla said, "Shut up."

"Shut up?" Chandra glanced behind her. "I wonder what Mammy will say if she see this"—she snatched a picture from the bed—"picture of Santa Claus?" Clearly, she was disappointed.

"You know him?"

She glanced at Jeeves contemptuously.

When their mother, hearing the commotion, entered the room, the early promise of a severe reprimand or even a flogging soon faded. "What going on here?"

"The two of them was pakpakkawing—"

Dulari glanced at Chandra sternly, cutting her short.

Kala appeared behind her mother, scrambled on the bed, and leafed through the pages. "Is Santa."

Jeeves was genuinely shocked. "You know him too?"

Chandra, her hands on her waist, looked on with dwindling excitement as her mother, uncharacteristically, launched into a long story about a pair of transparent plastic slippers with beaded fish-eyes she got once for Christmas. "My last present," she explained.

Chandra, tiring, slumped her shoulders and looked down at her bare feet, but Kala asked, "Why it was your last present?"

Dulari smiled. "People stop getting presents after seventeen years." She replaced the pictures carefully on the bed and stood up. "When they get married."

"Why we don't celebrate Christmas like all my friends in school?"

Dulari looked at Kala. "You remember what I tell you last year? And the year before?"

"'Cause Pappy don't like it," Chandra piped in.

"But all my friends—"

"Enough!" Kala was silenced by her mother's tone.

Narpat's reaction was more predictable. "What is all this airy-fairy nonsense I hearing about Christmas?" He had just finished eating and was sitting on the bench smelling of grease and sardine. He drew up a foot and rested his palm on his knee.

Kala ran into the bedroom and returned with all the pictures and post-cards. Sushilla pushed Jeeves in front, closer to their father. He sheaved through the papers. Jeeves felt his sister's finger stiff against his back.

Narpat looked up, and Jeeves noticed that he had singled out a post-card. "Who could tell me what wrong with this card?" Jeeves glanced at the white powder scattering around Santa Claus, who was standing on a roof. Narpat didn't wait for a response. "A man this size, standing up on a roof. You think that safe for the people inside, Mammy?" From the kitchen, Dulari glanced up at the area where Narpat had placed his hot-water contraption. "You notice this face and this belly?" He tapped the card. "A heart attack just waiting to happen. Roll straight off the roof." He pretended to be studying the card. "Diabetes. High blood pressure. Kid-neys ready to give up, grinding all that beef and pork whole day long." Jeeves tried to imagine this. "Lard, grease, and tallow mixing up and form-ing all kind of dangerous gas. A man like that shouldn't be around these chimneys and them. Because he like a bomb that could go off any min-ute." He smiled a little and then immediately grew serious once more. "This is what they teaching in school these days. That you could get something for nothing. Gifts. Not by hard work and dedication, eh, but just because is a special celebration. Gift-children. You could spot them from a distance. Big-big eye popping out from their head. Mouth always open wide. Tongue hanging out and rolling from side to side with short breath. Half of them will get a stroke by the time they hit thirty. The next half will end up in the rumshop." He glanced at his children. "Now tell me, who here want to be a little gift-boy or a little gift-girl?"

Jeeves was about to raise his hand but changed his mind.

During the first Saturday of the Christmas vacation, Narpat filled the copper one bucket at a time, with water taken from a standpipe lower down the road. Then he stripped down to his sliders, dashed a bucket of cold water across his body, and began lathering himself with carbolic soap. Afterward, he stood in the sunlight, allowing his body to dry. Chandra and Kala were in the kitchen at the time, helping their mother pick out the straw and sediments from the lagoon rice. Narpat stood upright, stared at the sky, and explained to Jeeves and Sushilla that toweling removed the body's natural shield. Then he went inside, got dressed in his gabardine trousers and starched cotton shirt, climbed onto his tractor, and drove away for his village council meeting.

In the afternoon Kala and Sushilla drew hopscotch and *peesay* squares between the trampled, greasy flowers. Later, when they went into the kitchen where Chandra was observing her mother turning the roti on the *tawa*, the iron plate, they were scolded for leaving greasy footprints and were sent to the copper. While they tiptoed to scoop out the water with an enamel bowl, their mother started: "Make sure allyou wash out the grease from between allyou toes. And careful leaning over the edge." She grumbled for a few minutes to Chandra, who attempted to look alternately sympathetic and aggrieved, then inquired loudly, "Where Jeeves? I hope he not climbing over the edge."

Jeeves, hearing his name, peeped from the porch. A few days earlier his head had stuck between the railings, and when he tugged in a panic, his ears almost came off.

Chandra traced a line on her palm tentatively. "I think that the tank might be dangerous for"—she hesitated—"little children."

"That is true," her mother said, surprising Chandra into a shy smile.

"It might have one or two crappo fish living in the water."

"And keewee too." Her mother dusted the roti and placed it in a basin.

"Yes. They teach me that in school." She bit her lip. "Every drop of water contain a complete universe of creatures."

"Look, you better go and make sure them children not doing any mischief outside."

Chandra walked purposefully to the porch. "What allyou *children* doing in the greasy place again? Ain't allyou just clean up?" She inhaled deeply. "Well, yes!" She glared at them and returned to the kitchen, but later in the morning, when from the kitchen window she spotted all three seated beneath the Julie mango tree, picking out pieces of narrowly sliced mango from a bowl and dipping the pieces into a mushy mixture of salt and pepper, she hurried out of the house.

"We having a pic-mic."

"Picnic," Kala corrected Jeeves, selecting a red juicy slice. She bit into the mango. "I think we need more pepper." She immediately ran to the bird pepper tree in their mother's backyard garden and returned with a handful of small grainlike peppers. She cut the peppers into tiny pieces and mixed them into the salt. Jeeves dipped into the mixture and almost choked from the pepper. He fanned his mouth with his palm and began to cough. Laughing, Kala fetched a bowl of water from the copper, and Jeeves drank, gargled, and spat. For the rest of the day he could only suck his thumb in short bursts.

When Narpat returned in the evening, he noticed Jeeves inspecting and blowing on his thumb. "I see we have a little blowfish in this house."

Jeeves, his cheeks swollen with air, could say nothing, but Chandra said, "He eat pepper. It all over his thumb too."

"I see." He chuckled. "You just discover what every culture all over the world realize. The value of pepper. Stimulate the enzymes. Put the body defense mechanisms on high alert." Then he shifted to Jeeves's thumb-sucking. Each time Jeeves placed a thumb in his mouth, he collected one thousand, four hundred, and twenty-three germs. He thought for a while, then said that cod liver oil was also an effective shield. Just like pepper. The children could not understand the connection. They looked on with growing interest as he reached to the ledge above Carnegie, retrieved a small plastic bottle, and took out a yellow capsule that he squeezed, burst, and massaged onto Jeeves's thumb. The boy giggled and sniffed his thumb. His smile disappeared instantaneously. He wagged and flicked his thumb as if trying to remove an insect. For most of that night he sniffed and wagged. Two days later he stopped sucking his thumb.

During the first week of the holidays, Jeeves ran around the yard and hung around his mother in the backyard garden while she planted pumpkins and cucumbers and eggplant and spiked a circular area with bamboo for her carailli vines. He grew bored and wandered into the porch. But he had not forgotten the magical celebration, and sometimes in the porch he imagined their old house covered in white dust and the chubby man who flew through the air pelting toys onto every roof. Then one morning he saw a scrawny boy, maybe three or four years older than him, clutching the end of a rope and dragging a bony goat along. The goat stood its ground, then bounded in the air and lowered its head. When it relented, the boy was able to drag it a few inches. This went on for a few minutes— the animal springing in the air, surrendering temporarily, the boy seizing the advantage. Jeeves looked on in fascination at this crazy, exciting game. He had never seen a goat at this close range, and he was struck by how much the animal looked like those he had seen on the postcards. And all at once he knew what he was going to include in his wish list.

When Sushilla had mentioned this aspect of the celebration, Jeeves had been enthralled—it just kept getting better—but he soon grew so exhausted by the possibilities that he could think of nothing beyond the dusty wind-up toys he had seen on the upper shelves of a Chinese grocery. Now his mind was blasted by the possibility of this playful, intelligent, inventive creature.

On Christmas Eve day, when Bhola, Babsy, and their daughter Prutti visited, Jeeves was not swayed by the bags of colored marshmallows and dried dates and the plastic packets of paradise plums they doled out. When Prutti, speaking with a painful correctness, launched into a speech about the gifts she expected to receive, his sisters threw sidelong glances at one another, but Jeeves was thinking of his pet.

"Ay-ay. I just remember. Where Narpat and the tractor? Like he making a lil trip to Port of Spain or what?" Bhola's hearty chuckle shook Jeeves out of his reverie.

After about ten minutes or so, Prutti stood up. "Moms, I think the sandflies is sucking very hard. I is getting a rash."

Now her parents stood up too, as if it were a prearranged signal.

"They live in a low-lying area, dearie."

"Time for Narpat to move out from this damn swamp, if you ask me. It look like he go forever be in cahoots with these damn ignurrent cane farmers and them. Car-hoots!" The word seemed to amuse him, and he exploded in a wet, squelchy laugh.

"Pops, I thinks we is forgetting something."

"Eh? Forget?" Bhola scratched his chin. "You sure?"

"I is most positively sure." Jeeves noticed how stiffly her hair was braided by two red ribbons.

"Oho. Oh shucks. I don't know how I coulda forget that. Okay, run in the car and get it."

"I believe it is presently in the rear seat of the automobile." Prutti walked outside and returned with a bulging plastic bag that she held before her mother.

"You do the honors, dearie. Was your choices in any case."

Prutti dipped her hand into the bag, felt around, and recited in a perfectly coached voice, "This plastic fine-tooth comb am for my cousin, Chandra."

She dipped again. "This bottle of Johnson Baby Powder am for my second cousin Kala. It has special healing ingredients." Kala, whose feet were usually bruised from climbing trees and jumping to the ground, snatched the bottle.

"Take it easy, take it easy." Bhola's small eyes seemed smothered by his pudgy cheeks.

"This angel bowclip am for my other cousin Sushilla. It appear quite pretty, if you asks me." Sushilla took the bowclip shyly.

"And now, this nice bumping ball is for my last cousin, Jeeves." She gave Jeeves the ball and glanced at her mother. "It should provide him with hours and days and weeks and months of amusement." Her mother smiled sternly.

When they were leaving, Bhola grabbed a chunk of flesh on Jeeves's buttocks, almost as big as the ball, and wrung. Jeeves screeched, and Bhola chuckled loudly. "Tell you damn father to leave these ignurrent cane farmers and come down to the city. Car-hoots!"

About five minutes after they had left, Jeeves took his ball to the porch. He bumped it against the floor, he bumped it against the walls, and in a moment of recklessness he bumped it on the wooden step, where it hit the roof and flew down the road. He gave chase, but a few minutes later he ran back screaming to the house, followed by a donkey. Assevero, the animal's owner, a wiry coco panyol who pried out finger yams and tannia from the lathro, shouted merrily, "Run fast, boy. This donkey like to eat little children." For the rest of the afternoon Jeeves gazed nervously at the road.

Narpat returned about five p.m. from his meeting, took one look at the empty bags and wrappings on the porch, and exploded. From beneath the Julie mango tree, the children heard him shouting, "I see Lord Lalloo pay a little visit today. Lord Lalloo, Lady Lalloo, and Princes Lalloo. And they bring all their poison with them. Where the four little diabetics? I better run outside and see if they faint away below some tree." He called out loudly. "Diabetics! Come here quick sharp."

When they were all lined up on the porch, their backs against the wall, he gestured to the tiny ants already swarming around the wrappings strewn on the floor, and asked if children with rotten teeth looked appealing. They shook their heads. He explained, as he had done so many times before, that children who ate sweets suffered from bad vision, palpitations, and dizziness. Worse, it prevented the mind from operating properly. "You know what happen when you throw in a dose of sugar in a gas tank? It shut down the cylinder one by one." Their mother came out, and the children were surprised to see her nodding in agreement when Narpat said, "Only a complete mule like Bhola will spoil children with all this poison. Damn jackass like him. Now clean up this mess here."

Because of Narpat's foul mood, Jeeves almost canceled his little plan, but it was too late; Sushilla had amended the letter earlier in the day, and he had already hidden away a pillowcase plucked from the clothesline outside.

That night he lay still in bed, his eyes focused on the ceiling. The wick was, as usual at night, let down, and the flickering light seemed to change the shape of the ceiling and the rafters each time he shut and opened his eyes. But this was difficult to keep up, and he soon found himself dozing off. Sushilla kicked his ankle. He sat up and surveyed the bed. Sushilla had one eye open, Kala's face was pressed against the pillow, and Chandra was frowning but her eyes were shut tightly. He crept out of bed, retrieved the pillowcase from the last drawer of the chest, and tiptoed out of the room. He opened the door slowly and was about to head for the Pavilion, the best place to put the pillowcase, Sushilla had advised, when he heard a slight shuffling. He looked up and saw Narpat at the other end of the room, his feet balanced on the window ledge, holding up a brown paper bag against the rafter. Jeeves tiptoed back swiftly to the room and lay in bed, contemplating the strange and complicating occurrence. Were his father and Santa somehow in cahoots? He heard a low chuckle from somewhere in the bed, but all eyes were shut.

This was too much. He felt the sudden urge to suck his thumb, but he had already lost his taste for soggy skin. After about half an hour, feeling drowsy once more, he tiptoed out of the room and looked up. No one. He sneaked the pillowcase with its letter to Santa beneath the bench and returned to bed, where he soon fell asleep.

He awoke the next morning to the sound of a cock crowing in the distance and, farther away, a dog yapping. A tractor drove along the road, chugging and growling.

He slipped out of bed, and when he opened the door, he saw in the muted darkness a slight bulge in the pillowcase. A tiny baby goat! He ran to the bench, closed his eyes, took a deep breath, and pushed his hand inside. Something soft and furry brushed his fingers and wriggled away. He dipped his hand farther in and poked around. His fingers closed around a small, quivering ball, and he was suddenly frozen with the thought that a hairy elf was still inside the pillowcase. He was about to loosen his grasp when tiny teeth sank into his finger. He yelped and pulled out his hand, clutching a snarling bat. He howled and released the bat, which bumped against his forehead, fell to the floor, and crawled between his legs. He bawled again, too terrified to notice his parents watching from one door and his sisters from another. The bat scuttled along the floor like a horrible deformed mouse, taxied back toward Jeeves, then flipped beneath the table. Jeeves dived in the opposite direction. He heard it flapping beneath the table, raised his head, and saw a pair of feet. A hand reached down, pinched the bat's wings together, and pulled it upward.

"Come, Mister Batman. Come and see what Santa leave for you." He got on his knees and saw his father swinging the bat from side to side. Then he noticed his three sisters peeping from the doorway. "Is a real nice fluffy little toy. Soft and cuddly. You only have to feed it once a day with a few drops of blood. You think you could spare that? Eh? Just four-five drops every morning."

The sisters tittered, and Narpat glanced sternly in their direction. "Come, let me explain something to you." Jeeves looked at the bat and stood his ground. "Come!" He jumped and took a few steps forward. "People who expect these gifts without doing anything to deserve it is nothing more than gluttons." He scratched the bat's head. "Say glutton."

"Glut-tin."

"Very good. Gift-people is glutton. Pigs is glutton too. No difference between the two. Now tell me. You want to be a glutton?"

Jeeves shook his head.

"You want to be a pig? Look at this bat here. Ain't it looking like a little pig?" He pressed a finger against the bat's mouth. The bat squealed and bared its fangs. The sisters rushed back to the room's doorway. Narpat flicked his finger and a drop of blood splattered on his merino. "That is what gift-people does do when they disappointed." He went to the window and pitched the bat outside. "Bite." Narpat returned to Jeeves. "Only a dishonest man expect something for nothing." His stern voice and his expression—his head bent slightly to the side, his drooping eyelids, his slack lips that made him appear both bored and amused—indicated that he was in one of his sermonizing moods. He explained that Christmas was a foreign celebration encouraged mainly by greedy shopkeepers just to make more profit. "You ever smell a goat?" His voice was lower now, signaling a shift in mood.

"I think they blight," Chandra said. "They does bring bad luck."

"Nonsense. Is because they does eat up everything that could fit in their mouth. Trip-trap, trip-trap went the hooves of the first Billy Goat Gruff as he trip-trapped over the wooden bridge." He reached into his trouser pocket and withdrew the page on which Sushilla had written the letter. "'Dear Santa, I want a ghote.'" He spelled the word. "G-h-o-t-e. What sorta animal is that? Anybody could tell me?"

Kala made a baa-ing goat sound; then Chandra joined in. From the corner Jeeves saw everyone laughing—his mother, his sisters, and finally his father. He tried to understand their merriment but could not rid himself of the memory of the bat bumping against his head and crawling between his legs.

That was the first and last Christmas occasion at the house, and from that moment on Jeeves developed two traits that would remain with him for most of his life. The first was a morbid fear of bats. The second was a tendency to tremble violently whenever he was angry or frightened.

On the last weekend of the holidays, Dulari surprised her children with an elaborate meal of *paymee* cakes wrapped in banana leaves, and *pone*, a cassava cake. She had spent the entire morning baking, and when Kala asked whether this was a belated Christmas feast, her mother said, "Just eat out everything before allyou father get home."

This was one of Jeeves's most pleasant memories of his childhood: unwrapping the banana leaf and discovering the fragrant, golden paymee within, the sticky pone clinging to his fingers, the delight on his sisters' faces; and his mother, uncharacteristically animated, talking of parties and encouraging the girls into carols; and when the table was cleared, her eyes still lively, explaining that this little celebration was their special secret.

On a Sunday evening in 1961, three months after Christmas, Narpat returned home leading a haggard, rust-colored cow, the rope tied around the animal's neck also wound in a *bamboochette* around its pointed, curving horns. Some distance behind, Kumkaran, a huge man with a hat barely fitting his head, and his pants held up with a fanbelt, was sweating and walking slowly while talking to the cow and to Narpat. Jeeves suspected that his wish for a goat had planted the idea in Narpat's head, but his father—and Kumkaran—offered a multitude of other, vague reasons. "Prime stock," he shouted to his somewhat terrified children, looking on from the porch.

"With me since the day she born," Kumkaran said emotionally.

The children noticed how different Kumkaran was from the cow, which was so skinny and morose, it appeared to be sick. Kumkaran looked to the porch and noticed Dulari. "A cow is a blessing on a household 'cording to some scripture or the other. Is why people does worship them all the time." He gazed at the cow reverentially.

"Only because it is a perfect recycling unit." Narpat slapped the cow's back lightly.

"Obedient, obedient beast. Treat her like me own daughter." Kumkaran pulled her ear roughly. "Eh, Gangadaye? Beti?" He tugged harder. The cow, tiring of all this affection, shook its head angrily, but Kumkaran held on to the ear. He glanced at the porch once more. "Allyou want to come and play with it, children?" Chandra and Sushilla ran inside, but Kala walked down the steps tentatively.

"It ever butt anybody?" she asked.

"Butt?" Kumkaran giggled guiltily. He squinted at the dung. "A cow is like a goddess, child." He grasped the other ear roughly and swung the cow's head toward him. "Bye-bye, Gangadaye. Pappy have to leave now."

Narpat dipped into his pocket and fetched out some bills held together with a rubber band. "I hope this is enough."

Kumkaran took the wad, flipping and fingering each note and inhaling deeply. "With me since the day she born." He seemed disappointed. "One bucket of milk every day. Tops. Used to make butter and ghee and *dahee* with all that spare milk. And she never hold back the milk. Just touch she they"—he kicked a teat—"and milk just start pitching out *tooroop tooroop*." Kala bent down and touched the teat. The cow kicked its hind leg, and Kala jumped back. Kumkaran smiled sadly. "And she so playful too. A blessing. A real blessing." He walked off, wiping his eyes with his shirtsleeve.

A horsefly settled on the cow's flank. The animal's skin twitched, and the fly flew off.

"How it could move it skin like that?" Jeeves asked.

"'Cause the foot can't reach so far. All animal have some special skill."

During the first week the cow ate up the surviving zinnias and marigolds, cleaned out the carailli vines, and leveled the *ochroes* and eggplants. The second week it shook itself free of its rope and, liking the shade of the porch, settled by the steps. Each evening Narpat brought on his tractor a bundle of cane stalks, which the cow chewed down lazily. Later he filled a bucket from the copper, stirred in some sawdusty flakes from a bag, and threw a handful of salt into the mixture. The cow dipped its head and drank noisily.

Jeeves was fascinated by all this: the animal's continuous masticating, the way it would swish its tail to flick away flies, and the energy it put into kicking away the bucket each time Narpat attempted a milking. The boy did not suspect then that the strange, unintelligible, almost lyrical Hindi words uttered by his father were obscenities. But Narpat persisted: he drove a stake in the ground, to which he tied the animal's hind feet just before he started milking; he stirred more flakes into the water; he brought home bigger bundles of cane stalks.

Each night he took in a quarter bucket, mostly froth, to the house.

Dulari witnessed all of this from the window while she was washing her wares. The children could sense from her silence that she was smoldering. Sometimes in the morning she went to her backyard garden, and with her hands against her back, the fingers clasping one another, she would survey the trampled machans and the now-withering stalks of ochroes and eggplants.

One afternoon she heard Kala screaming and rushed outside. Kala was on the ground, rolled up in a ball, the cow prodding her with its horns.

"Kala!"

Kala tried to roll away. The cow shook its head and stabbed a horn at her leg. She screamed and placed her hand over the wound, blood trickling through her fingers. The cow moved forward until it was over her, nudging her with its horn, turning her over with its snout, pawing at the ground with its front feet. Dulari looked around in panic. Her children were at her side, screaming. She too felt like screaming, but her throat was dry.

"Mammy." Kala's face was covered with mud and pieces of grass. Blood was dripping down her leg to the ground. Desperately, Dulari looked around once more. Then she ran to the side of the house and wrenched the pipe from Narpat's hot-water contraption. It wouldn't give. With her eyes still on her daughter, she braced one leg against the wall and pulled and twisted. When the pipe broke off, she almost tumbled to the ground.

Years later Jeeves would remember the scene in every detail. He would recall his mother pounding the cow on its back, getting between the animal and her daughter, and even when the danger was past, still thumping the horns. Only when she heard Kala whimpering did she drop the pipe and pick her up, cradling her like a baby, wiping her eyes, dusting her face. When she walked back to the house with Kala bundled up against her, Jeeves noticed that although his mother's face was stony, tears were running down her cheeks. The children had never previously noticed this expression, this mixture of frustration and exhaustion and determination. A bigger surprise awaited them in the night.

Usually when their parents were quarreling, they chose mostly Hindi words, and even then their mother's voice was low, pleading and finally despairing. Now she spoke in English. Loudly. "I want you to take a good look at this child here." She pointed to Kala, who was sitting on the Pavilion, her leg bandaged with a striped towel. Narpat seemed set to say something when she added, "Little bit again, and you would only have three children. Three children and a cow. A blasted cow."

If Narpat was surprised, he hid it well. He smiled, took off his tall tops, held them upside down, walked to the porch, and placed them by the doorway. When he returned, he was still smiling, but now his eyes were somber and calculating. He glanced at the bare table, then redirected his attention to his daughter. "Okay, tell me what happen?" He sat next to her. "Start from the beginning."

"The cow," she spluttered.

He loosened the bandage and tied it more firmly. "What happen, child?" He spoke gently.

"It butt me. Here." She pointed to the bandage.

"Anywhere else?"

She shook her head. "I don't know."

"Why it butt you? You was playing too near to it?" He glanced at the abrasions on her arms and shoulders.

She hesitated. "I wanted to take a ride."

"I see. A ride. What is the name of the cow?"

"Gangadaye," Chandra offered.

"Good. Very good. Gangadaye, not Black Beauty or Trigger or Silver or Nightwind. Gangadaye, a proper name for a *cow*."

Dulari must have noticed this shift in his mood; she seemed even more incensed. "Selling we that useless old animal. Damn cane farmer like him. Like all of them."

"You shouldn't condemn all—"

"All of them. Every single one. Canefield. Swamp. Dishonest people." Now she seemed incoherent, and when the children looked at her, they saw that she was crying.

"We have to learn to control these negative thoughts. They worse than all the poison combined." He turned to Kala. "The healing process will never function properly if the mind is not clear."

"If anything had happen to this child today. If anything had just happen . . ." She left the threat hanging.

Narpat stood up. "The cow will remain. People will never progress if they give in every time something bad happen. All the big cities all over the world spring up only because fire destroy some slum, or an earthquake level a useless settlement." He looked down sharply at Kala. "What lesson you learn today, child?"

"Not to play . . . to play near the cow."

"Good. Very good. The most valuable lessons we learn is always the most painful." He rapped his forehead. "'Cause we never forget them."

In the kitchen Dulari tapped her broom loudly. "Lesson, lesson all the time, and nothing to show from them."

When, less than a month later, Narpat got rid of the cow, his decision had nothing to do with the animal's disposition but rather with his discovery of the true reason for Kumkaran's eagerness to sell. The children tried to piece together this reason from Narpat's rage. "Never trust a man with a oily voice. A man who eyes does disappear every time he laugh. That sorta man no different from a engine with the noise hiding all the defect." He wagged a finger at his children. "Remember this good. Let it be a lesson to you. Not every grin is a smile." He continued lecturing for a while.

"What happen?" Dulari interrupted quietly

Finally he explained. Kumkaran's decision was motivated by his flirtation with a group of Pentecostals who had recently settled in the village. The Pentecostals had cautioned that primitive Hindu beliefs like cow-worshipping led to only one destination: hell. They had described this hell in every intimate detail.

"People who shed their skin like a snake whenever it convenient will never make progress. Moving from one superstition to the other." Narpat had calmed down slightly. "The sign of a weak people. Tell them anything and they will believe. Anything to make money. Thiefing in the day and praying in the night. You could see the weakness in their eyes. Ghee. Oil. Sugar. Fat. Soft pap instead of a spine." Dulari sat next to him, her chin bent on her palm, her eyes cast down, looking at the bare floor. "Places like here will never improve, Mammy. Everybody have a excuse in their back pocket." Narpat walked to the porch. "I going to give him back his cow. His daughter."

"Make sure you get back the money," she said, glancing up.

"He could keep the money. It will make him happier and fatter." He walked to the cow, which was chewing lazily.

She followed him outside, pleading. "We need the money. We just can't give away the cow for nothing. "

He unloosened the rope from the stake. "Come, Gangadaye, you going back to Pappy."

"We could fix up the wares stand. Or build a new cupboard."

Narpat was no longer listening. He stroked the cow's flank and led it to the road. "Show a thief some honesty, and you leave him stranded, like a fish out of water, suffocating in the air."

Kumkaran checked his urge to rush out and embrace the animal being led by Narpat because he knew that too much enthusiasm would hamper the inevitable bargaining. He had not anticipated his biting guilt each time he gazed at the empty pen, and once when he passed the knotted rope used to punish the animal, he muttered tenderly, "Beti." The idea that he had made a mistake ate him up, and worse, as a man accustomed to bartering, he felt cheated that he had exchanged countless gods and goddesses for a single deity.

When Narpat waved away his excuses about debt and expenses with a brusque, "I didn't come here to haggle. Give me what you could afford," Kumkaran was deeply touched. He played with the dirty fanbelt holding up his pants and coughed away the lump in his throat. "Gangadaye, beti. I hope you didn't behave bad. I hope you didn't forget your training."

"One cup of milk every day. Not a drop more."

Kumkaran tugged the cow's ear and swung the animal's face toward him. "That is true, Gangadaye? Is so you was behaving? What was the problem? You was too sad or what? Missing the family that you grow up in. That is why you didn't drop any milk? Eh?" He kicked a teat.

When Narpat walked away, Kumkaran was still chatting with the cow. The next evening he showed up at Narpat's house with twenty dollars hidden in his dirty mechanics' bag, which was jingling with spanners, pliers, screwdrivers, and an assortment of nuts. He leaned against the tractor. "Look like it need a little work." That evening he and Narpat removed the gas tank, knocked out the dents, patched the leaks with a sealant, and wrapped thin strips of rubber along the rusted lines. The next evening they dismantled the gear case and cleaned the wheels and levers with gasoline, greased the pulleys, and replaced the gaskets. Kumkaran, his face streaked with grease, said lightly, "When we finish, she will put all them fancy American buggies in they place."

"We could build a nice trailer with a door and a canopy. Gas shocks.

Hydraulic suspension. Could get them cheap from the bus company by the wharf in San Fernando."

Kumkaran was surprised that Narpat had taken him seriously. "Like a carriage?"

"A coach. Take schoolchildren on excursion trips to the zoo. People who getting married. Funerals."

"You think people will want they dead mother or father dragging about in a rusty tractor?" Kumkaran asked skeptically.

"The ride will be better than the destination." Narpat smiled at his joke and pounded a nut into place. "You know why Indians does favor cremation? To save on fuel. Just scratch a match by the corpse that puff up with gas and oil and grease, and it start sizzling in no time."

"Is exactly what the Pentecostal pastor say. The very said thing."

"They no better. Frightening stupid people with all this talk about the devil and hell." He looked up. "And heaven. Is a wonder none of these planes ever plow through it as yet. Nancy story for little children."

Kumkaran grew increasingly silent during the following days, until one evening he did not show up. Narpat was not bothered; he drew up plans for his trailer, and on the end of a cardboard box, he calculated dimensions, leverage, and tension. He tapped his pencil on the tractor's grille and explained to Jeeves, who was sitting next to him, that he could build the frame with teak logs and the wheels from the discarded rims of a truck.

Jeeves was transfixed; his disappointment at the departure of the cow lessened in the face of his father's ingenuity. Sometimes he was given a handful of nails or a small coil of wire, which he clutched carefully as he observed his father pounding, detaching, rearranging, and finally returning to his sketches to scratch out angles and adjust the dimensions of his diagrams. One evening Narpat crumbled up the trailer plan and began another. "It have all different sort of propulsion, you know. All different sort of vehicle. From a big fat ship to a box cart. The trick is the adjustment. Sizing down the apparatus."

Jeeves watched this new, smaller, and simpler apparatus taking shape, and even when it gradually grew to resemble a tricycle, he was uncertain because apart from a knotted chain and two ball bearings, it was constructed entirely of wood. He guessed it was complete when his father swept away the wooden strips and shavings in the backyard garden and invited him to hop aboard. Jeeves climbed on the tricycle and placed his feet on the wooden pedal. "Push," his father encouraged. "Push one pedal, then the other." But the wheels, not entirely round, were of solid wood, and the tricycle would not give. "Might have to make a few minor adjustments." Narpat tapped his sketch and went inside. After half an hour Jeeves gave up. In the night he rubbed his sore ankles and pulled out tiny splinters from his inner thighs.

"Stop digging and scratching," Chandra told him.

After a few days Jeeves realized that his tricycle was destined to remain stationary. But he also discovered during his teeth-grinding goading that it rocked a bit. He seized on the defect and soon he transferred his energy to rocking rather than pedaling.

One evening Narpat pushed his head through the window to gaze at his son rocking wildly. "Giddyap. We have to get a name for this horse of yours, Carea." He turned to his wife, "What is a good name, Mammy?"

Jeeves stopped rocking and stared at his parents. He tried to recall the cow's name. "Gangoo."

"Gangoo? That is the name of a top-class *dacoit*. Gangoo Mangalsingh. Kill forty-seven people." He twisted his fingers by his lip as if he were curling a moustache. "How about Gangaram."

"Okay." Jeeves, puzzled by his parents' mirth, resumed his rocking.

SIX

*I*n the months before Jeeves started school in September, he spent every morning on his rocking tricycle. His mother, who had previously shooed him inside because he often wandered out of sight, creeping beneath the house and straying into the backyard garden, was now content to see him rocking away. Occasionally he jumped off the bike and ran to her while she was collecting dried black sage and strips of bark for her chulha. He felt important when she allowed him to carry the small bundles to the kitchen, as he felt during the last Friday of each month when, following the trip to Lumchee's grocery, he helped to pack the tins of sardine and butter into the cupboard. The grocery trip, undertaken while his sisters were at school and his father in the field, was the highlight of the month. He would rush out from Janak's taxi into the cavernous shop, caught by the mingled fragrance of molasses and confectionery and dry goods. While Lumchee, a bony Chinese man with a hysterical voice, squinted over his oversize glasses at Dulari's list, Jeeves would gaze at the huge bags of sugar and potatoes set against the wall; and on the other side of the counter, the colorful tins and bottles on the lower shelves; and on the topmost, dusty unsold toys from previous Christmases. Frequently Lumchee would shout to his wife for some item, and she would walk with short, pattering footsteps to a gloomy back room. Sometimes she could not locate the item, and Lumchee would shriek to his customer, "No salmon, no salmon. Outtastock." While he continued his argument in Chinese, Jeeves would stare at the flies hovering around the stale cakes and hops bread in a dirty glass case atop the counter. He imagined they were chasing each other in a little insect game, and he would try to stir them by knocking on the glass. Often drunken men would wander through a side door from the adjoining rumshop, and then Lumchee would say, "Waitaminute," and disappear for about ten minutes. Jeeves would peep through the door at the disheveled men swaying from tall stools, spitting on the floor, and laughing merrily. Lumchee usually took about half an hour to go through a list, and on the way back, while Dulari was checking and rechecking the cost of each item purchased, Jeeves would imagine that he could still catch a whiff of the molasses and could still see the women who chatted with his mother, and the drunk men laughing and shouting. He spotted some of these villagers each morning while he was rocking away. At exactly seven he would see Sidney walking hurriedly to Chin Lee's sawmill, where he operated the bandsaw. Sidney's big head, crowned with flapping curly hair, was always inclined forward as if he were about to dash off in a sprint, but one morning when Jeeves was alone in the yard, Sidney stopped abruptly, whirled toward Jeeves, and twisted up his eyelids. Jeeves dismounted in a panic and fled inside. The next morning Sidney repeated his act, and from a distance his eyes seemed to be bloody eggs. Momentarily, Jeeves was frozen by this image, but when Sidney flicked out his tongue and whipped it from side to side, Jeeves tumbled from his tricycle. From then on he would venture outside only when he had calculated that Sidney had already passed by.

By that time Dev Anand would saunter by, whistling merrily and occasionally breaking out into a Hindi movie song. His real name was Balgobin Lutchman, but he always referred to himself as Dev Anand, his favorite Indian film actor. His fantasy did not end with the name, as he had developed the habit of wearing green scarves, saffron turtleneck jerseys, and spotless white trousers hemmed up an inch or so to make his striking red socks noticeable. Whenever he stopped to chat with Dulari, Jeeves would notice his wide-legged stance and his head bobbing back and forth and the cigarette jumping between his lips. On Fridays, Huzaifa pushed his Humber bicycle toward the mosque, more than a mile away. He had bought the Humber in a moment of weakness, but his short legs could not quite reach the pedals, and he was forced to goad it along the gravelly roads. No one had ever seen him on the saddle. The most interesting of these early morning strollers was Scaramouche because he always shouted to Jeeves, "Careful with all that speed, Sonnyboy. You going to tired out the horse in no time." He was a thin, gloomy man with deep wrinkles on his face. He wore oversize nylon shirts and spoke in a loud, rasping voice, even when he was conversing with Dulari, whom he called *didi*. Jeeves was surprised at his mother's annoyance with Scaramouche, who, oblivious to her impatient broom-tapping routine, was usually reluctant to leave.

One morning Scaramouche did not pass by. In the evening, Sidney, who was returning from the sawmill, told Dulari that Scaramouche had been found on the steps of his one-room shack. He had been severely beaten, and his long, flapping shirt was ripped and streaked with blood. Sidney was mystified both by the attack and by the identity of the attacker. He murmured something about the Outsiders.

A few days later Jeeves heard a dull thumping in the abandoned house opposite. He stopped rocking and gazed at the house. For the rest of the morning he glanced intermittently across the road, but he saw no one and soon forgot about it. The next morning, he noticed his mother gazing in the direction of the house, looking concerned. She had the same look that night when she was whispering to Narpat following his return from the canefield. Immediately he went to the porch, stepped into his tall tops, and headed for the tractor.

"Careful." Dulari followed him to the tractor, where he was unloosening a rope wound around an old steel box. "Maybe you should wait till morning."

They heard snatches of his response, "When you not sure about something . . . put the matter to rest once and for all . . . or you will never know."

"Could be just a strayaway dog or cat."

Narpat retrieved a long silver flashlight from his box, flicked the switch a few times, and tapped the base against the steering column. A weak light filtered from the flashlight, illuminating just a foot or two. "Local model. Don't last more than two weeks."

"Careful."

Jeeves felt a stab of fear and excitement as his father crossed the road and disappeared into the gloomy house. He had often heard his mother warning Kala about the snakes and black scorpions and hairy spiders and fearsome centipedes hiding between the rotting boards, and worse, invisible wraithlike creatures hovering around in the darkness.

Kala was at her mother's side by the road. Jeeves was about to join them when his father emerged from the house, his flashlight now just a dim flicker. Later in the night Narpat sent the children to their room, where they strained to hear the whispering.

Early the next day, a Sunday, the children were awakened by shouting. When they ran outside, they saw their mother standing at the side of the road watching Narpat push a lanky man from Samsoondar's abandoned house. The man was about a head taller than Narpat. He stumbled to his knees, sprang up, and flailed at Narpat, who ducked and lanced a hand upward, clamping his fingers around the man's jaw, pulling his head down until both men were at eye level. The children had no idea what was said by their father, but when he released his hold, the man ran down the road, holding his throat and cursing.

Now another man, short and wiry, with dark circles under his eyes and protruding teeth that made him look like a huge demented *manicou*, bounded from the house, hunched his shoulders, and hurled himself against Narpat, twisting at the last moment as if he were making a football tackle. Narpat caught his arm, spun him around, and flung him into the drain. He emerged wet and muddy, shaking his body like an animal. Jeeves began to giggle.

Dulari noticed her children behind her. "Get inside. Right now." They retreated reluctantly to the front step.

"This ain't over. This ain't over at all." Mud fell from the man's hair in little clumps.

"Don't let me ever catch any one of you in this place again."

"You is a blasted policeman or something? Eh? You don't know who you dealing with."

Narpat walked toward him, and he almost fell into the drain once more. "A little jackass. A stupid little thief. Weak and *marasme*."

"Who you calling marasme?"

"Take a look at yourself. Big pushout teeth—a sign of greed. Red, sickly eye. Meager body. Bad skin. Piles for sure. Blockage and congestion. No roughage in your diet. What you need is a good purge. A strong dose of senna."

He pointed to Narpat. "You better watch your blasted mouth, eh, mister. Who the hell you think you is?"

"Narpat. Remember that name good." The children noticed that their father was smiling. "Now get out from here, and don't let me ever see your face again. You and that other hooligan."

"What you going to do with the stuff?"

"You mean the jewel that you thief from Princes Town?"

"It wasn't from Princes Town." He hesitated then added. "Toobesides, we didn't thief the stuff."

"I will let the police decide that."

"Listen, mister, that stuff belongs to me mother. I was safekeeping it for—"

He stopped short. Narpat had skipped over the drain. "Go!"

The man walked down the road sideways like a crab, gesticulating and shouting, "You playing with fire. Careful you don't get burnup." He glared at the children. "You and your whole mothersass family better be careful."

Once more Dulari glanced back. "I thought I tell allyou to go inside. Quick sharp!"

From the porch, they saw their father entering the abandoned house and emerging after a few minutes with a small sugar bag wrapped into a bundle. "Will be back in a little while. Going to take this to the station."

"Hurry back."

But one hour, then two passed, and he did not return. Dulari sat at the table, her chin propped against her palms.

Narpat arrived in the midafternoon, grumbling about the slow pace of Janak's car and his tendency to load his children into it during every trip as if it were an excursion. "And after that little outing, guess what I see in Princes Town Police Station?"

"What?" Jeeves asked.

"A three-hundred-pound sergeant stirring a pot right in the filing area. I don't know how he could ever chase anybody down with all that blubber." He unbuttoned his shirt and stretched his arms to indicate the sergeant's girth. "You believe that? Making a cook right in the police station. I had to point out that Sunday is not a day off for the police." The children noticed that he was not annoyed, even when he repeated one of his favorite phrases: "This country going downhill, Mammy. Speeding pell mell. And the police leading the slide."

Throughout Dulari looked at him and said nothing. Once she inhaled deeply, as if she were about to interject, but she remained silent. Finally, she spoke a few words in Hindi.

Narpat grinned. "Criminals? They just full of mouth, that is all. Stupid young idlers who looking for trouble. Lochos and peongs. The real

criminal live in the town. Grocery owner. Doctor and lawyer. Cinema pro-
prietor. You could identify them by the size of their belly." When she murmured once more in Hindi, he added, "This house can't burn that easy.
Build with toporite and tapano and cedar. Good solid wood. Swell up with
water every time it rain. And we have our own fire extinguisher." He
pointed to the roof, where he had installed his hot-water contraption.
"First sign of fire, and that apparatus will start pitching water on all sides.
Sploosh." The children giggled. Dulari got up and went into the kitchen.
The children heard them talking late into the night, their father's voice
soft and cajoling but firm, and their mother's thin and desperate.

Two weeks later, on a morning following a flash thunderstorm that lasted
a little over an hour but that had rocked the barrel on the roof, awakening
Dulari each time thunder cracked through the night, Jeeves ran outside
and began to scream. That early in the morning wispy, foggy vapors curled
around the trees like floating cobwebs. Flying ants crawled from beneath
the house and flew shakily, before they dropped to the ground, their frail
wings already useless. At first Dulari thought Jeeves had been scared by
the ants; then she heard him screaming once more, "Gangaram, Gangaram." She rushed to the copper and saw him bending over his smashed
tricycle, his hands clutching a dislodged wheel.
    "What happen? The storm mashup the bike?" she asked, even though
she knew that neither the rain nor the wind could have destroyed the tricycle so thoroughly. When Narpat came out, she said, "I know this was
going to happen. I just *know* it. They say they was going to cause trouble,
and look what they do. Where the police now?"
    "The police don't have time with these minor matters."
    "Minor matters? First is the bike . . ."
    "What happened?" Kala asked sleepily, "The storm do that?"
    "Nothing to get upset about." Narpat flicked his hand up and closed
his fingers around a flying ant. "Look at this." Jeeves, still clutching the
wooden wheel, stood up. Narpat pinched out the tiny wings and shook
his hand. "See how it drop to the ground? Pull out the wing, and it get
helpless. Just now a lizard or a crappo will come and gobble it up." He
made a clucking turkey sound. Jeeves rubbed his eyes and smiled weakly.
    "First is the bike . . ."

"Then is the house." Chandra completed her mother's lament. Jeeves began to sob once more.

"Time to go to the field now." Narpat rumpled Jeeves's hair, collected his khaki sack from the step, and walked to the tractor. "I might come back a little later than usual this evening. Going to pay a little visit to the shantytown these Outsiders putting up in Dogpatch." He used the villagers' name for the area of flimsy one-room houses constructed of cardboard, plyboard, and dented aluminum sheets. Just before he climbed onto the tractor, he told Jeeves, "If you walk around with that wheel for a few hours, it will get your arms and legs strong like Dara Singh."

"First was the bike, next is the—"

"Shut up, Chandra." Dulari walked to the tractor. "Leave it alone. Is just a bike."

Narpat broke into a grin. "This country racing downhill, Mammy. The brakes cutaway. The people who call themself leaders have water in their vein. Water and rum." Just before he drove off, he shouted, "Is good firewood. The frame will burn for weeks."

Later in the morning Jeeves rolled the three wheels beneath the house. From time to time his mother walked to the porch and stared across the road. In the midafternoon she collected the remains of the frame and pushed them beneath the chulha. At around six in the evening, when darkness was beginning to set, she locked the front door and all the windows. Two hours later, when she heard a pounding in the front, she peeped through a crack and unlatched the door.

"Pheew." Narpat scrunched his face, and when Jeeves ran up to him, he said, "Whenever you keep all the windows shut, the germsy smell get trapped inside. All the cough germs and sneeze germs." Jeeves followed him to the Pavilion. "So you bury Gangaram?" Jeeves shook his head. "He was a little sickly anyway. That is what happen to sickly creatures. They don't last." He looked at his son's protruding knees and bony feet. "Sometimes you have to shoot them like what these racing people from Queen's Park Savannah does do with the damage horses that become useless." He cocked a finger at Jeeves as if he were pulling a trigger. "Pow!" The boy flinched and covered his face.

Dulari pulled Jeeves to her. "You frightening him." After a while she asked, "So what happened?"

Jeeves noticed the subtle shift in his father's voice as he spoke about the Outsiders who had appeared without warning on the outskirts of the village and had recently begun to expand and infiltrate, seeking out abandoned houses and unoccupied land. They were either unaware of, or didn't care about, land ownership. Now they were inhabiting fertile cane land. Jeeves gathered that these Outsiders—squatters, his father called them—had garbage piled around their shacks and quarreled all the time. Narpat explained that they were a potpourri of mixed and indeterminate races who had arrived from the other islands and from Port of Spain, and who had dozens of indistinguishable children from intermarriage. They were like parasites looking for an opening, a weakness. Most of the crime, the prandial larceny, the petty thefts, were committed by these infiltrators. Soon they would take over the village as they had done those bordering San Fernando. The government was encouraging this arbitrary resettlement to make inroads into opposition territory.

The boy felt his mother's arm stiffening when his father complained about the imposition of this alien lifestyle on idyllic little villages like Lengua, and about the genuine hardworking farmers gradually displaced from their land. "The most fertile land in all of Trinidad. Flood. Silt deposit. Topsoil from everywhere else wash down here." Now his mood shifted once more. He said that every disaster was accompanied by an opportunity that most people missed because they were too busy complaining and feeling sorry for themselves. The arrival of these squatters, he said, was a wake-up call to the villagers, a reminder that their values were being eroded nightly in the rumshop. He got up. "Come hell or high water, I going to stop this nonsense. Let these parasites take notice." He spoke loudly as if they were around the house, listening to him. "Somebody have to restore some order in this place."

SEVEN

On the morning of his first day at school, Jeeves listened impatiently to his mother congratulating Kala for having passed her Common Entrance exams, which had qualified her to attend the St. Stephen's College in Princes Town. Chandra had failed this same exam twice and now had to be sent to a private school, an additional burden for the family. "You nearly thirteen years old, Chandra, and this is your last chance to make a good future. This village is a bad place for girls with no education." While his mother was speaking to her two daughters and stuffing crayons and nursery rhyme books in his khaki bookbag, Jeeves was thinking of the school games Sushilla had often spoken about. Games with marbles and guava tops and *bois canot* bats. He couldn't wait to get out of the house.

On his way to school, he broke free of Sushilla's clasp to stare at dogs looking out from porches and chickens pecking about in yards, and when the straggle of schoolchildren crossed the road to avoid a dirty bison tied to a poui tree, he stood his ground and had to be dragged across the road by his sister. He was puzzled and offended by Sushilla's transformation from a petulant but sympathetic sister into a smaller version of Chandra. But as they approached the school and he saw little children in joyful motion he ran up the hill, his sister hurrying to catch up with him.

Then the whistle blew.

The games stopped; the children filed into lines. Jeeves was pushed by Sushilla into a line with small sleepy-looking children. A short wiry man in his late thirties with big sunken eyes and greased prickly hair emerged from the building with a whistle in his mouth. He was followed by an older man, tall, dark, and stiff-looking. Immediately the chatting stopped. The older man said loudly, "Good morning, children."

"Good morning, Headmaster Balkisson," the children chanted.

The Headmaster, his Adam's apple jumping above his tight tie, rambled on in a low, hoarse voice about the school's regulations and about values and purpose. "In this school our main purpose is to build character. First we lay the foundation. Then we put up the walls." He described this construction in minute detail, and by the time he arrived at the mantels and the arches, the younger students had lost interest. Jeeves was more interested in the man with the whistle who was moving between the lines and flicking a limber tamarind rod against his pants. Then the Headmaster finished his speech, and Jeeves noticed that three other teachers had joined him at the head of the assembly. From the back he heard, "Line number one. Put out your hands." The man with the whistle moved from child to child, examining the outstretched hands. Jeeves was beginning to be bored by this pointless examination, when the teacher swooped on a chubby boy, whirled him around, and in the same motion whacked four quick strokes on his back. The teacher bit down on the whistle. "Close up your shop immediately, Pariag. Nobody interested in buying potatoes this time of the morning." He pushed his rod into the boy's open fly and swished it around.

Jeeves's laughter was checked by the terrified faces of the other students. By the time the teacher had examined the first three lines, he had flogged about half a dozen children. A slim boy two spaces before Jeeves, with long curly hair, rubbed his eyes and sniffled. Jeeves began to grow increasingly concerned about his own dirty, chewed-down nails. Perhaps he would be spared because it was his first day. The teacher was now in Jeeves's line. "That is a nice rubber slippers you wearing, Dindial son. Your father send you to school to relax? Eh? And he forget to dress you up in matching pajamas." His voice was soft, and the boy jumped back with a startled yelp when the whip fell on his hand. The sniffing boy ahead of Jeeves pressed his hand against his mouth. Jeeves eyed the distance between himself and the teacher and briefly contemplated bolting from the line and dashing down the hill.

Just then a bony goat strolled out from behind the water tank at the side of the school and casually ambled toward the assembly. Some of the older students giggled. The younger ones looked on apprehensively. The teacher blew his whistle. The goat looked up and continued its journey. A few students broke the line, and the teacher rushed over furiously to them. More students scattered, and the teacher dashed to the head of the assembly, but the Headmaster had already departed into the school. Jeeves noticed a short balding teacher edging backward, away from the goat's trajectory. From the farthest line a boy shouted, "Is the Manager goat, Mr. Moonilal. You want me to catch it?"

"You touch that stinking goat, and you will spend the rest of the day jam up with it." He advanced on the boy. "Your father send you to school to learn goat catching? Eh?"

Mr. Moonilal turned when he heard a fresh round of laughter and saw a round man whose big head was covered with a dirty Wilson hat, his belly bouncing beneath his merino, running up from behind the school. "You blasted goat, you." He scrambled at the rope trailing behind the animal. Mr. Moonilal blew his whistle repeatedly while the Manager, almost astride the goat, pushed and goaded it away from the assembly. "You keep up this behavior, Mr. Goat, and I will throw you ass in the pot one day. Curry you backside good and proper." When the children howled at his pants dipping down his waist, he hitched them up with one hand and glanced back at the assembly. He had a slight squint matched by a distended lower lip that gave him the look of a lugubrious maniac. "Look at how you disturb these nice children. And make them see me in me nasty, holey home clothes." His voice softened. "You happy now? You please with yourself, Mr. Currygoat?"

The children hooted and clapped as the Manager dragged off the goat. Just before Mr. Moonilal furiously ordered the lines inside, the boy behind Jeeves said in a grave voice, "He holding the goat the wrong way. He have to tickle below the tail for it to move faster." Jeeves looked back and saw a stout, tough-looking boy with a big forehead and a stubby neck. Like Jeeves, he was wearing a rough homemade shirt and trousers.

Lengua government was a typical country school of about one hundred and fifty students and a staff of six. The barracklike walls were of whitewashed concrete, and wood hollowed by woodlice. The children were cramped together in long sturdy benches. There were no partitions separating the various classes, but the infants' department, into which Jeeves

was placed, was blocked off from the rest of the school with two huge
blackboards, on which were plastered pictures of animals, most of which
he had glimpsed in the *National Geographic*. Other animals, constructed
from papier-mâché, dangled from the cobwebbed ceiling. The animals
twirled and seemed to chase one another every time the breeze blew
through a gaping hole on the wall, just above a photograph of the Prime
Minister, smoking a pipe and squinting as if the smoke were hurting his
eyes. A jack spaniard's nest on his forehead looked like a horn, and whenever the photograph flapped, the insects bristled out. The room was dusty
with chalk and reeked of woodlice and turpentine.

The teacher's table was directly beneath the photograph, and when
the students were all settled, the teacher, Mr. Haroon, got up tiredly and
with a slight limp walked across to a brown cupboard set against a wall.
When he opened the door, Jeeves spotted cylindrical coils of drawing paper, a stack of copybooks, and on the lowest shelf several globs of plasticine. A cockroach scurried out from the lowest shelf, and the teacher,
startled, shrank back to his desk, from where he called a blocky boy to retrieve two lumps of plasticine. The teacher portioned out the plasticine
to each desk, returned to his table, closed his eyes, and for most of the
morning seemed to be fast asleep. Once or twice he looked up and gazed
at the children sleepily before directing his attention to an aquarium with
two turtles set atop a small cabinet to the left of his table. At ten-thirty,
just before the morning recess, the Headmaster entered the room with a
tall girl of about seventeen, with big eyes and a studious smirk. Immediately the teacher bolted up from his desk and began pacing through the
rows of desks, scooping up tiny pieces of squashed plasticine and pretending to examine their shapes.

"Is everything in order, Mr. Haroon?" The Headmaster placed his
hand on the girl's shoulder. "This term your student teacher is going to be
Kamini."

Kamini smiled shyly. Mr. Haroon attempted a smile, but it came out
as a toothachey grimace.

Kamini remained in the classroom when the whistle blew for the
morning recess and the children filed out the door just beyond the blackboard partition. Jeeves looked around for Sushilla but soon directed his
attention to a group of boys scampering up a mango tree with branches
drooping over the water tank. "Mango tree not so good to branch from.

What is your name?" It was the boy who had commented earlier on the goat.

"Jeeves."

The boy seemed surprised. "Jeeves? Where you get a name like that?"

"My father give it to me."

"I never hear anybody with a name like that. My name is Dhaniram, but I going to change it to Daniel. Daniel Boone Mahadeo. But for now you could call me Danny."

"Your father wouldn't vex if you change it?"

"Who care 'bout him?" Danny ran to the mango tree, scaled up the trunk, grabbed a branch, and nimbly mounted to a higher fork. When the whistle blew, he flipped back to the lower branch and jumped to the ground.

"Where you learn to do that?"

"I doing it my whole life." Danny whistled as if it were nothing.

When they returned to the classroom, Kamini was straightening the tables and Mr. Haroon was stooped before his table, his hands clasped before him. Soon after the children settled in, Kamini got out a book from the cupboard and read a story about a girl who, granted one wish by a water sprite, asked for straight hair and was given a magic comb. At the end of the story, the girl drowned. The teacher sniffed loudly, wiped his nose, reached over to the cabinet, withdrew a small blue vial, and flicked a few drops of liquid onto his tongue.

The infants' department was released an hour before the regular dismissal, and Jeeves, idling with the other students who were awaiting their elder brothers and sisters, concluded that in spite of his mother's warnings and his own apprehensions, school was rather interesting. He had enjoyed playing with plasticine, listening to Kamini's stories, and running around during the various breaks. He had even enjoyed the soggy biscuits and skim milk doled out to the infants in the afternoon. Most of the other students had blanched at its chalky taste and spat out the paste into their hands, but to Jeeves it was a relief from his purgative soups.

A few boys were sloshing in the tractor's ruts on the slope, but Jeeves realized that his loose canvas shoes, *washycongs*, would not permit this sort of adventure, so he ran around the school a few times and stared at the couteyah's dome rising from beyond the Manager's house, which was about one hundred yards from the school. On the way back he lingered to gaze at the colorful drawings of flying gods and demure smiling goddesses on the couteyah's walls. "Is bad manners to stare at the sadhus and them," Sushilla said impatiently.

When they arrived home, their mother was standing on the porch looking out anxiously. Briefly, Jeeves imagined that she had been worried about him, but after he had eaten and changed into his home clothes, she was still on the porch looking out. When she noticed him climbing on the railing, she asked absentmindedly, "How was school today?" He was about to tell her about his adventures with plasticine and about the goat when she added, "Don't worry, it will get better." Since she seemed so distracted, Jeeves went outside to the mango tree, climbed to the top branch, and tried to somersault like Danny.

His mother went into the house and returned with a rice sifter, and for almost an hour she slowly fanned the rice and picked out small black pebbles and straw. After she had cleaned the rice, swept the porch, and dusted out the mat on the front step, Jeeves wondered whether they were having special visitors. He finally got his feet over one of the branches and hung upside down, watching his mother walk to the backyard garden. His thighs chafed against the dried bark as he tried to swing toward a nearby branch. Eventually Dulari noticed. "Get down from there right now." He straightened his feet and fell on his back on the soft mud. He glanced at his mother, expecting a reprimand, but she was mulching her tomatoes and melongene and carailli.

At about six he spotted Chandra and Kala walking toward the house. Dulari rushed to the road to hug them both and asked about the schools, the teachers, the traffic in Princes Town, the idlers beneath the stores, and their journey home. Although her daughters were both exhausted, they seemed surprised by their mother's unexpected affection. When they revealed that Baboo's rickety bus detoured to Lothians and Monkeytown and Hardbargain before it dropped them off at Four Roads junction, from where they had to walk more than a mile to get home, she hugged them once more. Jeeves felt offended by his mother's indifference about *his* day at school and Sushilla emitted a few sniffles, but they both said nothing because they knew how easily her affection could transform into fury.

In the night, Jeeves heard her complaining to Narpat about how dangerous it was for young women to be walking through the solitary village roads in the late evening.

"Young women? Which young women, Mammy? What vice you putting in these little girls' head?" A little exercise was the best thing for them. It would strengthen all their bones and tendons, and furthermore, breathing in the cool country air would purify their lungs. When he was their age, he frequently walked five, ten, fifteen miles. He signaled the conversation had ended when he called Jeeves from the bedroom. "How much miles *you* walk today, Mister-man?" He patted a leg and hoisted his son onto it.

"It had a goat."

"A what?"

"A bony goat was running through the line, and a fat ugly man was chasing it."

"Is the Manager goat," Sushilla said.

"That Sookdeo is a first-class crook. Sook-deo, Crook-deo. Have a finger in every bobol and skulduggery in the village. He show up a few times in the village council meeting asking for this and that permit, but the only permit he really need is one to lose fifty pounds." Narpat continued talking for a while about his new favorite topic, the Outsiders, until Dulari emerged from the kitchen and reminded the children about the next day's school.

After a few days Jeeves fell into this new routine: the early morning oiling and dressing, the awkward journey to and from school in his oversize canvas washycongs, the rigid assembly inspections, the enjoyable play in the mornings while the teacher dozed, the lunch-period games like agouti and dog, and hoop, and cricket, and scooch, the stories told by Kamini in the afternoon, and the hour of freedom while he waited for Sushilla. He also grew accustomed to his mother fretting on the porch each evening until her daughters' return. Then one evening they did not arrive at their accustomed time. She tapped her broom loudly, paced up and down the house, slapped Jeeves for spilling his food on the table, and wrung his ears when she discovered his crayons and pencils in a messy heap on the bed.

By the time they arrived, she was completely distraught. But her daughters were too tired to care. They had missed the four o'clock bus and had to wait two extra hours. That night Narpat relented and agreed to leave the field early in the afternoons to get them at Four Roads junction. Dulari did not seem completely satisfied with this arrangement, but she acknowledged it would be safer. So for the next few evenings Chandra and Kala arrived atop the tractor, on either side of their father, reeking of grease and exhaust fumes. In the mornings they stared at the oil stains on their blouses, but Narpat made jovial plans about constructing a carriage with velvet seats and a silk canopy so they could arrive home like little princesses.

Chandra imitated her mother's fatigued sigh with her shoulders slumping, though away from her father's notice. But Dulari was more forthright. "We could use the same money you intend to construct a carriage to send them to school in a taxi."

"Money? What money? When you have all these Leyland bus junk up by the wharf in San Fernando with brand-new seat and nice smooth tire." The children settled in for an extensive discourse. "The government buy all these expensive vehicle from England but didn't have the sense to buy spare parts or to train technicians to repair them. Now they talking about independence. Who we fighting for independence from? Where all the guns and tanks? Where the martyrs? How many people here prepared to lay down their life for this so-called cause?"

"You mean like in India?" Kala asked.

Chandra frowned and bit her lip, but Narpat smiled and congratulated Kala. "That was a real independence."

"Mahatma Gandhi was a—"

"Jackass of the highest order."

Chandra brightened up at the rebuke of Kala.

"My teacher—"

"Is a top-class jackass too." He fished out a penny from his pocket and stared at its oily sheen, guessing that it had wound its way from a brass plate, a *tariyah*, offered as *dachina* to some pundit. "This side of the penny is love." He flipped the coin. "And this side is hate. Two sides of the same thing."

"The two is the same?"

Looking at the coin rather than at Kala, he answered, "Both give you a sense of power. Make you feel strong and superior. Two side of the same disease." He spun the coin toward Jeeves, and the boy tried to catch it.

Kala redirected the conversation to a more understandable issue. "My teacher . . . my book said that we are giving up slavery and bondage."

Narpat smiled. "How much slave you see on your way from school?"

"I believe I see numerous still working in the sugarcane fields."

"Kala!"

Dulari's warning came too late; Narpat was still smiling but his voice was cold. "If you walk through the whole of this island . . . if you walk from top to bottom, you will find only one group of people who never depend on anyone else for anything. Who don't line up for handout. One group of honest and hardworking people. And that is why everybody think they is slaves. Because they hardworking. Because they do all the work that the government supposed to do. Cut down forest. Maintain the land. Build roads. Clear drains." Now he glanced up angrily at Dulari in the kitchen. "All the honest people is slave, Mammy. All the lazy people free. The fat, rich, lazy people with cinema and four-five truck like Bhola. All the diabetics and them. Wheezing every time they count their money. Their eyes coat over with greediness. Surviving from one scheme to the other."

Only Dulari knew how much Narpat had been offended. "Time for everybody to go to bed." Kala seemed set to say something, but her mother shouted, "Now!"

Jeeves decided that *independence* was one of those curse words he had heard whispered from time to time by the older boys, but a few days later he heard it being repeated in the assembly by the Headmaster. "When we do get independence, all you little children will be able to walk proudly to school with your heads high. With a new sense of purpose and character." The Headmaster, musing on whether principals' salaries would be increased, drifted off into other benefits.

During the morning recess Jeeves asked Danny, who had grown into an expert on capricious information, about independence, and the boy replied casually that independence might have to be postponed. "I understand that fifty battleship flying down from England right now. Take what I tell you." Danny never explained the source of his dispatches, and he usually concluded with a confident: "Take what I tell you." A few days earlier Kamini had displayed a colorful chart illustrating the process of evaporation. After the class, Danny had revealed the chart was misleading. "I understand that is really the rainbow that does take up the water to eat the fish. Then it does drop it back as rain."

Jeeves was fascinated with Danny's stories. He thought of them while he was scratching out his sums and memorizing Mr. Haroon's nursery rhymes. Unlike his father's fables, and even Kamini's favored tales by Enid Blyton and Hans Andersen, Danny's stories took place in familiar, easy-to-imagine settings; and *he* was always the hero. Danny had begun school late and was nine years old, more than three years above the average age of the class. He was popular with the boys, but the girls avoided him. One of his major revelations was about the standard seven girls. He said that when girls were fourteen, they began to exude a sweet, sticky substance on their skins that made them smell more fragrant than younger girls and boys. "I understand that some people does collect this ooze and make cake and pie and sweetie. Put a few drops in Solo sweet-drink too. Take it from me."

Although he was talkative away from class, he usually stared morosely while Mr. Haroon or Kamini taught their lessons. He disappeared for about fifteen minutes each lunch break, and when Jeeves asked where he had been, he said that he was playing cricket with the older boys. Jeeves mentioned that he had never spotted him on the muddy cricket field at the back of the school. Danny scooped up a flat pebble and arced it over the Manager's house. He said that the clumps of bamboo at the far end of the cricket field concealed jagged landslips and ravines trickling between the roots of the immortelle and tapano trees. "Is a perfect nesting spot for river conch and cascadoo."

Jeeves recalled the tiny guppies he had seen during the canefield visit with his father. "You does catch them?"

"Sometimes yes, sometimes no." The ravines, he said, ran into a secluded valley overgrown with wondrous fruit trees. Golden mamesepote, and governor plums, and balata sweeter than any cherry.

"So you does eat these fruit and them?"

"Sometimes yes, sometimes no." He preferred to gaze at the deer and agouti and macaws and parrots and flamingoes and nimble monkeys.

Jeeves tried to visualize this place as a scene from *National Geographic*. He was captivated. "You think I could go there too?"

Danny shook his head.

"Why not?"

"It have a spirit. A prate name Papa Bois watch manning the place. He does get vex if too much people come visiting." Jeeves puzzled over this, but before he was able to ask about this prate, Danny ran to the mango tree and scaled up the trunk. In the afternoon, while Kamini was reading a story about a trickster named Anansi, Danny leaned over to Jeeves. "Don't tell nobody about this place, especially Kevin." Jeeves glanced at Kevin, a well-dressed boy sitting between two girls in the front row, his long curls scattering over his forehead while he guardedly molded his plasticine.

When he and Sushilla arrived home from school, they spotted on the table an assortment of pens, bowclips, rulers, pencils, erasers, four new bookbags, and a plastic bag with three pairs of socks. Sushilla rummaged through the pile, her eyes lighting up.

"Who is all this for?" Sushilla asked her mother.

"For everybody."

"I could have a bowclip?"

"One. *Only* one. And Jeeves, the shoes in that box is for you."

Jeeves opened a white cardboard box, unraveled the crepe paper, and retrieved a pair of new rubber shoes. He slipped in a foot and shook his leg. The shoe stayed firm.

"Where you get all this money? Daddy give it to you?"

Dulari returned to the kitchen without answering her daughter's question.

Jeeves was still wearing his new shoes, pacing around the house, when Chandra and Kala arrived with their father. The boy raised a leg to show off his shoes.

"Nice, very nice." Narpat took off his shirt, went to the window, and flapped it a few times. "I see Lord Lalloo pay a little visit today." Then without saying another word, he put on his shirt and returned to his tractor. The children all sensed that something was wrong, and from the slow, prolonged scouring in the kitchen, they knew that their mother was brooding over her husband's abrupt departure.

That night they listened to their parents quarreling and gathered that following Bhola's visit, their mother had journeyed with him to Princes Town, where she had purchased proper uniforms for Chandra and Kala and new shoes for Jeeves. Worse, she had borrowed two hundred dollars from her brother and had made arrangements with Janak to transport her two daughters to and from school.

Narpat argued in a savage, jerky Hindi, biting his words as if his teeth were clenched. When he broke into English, his children were able to piece together the reason for his anger. With all four children at school, their mother had too much time on her hands. She was now free to walk about the town like her sister- in-law Babsy, buying fancy nonsense. But he was more incensed by her debt to Bhola. In his entire life he had never borrowed a single cent. Not from the bank nor from family. Debt was a blight, a curse from which there was no return. It was a symptom of weakness; invariably it led to malice, rancor, and arguments. The two hundred dollars would hang around her neck and suffocate her. There was a moment of silence, and the children smelled the tangy Limacol their mother doused on her head when she was fatigued. Kala whispered from the wall separating the two bedrooms, "Mammy crying."

EIGHT

*I*n less than a week Narpat's wrangling settled into a more typical and generalized disapproval of the inadequacies he spied around every corner. He commented drily on the villagers who were up to their necks in debt, and who survived only on credit from Hakim, who stocked his small parlor with dusty tins of sardine and citrus concoctions; and Lumchee, the Chinese grocer. All the bars from Lengua to Penal on one side, and Rio Claro to Princes Town on the other, were swarming with drunkards. "They take a simple, innocent thing like cane juice and convert it to one of the worse poison on the face of the earth. Worse even than white sugar. And you know what will happen to these people? One day a piece of they liver will shut down, the next day the kidneys will join in." He got up and walked to the table, slouching and dragging his feet and flailing his arms. Kala tried to imitate his movements, then Sushilla and Jeeves.

Chandra sighed tiredly, and Dulari, setting her husband's food on the table, said in mock annoyance, "Come, Mr. Drunkard, you better eat this eddoes and sardine and watercress before it get too cold." Narpat turned to his food, squelching noisily.

Dulari smiled at Kala and Jeeves, who were still lumbering about. "All right, little drunkards. Bring allyou books and let me see what allyou learn in school today." While the children were fetching their books, Dulari placed her hand on her husband's shoulder. "Stop making that noise while you eat. It disgusting."

"The spit will speed up digestion."

"Oh gosh, man." She rocked her husband's shoulder playfully. This odd play was the only type of affection the children ever noticed between

their parents. This time though, unaware that their father was secretly relieved that he no longer had to leave the field early, they were surprised at
the swift resolution to the school busing issue.

Each evening Dulari examined their books with a grim steadfastness. She
pointed out the blotches and dog-ears and scratches and Jeeves's indeterminate scribbles. Chandra grew sullen and edgy during the examinations,
but Kala frequently volunteered to read passages from her literature
books: *Heidi*, and *Little Women*, and *Lorna Doone*, and *My Family and
Other Animals*. Dulari would close her eyes and listen attentively until it
was time to test Sushilla and Jeeves. But Jeeves could only recite a few
lines of puzzling, senseless nursery rhymes, and snatches of stories he
had picked up from Kamini. Occasionally Narpat joined in, especially
when Jeeves was reciting, *This old man / He played one / He played knick
knack* . . .

At school, the Manager popped into the infants' department with a
frequency that alarmed and irritated Mr. Haroon. One morning Danny
revealed that the Manager was Kamini's father, and soon she would be
appointed as a monitor, an intermediate stage between a student teacher
and a regular teacher. His sources, he said, were the older boys, who had
also revealed that Mr. Haroon's nicknames were Mister Morocoy and
Teacher Totsi. "My understanding is because of them two morocoy in the
aquarium. You never notice?"

Jeeves could not help but notice. He began to pay more attention to
Mr. Haroon's curious examination of the overturned turtles and soon developed a fascination with the animals himself. They were like the little
wind-up toys he had spied on the top shelf of Lumchee's grocery. They
moved slowly in little snaps, they playfully poked their head out, and best
of all, they seemed indestructible. They could be dropped, rattled, kicked,
and bounced.

Mr. Haroon always left school immediately after the whistle, allowing
Kamini to replace the plasticine and straighten the cupboard. Gradually,
Jeeves hatched his plan. For a few days he hung around, pretending he
was searching for a pencil or eraser, but there were always other students
legitimately searching for lost pencils and erasers. Then one day he was
left by himself. Swiftly, he dipped his hand into the aquarium and re-

moved one turtle, then the other. He placed them on the floor and withdrew to a safe distance. He wasn't sure what he expected of them, but he
had the vague idea they might slowly engage in a race. They pushed their
heads out and looked around but remained rooted. When Jeeves heard
approaching footsteps, he bolted out of the room.

The next morning the teacher's normally sleepy eyes were livid.
"Everybody stand up right now. The whole blasted class going to pay if I
don't find Lakshmikant and Pyarelal." The class realized for the first time
that the turtles had names. He questioned the students one by one. "Sa-
roop, you know anything about Lakshmikant and Pyarelal?"

"No, sir."

"Kevin, you know?"

"No, sir. Gospel truth."

Each student picked up the phrase as additional insurance.

"Tackoordeen?"

"No, sir. Gospel truth."

"You in the end row. The fat, dotish-looking boy. Who is your father?"

"Kumkaran, sir. Gospel truth. The lord will send me to hell to roast up
and fry like plantain if I lie."

"You know anything, Rodriguez?"

"No, sir."

"You sure?"

Rodriguez was too scared to invoke the gospel, and Mr. Haroon glared
at him. "I know you come from a well-known orange-thieving family, but
Lakshmikant and Pyarelal is not two rotten bags of yam on a donkey back,
you hear me."

Jeeves began to tremble, as did many of the other students who were
alarmed at Mr. Haroon's growing fury.

"You! Ramanand big-teeth daughter."

The girl began to cry, which infuriated Mr. Haroon even more. "Eh? I
wonder who crying for Lakshmikant and Pyarelal now?" Suddenly his
face softened.

Kamini seized the opportunity. "Maybe we should check the desks,
Mr. Haroon."

He seemed temporarily lost. "Yes, yes." But as the search progressed,
his rage returned. "Everybody line up by the partition. Indian file. March
quick. Left, right." His dissolute face took on an unhinged, menacing

quality. His upper lip trembled. "We going outside to look for them." The children, followed by a frustrated Kamini, filed into the yard. They searched the shallow concrete drain bordering the school, they poked beneath the water tank, they crept and scurried between the clumps of bougainvillea and dracaena the Headmaster had planted at the front of the school, and two boys climbed the mango tree. Mr. Haroon screamed at them. "Anyone of allyou duncy-head little jackasses ever see a turtle climb a tree yet?"

After about an hour the children returned to class empty-handed. For the rest of the morning Mr. Haroon got out an assortment of liniments and massaged his forehead and the back of his neck. Just before the lunch break, he dropped the lemon he was sniffing, bolted from his chair, and snatched a clump of plasticine that Dilpaul was compressing into a ball. "What is this lump you making here? Your mother?" The class was startled into silence, and Kamini slammed her book on a desk.

As they filed out for lunch, Danny whispered to Jeeves, "He wasting his time for nothing. Them morocoys must be halfway to Princes Town by now. Take it from me."

"They could walk so fast?" Jeeves had been musing over the idea that perhaps the turtles had absconded to Danny's secret spot at the back of the school.

"Walk? They does run and skip like anything when they ready." He hawked and spat. "Remember the story about the morocoy and the rabbit." He added ominously, "I think the teacher going mad. Don't surprise if a white van drive up to school and pack him inside."

But Danny was wrong on both counts. The turtles were found by a group of boys who had already established two goal posts and were kicking them around. When they were brought to Mr. Haroon, he shook them against his ear, pressed them on either side of his cheeks, then gingerly returned them to the aquarium. He withdrew a small tin from his cupboard and sprinkled some gray granules into the water. "Grind-up baby bones," Danny whispered. Jeeves was relieved that the whole adventure had been resolved amicably.

Things were going well at home too. Each morning Janak squeezed Chandra and Kala with eleven other children into his Austin Cambridge. In the evenings Dulari hummed her songs while she was washing her wares, and when Narpat returned, he grumbled thinly about the backwardness of the villagers. The children had never seen their mother as contented, especially when Kala was reading aloud from one of her novels. And now that she no longer had to oversee Jeeves during the day, she made modest but innovative renovations to the house. She draped a bedsheet decorated with teddy bears over the table. She tacked rectangular pieces of cloth on the seats of the chairs. She attached her cocoyea broom to one of Narpat's pipes from beneath the house and cobwebbed the rafters. She sewed new curtains and applied passepartout to pictures of cats and dogs, which she hung on the walls over the crevices and splinters.

After a month or so she had exhausted all the possibilities in the modest house, and gradually, almost imperceptibly, her mood shifted. She still listened to Kala's stories, but the humming in the kitchen stopped, and soon she no longer pretended annoyance at Narpat's teasing. When he glanced at the pictures on the wall and said, "It raining cat and dog in this house," she did not laugh.

One night she told him, "The children getting too big to hide behind the copper and bathe every morning." The following night she repeated the concern.

Narpat said lightly, "Somebody check the gramophone. It look like the record stick."

But she persisted. She mentioned the difficulty of filling bucket after bucket from the roadside standpipe. In any case, the copper was only useful during the rainy season. Narpat then went on at length about the lead, mercury, and calcium in the pipe-borne water and said that the Navet dam was a known reservoir for typhoid and cholera. People from the towns dropped like flies from these diseases every day. But when his wife said that the latrine was the source of more diseases than the dam, he shrugged and said nothing.

Jeeves, who was constantly frightened of venturing to the latrine at the back of the house, particularly during the nights, began to pay more attention to this ongoing negotiation. During a conversation with Danny, the other boy had casually revealed that jumbies and prates were best kept away by swearing. Whenever he went hunting at nights for manicou or agouti or lappe, he would safeguard himself by chanting, "Allyou nasty mothersass prate bitches, haul allyou hairy stones from here." Jeeves had been impressed at the rapidity at which these vulgar phrases rolled off Danny's tongue but during his hurried trips at night, it was difficult to share his friend's confidence. So he was overjoyed when Narpat, though voicing that he would never bathe in dangerous tap-borne water, gave in to his wife's insistence on an indoor toilet and bathroom.

On Saturday the official from the Water and Sewerage Authority, a small man with a drooping straw hat and a wilting moustache, departed with his stack of permits in his yellow van, disappointed that he had not been offered a bribe and intimidated by Narpat's imperious manner. Dulari and the children gathered around excitedly as their father hauled out five lengths of aluminum pipe from beneath the house, and cut, joined, and fastened. He had refused to allow a plumber to handle the job, and for the remainder of the day he knocked the pipes into shape and patched the leaks and dents with a stripped bicycle tube. The next day he drew his plans on the end of a cardboard box, whistling as he modified and adjusted. Jeeves felt a sense of ownership as he looked on happily at the maze of intersecting lines.

On Monday night Narpat returned from the field with four sacks of cement; on Tuesday, with a huge tub of sand. Each day he brought some new material on his tractor—bricks, boulders, boxing board, and melau, the white pebbles that glinted when rubbed against one another. He worked late into the night, allowing Dulari or one of the children to hold the gas lamp while he mixed the cement and cast the foundation just outside the back door. He permitted Kala to turn the cement a few times, but when Jeeves tried, the shovel stuck in the paste. "The hookworm fighting against the exercise," he said, smiling. When he tore down the latrine, he used the cedar and the aluminum sheets for the new structure. Throughout he gave a commentary on the money he was saving by doing the work himself. The children were excited by all of this: by being up so late, by assisting their father, and most of all by the emerging shape of the toilet and bathroom. But when it was completed, it seemed identical to the old latrine. Then Narpat returned one night with the toilet bowl, tank, and sink, and they marveled at the shining new porcelain.

Ten days after he had started his project, he turned on the valve just before the roadside drain and invited his excited family into the new structure. He pressed the lever on the tank and the bowl filled with muddy water. He flushed again and a brown rim formed around the water level. "New water. It will clean out." But muddy water also sprinkled from the Ovaltine tin that was perforated with numerous holes and tied with copper wire to the bathroom tap. He cupped his hands and tasted the water. "Mud mix up with some limestone and melau and sand."

"One of the pipes must be spring a leak," Dulari said.

He tasted the water once more. "The perfect thing for filtering out bacteria. Our very own purification plant. What we have here is the cleanest water in all of Trinidad." The children refused his offer to taste the water, but they were overjoyed that they would no longer be forced to bathe furtively behind the copper or slip out at nights to the latrine. "Hide away this plan good because you never know when we will have to consult it." Jeeves hid away the piece of cardboard in Carnegie.

Later Jeeves would think of his mother's "improvement and renovation phase" as responsible for his new sleeping arrangement, but at the time he blamed Chandra and Kala, whose complaints about sharing a room with their brother had escalated ever since they started high school.

Dulari tentatively suggested another room, but Narpat's innovatory mood had run its course. "I sleep in a old bench below a house for years," he said, not bothering to elaborate. Jeeves thought this was the end of the matter, but a few days later his father dragged out an old fiber mattress from the tractor. "Get it for next to nothing from Ramsingh. His daughter come back from England and don't want any old stuff again." He unrolled it in the living room next to the Pavilion and stomped on the stiff, protruding fibers. "Best thing for circulation. Stimulate every nerve in the body. Have the blood going top speed. Keep the *chakras* in prime shape. What you think?"

"Me?" Jeeves felt a sinking feeling in his stomach.

"Yes, Mister-man. You self. How old you is now? Five? Six? You getting too big to sleep with the"—he recalled one of Kala's books—"little women and them."

"Me alone, here?"

Narpat stepped away from the mattress. "Long ago in India and Persia, boys of a certain age had to pass through these tests to move on to manhood. Before the tests they was small and weak just like you. Couldn't shovel cement properly. No use to anyone." He snapped a finger. "But afterward they change into fighters and warriors."

"Just from sleeping in a mattress?"

Chandra tried to look bored, but she was delighted that Jeeves had been ousted from the room. Narpat smiled. "This is Trinidad. We don't have elephants or chariots here." That night Jeeves lay awake on the fiber mattress long after everyone else had fallen asleep. He pulled the sheet to his eyes and peeped at the bats flying through the eaves and hanging upside down from the rafters. He wrapped himself with the sheet, coiled into a ball, and listened to their shrill sounds. Then he heard other sounds: water dripping slowly in the kitchen sink, the chirp of crickets and grasshoppers, and a bird's faraway cry.

At school, Danny glanced at him sitting on the pavement while the other students played hoop, and three-hole marbles, and sheriff and thief. "They send you to school without food?"

Jeeves shook his head, surprised at his friend's question. When he explained, Danny, looking worried, said that bats were sly creatures that fastened their fangs on the necks of their sleeping victims. He added that the scissorslike mouth snipped the skin, so the tongue, shaped like a straw, could slip neatly into a vein.

Jeeves pressed his hands together and tried to hide his trembling. That night, covered with his blanket from head to toe, he listened to the bats flapping around the rafters. He fell asleep briefly and dreamed that a huge bat was clamped onto his neck. With the sheet around him, he wobbled up and stumbled into the bedroom. Sushilla awoke and, in the dim kerosene light, spied the sheet-clad body and screamed. Kala awoke and flung a hardcover edition of *Little Women* at him. Jeeves began to scream, a low, mournful sound. The sheet slipped off. From the other room Narpat shouted, "What going on there?"

There were hurried footsteps, and both parents rushed into the room. Jeeves tried to explain. Narpat was not impressed, but his mother said softly, "Come, you will sleep with us tonight." So that night Jeeves slept between his parents in a room smelling of Limacol and a strange comforting sweat. He enjoyed the warmth of his father's body and his mother's soft arms. When his parents fell asleep, he listened to Narpat snoring and noticed the rise and fall of his chest.

In the early morning, when the dew was fresh on the grass and Dulari was packing away her husband's lunch, Narpat pinched his son's neck and said, "Don't worry, we will deal with these bats and them once and for all." He looked down grinning at the boy. "Can't allow you to fail the test."

Jeeves contemplated his father's solution all day at school. An additional bed in his parents' room? Sleeping once more with his sisters? The construction of an additional room? But in the night Narpat returned with a clutch of thorny shrubs, two sour cherry branches, and a bundle of Chinese bamboo. He pulled the bench against the wall and arranged the shrubs and branches facing the eaves. "A perfect barrication."

In the night, Jeeves held the sheet against his chest and focused on the thorny barrier. The wind whistled through the shrubs, ruffling the leaves, but the bats were kept away. He slept soundly. The next day at school he ran after the football wildy, kicking and tumbling and imagining that the pain was his new muscles springing into action. Danny observed this new erratic fervor, and after the game, when Jeeves explained his father's protection, he said that he had contemplated suggesting that remedy but hadn't because snakes liked to crawl around the dried branches. The bats, he believed, were kept away by the snakes, not the thorns. Jeeves, still held by Narpat's talk of these marvelous transforming tests, was excited rather than disturbed by the notion of this new danger, and as Danny went on about snakes with human heads, and snakes with wings, and snakes that stood upright and looked you in the eye, he giggled nervously. Danny persisted. He revealed that once a cobra had spat in his face, and he had escaped certain death by grabbing the snake and biting off its tail. He said that this technique also worked with centipedes, scorpions, and spiders. He grimaced dramatically and said that occasionally he still felt the poison coursing through his body.

During the weekend, while Narpat was cleaning and greasing his tractor, Jeeves climbed onto the seat, placed his hands on the steering wheel, and tugged from side to side. He looked down at his father's oil-stained hands and shoulders. "This Farmall is your test?"

Narpat continued draining the oil into a plastic bleach bottle. "Yes, is a sorta test. But my real test take place long-long ago."

Jeeves stopped rocking. "It have more than one?"

Narpat wiped his hands with an old rag. "Every step you take is a test." He daubed some cloying grease on the axle and spread it around. Jeeves was disappointed that there was a multitude of tests. Some of his pride at sleeping alone faded. Narpat climbed onto the tractor and rocked the wheel to properly grease the axle. "My father was a cane farmer just like me. More hardworking than all the other farmers put together, and it show because he was able to extend from one acre to five to ten."

"The place you working in now?"

"A different field. Near the airport. The place was blazing with cane in those days. Now all that get convert into buildings. Like ugly concrete trains."

"And what happen to all the cane your father had?"

"Everything pass to his brother. He was the executor of the estate. A very dishonest man."

"Your uncle?"

"Was a common thing in those days. Brother thieving from brother. Most fathers use to leave their property in all their children name, as joint tenants, instead of dividing it up. It use to cause *commess* and confusion on all side. I was eleven years old at the time, and me and my sister and mother had no choice but to live with my uncle." Narpat was slightly breathless from the rocking, and his voice sounded harsh and clipped. "All three of us downstairs in that big house. In a small cardboard room. My bed was a nice little bench. In the morning, we went to work with his other laborers, and in the night we return with them. Working in my own father field for fifty cents a day. Fifty cents, Carea. And I save every penny. While my uncle son was driving about in his fancy car and going to the cinema, I was saving and saving." He rocked violently as if the wheel were stuck. "One night when we come back, the room was smash-up, with little pieces of cardboard and wood scatter all over the place. My sister begin to cry, but my mother just sit between all the mess and didn't say a single word. She didn't blame my uncle for robbing my father and she didn't blame him for smashing the room. She didn't say nothing either during the two weeks we spend sleeping in the back of a old 'bandon grocery own by a fella who went back to Portugal. Nothing when we move in the little one-room shack I build next to the land I was leasing."

Narpat dismounted from the tractor and rubbed his palms together. Jeeves watched the oil stains spreading evenly. "Why she wasn't talking?"

"She give up."

After a while the boy asked, "Like in a test?"

Narpat looked seriously at his son. "That is enough for one day." This was the first time he had elaborated beyond the brief cryptic references to his childhood, and Jeeves wished he would continue. The other students in his class had grand stories about their fathers: Rodriguez said that his father was a coco panyol who was eagerly sought out by the villagers for his Spanish prayers; Dilpaul's father was a former police officer who had been fired for not accepting a bribe from a county councilor; Danny hinted that his father was the county councilor; and even Kevin, who rarely spoke with the other boys, revealed that his father was living in America with three wives.

Jeeves also wanted his father to continue because he was intrigued by the notion of these curious tests. He tried to prod Narpat. "She never ever talk again?"

"She didn't get a chance. Fifteen days after we move to the little shack, she died."

"How?"

Narpat walked toward the house and pushed the bleach bottle beneath the step. When Jeeves came up, he swung him up the stairs. "She didn't realize that you have to fight hard for everything that you want."

"And you realize?"

"From the minute my father died."

"When I will know?"

Kala, who was reading on the floor, ran up to her father. Looking at his daughter rather than at Jeeves, he said, "When the time come, you will figure it out yourself." He pointed to his head. "This fella inside here will take care of it."

"You will help me?"

"All you have to do, Carea, is pay attention to the signs. They will be like little sticks waiting for you to pick them up."

NINE

*J*eeves soon grew accustomed to the welts from the fiber mattress, the wind whistling though the thorny shrubs, and the constant drip of water in the kitchen sink, but after Narpat's fragmentary account of his childhood, the boy's brief pride at sleeping alone gradually dwindled. He soon developed the idea that *real* tests sprang only from some immensely tragic event. His erratic, bristling energy increased at school, though, and he would frequently tumble in the field, trip over during hoop, and tangle himself in the branches of the mango tree. Dulari's attempts to reprimand him for the bruises and scratches were quelled by Narpat, who said that they were little badges of which he should be proud.

Then one day Jeeves received a major badge. His memory of the fall was fuzzy, and he depended on his classmates to fill in the blank spots. He remembered climbing the topmost branch of the mango tree to spy on the sadhus in the couteyah's compound. He recalled seeing the Headmaster's Morris Minor car beneath the Manager's house and a goat strolling around a sour cherry tree. He recalled dimly the crack of the branch and his swift descent to the ground, broken by the sprigs of foliage that had thrashed his arms and legs. He had regained consciousness at the side of the water tank, dazzled by the glare from Mr. Haroon's oiled scalp. Later there were several versions of what had happened. A few of the boys claimed to have made valiant, acrobatic leaps to catch him. Dilpaul insisted that he had fallen on his head, not, as Kevin maintained, spinning and floating through the air, and Danny, with a mixture of awe and envy, said that Jeeves was blight. He explained that it was easy to spot blight people: they were usually skinny with knobby kneecaps, bitten-down nails, and bulging eyes and were afflicted by bouts of trembling.

After he got home, Dulari fussed over him, asking several times whether his stomach or his head was hurting, and almost to appease her, he finally said that his neck was sore. When Narpat arrived, she was still massaging Jeeves with a concoction of Bengue's Balsam and soft candle. She spoke softly to her husband in Hindi, and he glanced at the boy's knees. "You turning blue, Carea. Just like one of these god on the almanac." He twisted his son's leg gently. "If this spread, we might have to cut it off, and you will have to hop about on one foot. We will have to get a crutch for you." Jeeves bolted up, and his father laughed. "This is how you know when the poison spreading. By the blueness of the skin. Gangrene."

Dulari removed her hand from Jeeves's chest. "Stop frightening the boy. Is iodine to stop any infection."

"Poison, poison." He got up and flapped his shirt against the window and returned to the Pavilion, sitting beside his wife. "You want to hear how dangerous all these drugs is?" Jeeves nodded. "When I was your age, my father and some other workers use to eat their lunch by the Caroni river. And they use to take off their tall tops and dip their foot in the nice cool water. What they didn't know was that a sly mister *huille* was peeping at them from the bullrush in the water."

"What is a huille?" Jeeves asked.

"A water snake, boy. With a head as big as a cow. And one day"—he leaned against the wall and drew up his legs—"one day the water start to bubble and froth up, and everybody pitch out and run away. Everybody but one worker."

"The huille bite him up?"

"Bite! It swallow him whole. Like a piece of potato." He opened his mouth wide, and Jeeves tittered. Now Kala and Sushilla came to the Pavilion. Chandra, who was helping her mother, peeped from the kitchen. "Everybody was afraid after that to go by the river, but one night my father had an idea."

He paused, and Jeeves said excitedly, "What? What idea?"

"He mix up a setta iodine and chemicals like Gramazone and Aldrex and he soak some chicken parts in the poison." He turned to Dulari and grinned. "And some white sugar and oil and butter too. The next morning he put all the poisoned meat in a sugar bag and fling it in the river. Two days later they find the mister huille floating in the water. Big like a train.

And when they cut open the belly, they find the sugar bag whole in his belly."

"And the worker too?" Sushilla asked nervously.

Narpat got up and went to his food on the table. "And cat and dog and goat and chicken too. A whole farm."

Sushilla placed her fingers against her mouth, and Kala bent her head and smiled. Narpat turned to his food and held up a *chataigne* seed circumspectly. "Poison. It never leave the body once it get a foothold."

"And what happen after." Jeeves wanted the account to continue.

"The story end, the wire bend, and the monkey break his back for a piece of *pommerac*."

The next day while he was walking to school, Jeeves marveled at his father's ability to transform a setback into an enjoyable tale; the world he created was always simple and fluid and controllable. That morning he was placed at the back of the class, next to Balack, a very dark, overweight boy with thick straight hair that fell in a mop over his forehead, and Mr. Haroon, originally intending Jeeves to spend the rest of the day recuperating in the last seat, either forgot about it the next day or preferred the arrangement.

He remained there for the rest of the year. Neither Mr. Haroon nor Kamini bothered him or his new seatmate. Their work was never corrected; nor were they asked questions. From time to time Jeeves glanced at Balack, his head bent low over his slate as he occasionally whipped out his tongue to clear away his running nose. Briefly Jeeves wondered whether this new arrangement was also a test, but not wanting to tempt fate, he decided to just enjoy this concession.

One morning after Kamini had read a story about an ogre she called a Skrattel, Danny leaned back and whispered, "Who this Skrattel monster remind you of?"

"The Manager," Jeeves replied immediately.

"No, no. Who in the class?"

Jeeves gazed around. He saw Balack digging into a nostril and began to laugh.

Mr. Haroon grabbed the edge of his table and got up slowly. He brushed past Kamini. "Stand up, boy. You think this is a funny story?"

Jeeves was roped in by the teacher's soft voice. "Miss Kamini describe the ogre like Balack."

The class broke into laughter, and Mr. Haroon returned to the front of the class, leaving Jeeves standing. He called Balack to his side. "You is a ogre, boy? How you feel to be called a ogre?"

Balack looked at the amused class and smiled. "It feel nice."

Mr. Haroon seemed distracted by the laughing students. "Nice? Then you really is a ogre. Go back to your seat right now."

After school Danny told Jeeves with a trace of admiration, "I thought for sure that Mr. Haroon was going to send you to the Headmaster office."

And Jeeves was astonished that he had escaped punishment and risen in his friend's estimate through the laughter of the class.

On the last day of that week, a new student who looked as old as Danny and just as tough enrolled in the class. He was a slim boy with a perfectly round head, black shining skin, and a frozen scowl. He was given a slate and sent to sit with Jeeves and Balack at the back. For the entire day he glowered at the class and glanced distastefully at Balack. After dismissal he bounded down the hill, which was unusual because all the smaller children waited either till regular dismissal or till they were met by an adult.

The new boy was one of only four black students in the school, but the parents of those students had lived in the village as long as everyone else and were well known. Danny conjectured that the boy had come from Port of Spain, or worse, from one of the small islands. He said that they chose small remote areas like Lengua to escape detection. "It have only one way to *cife* them out. They have this big bump on they tongue that prevent then from saying some words"

"Like what?"

Danny scratched his head. "You ever hear him talk yet?"

"He does keep quiet all the time."

"They can't say *box* and *dog*. What is his name?"

Jeeves tried to recall the boy's name written on his copybook. "Kassie."

"Kassie? You sure? The only Kassie I ever hear about is a pundit fella from Penal." He grinned. "Must be his black outside son."

Jeeves could not understand the joke. The next day he tried to engage the new boy in a conversation. "What is your name?"

"Why you want to know that?"

"'Cause my friend say that black people does have funny name. And you write Kassie on the slate yesterday."

"Who does have stupider name than all these country bookie? Ram this and Ram that." He thumped his plasticine on the table. "My name is Quashie. And in the future, mind your blasted business."

The following day Danny said, "Quashie? Is a real funny name, if you ask me. Two to one, he is a small islander. Get him to say *box*. Or *dog*."

After the lunch break Jeeves recited, "A for apple, b for . . ."

"Belly pain." Balack grimaced out the word, which was an accomplishment because it was the first time he had spoken in class.

But Jeeves was annoyed. A few minutes later he tried again. "What is your favorite pet?" He added hastily, "Not you, Balack."

"Parakeet," Quashie said hesitantly.

"What about dog?"

He glared suspiciously at Jeeves. "If you have any damn puppy you trying to give away, I don't want none."

"Don't have no puppy."

"Then don't want no dog either."

"He smart like anything," Danny said contemplatively. "You have to trick him to say *box*."

Jeeves, however, decided to tap a higher authority. He had recently developed the habit of hanging around while his father was repairing his tractor, at first to avoid his mother's new obsession with his homework but gradually because he felt a sense of importance whenever he was asked to pass a pliers or spanner or when his father explained, as to an adult, some technical term. He marveled that less than two years ago he had been forbidden to go outside when it was dark and that he had strolled around the house in a nightie. Sometimes he wished for a swift surge to adulthood so he could be as strong and independent as his father, but from the conversations with Narpat, he gathered that the road to maturity was paved with test after test. That night he told his father, "A new boy come in class today."

"So he is your new friend?"

Jeeves pondered this. "My other friend say he come from another island."

Narpat grimaced as he secured a nut. "What island?"

"I don't know the name."

With the handle of his wrench he tapped the nut. "Guyana, Grenada, Tobago, Jamaica?" The names seemed to echo the sonorous tapping. "What is this fella name?"

"Squashy." After a while he added, "And he could say *dog*."

Narpat's lips tightened in one of his humorless smiles. "Most likely he living in Dogpatch. Keep an eye on him. Watch your books and pencil, and if he causing you any trouble, let me know."

The next day Jeeves lost a black crayon, but when he glanced around, he noticed it sticking out like a chimney from one of Balack's plasticine inventions. Each morning while Jeeves strained to hear Kamini's story, Balack painstakingly wriggled tiny pieces of plasticine into miniature trays, tires, and hoods.

"This damn stupid place," Quashie said.

"Is a nice school."

Now Quashie directed his attention to Jeeves. "Who say so? You? And who talking about the school in the first place?"

"What place then?"

"Over here. With only stupid cane and stupid house on long post and stupid animal tie allover the place."

"It never had all these things in your island?"

"What damn stupidness you talking now? I come from Port of Spain. The town," he said proudly.

Narpat had often described the island's capital as a huge, dusty, disorganized city where people routinely dismounted from some overcrowded boat and constructed a shack on the nearest plot of unoccupied land. Many of the newcomers chose the northern range, and their houses hung precariously from slopes and foothills. "I hear people does live like bachacs in that place," Jeeves said.

"And over here they does live like crab. Bathing in the mud whole day and running back to the bush in the night. With little children speeding around with no pants."

"So why you come then?"

"Is none of your damn business."

Jeeves decided to leave the new boy alone. The rest of the class had already developed this attitude, and during each lunch break Quashie leaned against the wall and watched the other children playing cricket and football. Once Jerome, one of the four black students at the school and the captain of the football team, placed a hand on his shoulder and whispered something, but when the other boy returned to his game, Quashie remained against the wall, staring sourly at everyone. In the afternoon he said, "*Dhal* water." A few minutes later he added, "That is why they does play sports like little woman. All that dhal water they drinking make them weak."

"Who?" Jeeves asked, a bit surprised because his father had offered the same dietary assessment.

"Everybody in this stupid place. All the country bookie and them."

"What allyou does eat in Port of Spain?"

"Good food. Pudding and souse and all kinda meat." He caught himself. "Mind your damn business."

Danny provided the missing details. "They does eat anything that fall on the ground or get bounce down."

"Like what?"

"My understanding is that it have no cat or dog in Port of Spain again. Take it from me. You better be careful because two to one, he might get real hungry one day and eat up you or Balack. Or maybe you alone because Balack too nasty. I think I better start walking home with you just to be sure." Danny, who was offended by Jeeves's growing friendship with Balack, was pleased to once more walk home with the two boys.

When they arrived home, Sushilla told her brother, "You choose the two worst boys in the class to be friends with. That nasty one and now this other one who does look like a little criminal. Just now you will come friend with the lil creole too," she added disapprovingly.

And that was exactly what happened. On Friday, Danny was showing off in the mango tree, sprinting from branch to branch and hanging upside down. Quashie passed by Jeeves and said aloud, "Just like he monkey god." Balack, who was collecting pebbles to augment his plasticine vehicles, stood up. "The old lady tell me that people from around here does pray to goat and monkey and rat," Quashie continued.

"Which old lady?"

"My mother, stupidee."

Although there were a few calendars with Hindu gods and goddesses in the house, Jeeves and his sisters suspected that they were tolerated by Narpat only because they gave him an opportunity for argument. "Your old lady crazy."

"Monkey god." Quashie sniggered.

Balack walked to the mango tree. When the bell rang for dismissal, Danny rolled up his copybook and ran after Quashie. "Which monkey god you talking 'bout?"

Quashie turned and said calmly, "Yours."

"Your mother is a monkey. Your father too. All of allyou people is monkey." Danny shouted and lunged at Quashie, grabbing his collar and spinning him around. Although Quashie was caught off guard, he soon regained his footing, and the two boys danced around in a lock, each trying the throw the other to the ground. Quashie was taller, slimmer, and nimbler, and Danny more compact and stronger. Neither was willing to give ground. Then Quashie skipped suddenly to the side, crooked his leg against Danny's, and pitched him to the ground. Danny kicked out savagely, and soon both boys were on the ground rolling and tumbling over each other. On the ground Danny had the advantage, and he managed to get astride the other boy.

Then it was over. Mr. Moonilal hauled both boys up, Danny first. He swished his whip in preparation before he unleashed a range of strokes, twisting his wrist so that the blows came from all angles. "You think this is your father backyard, eh? You think this is Golden Grove jail? How much years your convict father get? Six? Then is six more for you." The other students had never seen Danny so defenseless. He was slumped to the ground, his hands covering his face. Mr. Moonilal turned to Quashie. "And you. You think this is some mashup Port of Spain school where half the students don't know who they father is? Teaching steelband and bad johnning? Well, we have different values here. Let me show you."

"No," Quashie screamed. "No!"

"Eh? But what happen to you and all?" Mr. Moonilal was shocked into dialect.

"You can't beat me like that."

The teacher recovered somewhat. "I can't beat you? My crosses, I forget." He glanced around at the other students. "Remind me who is the teacher here and who is the student, please."

"Touch me, and I will tell my mother."

That stopped Mr. Moonilal dead in his tracks. He was accustomed to the passive village parents who usually unleashed a fresh burst of punishment on their children if they complained of a beating at school. But the town parents were a different matter. They had dozens of outside children. They waltzed in and out of jails. They armed themselves with guns. They would think nothing of exacting savage revenge on a teacher.

He turned to the gaping children. "Eh? What allyou little wretches hanging around here for? The matinee finish." He swished his whip, and they bolted. He turned once more to Quashie and smiled stiffly. "You notice the kind of values we have in this school? You better get accustom to it real fast."

Jeeves was too scared to go to Danny, still kneeling on the ground and staring blankly at the few onlookers. Quashie went instead. "Your father really in Golden Grove?" Without saying a word, Danny got up and ran down the hill. He stumbled into a tractor rut and, with his clothes now soiled with mud, continued down the hill.

Quashie loped over to Jeeves and Balack with a slight swagger. Jeeves asked him, "You wasn't 'fraid?"

And Quashie slipped into a pose with which Jeeves would grow familiar: he made a half-step so that one foot was slightly before the other, dangled his arms like a runner loosening, and said very casually, "Who? Me?" That afternoon for the first time he hung around until regular dismissal. The next day, when Jerome ambled over for a quick greeting, Quashie ran off with him. Afterward he announced to Jeeves and Balack that he would be trying out for the football team. Jeeves didn't pay much attention because he was focused on Mr. Haroon, who was uncharacteristically walking through the class and mopping his face with a chalky rag that left white trails on his harassed face. He retrieved a book from his cupboard, coughed loudly, and without announcement began reading, in a lugubrious voice, a poem about an Indian who had been peacefully gathering shells when he was beset by conquistadores. He closed the book and, in an absentminded voice, droned on about peaceful communities upset by the intrusion of strangers. Mopping his face and scowling, he mentioned that he had always enjoyed teaching the infants' department because of his affection for little children. They could be molded like plasticine. They were innocent. They brought no distress to their teachers, no reprimands from the principal. He rambled on about unacceptable changes and faded into incoherence. Jeeves was fascinated by the teacher's pained expression.

When the bell rang for lunch break, and Balack slogged to the drain to collect his pebbles and Quashie ran off with Jerome, Jeeves followed Danny, thinking he would catch up with him in the magical forest. But Danny circled to the other side of the school, to the plot just ahead of the Manager's house. He sat beneath a guava tree, pulled out an oily paper bag from his pocket, and withdrew a single slice of roti that he placed on his knee while he refolded the bag. Jeeves had meant to join his friend, but he felt that Danny, eating his modest meal by himself, would not appreciate the company, so he returned to the other side of the school. He felt sorry and guilty to have witnessed Danny's humiliation and also for having seen him sitting alone, consuming his simple meal, but after school, the other boy said, "I think I going to buss through the track at the back and then tack back to the couteyah."

"Why?" Jeeves asked.

"Why? 'Cause I want to see if the sadhu have a tail coil up inside he *dhoti*." He hawked and spat, and Jeeves realized that Danny's casual bravado had returned. "Who going?"

Balack began slinking away, and Quashie pushed his hands in his pocket.

"Me," Jeeves said.

Danny turned to Jeeves, surprised. "You sure? You not 'fraid?"

"No. I want to see the tail."

"It will be dangerous."

Jeeves thought of his father's fables. "I still want to see it."

Now Danny seemed undecided. He narrowed his eyelids. "Better I go alone this time and report back what I see. Like a scout."

When he left, both Balack and Quashie seemed relieved. "Why allyou didn't want to go?" Jeeves asked.

"You is a stupidee or what? Suppose—" Quashie stopped short.

"Suppose what?"

"I hear they does sacrifice people in them place."

"Who tell you that?"

"The old lady. And that if you touch one drop of that holy Indian food, you could get possess for life."

The next day Danny confirmed Quashie's trepidation. The couteyah, he said, was guarded by a two-headed cobra that had prevented his entrance into the building. Before the cobra had chased him away, however, he was able to glimpse a group of sadhus floating on stiff cardboard clouds around a smiling demon with a horned helmet. "From what I cife out, he is the main raksha. I think he is some kinda cannibal. Take it from me."

"You really see them thing?" Quashie was too frightened to maneuver into his breezy pose.

"Must be true because I spot the exact scene in a almanac at home." Jeeves was excited by all of this.

Danny lowered his voice. "And the raksha had a real big belly. Two to one, he does eat children. I think I see a few of them jumping up inside him."

"How children does taste?" Balack asked seriously.

"Like chicken. Only a little more salty." While they were walking home, Danny hinted that he had spoken to one of the lesser demons and had been granted a secret wish that somehow involved Mr. Moonilal.

$\mathcal{T}$hree months following Danny's visit to the couteyah, a new teacher was introduced to the assembly. He was a young, nervous-looking man who, unlike the other teachers, wore crisp suede cardigans, corduroy bell-bottoms with huge stylish belt buckles, and round tortoiseshell sunglasses and styled his hair in an unruly mop. Everything about him was thin: his moustache, chin, and nose; his pointed shoes with two-inch heels; even his striped tie slung stylishly over a shoulder. "This is Mr. David Doon," the Headmaster announced. "Fresh from Canada. He will be helping out in the infants' department and standard one. He is on a probation. Now say *probation*."

"Pro-ba-shun," the children chorused.

Mr. Doon looked crestfallen; he stroked his tie sadly.

The few hours that Mr. Doon spent in the infants' department seemed to distress Mr. Haroon even more. He sipped and sapped from a variety of tiny vials while the new teacher walked though the classroom, clasping and unclasping his fingers and murmuring mysteriously to himself. On his second day, without any warning, Mr. Doon said in a high-pitched voice, "Book sense is nonsense." Mr. Haroon jumped. Mr. Doon strode over to the last desk and surveyed Jeeves, Balack, and Quashie. "In Canada, we don't spurn kids who are differently abled. To *us*, these kids are special. Now repeat after me, 'Book sense is nonsense.'"

He belabored this slogan several times during the day, and whenever the class was slow to respond, Kamini would chirp in an exasperated voice, "Kids!" He placed Quashie on the front bench and spoke ardently about affirmative action and the backseats of buses, but the boy was deeply suspicious of the move and kept sneaking back to his regular seat.

Mr. Haroon restocked his cupboard with droppers and lemon slices and tubes of liniment. The room now smelled of camphor and menthol. Then unexpectedly he got a reprieve. Mr. Doon began taking the class outside, to the water tank and the bougainvillea and dracaena at the front and occasionally to the cricket field at the back. "Creative visualization," he told the confused children. "Look at that leaf there. What sort of leaf do you think it is?"

"A *chicito*," Rodriguez volunteered.

"To you it is a chicito, but to me it is more. Far, far more." The children waited for an explanation, but Mr. Doon was now lost in his examination of the leaf. Another day he pointed to a scissorstail circling the field and, in his high-pitched voice, sang, "O lovely scissorstail, how graceful doth you fly. While other creatures tread the ground, your domain is the sky." He looked down, his eyes slightly glazed, and confessed to the class, "I was a budding poet in Canada. Part of the underground literary club," he said mysteriously. "Had quite a few pieces published in journals, too. The guys there said I was a first-class poet, but to me"—he hesitated and fondled his tie—"it was just a hobby. Now who can tell me what a poet is?"

"A guy who write poetry," Kamini said.

He nodded graciously. "A first-class response. But a poet is more than that. Far, far more. He is a man or a woman who is just bursting with ideas and joie de vivre. He is a mystic and a seer. A lonely creature walking the roads of life dragging his dusty imagination like a leaden tail."

Sitara burst through the teacher's contemplative mood. "What is a seer, sir?"

"I think is a sadhu," Danny whispered to Jeeves. "The same sorta tail."

"A *obeahman*," Kevin shouted.

Kamini clucked disapprovingly, but Mr. Doon was more charitable. He stroked his tie. "'O omniscient seer, how wisely doth thou preach. Thou hast traveled far to enchanted lands, we can never hope to reach.'" He released his tie. "Culled from one of my pieces in *Exile*."

Kamini's eyes widened in awe and admiration.

"*Now* who can tell me what a poet is? He is a man bursting with . . ."

The class went silent.

"Kids!"

Rodriguez tried to recall the strange words the teacher had used. "With jaundice."

Mr. Doon seemed confused, then said, "With joie de vivre. With joy of life. With music in his head, beating, beating, beating all day long. And the most amazing thing is that each of us"—he gestured to the children— "has a poet drumming away inside us."

After school Balack said: "I have a poet inside me belly."

Quashie said: "I have a uncle in the States. He going to send for me one of these days. He promise that in a letter."

Jeeves said: "I have a father who does say the same thing like this teacher. 'Bout ideas and futuring."

And Danny said: "I have a good feeling that one day a white van will pull up in the schoolyard and drag Mr. Doon inside. Give him a big, fat injection in his bottom."

But Mr. Doon's popularity grew at school. Although he had spent more than half of his twenty-four years in Trinidad, he rarely referred to his childhood, and from his accent, his clothing, his conversations, and his references to strange, exotic animals, the students and the other teachers considered him a bona-fide foreigner.

At the end of the school year, he followed Mr. Haroon and his class into standard one, and Kamini, with the help of her father, also transferred. She started wearing new frocks and colorful silky scarves, which she continuously tugged and adjusted. Mr. Doon carried the class farther afield to the brink of the playground, where there were stunted wild guavas and blacksage and jumbie-bead bushes and a withered poui. Once he looked down at a small muddy ravine. "O mighty river, how powerful doth thou flow. No wall, no fence, no barricade can cause your course to slow."

He caressed his tie.

Kamini fingered her scarf.

Mr. Doon made the students sit at the edge of a landslide, their legs dangling against the exposed mud. The class waited. The teacher stared down. Some of the boys swung their feet in boredom, dislodging small pieces of mud. After about twenty minutes of silence, he intoned, "Emotion collected in tranquility." He got up and dusted his trousers. "I am a Wordsworthian. By nature, not nurture." No one really knew what he was talking about. During staff meetings too, he spoke mysteriously about in-

teractive learning and community-based models, and when he learned of
the school's budgeting problems, he suggested a bazaar involving the entire village. The Headmaster, initially cold to the proposal, eventually ap-
proved when Mr. Doon explained that the bazaar would not only be an
ideal fund-raiser but would also advertise the school.

The Manager's visits to the school increased, and there were frequent
muddy trails on the classroom's floor. He looked on approvingly at Mr.
Doon lecturing in his foreign accent, and sometimes he followed the students outside. One day he told the teacher, "All these 'telligent poetry you
does be rhyming out, Teach, my stupid opinion is that you should heap
them in a book."

Mr. Doon flung his tie over his shoulder. "How can I profit if I gain the
world and lose my soul." The Manager was taken aback by the teacher's
vehemence, but he began purring while the teacher explained, "My cre-
ations are like birds, graceful only when they are allowed to soar unfet-
tered. Once they are caged, they fall to the ground like lumpen lines.
Kicked aside and trampled."

"I see what you mean," the Manager said.

"But what about these poems you had in the Canadian magazines?"
Kamini asked.

"Test flights. Quite different from packing them like New Brunswick
sardines in a single tin."

The Manager told him, "You know something, Teach? You remind me
of meself in me younger days. When I had all these big-big hope and
dream." He stretched his arms, and his merino tightened even more
against his belly. "But when you take wife and half a dozen children spring
out, then you have to keep all you stupid opinion"—he corrected himself
hastily—"I mean all you dreams and hope to yourself." He said dreamsanhope. "Now wife gone, and all the *neemakaram* children move out. Just
me and this little girl here."

Kamini frowned and said stiffly, "My father is a simple guy."

"Simple yes, but I still have all me dreamsanhope pack away inside me
whole heart."

A small dog emerged from the blacksage and slunk up to the children.
The Manager snatched a stone from the ground. "Haul you nasty little ass
away from these nice children." He flung the stone. The dog yelped and
ran back into the bushes. "Belong to these damn lochos who does go to

catch conks and crab and buss out behind my house like if is they father property." He cupped his palms against his mouth. "If ever I catch anybody in my property, they father go have to buy a new foot or hand for them."

"Kids!" Kamini shushed the giggling children and, with an exasperated look, turned to the teacher. But Mr. Doon was gazing intently at the bushes.

"Sorry, lil children," the Manager said in a sugary voice. "Is how these locho and them does drive a simple man to behave sometimes. Simple but experience. Organize all kinda fund-raiser in me life. Waiting a long time to try me hand at school bazaar. Could organize all the eats and drink and games. Darts and bran tub. Eh, Teach?"

But Mr. Doon was still gazing at the blacksage. His hand trembled toward his tie. "O modest mongrel, how humbly doth thou slink. To give thee bone or meal or drink, we seldom ever think."

At home, Jeeves—like many of the other students—mentioned the new poetry-spouting teacher who had promised to put an end to the arbitrary flogging of students and who talked mysteriously of yellow school buses and multi-exceptionality classes. Kala seemed interested in Jeeves's account, and one evening she told him, "In some countries, is against the law to beat children."

"Really? How you know that?"

"I read about it."

Jeeves thought of this for a while. "And in these place they don't do hard sums and handwriting exercise too? The new teacher don't do any of that. Only Mr. Haroon and Miss Kamini."

Narpat, who had been listening from the Pavilion, said lightly, "In less than a year they will chase him outta town. And you know where he will end up?"

"Where?" Jeeves asked.

"In the madhouse. Half the people there is teachers who study abroad."

The next day Jeeves mentioned his father's revelation. Quashie was skeptical, but Danny agreed immediately. "I think Mr. Haroon spend some time inside too. Every holidays he does have to go to St. Ann's for injection."

Jeeves began to pay more attention to his teachers. He was intrigued by Mr. Haroon's tormented expression and his conversations with Lakshmikant and Pyarelal. He strained to hear what the teacher was muttering to his turtles, discounting Danny's theory about training the animals to speak and spy on humans. He brought up his work to the teacher and heard him whispering about burning down the school with its old wooden walls and ramshackle cupboards and tables.

At the fortnightly staff meetings, the Headmaster now asked Mr. Doon rather than Mr. Haroon about the class, and he always responded briskly with an impressive wordy account. Mr. Doon was younger than any of the other teachers, and they all deferred to his mini-lectures. They agreed readily too when he suggested the Manager be included in the bazaar's committee.

During the following days Mr. Doon seemed oblivious to the other teachers' distress while he spoke to the class about fascinating games like curling and ringettes and hockey, or when he announced that he had encouraged the principal to pave the yard with oilsand, or when the oilsand, deposited by the Manager's Bedford, melted and swelled in gummy balloons that clung to tiny shoes.

On the day following the paving, when Jeeves arrived home, his mother took one look at his shoes and hauled him roughly to the bathroom, where she listened to his account. Late in the night she repeated it to his father. Narpat took off his boots, held them upside down to allow the small pebbles and straw to fall out, and listened patiently to his wife. He called Jeeves, pulled up his eyelids, tapped his chest, kneaded his stomach, and gave him a clean bill of health. In fact his examination showed that Jeeves's health had improved slightly. Jeeves, wanting to impress his father, said that the paving, though carried out by the Manager, originated with the teacher from Canada. "I don't think Mr. Haroon like him. Or the Manager-mister who does come in the class all the time."

"How you know that, boy?"

"I does listen to them in class."

"I see. And what lesson you learning from all this eavesdropping? Eh?" He pushed the boy gently. "Run down to the rumshop quick sharp and tell everybody."

Narpat seemed set to deliver one of his lectures, but Dulari interjected, "Look at the nasty floor. Look at all the tar."

"Going to fix that tomorrow. Some turpentine will wash it out clean." He went to the table and began chewing noisily.

School was out the next day, so neither Jeeves nor Sushilla knew of their father's visit to the Headmaster's office, nor of his stern lecture on the proper methods of asphalt paving. "We not talking about building character here," he told the Headmaster. "We talking about laying a proper foundation and establishing a proper drainage system. Any fool could understand the process."

A few teachers drifting in and out of the office were surprised to see this rough-looking man, his sleeves rolled to his elbow, his shirt unloosened to the third button, explaining as to an illiterate, his illustrations drawn on a piece of cardboard. After Narpat had left, the Headmaster opened and closed his drawers roughly, and when Tara opened his door, he barked at her, "You don't have any lesson to prepare for tomorrow?" A few minutes later he strode into Mr. Haroon's classroom. "This is not a sick bay, eh. Why you don't use this time to remove them posters that hanging on the wall since the school build." Mr. Haroon rubbed his eyes and mentally began another letter.

One week later the Manager came into the class with a folded sheet of paper. Mr. Haroon gazed at the clumps of mud on the Manager's boots. "Morning, morning, little children," the Manager said loudly as he walked to Mr. Doon, who was standing against the blackboard. He fanned his face with the folded sheet. "This place so hot and sweaty. Not like the republic of Canada. Just the other night Kamini pull out a atlas and show me all them Canadian place like Otwaroo and Coobeck. I like how Canada shape up too. Like a nice slice of roti cut up neat and proper. Not like Trinidad, which does remind me of a squingy paper bag wring up on the four side." Then he got down to the real purpose of his visit: the school bazaar. "I understand that plenty dignitary will be attending, and in my stupid opinion we have to show them that although Lengua is a little mashup place, we still have we dreamsanhope." He glanced at the sheet in his hand. "Ay ay, I almost forget this here. I write down some little snacks for the bazaar." He unfolded the sheet and, with his nose almost touching the paper, read: "'Doubles, eight cents apiece. *Phoolorie*, five cents a dozen. Egg cake, five cents a slice. *Eggless* cake, three cents a slice. *Chillibibi*, penny a pack. *Channa*, only one cent a pack. Meals consisting of cassava, peas, and one piece of chicken, fifty cents. *Tambran* ball, mango *anchar*, *toolum*, and pommecythere, just three cents each.'" He paused and cleared his throat. "'All the above items will be supplied by Ramsoondar Samodie Loknath Sookdeo Esq., also known popularly and humbly as the Manager, and will be prepared under extreme sanitary condition so no kids will get dysentery or any nasty diseases.'" He folded the paper. "Is Kamini who write this. I get too old to keep on using all these big words. It does make me 'barass." He feigned a brazen shyness. "She wanted me to prepare some Canadian dishes too, like doughnuts and apple cakes and *umlettes*, but we didn't have the 'gredients."

Mr. Haroon observed what he took as a conspiracy with a growing sense of unease. One morning he cleared out a portion of the blackboard and wrote in an Old English script: *A classroom is a place of learning, not of chatting.* And beneath: *Please take off all dirty boots when entering the room.* When the Manager saw the sign, he commented wryly, "It look like Haroon get tired of writing letter to all them ministry people. He writing on the board now." He recalled one of Mr. Doon's oft-repeated adages and added, "My stupid opinion is that too much book sense is nonsense."

That same day Mr. Haroon was forced by the Headmaster to write twenty-three letters, one to each parent. He spent the entire day writing his letters outlining the parents' expected contribution to the school bazaar and itemizing the pastries and sweets that should be donated. He resisted the urge to sign each letter: *I Hamza Haroon, in a manner of speaking, Hostage and Victim.* At the end of the school day the students folded the letters and pushed them into their bookbags. The next day Jeeves handed him a two-page epistle. He read absentmindedly, intending to throw this letter, together with the others, into the bin, when he stopped abruptly and began rereading from the top. He read with growing excitement of this parent's annoyance with the list sent the previous day. Not one healthy item, the parent wrote. Bazaars in times past were glorious events where acrobats and wrestlers displayed their strength and flexibility, where foreign merchants displayed wares from every corner of the globe. They were not money-making ventures profiting from the sale of poison but circuses and carnivals rolled into one. They never left a trail of heart sufferers and diabetics and children bloated with gas and toxins.

Mr. Haroon glanced at the student who had brought the letter; though he had never paid him much attention, he recalled that the skinny boy with a thin, slightly pointed upper lip and huge, faintly moronic eyes had been up to his desk rather frequently with a number of frivolous problems. The name on the letter seemed familiar too. "What sort of work your father does do, boy?"

"He is a cane farmer."

"A cane farmer?" Mr. Haroon seemed disappointed. He shouted to Kamini, "Bring the attendance here, girl." He flipped through the dog-eared folder. "Yes, yes. Narpat Dubay. I hear about him in the village council meeting." Jeeves was surprised that his teacher was familiar with his father's name. "You have a sister name Kala, not so? Was in my class too. Bright girl, but use to argue too much for her own good. And another sickly sister who use to be coughing in class all the time." Jeeves was astonished that students were clumped together into families, and while he was walking to his house, he worried that this blurring of hithero private business meant that his frequent floggings and Narpat's dietary injunctions might also be in the public domain. But when he arrived home, a bigger worry awaited him.

"A charity," his father thundered. "But guess who pocket the money going into?" Jeeves remembered his friends' excitement earlier that day. Dilpaul was brushing up on his dart-throwing skills with an ice pick. Danny had revealed he had sandpapered all his fingers so he could locate the expensive toys hidden at the bottom of the sawdust-filled tub, and Kevin had confessed that his mother had already purchased a new outfit for him. Jeeves glanced hopefully at his mother when she explained to her husband that both children had been looking forward to the festivities. But Narpat would have none of it. "Not everything that you want in life will fall from the sky. It have people who does spend their whole life not doing anything because they alway hoping for some miracle round the corner. They will stay home all day rocking in their hammock waiting for the outcome of some nonsense a pundit predict. Wasting money on *whe whe*. Gambling on horse. This country going downhill, Mammy. Everybody looking for a free ride. The train leaving the track. Check the engine." Jeeves grew increasingly disconsolate as his father's lecture on discipline blossomed.

He lay awake that night and was surprised that there were moments of such complete silence, he felt that he was alone in the house, but when he concentrated, he realized that the silence was not an absence of noise but a quiet harmony where the chirping of the crickets and grasshoppers and the faraway cry of the frogs blended into each other. He realized too that he had grown accustomed to the drip of the kitchen sink, and that other sounds no longer registered because he had grown too used to them. He tried to separate the sounds and imagined he could hear a faint trilling laugh, like a child enjoying a game.

The next morning when Jeeves awoke, Kala and Chandra had already left for school, and when he spotted Sushilla sulking by the table, he remembered his father's injunction. He was about to cry when he spotted his mother tapping her cocoyea broom. He recognized the mood: fatigue and anger and frustration. At ten in the morning his mother led him to the bathroom, turned on the tap, and waited for the water to sprinkle. A few minutes later she threw some powder on his back and left him alone to ponder this strange development. When she returned to dress him, she informed Sushilla that she could attend the bazaar. The girl ran and hugged her mother.

"Me too?" Jeeves asked.

"Yes. You too."

They left the house waving happily to their worried-looking mother.

While they were running down the road, Jeeves recalled his mother's warning while she was fastening his shoelaces: "Don't tell anybody about this. Is our little secret. Me and you and Sushilla."

"This secret like the one we had for the Christmas holidays long time?" he asked his sister.

"Is only a secret from Pappy. So you better keep your mouth shut."

ELEVEN

*T*he assembly area was congested with long wooden tables dragged from the school. On the tables were buckets of red mangoes, and bunches of ripe bananas, and jars filled with pommecythere anchar, and cakes with multicolored icing. Parents stood behind pails of soursop ice cream and baskets of phoolorie and doubles and oily sweets. Some of the parents tried to cajole the students by holding up the delicacies. "*Kurma* and paymee. Hot and sweaty." Teachers strode grimly through the crowd, occasionally peering at the money boxes on the tables. The Headmaster was wearing an old tweed jacket, and some of the other teachers, ties and white cotton shirts. Jeeves walked by the assembly to the games section. A group of older boys were attempting to dislodge a pyramid of milk cans with flannel balls, and dangerously close to a gathering of curious younger children, some young men were pelting darts at a board stuck on the mango tree. There was much laughter and shouting whenever a dart came close to the bull's-eye. Jeeves searched about for Danny and Balack and spotted Mr. Doon, his hands clasped against his chest, gazing at the Manager coaxing some nervous girls to mount his bemused goat. "Five cents a ride. Only five cents." But whenever some child got astride the goat, the animal refused to budge, and the Manager shouted, "Look, move you lazy ass and give these nice children a ride, otherwise is the pot for you. Curry you bambam good and proper."

Jeeves contemplated spending his ten cents on a ride but instead paid for a dip into the bran tub. He plunged his hand into the wet sawdust, felt around, and brought up a brass whistle wrapped in gift paper. He tried again and retrieved a solitary marble. He pushed both into his pocket. A loudspeaker hummed and buzzed, and a parent, after much tapping and testing, announced the drawing of a raffle. The winner got a bunch of mataboro. The Headmaster began to speak in his low voice. He thanked the parents and the teachers and diverted to a lecture on building character. Now that Jeeves had spent the money given to him by his mother, the bazaar began to lose its appeal. He searched once more for Danny and recalled his friend talking about rakshas floating within the couteyah's compound.

He ran down the hill and paused to stare at the *jhandis*, religious flags, flapping above a spreading neem tree. He pushed open the gate and walked into the compound. He now saw that the wall murals he had spied from a distance were arranged in panels like a comic, but he could not understand the connection between the flying gods and a monkey-man holding a mountain aloft. One panel depicted a group of children with adult faces; another a man stringing a bow. The aroma of burning oil and camphor and stale flowers percolated from behind a slightly open door. When he pushed open the door, he saw that the windowless room was gloomy but for a small *bedi*, a ceremonial tray, directly beneath a skylight on the dome. In the center of the bedi was an arrangement of flowers surrounding a cylindrical black stone. At the side of the stone was a *lotah* half filled with milk and a tariyah partially covered with flowers. He dipped his finger into the milk and flicked his finger on a hibiscus. A coin glittered dimly. He stirred around the flowers and noticed that the tariyah was filled with coins. He removed a penny, slipped it into his pocket, and rearranged the flowers. He heard a dull thud at the end of the room and in the gloom saw a figure stirring from what seemed a bed. He froze, but as the man lunged at him, uttering harsh Hindi words, Jeeves turned and bolted from the room. He stumbled just before the outside gate, bruising his knees. The man was almost upon him when he pushed open the gate and fled down the road.

Of all the beatings Jeeves ever received from his mother, he remembered this as the worst. When he arrived home, he had at first hidden beneath the house amid his father's junk, but after a while the acrid smell of chinneys, little brown caterpillars, and the sting of crazy ants flushed him out. He went to the Julie mango tree and tried to hide between the branches, and after an hour or so of safety, he calculated that he had escaped. His mother was in the kitchen when he tiptoed into the bedroom and, fatigued by the day's excitement, fell asleep.

He awoke from a dream in which he was encircled by a huge snake dragging him into a hole. He opened his eyes and saw his mother above him, her face twisted with rage. "I didn't know I was minding a little thief in this house." He braced for the blow, but she dragged him to the living room. He noticed his sisters arranged like offended statues on the Pavilion. Slap! His father was at the table, eating slowly. He counted five slaps, then six, and as he tallied, the pain blurred so that he was able to hear his father chewing and also catch each of his sisters' expressions. "Thiefing from a couteyah, of all places. Letting everybody from the village know we have a little thief living here." Ten! How long was she going to keep this up? "Just like the lochos and peongs who living in Dogpatch. Maybe we should send you to live there. Live in one of those mashup shacks and eat nasty food. Live like a bachac with the other Outsiders. This country really going downhill when little children take up thiefing and trespassing."

As he was led away to the bathroom, his father said, "One violation does always lead to another. Who give him permission to go to the bazaar?" When the water hit his body, the pain all at once washed over his arms and back and shoulders. He stiffened, fighting his tears; and suddenly he knew why his father had not taken an active part in his punishment: he had passed a major test.

Following each flogging, his mother would come to him with a bowl of Quaker Oats and rub his back and shoulders while humming a Hindi song, but this time it was Kala who came. She told him that their mother was angry because she had trusted him and he had let her down. Jeeves noticed she was sounding like their father, but when he sniffed and wiped his eyes, she began to talk about her time at the Lengua government school, and about how happy their mother had been two years ago when she had passed her Common Entrance exams. This didn't make Jeeves feel any better because he was still at the bottom of his class, and save for the story sessions conducted by Kamini and Mr. Doon, he hated every subject. He wanted to be as grown-up as Chandra or as smart as Kala. Even Sushilla, who sulked when she was offended, had a beautiful singing voice and could draw beautiful and realistic pictures of angels.

The Monday after the bazaar, while Jeeves was laboring with a block of sums written on the board, the Manager, outfitted with a pair of clean shoes and a new merino, stormed into the classroom. "Teach, I begging you to carry me when you rent that plane to float back to the republic of

Canada." He spoke loudly. "This place is not a good place, Teach. People here too *mauvais langue* and gossipy. Just imagine people saying that the Headmaster asking for billsanreceipt for all the thing that get sell in the bazaar. What is a billsanreceipt? My stupid opinion is that is just a piece of paper." He snatched a sheet from Balack's table. "Just like this. It here *now*." He crumbled the paper. "Now it *gone*." Balack began to sniff. "I don't know where the Headmaster picking up all these foreign vice from?"

The next day he was more direct. He barged into the class waving a piece of paper. "Everybody does want to kick a man when he down." He flung the sheet on Mr. Doon's table. "Read it. Read it good." He stabbed the sheet with his thumb. "'Please provide bills and receipts for the above items. Sign, the Headmaster.'" He looked squarely at Mr. Doon. "When a man down everybody does want to take a lil kick at him, but I not going to put up with this nonsense." He tweaked the bags beneath his eyes. "How allyou expect me to produce all these billsanreceipt when I throw them away the same night self? I hand over every black cent I make in the bazaar. What I need billsanreceipt for? Eh? My word is my bond."

Mr. Haroon, who had tolerated the Manager's noisy intrusion for almost a year, got up suddenly and shrieked, "Get your ass out from this class right now."

"Eh? Get out? Who go put me out?"

"I, the aforementioned Hamza Haroon, in a manner of speaking—"

"You? A damn sickly mingpiling man like you? If I blow too hard, you go drop."

"Dad!"

Mr. Haroon's brief defiance withered. Mr. Doon scribbled furiously. The Manager frowned and said, "Ay-ay, Teach, what you writing down? Is a record you keeping of this record? You and all?" He snatched a rusty divider from the table. "Take this, Teach, and jook me in me whole heart. Jook me good and proper." Mr. Doon continued scribbling. "Allyou bitches. All of allyou."

"Dad."

"I didn't start the battle, but I go finish the war." The Manager, wavering between self-pity and rage, now felt a dry, empty exhaustion. "Write. Write all you want. You is a ejucated man. That is you privilege. But see if that record you recording don't land you up in the Royal Jail. Jails here not like nice Canadian jails, eh. Once you get inside, you bottom in clear and present danger." And he strode out of the class.

Mr. Doon's records had nothing to do with either the bazaar or the Manager, and later in the night, in his mother's modest flat in Cocoyea, which smelled of bay rum and camphor, he could barely contain his excitement. In his coilspring notebook, he wrote: "Irony of ironies! Just when I had concluded that this desolate village could not sustain my abundant poetic appetites (Where were the surging mountains, where the misty bowers, where, indeed, the rustic paths leading to quaint cottages?) divine hands thrust in my path another type of material." He paused in his writing to recall, first of all, the colorful bazaar, then the scene in the classroom the next day when a trembling Jeeves had stood in the corner, his head bent, as the Headmaster summoned Kevin to confirm that the boy had been seen running out of the couteyah, then launched into a vengeful tirade about the boy's father, a village despot who thought nothing of foisting his eccentric ideas on everyone. "I am humbled by the realization," he wrote, "that divine hands must have guided me to this sorry village of local Micawbers, Chuzzlewits, Pickwicks, and most significantly, a local Pip."

The Manager never produced the receipts, and to Mr. Haroon's relief, he stopped waltzing in and out of the school. But he was deeply hurt that the Headmaster had cut him off. Every night he worried that Kamini's hope of promotion to a monitor was threatened. He felt trapped and helpless, surrounded by enemies: the Headmaster, Mr. Haroon, Mr. Doon, the neighbors who he was certain were whispering behind his back, even the insolent students laughing and shouting all around him. He fantasized about various traps he could lay for these students: deep holes concealed with leaves or a few coral snakes released in the shrubs. But like most despairing people, instead he sought allies. He began showing up at the village council meetings, and while Narpat, whom he had always considered a braggart, stood up and berated the other villagers, the Manager contemplated how far he had sunk. *Just a couple hundred dollars I thief from the bazaar*, he thought. *After all the blood and sweat I give to the school, the least they could do is say, "Take the money, Manager. You deserve it."* During one meeting while he was sitting at the back, his arms folded across his belly, Janak mentioned the rumored plans for independence and inquired whether the village council would hold some sort of function. Narpat replied that independence, if it came, would change nothing.

After the meeting, as Narpat was walking to his tractor, the Manager said, "But ay-ay, Narpat, I didn't know you could make so much good points. I like how you was firm with everybody."

"You have to be firm with people who does behave like little children."

The Manager didn't like Narpat's tone, but he was desperate. "I agree one hundred and one percent. Is my stupid opinion that Janak want function just so he could get work for his lickup car."

"That is his profession, and he is entitled to it."

"I agree one hundred and one percent, but some of these fellas don't realize that book sense is nonsense." The Manager waited patiently while Narpat expounded on the value of pain and hard knocks; then he blurted out, "In my stupid opinion some of these ejucated people think they way is the only way. Like the so-call Headmaster." He lowered his voice. "Is none of my business, but that same Headmaster who does be preaching 'bout values, eating beef and pork like it going outta style. Right in my own house. Is none of my business. I just stating the facts."

"In your house?"

The Manager saw his error, and his melancholy mood returned. "People does think they could treat my house as a pig pen just because I is a low-class *chamar*."

"That is the cause of three-quarter of Indian people problem."

"Eh? But you yourself is a Brahmin."

"What is a Brahmin?" Narpat asked. The Manager struggled for an appropriate response, but Narpat continued, "A Brahmin is a fella who main goal is to instruct. Not to make money from all sorta scheme." For the next half an hour, Narpat explained the origins of the caste system and its perversion, after centuries of conquest and occupation in India, into a rigid and impractical doctrine. "How much of these proud and educated people you think it had line up in Calcutta to come here and do slave work?"

At the end of it the Manager felt more exhausted than ever, but while he was walking home, one of Narpat's analogies stuck in his mind. Narpat had likened the invasion of India by the Mongols and the Arabs and the

British, to the appearance in the village of the Outsiders. Just like the invaders of India, the Outsiders were introducing a system of values alien to the village.

After the next village council meeting, he told Narpat, "For the last two weeks, I thinking and thinking about this function that Janak pushing for. Just last night I tell meself, 'You know something, Manager? This might be a good 'portunity to invite up Googool, the MP for the area. He bound to show because election right around the corner.'"

Narpat's distaste for the Manager was matched by his antipathy toward politicians. "These fellas does come just before election and promise the moon and the star. And you don't spot them again until the next four years making the same promise to dotish people."

The Manager was reminded of how difficult it was to sustain a conversation with Narpat. He shunted away his irritation and concentrated on the bigger picture: the opportunity to establish important contacts and open his campaign for the county council elections. "I agree one hundred and one percent. Just last night when I was talking to meself, I say, 'You know something, Manager? I feel that we need some sorta newspaper fella for these 'portant meeting.' Somebody like Partap, the cripple fella, son. To write down all these promise and them. Make it like a public will and testament with the whole village as executors."

During the following mornings he gazed wistfully at the children walking up the hill. He had lost the taste for shouting curses at them. Sometimes he tweaked the bags beneath his eyes and sobbed. "Nobody bothering with the chamar again. He too low caste for anybody to pay any attention."

One lunch break a ball rolled beneath his house. "But ay-ay, why all-you standing up like statues so? You expect the ball to roll back by itself?" The two boys glanced warily from the ball to the Manager. "Ain't you is Jugoon boy?" One of the boys remembered the Manager's crude reference to his mother a few days earlier and was about to call him a fat nastiness, when the Manager came down the stairs, the wooden planks creaking with every step, retrieved the ball, and threw the ball to the boys. During the week he sent greetings to several mothers, and occasionally he appeared with a ball that he claimed he had found in a hole. Gradually he felt a gnawing trickle of goodwill toward the school, the children, and their mothers. If only he could reestablish some sort of relationship with

the principal. In the mornings while he brushed his teeth and gazed pro-
prietorially at the children, he racked his brains for an opening. He
thought of alerting the Headmaster that there was a communist and in-
stigator operating in his school, but his once-reliable source of information, his daughter, was either unwilling to discuss Mr. Doon or did so in
an unintelligible accent, which infuriated him.

Then one morning, just after nine, the Headmaster's car, parked on
the road, was damaged by a tractor. The Manager whipped out his toothbrush and ran down the steps. The Headmaster and two teachers were
inspecting the damage. The Manager stood behind them and said, "Public thoroughfare. They have the rightaway."

One of the teachers said, "These Farmalls does speed through here
like if is a highway."

"Public thoroughfare, as I say."

The teacher grumbled some more. The Headmaster ran his fingers
over the dented bumper.

"They not liable one bit," the Manager continued. "Now if it was park
below a house, it would be a different matter. No thoroughfare. No rightaway. One hundred and one percent liability." Ten minutes later the
Manager fussily offered directions up to his house, even though the Headmaster had driven along the bumpy, muddy road to his garage for close to
ten years. The next day he coached the standard seven boys into the
proper method of pounding out the dent, filing away the rust, and spreading the paste and filler. The Headmaster stood by silently, with a new appreciation of the Manager's worth.

Throughout that week the students noticed old junks from the village
hauled up the hill. During the Friday recess Jeeves asked Danny, "How
come all these standard seven boys get to leave class and go below the
Manager house?"

"To fix these old cars. The Headmaster getting a cut."

"A cut?" Jeeves asked. Danny made the scam seem exciting and illicit.

"Yeah. I think I will go and investigate after lunch."

"Below the Manager house? I could come too?"

"Nah. You too small. They will pick you out."

When classes resumed after lunch, Danny was not in his seat. Jeeves
was sure that his friend would be found out and punished, but no one no-

ticed. After dismissal Danny called out to Jeeves on the road, "Anybody miss me?"

Jeeves shook his head. "Where you was?"

"Where you expect? Below the Manager house."

"I didn't see you there."

Danny fished into his pocket and retrieved a key. "From one of the cars."

"You thief it?"

"Take it."

"What you going to do with it?"

"Watch." Danny threw the key in the air. It disappeared behind the couteyah's wall and fell with a clink somewhere within the compound.

"You going back on Monday?"

"Nah. Guess who I see going up the Manager house?"

"The Headmaster?"

"Kevin mother. A lady name Cecilia. I think is his girlfriend."

Jeeves laughed at the idea of the fat, dirty Manager having a girlfriend.

The next week the Manager walked up to Mr. Haroon, whose distaste of his easy familiarity had returned. "Morning, Mr. Haroon. I like these new pictures you hang up in the class. This school need more teachers like you, if you ask me. Not like some of these other teachers who only bringing in foreign vice. Recording they record in they book all day long. Why they don't write something useful instead. Like a letter." Mr. Haroon looked up, and the Manager noticed the little tremor of excitement rippling through his ailing face. "Not a big long letter. Just something simple to Googool, inviting him down to address the crowd in a speech of he very own choice. Simple letter yes, but we need a professional letter writer when we inviting these special guests. You could make me, the honorable, humble Manager the RSVP." He spoke loudly and noticed Mr. Doon glancing at him and scribbling. "Well, think about it," he said, walking over to Mr. Doon. "Good day, good day, Teach, how the recording going?" Mr. Doon closed his notebook. "You know, Teach, just last night I was talking to meself and I say, 'You know something, Manager? Why you don't pick up writing too?'" He sat down on Dilpaul's desk, whipped out a dirty copybook and a bitten-down pencil, and wrote laboriously: Point number one. Fight fire with fire. From time to time, he moistened the pencil's tip and peeped at the confused teacher.

That day the Manager left the school with a meditative smile. Order had been restored; his plan was now back on track. Late in the night, with his copybook on his lap, he shouted from the gallery to his daughter, inquiring about the spelling for *revenge, calculate*, and a word he had heard several times in Mr. Doon's classroom, *parable*. He pronounced the word *prabble*.

Part Two

hen the date for independence was finally announced by Dr. Rawlin Gibbons, the reclusive Prime Minister, he skillfully hinted that both the general and the county council elections would be held in the week following August 31, 1962, the day of independence. The Trinidadian flair for fete and carnival rose to the occasion. Paintings and murals were commissioned. Political hopefuls kept their cards close to their chests, throwing sly hints about their political aspirations and about their sudden annoyance at the island's low international status. But in the villages, life went on as usual. Cane was planted, cut, and weighed, and the fields were burned in preparation for the next year's growth. Some of the older villagers expressed their fear of independence and cited the leader of the opposition, Dr. Sohan Bhandara's, prediction of anarchy. In these villages the only visible signs of the impending independence were the celebrations organized by the schools during the week prior to the vacation; most of the observances were forced on the reluctant staff via ministry directives. But at the Lengua government school, there were more diverse motives at play.

At night, Narpat saw, interspersed with his children's books on the table, faded pink-and-yellow pamphlets with the government's stamp. One evening while he was sitting on the porch, cleaning the mud from his tall tops, he heard Jeeves reciting from one of the pamphlets and Kala attempting to correct his pronunciation. "Come, boy," he called, when Jeeves had finished the exercise. Jeeves came immediately and followed him to the tractor. "We going for a little ride. You study enough for one day."

"You not going to eat?" Dulari called to her husband from the front door.

"Later. I have to go to the weighing scale for a while."

The scales in Lengua and other cane-farming districts were built adjoining the railway lines that transported the farmers' cane to the British-owned sugar factory, Tate and Lyle. Jeeves had visited a few times with his father and had always been transfixed by the crane plucking up bundles of cane from tractors and bull carts on the weighing bridge and depositing them into the carriage. On his first visit the crane had reminded him of a giant praying mantis holding its victim aloft.

Narpat parked his tractor at the end of a line of bull carts. "This is the time of the year that all the farmers does wait for. You see that woman across there?" Narpat pointed to a woman standing next to a bull cart. She was wearing a wide-brimmed hat and a cutlass slung in her belt. "She working in the field since she was a child. A couple years ago she had a baby right in the field. And three weeks later she was back to work. Not so, Lakshmi?" he shouted to the woman as if she were part of the conversation.

The woman glanced back, waved, and whispered to a girl standing by her side. "She was as pretty as your Mammy one time, but now her face get cut up from the stalk, and hard from working in the sun whole day. Her little girl going to get the same way in no time. And for what?"

"That is why Chandra and Kala and Sushilla don't go with you to the field?"

Narpat shouted greeting to a group of farmers clustered around a boxy little building next to the scale, then turned to his son. "Independence shouldn't mean drinking and feting. It should mean walking with your children halfway down the road."

"Which road?"

"It mean giving them a start, Carea. So they wouldn't have to sell cane to the factory for next to nothing."

"Then why they does sell it to the factory?" Jeeves was about to repeat the question when his father dismounted from the tractor. The train was slowly chugging into view. Jeeves stood on the tractor's seat. The setting sun added a fierce sparkle to the rusty train, making its progress from the crimson-tinged field seem deliberate and frightful.

On the way back Jeeves, still struck by his vision of the train, didn't notice his father's silence, but when they stopped by a coconut vendor to purchase two nuts, the boy heard Narpat talking to the vendor about the upcoming county council election and the local school's celebration.

During the week preceding the celebration, Narpat read through the stream of directives issued by the Ministry of Education. One evening he summoned all his children to the Pavilion. Chandra came from the kitchen, Sushilla from the bedroom, and Kala from the porch, where she had been reading aloud to Jeeves. Jeeves followed her. "Line up, line up," their father said jovially. "Time for a little quiz."

Kala stepped forward.

"Question one," he said. "What is independence?"

"It mean to be free from colonial domination and to enact your own laws."

"Good, good, Kala." He pointed to Chandra. "Question two. What is independence?"

"You ask that already," Chandra replied.

"Okay. Question one, part two." Chandra bit her lips and glanced at her mother, looking on from the kitchen's entrance. "Hurry up, girl," Narpat said. "You nearly fifteen years old. You should know the answer right off the bat."

"It mean . . . to be free."

"Good, good. Part three. Sushilla. What is independence?"

She came forward shyly. "Different color paper from school. And speeches."

"Very good. Your turn, Carea."

Jeeves wished he had thought of Sushilla's response. He tried to recollect the Headmaster's speeches on the subject. "It mean that the Headmaster going to get more money."

Dulari came from the kitchen, laughing in her soft, almost soundless manner, with her hand against her mouth. Narpat too was chuckling, and Jeeves guessed he had said something funny.

Later in the week, when Narpat learned that Kala had been selected by her teachers for an interschool debate on independence, he practiced with her and gave her hints and pointers that were useless because they all came back to the plight of cane farmers.

Narpat arrived for the school celebration just in time to see the Manager daubing a dirty rag across his face as he walked to the stage. He listened to the laughter and the applause following the Manager's speech. "Ladies and gentlemen and nice little boys and girls, I is not a ejucated man like the other honorable guests, so I promise not to use too many long-long words. In fact, on a point of order, I first and second the motion, that the speeching part of this honorable function come to a end, and I first and second the motion, that the eating and drinking part come to a beginning."

Narpat walked away disgusted; he had come to challenge the special guest, Dinesh Googool, the incumbent MP for the area, but the politician had delivered his speech and hurried away.

Two weeks later he got his opportunity: Mr. Googool had accepted the Manager's invitation to address the village council. All the meetings of the last two months had centered on the pressing problem of land ownership. More than a third of the cane-farming land in Lengua was part of an estate owned by a retired magistrate from Port of Spain. The magistrate, now bedridden, had named his son executor of his property. The son issued notice he was selling off the estate. The farmers who had cultivated the land for more than twenty years were angry and fearful. "How he could do this?" they asked during the meetings. "Because it is his legal right," Narpat answered. "Any of you bother to get deeds? Any of you bother to survey your property?" The farmers pleaded ignorance of these legal matters. "Then you all like little children begging a stranger to take away your toy," he retorted. A few of the older villagers said in a resigned voice, "The same way he thief out we land, god will thief something bigger from him." Narpat laughed at them. "You think god have time to bother with people who can't take care of themself? You think he have time to step in every occasion a fool get cheated of his property? Then he will be busy every second of the day."

In the rumshops, the farmers complained about the politicians and felt that everyone in power was in a complicated conspiracy to cheat them. While Narpat chastised the farmers, the Manager moved from bar to bar, consoling and flattering.

The night of the meeting the little post office was packed with farmers who had never previously attended. They stood at the back, many of them still in their grimy field clothes. The Manager moved through the crowd, shaking hands as if he had not seen these farmers for years. "Googool go be here in a little while. Send the invitation meself. Get a long-long reply in one day time."

Half an hour later he was less effusive. "Bad road. Landslide. Poor Googool must be get lost."

Premsingh, a burly farmer with a handlebar moustache and a tattoo on his forearm, jabbed a finger at the Manager. "How he could get lost when he own nearly half of Ramgoolam trace, just five miles from here?"

"Eh? Nearly half?" The Manager pretended this was news to him. An hour later, when Googool had still not turned up, he retreated to a corner of the room and began fanning himself with his hat.

The farmers were now arguing loudly among themselves. "Who the ass he think he is to make big people wait like lil children?"

"Is so them fellas does operate."

"We should go to he house and drop some good cuss on him."

"Think because we don't wear jacket and tie, he could ride we like jackass."

"They could only ride us if we allow them to get on our back." Narpat had been sitting at the table at the front, poring over an old map. Now his voice cut through the room, silencing the angry farmers. The Manager stopped fanning. "Who is Googool? A doctor? A lawyer? Who put him in Parliament? What trade he have to fall back on if we throw him out?"

The flurry of questions confused and silenced the farmers. The Manager said, "I think he is a LLB."

"A LLB, my ass. He is some kinda JP."

"A *Jamette* politician," Premsingh said.

"You mean he is not a real LLB?" The Manager was disappointed.

At that moment Mr. Googool, preceded by his chauffeur, walked into the post office. He removed his tweed jacket, gave it to his chauffeur, and glanced at his watch. The Manager's worried look evaporated, and he began to purr loudly, as if he were simultaneously clearing his throat and giggling. The chauffeur, a short man with a great mop of hair swept back stylishly into a ducktail, frowned at the Manager and in a swift, sweeping glance, conveyed his displeasure to the crowd. Narpat carefully folded his map. "Tonight we are lucky to have our parliamentarian for the area to discuss our concern and represent us in this legal matter of the land ownership."

The crowd applauded.

Mr. Googool withdrew a sheet of paper from his shirt pocket. The chauffeur shifted from one foot to the other, trying unsuccessfully to look like a badjohn. Mr. Googool stepped forward and lowered his glasses over his huge bumpy nose. "My loyal constituents, who have elected me as your esteemed parliamentarian, I come to you tonight, with a list of our— and I stress the word, *our*—achievements. We have built two bridges at Samlal trace, repaired part of the landslide at Crappo Patch, provided electricity and water for the fortunate residents of—"

"We know that already," someone shouted.

"We want to know if you going to settle the matter with the deed."

"In any case, the bridge no better than before, and the access road only accessible to Farmall," Janak said laconically.

The chauffeur stepped forward, folded his arms over his chest, and rocked back on his heels. The Manager tried to defuse the situation. "Honorable ladies and gentlemen. Special invitation. Speech of he very own choice. Go 'head, go 'head, sir."

Mr. Googool seized the brief lull. "As we all know, the general election is just 'round the corner, and I plan to extend water and electricity to every single house in my constituency. That is my humble vow."

The Manager clapped and shouted, "Yay, yay." The rest of the crowd glared sullenly.

"What is the blasted point in putting water and lights on the land, if we going to lose it to some old schemer in Port of Spain?"

Mr. Googool flicked a glance at his watch. The chauffeur said, "Independence. Freedom for all. Mind, body, and soul."

"Yay, yay."

Mr. Googool brightened up and recited. "What is independence, I ask you? Is it just writing our own constitution, or is it the final step in our emancipation from slavery and bondage?"

"Yay, yay."

Mr. Googool nodded and acknowledged the Manager's acclamation. "Ladies and gentlemen, in 1834—"

"We not interested in any 1834," Premsingh said.

"It have anybody from that time here?" Janak looked around exaggeratedly. "No, I don't think I spot anybody."

"Yay, yay." The Manager caught himself and said quickly, "I think in 1834 they leggo all them slave what use to be living in cave and thing.

Learn that in standard seven. From teacher Pariag. Remember him and his whip name King George?"

Premsingh had had enough. "Look, shut you fat ass. We didn't come here to talk about Pariag. Not 'bout no damn slavery either." Some of the farmers began to shout curses.

"Peoples, peoples," the chauffeur said. "Mr. Googool make a great sacrifice to come here today to—"

"Then he could haul he ass back to Corinth."

"Without any of we vote."

Mr. Googool pushed the prepared speech in his pocket and looked at the chauffeur.

"Special invitation," the Manager pleaded. "Speech of he very own ejucated choice." At that the crowd erupted, and the Manager donned his hat and wisely decided to keep out of the commess.

"Mr. Googool, sir, don't forget the next meeting in St. Croix in half an hour time. Big crowd. Big, *big* crowd. Waiting patiently just to hear you."

Narpat interrupted the chauffeur. "Mr. Parliamentarian, *sir*, before you leave, I want to know if you intend to look into this matter of the deeds." He spoke slowly, as if addressing a truant child.

"These thing take time. Googool is a busy man."

"Keep you lil mingpiling ass shut," Premsingh shouted to the chauffeur. "Is no damn taxi permit we talking about here." Everyone but Janak thundered in agreement. The chauffeur tried to look menacing.

"Consider it done." The crowd was immediately silenced by Mr. Googool's desperate acquiescence.

"Then we would like to have that in writing." Narpat read from a sheet of paper in his hand. "I, Mr. Dinesh Googool, the parliamentarian for the Naparima constituency, promise to have the issues of the farmers' deeds resolved before the next election, or forfeit all the votes in the district of Lengua."

"Don't sign it. Don't sign no damn paper."

"I warn you already to keep you ass quiet." Premsingh and another rough-looking farmer advanced on the chauffeur.

"The lord giveth and the lord taketh away back in his wisdom to behold," Kumkaran chanted.

Mr. Googool looked at his chauffeur running from the building and the crowd closing in and blocking his own escape. In a single glance, he

gauged the hard rough faces, the facility for violence, and the desperation
that strengthened these illiterate villagers. He saw Narpat looking at him
with a harsh smile and, seated at the back, a young man with a flourishing beard and huge woman's sunglasses. When he signed Narpat's prom-
issory note, the crowd for the first time applauded. He flashed a half-dead
smile as the crowd allowed him to return to his car.

The meeting had ended on a sour note for the Manager. Although he
had rushed to console Mr. Googool, the chauffeur had sped off, almost
running over his toes. Later, as he mulled over the meeting, he convinced
himself that his botched plan was somehow due to his caste, and for the
next few days, he muttered to a number of confused and impatient villagers, "People does think that just because I is a low-class chamar, they
could treat me like if *corbeau* shit on me. Everybody in this place want to
mashup me foot. Bounce me down like a dog. Throw me carcass in the
drain." Sometimes he elaborated. "Everybody want to make me a scrapegoat. Me, the honorable Manager of Lengua government school for donkey years, suddenly come a *wothless* scrapegoat."

Less than a week later the Manager had cause to sink into an even
greater gloom. Using one of his many disguises—this time thick horn-
rimmed glasses, a fake beard, and a long billowing shirt reaching his
stumpy legs—Partap's son, a young journalist who worked for the *Evening
News*, had attended the meeting, and his report, when it appeared in the
Friday edition of the newspaper, portrayed Narpat as a brilliant legal
strategist and Googool as a corrupt and inept politician. The article—
"Googool Gallops from Grievous Gang"—had two important consequences: knowledge of the humiliation inflicted on Mr. Googool was no
longer confined to Lengua; and Partap's son, who often disguised himself
as one of his comic book heroes, gained a brief notoriety.

The evening the article appeared, Narpat read it to his wife and children and pretended it was nothing. "What these fellas . . . this Partap son
know about legal strategy? He take a principled stand and change it in
something else. Make me sound like a big-shot lawyer or something." But
he was secretly pleased. The following nights before he went to bed, he
withdrew the article several times. One night he muttered to himself, "He
make me look more important than Googool." He lay awake in bed imagining he had defeated Googool in the general election and that soon afterward he had formed an organization representing cane farmers. He

imagined he was able to negotiate a better price for cane from Tate and
Lyle, and that he eventually succeeded in having farmers installed on the
board of directors.

But he knew that Googool would be able to hire taxis, rent loudspeakers, print bills and posters, and throw fetes in all the rumshops in
the constituency to bribe the wavering voters. The general elections were
out of the question; not so the county council election, which was confined to Lengua and the neighboring Monkeytown. Most of these villagers were already familiar with him, and Gopaul, the incumbent county
councilor, a worn asthmatic, spent more time convalescing in various
nursing homes than representing the constituents. One night he told Dulari he intended to fight the county council election as an independent
candidate. On subsequent nights she brought up all the problems he had
already considered.

But once the decision was made, Narpat stopped talking about the
elections at home. In the evenings he repeated his torturous fables to his
children, and when his daughters made some excuse and sneaked away,
he turned to Jeeves. His fables were of free will and duty and community
service and solemn promises, and Jeeves, though paying scant attention,
was occasionally struck by the image of stern wrinkled animals seated
around a cave, gravely debating some esoteric issue. He hoped his father
would imitate some funny animal mannerism, and when he didn't, Jeeves
grew bored with the lengthy pauses and with the fables themselves. The
boy tried to establish some thread, but Narpat jumped from story to story.
Frequently Jeeves fell asleep during one of these intervals.

When all the children were finally asleep, Dulari approached Narpat
with her concern about the decaying walls and the meager furniture. She
worried about this new direction into which her husband was heading,
and about the money that inevitably would be diverted.

"Material possessions should be as humble as possible; otherwise we
will always worry about their value or whether they match the neighbors'."
This late in the night, Narpat's voice was soft and gentle.

"Is just a matter of convenience."

"It *start* with convenience. Then it move to competition. And excess.
On and on until nothing could satisfy again."

"Sometimes I get tired of cooking in the chulha and blowing and blowing the fire all day. I not young again, you know."

"And sometimes I get tired from working in the field from five in the morning to five in the evening. But every bit of tiredness is a joy. The more exhausted I get, the happier I become." Without looking at his wife, he added, "And you still young to me, Mammy."

They would go to their room then, but the next day in the field his mind would drift back to the elections. *Nothing is ever accomplished without sacrifices*, he thought. *Anything that comes easy is either valueless or makeshift.* And in this mood his decaying house and its modest furniture were invested with a sanctity far beyond their worth. While he was hacking away at the cane, he would recall too the treachery of his uncle, and the older man's single-minded pursuit of wealth. His uncle's riches had brought no joy: he grew fatter and unhealthier, and his choleric face would darken with rage at imagined conspiracies involving his workers, his neighbors, and his nephew, whom he had defrauded of his inheritance. One afternoon Narpat realized that his visceral dislike of the Manager was because his fellow villager reminded him of his uncle. On the day he spotted the Manager's election handbill affixed to a telephone pole, he journeyed to Princes Town and registered his own candidacy for county councilor.

THIRTEEN

*E*ach morning during the preelection period, the Manager gazed out from his gallery and thought of the power and wealth he could access as a county councilor. In spite of his setbacks, he knew that if he bribed a sufficient number of people, his chances would be excellent. He had pulled himself out of poverty through his constantly replenished faith in shortcuts and bobol. When his wife and six of his seven children, fed up with his bribing, deserted him, he accused them of treachery but also of stupidity. Kamini was his jewel because she had remained with him, and he routinely promised her all his ill-gotten assets.

One morning as he was staring at his goat, he called out to his daughter. She emerged from her room dressed in pants and a jersey instead of her usual bodice and skirt. He glanced disapprovingly at her new outfit. *"Aray!"*

"I am going to the post office."

"Eh? Who you posting letter to every day now? Mahatma Gandhi?"

"The guy is dead, I think. Gee, look at the time. I gotta run."

She walked past the postal agency, crossed the road, and headed for Lalbeharry trace. At about four p.m. that afternoon Janak, returning from a trip to Princes Town, spotted her walking to the trace. He drove on for a while, then made an abrupt U-turn in the direction of Lalbeharry trace.

When the Manager heard of Narpat's candidacy, he began his campaign in earnest. He greeted villagers he had never spoken to with an effusiveness that made them instantly suspicious. "But ay-ay, how Nabes, how?

Just the other day I tell you boy from school to tell you hello on my behalf, but children these days too forgetful."

One day he drove his Bedford up the hill to his house and brought it to an abrupt stop. He slammed the door. "Tick. Nothing but tick. This whole village fulla tick. The minute they hear a honest man taking up politiscing, they does sharpen they teeth to start sucking. They wouldn't be happy until they suck me dry." The first week of campaigning had been a disaster. Initially he had been met with a stony silence, but as his intentions became clearer, he was forced to listen to a litany of complaints. He walked up the stairs grumbling. "Every blasted body in the village have a sick son or daughter or some debt they can't afford to pay. Tick on all side. This whole blasted place only fulla tick and crazy kissmeass people. Diggers and jookers!"

Kamini looked up. "Is exactly what David—I mean Teacher Doon—say."

"Eh? He say that? Who the ass he think he is to criticize poor people for no rhyme and reason?" But after his anger had cooled, he asked his daughter, "You think Teach might be interested in writing one or two small speech for me? Nothing too fancy. Just a few words for the election."

"I will ask him. I guess he will."

The Manager was astonished at his daughter's confidence. He dug into an ear and flicked his finger. "Maybe we could get him to draw up a few poster. Stick them up in Polly rumshop and Hakim parlor and in the post office."

"Gee, I think mebbe you will need a photograph for that. I think mebbe Partap son does do photographing part-time."

"Who? That damn kissmeass scamp? I don't want to hear nothing about him. He crooked just like he lazy, hop-and-drop father." But the Manager couldn't discount the appeal of his daughter's idea, and later in the night he rummaged through the cardboard grip beneath his bed. He threw aside unpaid bills and an old summons to appear in the Princes Town court. Finally, he turned up a photograph taken when he was a driver at Baboo's bus company. The photograph, taken during an excursion to Maracas bay, showed him kneeling before a pot, his belly almost covering the rim. He gazed at the picture fondly, then threw it aside. Eventually he went to Yip's photo studio and posed fussily for two passport-size pictures. "For election," he told Yip, a short, harassed-looking Chinese with long, skinny arms. "Need a nice background. You have any waterfall? Or some palace like the Taj Mahal?"

"No background for passport."

"Eh? Not even a small stupid mountain self?" He left the studio in a bad mood. "What the hell he think this place is? Hong Kong? Can't give a man a small stupid background self."

Every night he dictated the day's expenses to his daughter, grumbling about ticks and chiselers. "They only dreamsanhope is to suck out a honest man like a ripe mango, then pelt him away. But let them continue sucking." Sometimes he had an inspirational moment and would command his daughter, "Prabble number ninety-four. Dog that 'custom sucking egg never stop until they see a bigger dog reflection in the water, then they leggo the bone."

During every meeting he withdrew glasses with thick foggy lenses and, adjusting and readjusting to much applause, read from a light blue binder, "I, Ramsoondar Samodie Loknath Sookdeo Esq., known to all and each as the popular and humble Manager, do honestly, candidly, and singlehandedly give a guarantee to right the wrongs, and good the bad, of this little bower we call Lengua." The crowd clapped and hooted at the slippery Indian accent he slipped into whenever he read from one of Kamini's binders, seducing him into even more promises.

Most mornings of that month he stood in his gallery, smoking and surveying the men and women limping up the slope toward him, their faces contorted into bogus suffering. He greeted each with a controlled cheerfulness, and it was only after they had left that the bind of his anger tightened. "Kamini, come here and write down this prabble: The road to poordom is paved with wicked bitches. And this: Selfsame bitches will squeeze out every last drop of milk from a honest man breast. Okay, read it over for me. And you better change milk into sweat." But even while Kamini was reading, his depression lifted, transformed into robust images of him being chauffeur driven, the window rolled up while he listened to the day's news on the radio. He imagined foreign news, not brimming with troublesome demands but soothing and romantic. This morning a volcano suddenly erupted in Rome, killing a million people. The war between India and Pakistan has wiped out another five cities. An earthquake destroyed half of Venezuela.

One day he had an unexpected visitor. "How you father, old man Partap, going? It cross me mind this very said morning to visit him, but the election business have me too busy." He crumbled his hat and stared sorrowfully at the ground. "These days I visiting all the hop-and-drop, brokofoot people in the district. All the 'digent people too. And them what husband leave them and wife leave them and neemakaram children 'bandon them." He slammed his hat on his knee. "All these bitches. All the jookers and diggers." He glanced up suddenly and wiped his eyes with his crumbled hat. "But that is me job. If the Manager don't see 'bout these people, who else will see 'bout them?"

Partap's son fished into his lab coat and brought out a chewed-down pencil. "I would like to get some meaty thoughts on the campaign. How do you plan to combat the boondoggle in agriculture? And what steps have you contemplated to bring the different races together in the district of Lengua?"

"Races? Bring them together? Why?" The Manager glanced suspiciously at the journalist.

"Routine questions. Must be asked. At all cost." He nibbled his pencil. "Okay then, do you intend to be a partisan or a mugwump?"

"A mugwump, man? You mean I reach so low now where a honorable journalist could just walk in my house and call me these insultive names cool-cool." After Partap's son had left, the Manager shouted to his daughter. "*Aray*, where you dress up and going?"

"To the post office."

"Go, go!" He flicked his wrist. "And if you see any of them mugwumpy bitches coming up here, tell them to haul they jooking and digging ass away." But Partap's son had given him an idea, and early the next morning he journeyed to Dogpatch, the Outsiders' settlement. The men lounging on their steps gazed indifferently at his approach and at the bags of sweets in his hand. "Where all the little children gone?" He peeked around sourly. "Have some gifts for them. Paradise plum and cough drops." A shirtless boy emerged with a dog from beneath a house. The boy took the bag of sweets.

"I want a dollar."

"Eh? A dollar?"

"Gimme a dollar."

"Nice sweets." The Manager shook a bag.

"Gimme a dollar."

The Manager glanced at the man watching lazily from the step and at a woman with a dress hitched high on her broad hips standing at the doorway. "Children nowadays. They too smart." He dipped into his pocket, fishing for the smallest coins. "Two ten cent and three one cent. That make it twenty-three cent." He hurried away, mumbling and cursing. "Hello Partap son, you neemakaram bitch, I have a nice article for you. Write down this: The Manager today bring all the race together when he donate twenty-three cents to a damn blasted little scamp." He never returned to Dogpatch, and in each subsequent speech he now vowed to "put a complete full stop and next punctuation too on all them outside people who soaking inside the bower of Lengua."

Narpat addressed just one meeting, held in the small post office used also for village council assemblies. He came to the meeting directly from the field and wore his rough khakis and tall tops caked with mud and bits of straw. "I didn't have time to change in fancy clothes," he said as he strode to the front. "I am a working man. Just like most of the people here." He glanced at the crowd. "And working people have to be strong in mind and body. Look at me. Not one drop of oil and not one spoon of sugar in this body for the last five years." He rolled up his sleeves and shifted to a wide-legged stance. "That is why nobody in this mashup post office could last more than two minutes against me. Not even these little children"—his lips curled into a mocking smile as he gestured to a row of young men— "half my age." He grasped a handful of hair. "Thick like the day I born. This chin here could take a thousand blows." He cuffed himself, rocking backward, and the young men, those who didn't know him well, straightened in their seats and gaped at this slim, well-built man who might have been good-looking when he was younger, before the harshness set in.

"Take a good glance around you, and see how much unhealthy people it have here. Watch how puffy and sickly Kumkaran is. That big belly full of gas and bile acid and pollution just waiting to explode." Kumkaran tried to maintain his dignity, but his sleepy eyes and slack features didn't lend themselves to his effort. He was trembling with rage, and if anyone but Narpat had insulted him in this manner, he would have strode to the front and knocked him down.

"Kumkaran can't help it because it in his blood. No different from the

majority of Indians in this village. Soft and sickly-looking. Puff up from all
that sugar and oil. Fry this, fry that. Bile and mucus leaking from every
outlet. Muscles turn to pap. Gallbladder and kidney trouble. Indigestion
and peptic ulcer. Now compare that with the things Indians use to eat
long ago when they wasn't afraid of anything. When nobody could come
to their village and outsmart them." He tapped his chest and reeled off a
list of unfamiliar grains: kamut, spelt, amaranth, teff. "And that is the exact reason why these black people, the *kirwals*, so healthy. Boil yam, boil
dasheen, boil plantain, boil breadfruit. Everything boil." Humphrey, one
of the three blacks in the crowd, crossed his legs and elegantly dusted his
trousers. "Don't mind they does borrow all these things from their neighbor backyard." The crowd erupted. Humphrey stopped dusting. The villagers who knew Narpat well realized that his irritation was shifting and
inclusive. His criticisms of local Indians included everyone not only in
the village but in the entire island. Sometimes they suspected the span of
his dismay encompassed every single person but himself; all who had
lived and died since his Aryans fell from grace.

"In this campaign you will hear all sort of promise about building road
and draining field and repairing bridge. But what that will change? Anything at all? The road will cave again in the next rainy season, the drain
will clog up in a week or two, and the bridge will collapse when one
loaded Farmall pass over it." He paused, then added, "I want to make a
different kind of promise tonight. What I promise to do is to wipe out
prejudice, superstition, laziness, jealousy, and with Janak help, gossip too.
Mauvais langue. People running their mouth without knowing the facts
and figures." The young men, mistaking this for humor, exploded with
laughter, and Janak sank in his chair and looked around furtively. "But in
order to do this we have to start with our own children. Pound it in their
head." He hammered a fist on his open palm. "Pound, pound, pound."

Kumkaran placed his hands on his belly and drummed his saffron-
colored shirt. "You talking my language exactly."

Narpat ignored Kumkaran. "When last anybody here went to Port of
Spain?"

Janak raised a hand.

"That don't count. You is a taxi driver. That is your job."

Janak folded his arms.

"Anybody know who is the Prime Minister?"

"Rawlin Gibbons. Short little fella. Write one setta history book. Does talk like if he have to pay for every single word. Like a duck that gone to school and learn to quack out a few nursery rhymes. Talking now all the time 'bout this independence nonsense. My understanding is that he don't like Indians." Janak spoke slowly, emphasizing each word as if he were teaching a slightly deaf child.

"And who elect him? Who put him there?"

"Cane farmers catching we ass as usual and everybody looking in the next direction. For six months of the year we in the field from morning to night. And what we have to show for it?" Soogrim, a balding cherubic man with an uneven handlebar moustache, looked around pleadingly. "That is why it have so much 'bandon field all around. All the help going to Port of Spain. All them illegal immigrant from Grenada and Antigua and Guyana getting more help than we own Trinidadian people. And the worse thing is that they settling all over the place like crazy ants."

Narpat's smile broadened, giving him a mocking, inquisitory expression. "I apologize. I see that people here up-to-date. We know exactly who to blame. For flood, for drought, for bad debt, for our sickly children, for the land deed, for everything. A village of complainers looking for a excuse. My ambition is for everybody in this crowd"—Narpat gestured with his hand—"to start thinking more progressive. To become futurists. To concentrate on what we could change rather than what already happen. Futurists. Remember that word good." He tugged at his lower lip and surveyed the crowd imperiously.

Ali, a perpetually drunk worker at Chin Lee's sawmill, struggled up. "Like a prophet?"

"A prophet is a salesman. Retailing salvation. A futurist prepare for tomorrow by proper planning. When was the last time anybody here had an idea?" Several hands went up. "Something that nobody think of before." Some of the hands went down. "An idea that could stand the test of time." Only Huzaifa kept his hand up. Narpat gestured to him with his chin.

"My idea," Huzaifa began, rising with a purposeful slowness to his feet, "is passive resistance." He gazed meditatively at the ceiling and smacked his lips after each word. "I believe we should block all the roads and prevent incoming and outgoing vehicles from using the village. Scatter some log and light up some old tire. Give the children some placard to hold up too. No representation without land deed."

Janak raised his hand angrily. Narpat ignored him. "The few cars that use the roads are all from the village. You think we should block them from coming and going? Besides, passive resistance is not a new idea. Gandhi thought of it already."

"Yes, Gandhi." Huzaifa shifted from foot to foot. Reluctantly he sat.

"Now you all go to your homes and think of what I propose for this village."

"How you going to settle the land deed?" Premsingh asked.

"The land deed is one part of the puzzle. You can't settle it without fixing the other pieces."

After most of the crowd had drifted away, a tall young man with a ginger moustache, and long hair parted in the center, came up to Narpat. "Could I bother you for a minute, sir?"

Narpat had noticed him sitting at the back with Partap's son. "Go ahead."

"Well, I am writing a paper on Panchayat and the politics of the village, and—"

"Where you from, young man?"

"From the University of Edinburgh. It's in Scotland."

"And you want to know about Panchayats? Well, this is not a Panchayat. Is a meeting which suppose to tell everybody who was here that nobody will help them if they don't make the first move."

"So, was anything settled here tonight?"

Narpat smiled. "That depend on how much business the rumshops do tonight."

Later that night in the rumshops, the farmers put aside their disappointment that Narpat had not really dealt with the land settlement issue and made jokes about his dietary obsessions; nevertheless, they were reassured by his easy confidence and brashness. For the remainder of the election period, Narpat made no other public speeches. He sat on the Pavilion after returning from the field and considered the measures he might implement to improve the lives of the villagers. His wife tried to draw him into easy conversations, but he said nothing and after a while she too fell into the mood.

On nights when Narpat was away, Jeeves would see tiny sparks flitting in the kitchen, and he would know that his mother was before the chulha,

slowly stirring the burnt wood. At Chin Lee's sawmill some of the older
boys had spoken of the election, and when Quashie boasted about the violent campaigns in Port of Spain, Danny had countered with a story about
a policeman who had been set ablaze during a particularly riotous con-
test. Now Jeeves wondered whether his mother was worrying about this
danger and whether she would be consoled if she understood that this
whole election business was nothing more than a test. One afternoon he
asked Kala, "Why Pappy fighting in this election?"

"To help people from the village."

"Why?"

"I think he want to make them more independent."

"How he could do that? He will quarrel with them? Or tell them
stories?"

"Teach them about history." She diverted to a confusing lecture on
Columbus, slavery, indentureship, sugar, the mercantile system, and independence, and at the end of it all Jeeves decided he would no longer
ask his sister for any clarification. In the late evenings he would listen to
Sushilla singing the proposed national anthem, which he'd also heard at
school: "Forged from the fires of whip and chain / The spark burning
bright on the freedom train . . ." In class he listened to Mr. Haroon murmuring to Lakshmikant and Pyarelal about the projected benefits of independence.

Danny whispered to Jeeves, "Wouldn't surprise me if them morocoy
jump out of the tank and run away again."

Jeeves said nothing, but after school he told his friend, "Was me who
take them out. I wanted to tell you long time now."

He felt safe with this belated confession, but Danny stared at him dis-
believingly, then turned away, kicked a pebble on the road, and skipped
over a pothole. Jeeves quickened his stride to catch up with his friend.
Then Danny told him, "Kevin and some of the other boys say it was me
who do it."

"They stupid. I will tell them it wasn't you."

"You will really tell them? Why?"

"Because it was me who let them out."

Danny glanced at Jeeves before he said, "I don't care. Let them think
what they want." He spotted Dev Anand, one of the village characters,

and crossed the street to join the man. "I will catch up with you tomorrow," he shouted to Jeeves.

But the next day he did not show up at school. And in the two months preceding independence, Jeeves noticed that his friend was increasingly absent from class.

ndependence day, like all other celebrations, left Narpat in a sour mood. While he was driving to the field early one morning, he noticed the rumshops already open and knew that in a short while they would be noisy with farmers spending a fortnight's wages in a few hours. The next day they would complain about the government, their families, their neighbors. This early in the morning the air was clouded with a cool, damp fog. Narpat attached the plow to his tractor and maneuvered between the furrows, tilling the burnt stalks and the rotting leaves into the soil. The fields were deserted, and the only sound was of his tractor chugging sluggishly, like a ghostly tank snatched from another time.

When the sun rose, he parked his tractor on the muddy track, took off his shirt, folded his trousers' hem into his boots, and began slushing through the shallow ravines that separated the field into even plots as he cleared the banks of trash dislodged by the plow. When, just before midday, he climbed out of a ravine, the mud on his chest and arms had caked into a thick crust, which scattered like powder when he dusted himself.

The workers from the adjoining fields would usually congregate beneath the hogplum tree now, squatting on the gravel track, unpacking their meals from aluminum icy-hots. While they ate, they would chat about the current price for cane or about the dishonesty of Tate and Lyle, or listen to Narpat's lectures on self-reliance. They were tough, wiry men, their bodies hardened from working in the fields since they were young. They were usually quiet and taciturn, but occasionally they quarreled among themselves, some of these arguments continuing in the rumshops.

Today Narpat sat alone beneath the hogplum tree. He missed his audience, and when he had finished his meal, he propped his back against the trunk and imagined the conversations of the farmers as they grew increasingly drunk. Perhaps they were uselessly speculating on the higher price for each ton of cane. They had forgotten the land they worked was not theirs, that it could be snatched away. He recalled the promise he had first made almost forty-five years ago as he had gazed at his then-modest field: Even if I have to die in this field, no one will take it from me.

Independence. Just another excuse to drink and fete. Like prisoners let loose for a day. No wonder his daughter had compared cane farmers to slaves. For the rest of the day, while he plowed and tilled, he contemplated the various reforms he would institute after his victory. Once the land-ownership issue had been resolved, he would guarantee a higher tonnage, and he would pressure the MP, Googool, to build better access roads and clear the rivers and ravines and increase subsidies for fertilizer and agricultural equipment. If Googool made excuses, he would mobilize the farmers to march to his constituency office and if necessary to Whitehall itself. And throughout all these reforms he would train the villagers to think constructively and to plan for all exigencies. Force them to become futurists.

If he hadn't been so preoccupied during the following days with the farmers' problems and his shifting solutions, he might have noticed, opposite his house, a tall yellow pensive-looking man who must have suddenly developed his neat potbelly, because he still walked with the sprightliness of the slim, poking around the abandoned property. First, he came with a variety of measuring tapes, spirit levels, T-squares, and strings wrapped around two bobbins. He climbed, stooped, knelt, and dangled from the rotting lintels, measuring and marking with a stick of carpenter's chalk that he occasionally placed between his teeth, his drooping moustache enlivened. A few days later a plumpish woman with thick eyebrows shading her small eyes, and two lanky adolescents with unbuttoned shirts, streamed out of a Vauxhall with the older man. The woman, wearing her orhni stylishly, disappeared into the house, but the two teenagers, looking bored and a bit annoyed, hung around in the yard while the man pulled out the dried vines from the sagging fence, cutlassed the razor grass, and raked everything into a big pile. He went to his car and returned with a tin of kerosene and sprinkled the fluid over the pile. Only when the fire roared to life did the two young men show any interest.

They ran around throwing bottles and bits of green rabbit grass into the fire. One of them shouted, "Yay, man," as a bottle cracked and exploded. The woman emerged from the house, wiped her chin with her orhni, and said something to the young men, but they ignored her. Then the flames died and they returned to the car, looking bored once more. For the remainder of the evening, while the couple cleared and cleaned, they stayed in the car, listening to Indian movie songs and occasionally flicking glances at Narpat's house. When Dulari spotted Chandra on the porch, she ordered her daughter inside.

Narpat glanced across the road. "Wouldn't surprise me if that whole house burn down the way they setting fire on all side." This was his only comment on the renovations.

On the morning following the election, just before the results were announced, an old Thames Trader truck stopped before the house. The two young men sitting atop the dangerously swaying lumber jumped from the truck and sat on the steps while the workers offloaded the cedar boards, scantlings, and a few lengths of baseboard. Dulari was sweeping the front yard, anxiously awaiting the results. When a Vauxhall pulled up, the woman with the orhni crossed the road, looking up and down, as if in this quiet area she expected cars speeding by. Dulari stood up and shook her broom loose of the dirt. "How, didi?" the woman said.

"I just cleaning up the yard." Dulari was suddenly conscious of the woman's gold bangles and necklace, and her own shabby clothing.

The woman adjusted her orhni, and her bangles slipped down her hand. She had all the mannerisms of the rural rich: fussy gestures that drew attention to her jewelry, a measured, fatigued manner of speaking, and a downward twist of the lips that seemed set to signal some trivial irritation. "We trying to put this place in order but is a whole ton of work. I can't imagine that it really had people living in that house. Poochoon keep saying that all we have to do is change the roofing into Aluzinc and build some new concrete walls and replace all the flooring with ceramic tiles and these old window with louvers but"—she sighed tiredly—"is a whole ton of work."

Dulari grew shy in the face of the woman's confident plans and her fatigued expression. "Is a good spot."

"I don't know what get inside Poochoon head to buy this property behind god back. But when he set his mind on something"—she glanced at her husband smoking contemplatively over the jutting ends of the cedar—"he does see it through come hell or high water. Them mans!"

"So you all from the countryside?"

"Siparia." She exhaled in a series of rhythmic groans. "A two-story house in a corner spot. Grocery and supermarket right round the corner. Cinema half a mile away. But Poochoon, when he set his mind on something, nobody could get him out of it." She sounded more exhausted than ever, but her eyes were watchful. "Night after night I ask Poochoon if he know what he doing. All his *chelas*, his disciples, beg him and beg him to reconsider as if they don't know how stubborn he is. He never ever take any advice, this Poochoon. His way is the only way," she said proudly.

"Just like my husband." Dulari realized that the woman was boasting, and although she had always been frustrated by Narpat's stubbornness, she wanted to impress her. "You must be hear about him."

"Hear?" The woman smiled and cleared her throat. She held the smile in place until she was ready to spit. But she swallowed. "The only thing I does hear is these chelas lining up in Siparia begging Poochoon to forget this stupidness. Poor chelas, losing the best pundit in the area."

"Poochoon is a pundit?" Dulari asked uneasily.

"Yes, didi. Chelas lining up by the doorstep day and night, night and day, dropping a whole ton of dachina. I notice you and all does have a few visitors," she added disapprovingly.

"Is for the elections. I don't know what get in Narpat head to get involve in this election-selection business. But he always say that he not interested in making money. Just helping out other people." And Dulari realized with a bit of surprise that not only was she imitating the other woman's fatigued manner but she was boasting of a quality that had always dismayed her.

The woman smiled guardedly. "Is exactly what Poochoon does say to me. He does say, 'Radhica, some cut out to do the work of god and some cut out to do the work of man.' Anyways, didi, I should go and help him now." She adjusted her orhni, allowing her bangles to shimmy.

Late in the evening, when Radhica and her family were getting into the Vauxhall, Dulari had her victory. A pickup van with a dozen or so men crammed in the tray came to a screeching stop, and Partap's son, swaying as if he were drunk, stood up. "Against all odds, Mr. Narpat, cane farmer extraordinaire, unorthodox campaigner, and self-styled futurist, this evening registered a stunning victory in the county council elections." While the other men were cheering drunkenly, Partap's son sat and contemplated the next sentence of his newspaper article.

The woman, pretending she was not listening, waved, and as the car pulled off, her bracelets rattled against the door.

Shortly after the results were announced, the Manager locked himself in his room, thrust a length of pipe through the door's latch, stood on his bed, and surveyed the crossbeams on the ceiling. When he heard the pounding on his door, he shouted, "Leave me alone. I have one last, clos-ing, final thing to do. I hereby issue instruction for my body to be trans-ported to the Laperouse cemetery to be buried in a section with all the other low-class chamars and scrapegoats. Let the mourners gather at the house of mourning before take off to the cemetery." Suddenly anger, sharp and bristling, displaced melodrama. "All them bitches who eat me and drink me out. Tell them to gather together for one last, closing, final piece of chiseling. The jookers and diggers."

"Daddy!"

"Leave me alone, man. Leave me alone. I is just a ordinary mugwump. You hear that brokofoot Partap son say that with he own teeth." But the Manager had little appetite for suicide, and the image of his body swing-ing slowly from the crossbeams, his pants soiled, while those he had bribed and feted gathered around, revolted him. "I going out like a man," he shouted. Eventually, he climbed down from the bed, removed the pipe from the latch, brushed aside his daughter, and rushed to the railing out-side.

"Daddy! Don't!"

He leaned over the railing, fished in his pocket for a cigarette, and lit one. He took deep, prolonged puffs as he imagined the scene of merri-ment at Narpat's house.

In fact, the little crowd that had gathered at Narpat's residence soon re-alized there would be no celebrations that night. He walked grimly through the crowd, accepting congratulations and shaking rough, cal-lused hands. Finally he climbed onto the tractor, and Soogrim shone a flashlight on him. "Tonight is not a night for celebrations," he began, silencing the crowd. "It have nothing to celebrate. A man win. Another man lose. The problems didn't go away. Cane farmers still getting a bad deal. Tate and Lyle still underpaying us. The government still playing the fool. John Public still think we is worthless bonded laborers. Some of us act as if we believe this too. And we still don't have any deed for land we work for more than twenty years." He paused, and the weak light emphasized his joyless smile. "When all that change, then and only then we will celebrate. Now go home and think about the future of this little village."

The farmers who had gathered at his home that night vainly expecting a fete did not go home; instead they went to the rumshop. But they were not disappointed, and these men who had frequently avoided him now said, "We need a man like Narpat in these people tail. A fighter." And, "Just let Googool try any of his nonsense now. Narpat will fix him good and proper." Someone added, "I know him a long time now, and the thing I could say about him is that he have a plaster for every sore."

Late in the night, while his supporters feted, Narpat lay awake and contemplated his plan of action. His wife gazed sleepily at him. "Is time somebody straighten out this mess, Mammy. Is high time. Somebody have to put the brakes on the slide." She fell asleep, and when she awoke a few hours later, he was still propped against his pillow. He had always scorned the villagers' talk of karma, but that night he thought: *This is my destiny. This is what I was born to do.*

The bacchanal surrounding independence and the election had also reinforced Mr. Doon's sense of his own destiny. He had listened to the independence calypso, "Don't Leggo," ceaselessly played on the radio. In the weeks prior to the election, he had read the papers avidly and groaned when he heard of the public argument that had broken out between two of the island's foremost artists, commissioned to create a mural of Trinidad. The Indian painter had railed against the Orisha-inspired symbols of his co-painter, and the black painter had fumed about the gaudy, mystical images of his fellow artist. The population had taken sides. On the radio, Mr. Doon heard a trade unionist pledging his support to a mysterious campaign to change the island's name and, on another station, the head of a Hindu organization prophesying a serious hurricane on independence day. Rival religious groups predicted earthquakes, floods, and volcanic eruptions and stopped only when they had used up all the natural disasters. In the nights, as the smell of liniments and camphor percolated through his mother's modest flat in Cocoyea, he had watched from his window a neighbor alternately flogging and lecturing his dog, and he had contemplated his material. *Crackpots*, he thought. *This place is teeming with crackpots.* In the months following Narpat's victory, he had attended all the village council meetings and had listened intently to the guests. Professors from the Centeno Agricultural College had arrived with charts illustrating sugar plantations in Mauritius and Fiji, officials from the Ministry of Agriculture with mildewed pamphlets on squatting. An assortment of aldermen, retired magistrates, businessmen, and solicitors had followed, all of whom delivered lengthy speeches with quotes from religious texts and from authors they had been forced to study years ago. Each was excoriated by Narpat for wasting the villagers' time. Eventually, seething in frustration, Narpat had delivered a long discourse on the history of sugarcane in the island.

One evening Mr. Doon had journeyed to YesRead bookstore and asked Huzaifa, the lone clerk, "Could you fetch me a thesaurus, my good man?"

Huzaifa had been confused both by the request and by the accent. "What is that exactly?"

"A dictionary of synonyms."

"Oh, I see. Why you didn't say so?" Huzaifa returned with a stack of dictionaries. He noticed Mr. Doon's frown. "These wouldn't do? All the schoolchildren does use them. What word exactly you looking for?"

"Crackpot," Mr. Doon had said. "I've used it too often. I need a word of a similar hue."

Huzaifa seemed both surprised and disappointed. "That is a nice word. Almost as nice as *holdings* and *chattels. Vouchers. Deposition.*" He had recently stolen some books on property rights. "*Binding. Affidavit.*" He nibbled his nails expectantly while Mr. Doon counted his change and hurried away. *Maybe I should carry some of these books for Narpat*, Huzaifa thought. *Set up a little office and settle all the receivable invoices. Ledgers. Requisition.* He closed his eyes.

FIFTEEN

*I*n the village, Narpat usually got his own way, and he anticipated a swift resolution to the problem of the property rights. But the world beyond Lengua held its own rules, and Narpat's intractability, which inspired a grudging respect from the villagers, was viewed in the cramped lawyers' offices in Princes Town and San Fernando, and the government departments in Port of Spain, as nothing more than a nuisance. The harassed-looking lawyers, uncomfortable in their tweed jackets, a symbol of their Cambridge years, peered from behind stacks of old files and cited unresolved cases of ligitation, some as old as twenty years. The government officials glanced at Narpat's rough country apparel and, expecting a shifting obsequiousness, were startled and affronted by his forthrightness. And they blocked all his arguments with tortuous bureaucratic subterfuges. A middle-aged official with a bored drawl told him, "The problem is that allyou country Indian does sue like if is a style. Is that what clogging up the system."

"And fellas like you unclogging it, not so? Bright helpful fellas like you?"

The official, startled out of his drawl, said, "Listen, mister, if you not happy with my help, you free to go elsewhere."

"And I will bounce up the same slackness. People sluggish with piles and constipation. Operating only on one cylinder. "

"Look, mister . . ."

"I going to the top. To the Prime Minister."

The official relaxed; he glanced at his co-workers and grinned.

At home, Narpat's family, already familiar with his broad condemnation of the village Indians, now listened to his criticism of other races.

"When some of these British fellas abandon the island, they leave behind nice buildings and nice laws. What they didn't leave was people in these buildings smart enough to interpret the laws. All you have now is a set of jackasses dress up in jacket and tie and pretending they know what they doing." Kala was always keen to debate her father on anything pertaining to independence, but when he moved on to the more amorphous discussion of duty, she and her sisters cited their homework and retreated to their room. And Jeeves, alone with his father, was anxious to please him and would ask questions like, "Why is only your duty to see about these farmers?" To which Narpat would reply, "Because I don't give up. I like a old boxer dancing around the rope." One night he told his wife, "I going to the top. To the Prime Minister himself."

"To who! You think he will have time for you?"

"That is his job. That is what we put him as Prime Minister for."

Narpat's letter to the Prime Minister was reported by Partap's son in a one-paragraph article and created a minor scandal in the village. The enraged Manager shouted to his daughter, "Write down this. Prabble number one hundred. The dog what see it shadow in the water and leggo the bone want to live in the bower all by itself." In the rumshops, some of the farmers speculated on the Prime Minister's reaction when he received the letter. "I sure he never get a letter like that before. He bound to reply."

At school Quashie asked Jeeves, "Your father really write a letter to Mr. Gibbons?"

"Yeah. A big long letter. Twenty page in all."

Quashie whistled admiringly.

During each meeting the farmers inquired about the Prime Minister's response. They encouraged Partap's son to write a critical article about the Prime Minister's private life. Say that he have half-dozen children scatter all over the place. Say that he does talk to spirit and prate.

The letter was never acknowledged, and Narpat blamed Googool, he blamed Tate and Lyle, he blamed the Prime Minister, he blamed the lawyers and aldermen, and finally he blamed the villagers who came to his house with their complaints and who grew sad and reproachful when he explained that he was unable to assist them. Frequently, he would berate them for not anticipating these problems and for their inability to look after themselves. It was not karma, he explained, or the malevolence of mysterious officials that had brought them to their state, but their own weaknesses. Sometimes Narpat's lectures released these supplicants from pretense and they would rub their hands together and curse their condition and talk about the blight of poverty. At that point, he would call out to Dulari for a few coins.

Initially Dulari had been thrilled with her husband's new status, and when her brother Bhola and his wife had visited, she had fussed about Narpat's duties and about his beleaguered constituents who expected him to single-handedly ease all their burdens. She was also able to match Radhica's air of mordant fatigue, and if a visitor had spotted these two women chatting across the road while a battalion of trucks and vans deposited hollow clay blocks, cement, sharp sand, laminated sheets, and truckloads of lumber, each load a different color, this visitor might have assumed that the conversation was a brief respite from some laborious construction. But things were not working out the way Dulari had anticipated. Narpat's duties took him away during unpredictable hours, and he returned harassed and brittle with annoyance. He gave away most of his county councilor's salary to the supplicants, and Dulari, who had always felt trapped in the village, now began to take an even dimmer view of its inhabitants. She studied the house opposite. Each week some old broken section was knocked down and replaced with a modern substitute, so that in a few months a two-story concrete house with Bermuda tile roof, panel sliding doors, casement windows, and eggshell-blue walls rose from Samsoondar's dilapidated property.

One morning Radhica came across the road and beckoned to Dulari. "Ever since we move here I wanted to invite you, didi, but with all this renovation-penovation . . ." She patted her cheek with her orhni as they entered the house; and Dulari, who had noted the external repairs and had often imagined the kitchen and the living room, was startled by the glossy lacquered walls, the decorative mirrors and tiles, the sparkling furniture, and the spotless kitchen with its fridge, stove, and oak cupboards. "We still have some work to do." Radhica passed a finger over a minor brush mark on the wall and frowned. "Poochoon does always say that a clean mind could only operate in a clean house."

When Dulari returned to her chulha, stirring the milk, she knew that she would never be able to reciprocate the invitation. Later that morning, while she was sweeping the yard, she gazed at her own house, built on uneven posts, a barrel perched uselessly on the roof, and at the rotting walls, the old wooden windows, and the knot grass sprouting from the asphalt's wedges. Her house, always a source of frustration, now became an object of shame. Even her air of fatigue faltered when pitted against Radhica's more polished performance whenever the other woman complained about the huge rooms she cleaned each day, the ceramic tiles she mopped, the windows and sliding doors she polished.

Nevertheless a strange friendship—part competition, part genuine amity—developed between the two women, and it became routine for them to greet each other ponderously every morning before they launched into their conversation.

Narpat, rarely at home, was unaware of this blossoming friendship. He had, though, developed a swift distaste for Radhica's two sons—lochos and peongs, he called them—who lounged about in their gallery with their oversize unbuttoned shirts flapping like capes when they slid down the banister, hooting and laughing. Then one morning at four a.m., when the village was still wrapped in its nighttime silence, he was awakened by the piercing wail of a conch. He sat up in his bed. "Who blowing that damn thing this time of the morning?"

"Radhica and them," Dulari replied sleepily.

"What happen? They open a fish market?"

"They blessing the house today. According to the *patra*, is a good day. Radhica husband check it himself." She hesitated then added, "He is a pundit."

"A pundit?"

Dulari recognized the edge in his voice. He got up and went to the bathroom, and she heard the trickle of water. When he returned with a wet towel draped over his shoulders, she told him quietly, "They invite us to the blessing."

He put on his work clothes, and Dulari went to the kitchen to prepare his meal. He ate moodily, flinching each time he heard the conch's wail. He walked to the tractor, started it, and idled its engine, the exhaust belching black towels of smoke. As he was pulling out, he shouted to his wife, "When you go to the fish market today, make sure you buy five pounds of salmon and some sardine." The tractor jumped across the drain and romped down the road.

In the late evening he glanced at his bright-eyed children and knew they had been to the house blessing. That night he lectured them extensively on the devolution of the caste system from a practical meritocracy in ancient India to an oppressive and inflexible hierarchy maintained by the Brahmins to safeguard their authority. He related stories of local pundits masquerading as true Brahmins. He mentioned Pundit Harridath from Debe, who conducted illicit liaisons with many of his female chelas, and Pundit Samsoondar from Felicity, sought after because of his prodigious chanting capability. "This man could chant a mantra nonstop for two hours. You know why?"

"Why?" Jeeves asked sleepily.

"Because he couldn't do anything else. Couldn't read Hindi, couldn't read Sanskrit. So he learn out a few mantra and pretend it was a special skill. And these *gaddahars*, his chelas, use to chase him all over the place, because they really believe it was a unusual talent." The Brahmins, though, were not only charlatans; they were the main perpetrators of the Indians' unhealthy diet. He rattled out a few sweetmeats. *Ladoo. Halwa. Gulab jamoon. Batassa.* The children laughed at his nursery rhyme intonation. "Sugar. Oil. Butter. Fat. They should charge every one of these fellas with murder. For killing ten, twenty people every day." He capped off his lecture by emphasizing the glory of Aryan India, when there were majestic armies of elephants, and fierce warriors, and codes of honor, and an ayurvedic system of medicine that could cure any ailment. "Scholars living in caves in the mountains meditating for half their life to solve some puzzling riddle."

"What riddle?" Jeeves asked.

"Any riddle, boy. Nothing was too difficult. Nothing was beyond their ability once they put their mind to it."

At the next village council meeting, he said, "The Prime Minister has refused to acknowledge our letter. What should we do with this riddle?" The villagers looked at one another. "Give up? Leave it in the hands of god?" From his emerging smile, the gathering knew he had a plan. "What about if we force him to take notice? What about if a delegation of farmers march around his official residence at Whitehall?"

But the villagers' taste for Gandhian resistance crumbled soon after the meeting, and even though the planned protest was reported by Partap's son, on the appointed day Narpat was joined only by the journalist,

Premsingh, Huzaifa, Soogrim, and Janak, whose taxi they had hired. By midday, however, the small delegation had attracted the attention of a few dozen vagrants and idlers who marched around Whitehall chanting "We is people too" and "Give peace a chance" and "Don't leggo." During a brief lull, one of the stragglers, a recently released patient from the St. Ann's madhouse, produced a battered trumpet and blew a stuttering tune that some of the idlers agreed was from *My Fair Lady*. By three o'clock the crowd had swelled to thirty, by four to almost fifty, with a half-dozen professional protesters who usually hung around Woodford Square. Narpat's protest now included demands for a new steelband yard in Belmont, the resignation of the Commissioner of Police, an Indian radio station, and the revocation of independence. Partap's son saw a major article.

The vagrants were the first to leave, hurrying away to secure their spots on the pavements. The professional protesters glanced guiltily at their watches and sneaked away. The idlers left soon after. On the way back, Janak made several morose pronouncements. "Half an hour again, and the police woulda be in we tail. Spot a few of them on they horse hiding by a snackette on Abercrombie street. The first slip we make, and they baton woulda be out. See some of them Marabuntas too," he added, referring to the government's alleged secret police composed of criminals.

"We could have lay down on the road," Huzaifa said. "Let them beat we as hard as they want. For the sake of independence."

"What independence? We get independence already," Janak said.

"The small rural protest soon outgrew its limitations and burgeoned into a clarion call for justice and equality." Partap's son rehearsed his article.

Huzaifa, trapped between Premsingh and Soogrim, lunged forward. "Salt!"

"We accomplish what we set out to do," Narpat said. "In this place the important thing is the size of the crowd."

Janak didn't like Narpat's tone. "We don't even know if the Prime Minister was in the building. Since he win election, he disappear again. I hear that he have a setta secret passage leading to river and mountain and beach and hoehouse."

"Salt! We should collect salt like Gandhiji. Let we go and collect salt in Maracas bay."

"It have no salt in Maracas," Janak said, shattering Huzaifa's fantasy. He remained silent for the remainder of the journey.

Five days later his fantasy was reignited. Huzaifa rushed home with the *Evening News* flapping in his hand. "Look! Look it right here. On the front page to boot."

His wife, Salima, a big dark woman who towered over her husband, glanced disapprovingly at the newspaper. She had been fuming over his transformation into a Gandhian acolyte. "It don't have no picture," she said.

"A thousand words is better than a simple picture," he replied, confusing and angering his wife. "And it have a good few thousand here. Two thousand, three hundred, and twenty proper."

"They shoulda drop a two-thousand-dollar fine on allyou tail for disturbing the peace."

"Wouldn't pay a single cent. Let General Dyer do his worse. Go to jail instead." The idea appealed to Huzaifa.

His wife noticed his serene expression. She snatched the newspaper. "Where your name? I not seeing any reference to any Mahatma Muhammad. The Muslim Gandhi. Where you?"

This was Huzaifa's true disappointment. Partap's son's article had mentioned just Narpat and focused on the multiethnic nature of the crowd. There were several references to "Trinidadian rebels with a cause" like Butler, Rienzi, and C.L.R. James. But no mention of Gandhi. None of Huzaifa. He retrieved the newspaper his wife had flung on the floor and refolded it carefully.

"Where you going now, Mahatma? To collect salt from the ravine at the back? Why you don't use that bike you never get ride yet?" Huzaifa walked through the front entrance smiling. "You better bring you lil ass here this evening if you know what is good for you. That back window still need repairing." This was another advantage to Huzaifa's new belief in passivity, and around the house were several unfinished projects: a window dangled from one hinge; half of the kitchen wall was painted in bright green, the rest covered in its original flaky brown; a quarter of the backyard was clean, the rest covered with paragrass; a clothesline sagged between an aluminum rod and a makeshift shank; the virgin bicycle was propped against an outside post.

"I am going to visit Narpat," Huzaifa said in what he hoped was a meditative voice.

"Who? Nehru? Mahatma and Nehru planning to start the revolution?"

Huzaifa liked the analogy. "God is love, Salima." He was too far down the road to hear his wife's savage curses.

Narpat read the article carefully while Huzaifa stood erect, his eyes half closed. "Is a nice article but nothing about the deed and them."

"I think Partap son hint at it in paragraph four. Third line."

Narpat read the reference aloud. "'The plight of the farmers in the neglected agricultural community of Lengua, with a population of just over four hundred, was a focal point of the protest.'"

"A lil hint but is still a hint."

Narpat reread the article more carefully, and when Dulari came to the porch, he read a few paragraphs for her. Her eyes brightened, and she called out in her new fatigued voice to her children. "Allyou father in the papers again." Her daughters peered at the newspaper for a photograph of their father and, finding none, lost interest. Jeeves hung around for a while. "What they say about you?"

"You have to learn to read, boy. It will protect you against all sort of superstition."

Huzaifa nodded. "When I was a little boy, I used to read one half-inch book per week." He indicated the thickness with his thumb and forefinger. "Nowadays I does read a one-inch book per week." The space between his fingers widened. "And when I in the mood, I does tackle a one-and-half-inch book."

The Manager read the article the following morning. Sunday mornings he usually lounged in the gallery, smoking and reading the newspapers and hawking on the steps. Occasionally visitors dropped by to negotiate the price for a load of sharpsand or gravel, or to talk about their children at school, and although the Manager rarely placed these children, he doled out advice liberally. But now the visitors had almost dried up. In a rage, he shredded the page and scattered the pieces on the floor.

He gazed at the pieces and lowered his body tiredly onto his hammock. Kamini, her face blazing with rouge, emerged from the house, glanced at the torn newspaper, and said, "I am going down to the post office for a while." She hurried down the steps before her father had an opportunity to vent his rage, but he called after her, "When you finish lick stamp, I want you to walk down to Lumchee shop and get about eight feet of rope and some soft candle."

Kamini hesitated. "Daddy, you shouldn't talk like that all the time. What people will say if they hear you?"

Mention of "the people," the broad mass of ungrateful voters, rekindled the Manager's anger. "What people? Them mugwumpy, scrapegoaty bitches and them? The jookers and diggers? All of them could kiss my nasty ass."

"Daddy!"

Kamini walked away hurriedly. Later, when she had detoured from the post office to Lalbeharry trace, where Mr. Doon was waiting in his Prefect, blowing smoke through the window idly, she did not mention her father's poetic fancies but rather his frequent threats about suicide. Mr. Doon took a deep drag from his cigarette and contemplated this bit of information. *The despicable squire was found swinging from his joist by a dappled assortment of chimney sweepers who proceeded to ransack the tenement in the hope of locating the ill-gotten treasure he had surely hoarded within the panels of the building. Pots and pans were overturned, clapboards removed, the attic scavenged, the basement combed.*

"What you mumbling about, David?"

"One of the mysteries of nature is how a man like your father could have generated a creature like yourself." His voice softened. "Roll up the window, please."

But Mr. Doon's book was not going well. He had been excited on his return to Trinidad by the untapped Dickensian world he saw at every corner. Late in the nights in his mother's flat, he'd push aside his coilspring notebook, close his eyes, and imagine the editors of *Descant*, *Exile*, and *Fiddlehead* sending down special emissaries to coerce him into writing a piece. Occasionally he would peep through the louvers at the neighbor reading intently from a crumpled magazine to his dog. This blasted independence come and gone like a breeze, he would think sadly. Where were the riots? Where the stirring speeches? Where the partition with entire villages uprooted? Where the raw material for a controversial but universally acclaimed novel? Occasionally the students at Lengua government school would see him, his tie loose around his neck, his hands clenched against his back, staring at the playground and muttering.

"Look out for the white van any day now," Danny told Jeeves.

$\mathcal{T}$he year of independence and of his father's political victory was one of Jeeves's happiest: his father's prolonged absence and his mother's long conversations with Radhica allowed him the opportunity to slip away to Chin Lee's sawmill, where a group of other village boys were already playing football, cricket, and scooch. Soon they grew bored with these games and, drawing inspiration from television shows, fashioned wooden lances and swords resembling those in *Ivanhoe* and *Robin Hood*. Some of the boys mimicked popular television characters like the Riddler and the Green Hornet, and Janak's eldest son, who hung around with a mock sawdust-filled cigarette, said, "Have no fear. Zachary Smith is here." To which the smaller boys would respond, "Danger, danger, Dr. Smith."

In the bushy spot separating the school from the Manager's property, Danny, when he was in school, instructed Jeeves to close his eyes and slow his breathing. "In a little while you will come one with the animals, and hear all of them talking." Jeeves heard nothing, but later Danny translated the silence into a riveting drama where the ocelots and snakes and birds and lappes held parties, plotted against one another, and occasionally planned an attack on a human. Danny also taught him how to drive a nail into a pyramidal guava stump to make a top, and to flatten the crown of a soft drink to make a *zwill*, a whirring miniature blade controlled by a length of twine. He demonstrated how, with a candle stub, a rubber band, and a wooden bobbin, he could create a wind-up truck, and one morning he brought a ball that seemed to be swathed in rubber bandages. "Make this meself from a rubber tree. Make 'bout a hundred cut and the next day all the sap does harden to rubber." He told Jeeves about the chataigne tree, which oozed a sticky *laglee* used to catch birds, and other plants that screamed and sang when they were cut. When Jeeves asked to see these trees, Danny said that it was tricky business and that he would first have to get permission from Papa Bois.

"The forest watchman?"

"Yeah, but I can't promise anything because he not in a good mood these days. Too much hunting going on. A lotta baby animals getting wipe out. Rodriguez father and Sidney does go hunting for manicou and 'gouti every night. Bounce them up a few time."

"They spot you?"

"Nah. I get one with the forest. Sorta invisible." Whenever Danny showed up in school, he would explain his absence by saying he had been "studying the animals."

Sometimes at home Jeeves pretended he was invisible, and he was only jerked out of his fantasy when his mother said, "You ignoring me now? Or you busy dreaming up fancy schemes like your father?" One morning while he was attempting to become one with the house, she slapped him and said, "How much time I must ask you to do a simple thing before you pay attention? Eh? Of all my children, you will come out the most useless. I could see already that I will never be able to depend on you for anything. You following a good example."

But I invisible, he thought.

Later, when his mother was chatting with Radhica, he slipped away to the sawmill and, with the other boys, safely engaged in his fantasies. Occasionally he broke from the group and strolled to the back of the sawdust pile, toward the bamboo groves. He recalled the stories told by Kamini and he thought: *I am Martin Rattler hunting for adventure, King Arthur searching for Excalibur, Theseus preparing for the rites of manhood, Jason voyaging for the golden fleece, Odysseus moving from adventure to adventure.* He liked the idea of the heroes' sacrifices, and sometimes, listening to the groaning, creaking bamboo, he recalled his father's talk of ordinary men transformed into heroes by passing some mysterious test. Occasionally, he tried to interest Narpat in these fantasies and was disappointed when he was met either with a stony silence or a lecture about backward societies. Now the lectures were dense with references to laws and regulations and public servants. One night he overheard his father saying to his mother, "I have no choice but to see about the deeds. They depending on me."

"Depending? These is big, seasoned farmers. Why they can't see about their own problems? Why you alone have to bear the weight of the entire village? Why your family alone have to sacrifice?" Jeeves thought of his mother's frustrated plea and of his father's characteristic recital while he was playing in the sawdust, and in his fantasies he imagined himself miraculously rescuing his father from throngs of berserk farmers, from frenzied animals, from conniving uncles. He imagined removing his mask and watching the surprise and delight on his father's face.

You?

He stood with his hands on his waist and smiled.

It was you all the time? Little Jeeves?

He grinned.

At home, he was distracted from his fantasies by his mother's frustrated voice. "This village is a real trap. Bit by bit it will eat up every single person who remain here. Bit by bit. This place will never change."

But in the year following Narpat's victory, as the government halfheartedly instituted a few of its election promises, change came grudgingly to the village. Asphalt roads were repaired, access traces cleared and widened, and a few new cars appeared in recently paved garages. An old pickup van, its tray laden with carite and carailli and moonshine, and tiny shrimps looking like bleached cockroaches, crawled through the village, its approach signaled by its hoarse horn. An abandoned lagoon was cleared, drained, and filled with mud. The village boys descended on the dredged lagoon. Cricket teams were picked, talent unearthed, and in a short while Lengua was able to offer up a squad for the Southern Cricket League.

The games were halted for three months during the rainy season, when the pitch reverted to a lagoon. The harsh thunderstorms swallowed up other improvements: asphalt buckled and sank, rivers overflowed, vegetables were ruined by the muddy water, and small cobwebby cracks appeared on many of the renovated houses. Bisons and dogs shook off swarms of mosquitoes and sandflies. An epidemic of dengue fever spread from Debe, and government workers sprayed a couple drains and some water containers. Children fell ill, many from the chemicals. Pundits were called in. The government workers returned with their spray cans when cases of malaria were discovered.

The Brahmin, Narpat's neighbor, prospered. His services were sought to safeguard against further disasters. He blessed dozens of houses, re-cited protective mantras for others, and conducted daily *pujas* that prom-ised prosperity and good health. His own prosperity was announced through the elaborate renovations to his house. His lawn was dug and re-planted with glistening silvery shrubs and ginger lilies and dwarf pomme-cytheres. He built two massive Grecian columns on either side of the front gate, and installed decorative fretwork on the front ceiling. One af-ternoon, a van deposited an enormous lotus-shaped wicker chair. Now he smoked and sang and shouted greetings to his chelas from the chair.

In the evenings while Dulari was awaiting her husband, she glanced through the front door at the Brahmin and his wife sipping tea in their gallery. She thought of her parents' home in Charlieville. There was a bal-cony lined with potted oleanders and zinnias and marigolds. Villagers dropped in to greet her father, a quiet lawyer's clerk. Her mother was usu-ally in the small, cozy shop chatting with other women. There were fruit trees in the yard and a swing where she had rocked and imagined that her life would always be as pleasant.

One night she told her husband, "Every week Radhica and them buy-ing some new furniture."

"With money they swindling from poor, stupid, superstitious people."

"That is his job. He serving a purpose in the village."

"I see." He walked to the porch. After a few minutes he shouted, "You want a house like the Brahmin, not so? Is that house that causing all the jealousy. Envy." He ground out the word.

She went into the kitchen, removed the pot of milk from the chulha, and placed it on the rickety cupboard. She wrenched out a hand of ba-nana suspended from a nail on the wall, tore open the green skin, and be-gan chopping the fruit into coin-size slices. Narpat heard the sound of the knife slamming against the chopping board and walked out of the house. Opposite, the Brahmin was standing straight against the banister, smoking and gazing at his newly constructed fence. He flicked away his cigarette, walked across the gallery, and lowered himself onto his lotus-shaped chair. He withdrew a book from a side table and began to sing in a loud, quivering voice. He rocked his head from side to side and, with the book in his hand, made twirling motions as if he were directing an invisible orchestra.

Narpat started his tractor, opened the radiator's cap, and fetched a bottle of water from the copper. By the fourth bottle, the Brahmin had retreated inside his house. Narpat capped the radiator and switched off the engine. He saw his wife looking at him from the kitchen window.

Three days later the Manager's truck pulled up with a brand-new couch and six morris chairs with maroon felt cushions fastened to the tray with a jumble of ropes. He had been surprised when Narpat had walked into his yard and inquired about the cost of transporting the furniture.

When, the next day, the truck stopped by Narpat's place, the Manager held on to a canhook at the edge of the tray and hoisted himself up. Narpat had already unloosened the ropes, and both men slid the couch off the tray and carried it into the house.

"Morning, morning, everybody." The Manager was breathing heavily and sweating. He straightened and glanced at Dulari. "New couch. New chair." He dropped his end. "New table coming later to replace this old one?"

"Will build it myself. Special design." Narpat lowered the other end.

The Manager gazed around the bare house. "Allyou already throw out all the old furniture from the living room to make space, eh?" He motioned with a leg. "Good spot for the couch in that corner." His ankle swiveled. "And the chairs and the special design table will fit nice 'cross they."

Dulari walked from one end of the living room to the other, calculating distance. Jeeves trailed her, mimicking her long strides. The Manager glanced at Jeeves, surprised that a robust man like Narpat had such a sickly-looking son. "Boy going to school?"

"Boy, you going to school?" Narpat relayed the question to his son.

"Going to school on a train."

Only Kala noticed the Manager's dry grin; the other children were helping their mother arrange and rearrange the couch at different spots in the living room. Finally she positioned it at the side of the front door. Then she lined up the five old chairs against the wall and, with much appraisal and adjustment, arranged the new morris chairs around the mora table. When the Manager left and Narpat returned into the house, she was still gauging the new furniture. "Nice chairs," he said. "Need a nice table to go with them. A spinning table with a ball-bearing base. Put the milk there." He motioned with his hand. "Put the vegetables there. The beans across there, and the rice on that end. So whatever you want, you just spin the table and it right in front of you." He spread his arms and spun around as if he were dancing. The children giggled. "A dancing table."

"Dance all the food straight to the floor," Dulari said, smiling.

"Not if I weld on a big chunk of magnet to the bottom. You will have to practically pull out the cup and plate from the table."

"I will have to take the whole table to the wares stand when I want to wash cup and plate."

Dulari must have known that Narpat's magnetic table would never materialize, and for the remainder of her life in the house, the six morris chairs with felt cushions enclosed the old table. She grew strict with her children, particularly her daughters, reminding them over and over of the sacrifice in sending them to high school. In the mornings she swept the floor so briskly that the ends of the cocoyea broom caught and splintered between the wooden planks. In the nights, while the children were doing their homework, they would hear her singing mournful songs from *Guide* and *Dosti* and *Mother India*. Sometimes after she had inspected their homework, she would relate little incidents from her childhood: going to the drive-in with her parents, celebrating birthdays with her cousin, making excursions to the beach and Blue Basin and Caura valley. Melancholy invariably led to a stony resignation, her only utterance being, "Is my luck." Yet during the two years before Narpat's tenure as a county councilor came to an end, she got many of the items she had fussed about. She got a twelve-by-fifteen diamond-patterned linoleum, with which she covered the ugly living room floor, and a few weeks later a laminated coffee table with bowlegs, which she placed before the couch. Both the linoleum and the coffee table were purchased with money borrowed from Bhola, and after the inevitable argument with her husband, she busied herself in the kitchen, singing her sorrowful movie songs.

A month after the purchase of the coffee table, Chandra complained that she had heard a sound outside the window as if someone were prowling about. For two weeks Narpat listened to his wife's complaints, and each night he repeated his response. "Glass louvers, eh. Make it easy for these so-call prowlers to peep inside." Sometimes he switched to a sneaky voice, "That is Kala pretending to do her homework? That is Chandra and Sushilla following their mother about? And that is Jeeves peeping out at me? I better grab him. Plonk! Plonk!" But eventually he gave in, and the wooden windows were torn down and glass louvers installed. Narpat did the installation himself, and the louvers, slightly misaligned, never closed properly, and the children were afraid to force the latch into place.

Finally she got electricity. Previously he had argued about the cost of extending power to his house from the junction to where the nearest pole was situated, a half-mile away. Dulari knew this was a major expense, but each morning she listened to Radhica complain about the portable generator's inability to power her stove, her fridge, her television, and her fans. "I does have to unplug the fridge every evening when Ray father watching his television shows." Now that Radhica had grown familiar with the other woman, as a mark of respect, she had stopped referring to her own husband by his name. "You can't imagine how hot the place does be then." She exhaled loudly, waving her hand before her face. "But he can't do without he *Lucy* show." Her lips crumbled into a slack smile as if this were an indulgence she barely tolerated. "And Ray and Jag too does be stick up in front the television, watching these pow-pow gun-shooting show. Everybody getting too modern, if you ask me." After these conversations, Dulari would return to her kitchen to finish the evening's meal. She would rearrange the smoldering wood in the chulha and blow the fire to life until her eyes were red.

One morning Radhica told her, "I think we should have left the big Phillips set in Siparia and buy one of these little matchbox set instead. But when you get accustom to something, how you could do without it? You could imagine Ray father watching he *Lucy* in that little matchbox?" After a while she added, "At least we don't get these outage-poutage every night in we generator." But increasingly she could not disguise her frustration with the spoiled food in the fridge, the flickering lights, and the inconvenience of daily refueling the generator. "I don't know why we move to this place."

A statement uttered by Dulari for so many years; yet she always responded with, "Is not a bad place. It very quiet and peaceful." She was irritated by Radhica's boasting, irritated at being forced to defend the backward village, and each day her irritation was kindled by the chulha, the sooty lamps, the vegetables soaked in water to retain their freshness, and the bloated heat pressing down from the aluminum roof. The children joined in the fantasy; they imagined ice-cold water and iceblocks and lights controlled with a flick of the switch. Chandra began to complain of headaches from studying in the dim lights, and Sushilla said the smoke irritated her throat. Each day the children testified to their deteriorating eyesight.

Then one evening a yellow government van dropped off an electricity pole about a hundred yards from Narpat's property, and later in the week another yellow van offloaded about a dozen men who smoked, drank, rested, played cards, and yet managed to dig a hole and plant the pole. The following day the van braked noisily by the pole, and a scowling, wiry man unraveled a ladder, scooted up the pole, connected some wires, scooted down the pole and dragged the other end of the wires up the road. After a great deal of rattling and shaking, he managed to fold the ladder. He walked across to the Brahmin's house. "The county councilor fella living here?" The cigarette between his lips jumped up and down.

"Across the road," one of the boys said.

The electrician looked skeptically at the small house and played with the cigarette in his mouth, calculating the bribe. Finally he spat out his cigarette and walked back to his van.

The extension of electricity to Kanhai trace was the only instance when Narpat's political position resulted in personal benefit, and in the following months Mr. Doon listened to gossip about it in the rumshops. But it solidified the friendship between Dulari and Radhica, and it paved the way for Dulari's children to sneak across the road to watch television when their father was away.

Narpat did the wiring himself. He sketched a number of plans, walked around the house, tapped the walls, stared at the rafters, and added modifications. Eventually he threw away the paper. One evening he returned with a bolt of wire wrapped around a huge bobbin. He split the wire with his teeth, snaked it along the ceiling beams, slipped it through the rotted holes in the rafters, and tugged it down to the walls. Jeeves jumped to pull the wires, but he was scolded by Dulari, whose purposeful fatigued look had returned. Sometimes the wires disappeared in odd spots like behind Carnegie, and then Narpat had to retrace his steps. When he ran out of electrical wire, he pulled out a jumbled tractor's harness from beneath the house, bit off pieces of greasy filaments and cables, and with these joined and tied, completed the job. He placed the outlets in unusual places, some too high to be useful and others almost jammed against the floor. When the house was connected by the scowling electrician in the yellow van—its final appearance in Kanhai trace—the lights flickered and dimmed, but no one cared. "Careful, Jeeves," Dulari cautioned. "Don't switch on the lights so often. You will burn the fuse."

"Fuse?" Narpat said.

Wiring the house had energized him. He had enjoyed the random modifications and substitutions of outlets and unions and wires. And everything worked. The energetic inventiveness remained with him for a while, and he installed several outlets and useless plugs and sockets along the walls.

"Preparing for Christmas," Dulari joked.

He removed the bulbs and replaced them with fluorescent lamps, which flickered dimly and buzzed. "Voltage too low in this area." He thought for a while, then took one of his wife's brooms and rubbed it against the long cylindrical lamp. The bulb buzzed into brightness. "Need a little contact, that is all." The children soon grew used to the droning and the ritual of rubbing the broom against the bulb, and Jeeves, who slept beneath the longest and noisiest, discovered several new species of insects. Occasionally he would awaken and see his father on the Pavilion, a book on his lap. "Why you waking so late?" he would ask. And his father would reply absentmindedly, as if he were reading from one of his books, "Every problem have a solution attached to it. Like a tractor and a trailer."

"You trying to find the solution?"

His father would remain silent, but a few minutes later when Dulari came from the kitchen, he would tell her in a low, subdued voice that his tenure as a county councilor was coming to an end and he had not yet settled the property rights. "I never make a promise that I didn't keep."

"Is not your fault that they seeing this problem."

"I make a promise," he said after a while.

And just before his incumbency concluded, when the farmers' disappointment had turned to rancor, when his belief in his own abilities was sorely tested, he was able to settle the issue. One midday Stewart, the owner of the estate, arrived from Port of Spain with his surveyor, a slender mixed-race man of about thirty. Narpat heard the commotion in the distance but paid no attention. Then an urgent summons was relayed to him. He arrived and saw Stewart and his surveyor, both wearing ties, both sweating in the sun, standing within a circle of angry, frightened farmers. The two men from Port of Spain, with impressive ledgers in their hands, were talking about trespassing, prosecution, and imprisonment. Premsingh, the usual ringleader, was cowed and useless. Some of the other farmers held their machetes loosely, uncertainly. Narpat pushed his way through the crowd. "What going on here?"

"We come to survey the property," Stewart said angrily. "My property." He tapped his ledger.

"Survey the property for what reason?" Narpat asked.

"Subdivision," the surveyor said curtly.

"To build house on land we working for we whole life. Just come all of a sudden and take it away." Soogrim was close to tears. "What will happen to my children? You want me to put them on the street? Send my daughter to work in the clubs and them? Eh? You will be happy then?"

"Our own rightful property."

"That is a damn lie."

Narpat turned to the surveyor. "You want to survey the land? Okay, go ahead and survey it."

"At least somebody in this blasted place—"

"But not a single house going to build here. Not one."

"Mr. Cane Farmer, if you understand the law—"

"I understand the law very well, you little tout. And I telling you that not a single house going to build in this canefield."

The surveyor tried to maintain his dignity. "And you going to stop we? Stop we *and* the police?"

"Listen"—now Narpat turned to Stewart—"you could come here with the police and survey the land and drive your stakes in the ground. But in the morning all the stakes will be missing. Same with the bulldozers and backhoes. You put up a single house, and in the morning it burn to the ground. You see all these burnup canefield all around." He gestured with an idle wave. "We cane farmers know how to set fire. How to control them. How to guide them. We doing it all our life."

"Arson," the surveyor spluttered. "A good five years in jail for that."

Stewart looked from Narpat to the burnt fields.

"But they are reasonable people too. They know they pay for the land, and they expect to work it as they see fit. More than twenty years now they put down money on this land, you understand? More than twenty years it providing a livelihood for their family. They didn't suddenly appear like bachac and claim ownership. You think they did imagine that twenty years later some family member would appear with a little tout who suffering from a bad case of rickets and say, 'Everybody clear out. We putting up house.'"

Mr. Stewart looked thoughtfully at his surveyor, who said, "We coming back, we coming back. *With* the law. Then we will see who is a tout who suffering from rickets."

"The law?" Narpat recalled his frustration with the clerks in their Port of Spain offices. "What law give allyou town people the right to come to the village and bulldoze agricultural land like a piece of useless swamp? What law give you the right to destroy any property that in the way?"

The surveyor punched his ledger. "This law. It right here."

"And what law will protect allyou from people who see their life going up in smoke? Check your ledger for that ruling. Just remember. Reasonable people, but they know how to set fire and how to control it. Taking away a farmer land is like taking away his life. Now go." He gestured to the road.

"We coming back."

"Come. We invite you. We is hospitable people. We will prepare a grand feast. Just set the date." Now for the first time, the farmers laughed.

"With the long arm of the law."

"You should see about that rickets first." Narpat spoke as if he really meant it. "Get out from your office and spend some time in the sun." He motioned to the farmers. "Like these people here."

"We coming back with a topnotch lawyer."

"You better bring a magistrate too."

But they never returned. Stewart, acting on the advice of a family

member, had assumed that subdividing the estate would be a simple
process. He didn't have the stomach for a protracted battle, and besides,
he had heard stories of these rural Indians and their cutlasses. Maybe, he
thought, the farmers were extricating him from unnecessary expense.
The estate was in such a backward place anyway. Behind god back. Who
would want to buy houses in such a place? He was surprised that he had
not thought of these problems before. So he decided to offload the estate
with the stipulation that the farmers pay for the surveying and all the legal fees. They agreed happily, with Narpat supervising all the arrangements. Partap's son squeezed out another article, Narpat was again in the
good graces of the villagers, and Dulari was once more able to claim par-
ity during her conversations with Radhica.

Narpat was not caught in the flurry of compliments; he had doubted himself, had come close to surrendering. In the canefield he saw himself as
distant from his family, his enemies, the entire village. The last of his
breed. And during this period of distance and detachment, he was able to
see his future clearly. He had worked honestly, avoided the vices of the
other farmers, lived his life according to a stringent moral code. He contemplated the purpose of his life, the innumerable sacrifices, the early
death of his father, his struggle to possess his own field, his political victory, the land settlement, and he knew that these events had in a sense
singled him out. His entire life had been a struggle against negligence and
idleness. He had seen his father, so strong and focused, slip into the haze
from which he never recovered after his canefield was stolen from under
him, and he had seen his mother, ever dependent on her husband, sinking into another kind of gloom, useless in the face of her brother-in-law's
pilfering.
     When he was twelve, his cousin had taunted that Narpat's father had
died from craziness. He had leaped at the boy, pummeling him on his
head and arms and chest, too enraged to notice his own strength. His uncle had flogged him with a cable, which had cut deeply into his back and
shoulders. He threatened to throw the family out into the road, and
Narpat, who had been offended by his mother's silence during his flogging, saw how easily tears now flowed from her eyes; how gracelessly she
begged and groveled. For a moment, he wished that his uncle's fury would

be reignited and that he would turn on this woman whose hands were pressed against his feet. Nine years later she passed away, and Narpat felt neither grief nor regret, just brief wonder at how little she had left behind.

He had changed in those nine years, become tough and stubborn and watchful, and soon the anger at his uncle's cruelty and his cousins' taunts was displaced by a ruthless observance of their grand follies. So he was not surprised at his cousin's accident at the drag-racing strip at Wallerfield, the boy pulled unconscious from his wreck and a month later set in a wheelchair, where he would spend the rest of his life. Nor was he surprised by his uncle's deterioration into diabetes. Ten years after he had left his uncle's house with his sister and his mother, he had visited the old man and had seen an almost lifeless creature, berating the boy for having neglected him, still trying to bully, still trying to raise his useless leg to kick. Around him were his idols, upon which he daily conducted ceremonial ablutions, testimonies to his high caste. And at that moment Narpat saw—more than during the destruction of their downstairs room, the construction of his little shack, the death of his mother—at that moment he saw how much he had grown apart from everyone. Owing no debts. Obligated to no one. Free. Strong. Apart. The land settlement reminded Narpat of the qualities that had enabled him throughout his life to overcome every single obstacle, and his children often heard him saying things like "A man without a mission have no purpose in life" and "The biggest battle is to understand this purpose. We fighting this battle from the minute we born to the moment we die." Occasionally he elaborated, gazing at Kala rather than at his other children, as if she alone could understand what he was saying. "People believe the main aim in life is to make plenty money. Build new house. Buy fancy furniture. Eat unhealthy food. Own cinema and truck. But tell me what they will leave behind? What people will remember them for? For their stinginess and bobol? How all that money will benefit anyone else?" At other times his voice would soften. "Every single person have one special purpose."

"What is my purpose?" Jeeves would ask seriously.

And Narpat would smile and ruffle his son's hair. "Only you could figure this out, Carea."

"What if I can't figure it out?"

"Then you will end up like these mad people you see marching about in Princes Town." He would rise from the Pavilion and, with his hands clasped against his back, pace up and down briskly and mumble like the mad people. Jeeves would imitate him until Dulari peeped from the kitchen and reminded her son of his homework. "Come here, madboy, and read what you do in school today." Jeeves would persist. On succeeding nights he asked his father the same question: "Suppose I can't figure out the purpose?"

One night, with Jeeves sitting next to him on the Pavilion, Narpat called his daughters. "Time for a little story."

Chandra came reluctantly from the kitchen, her hands dusty with flour, a trace of irritation on her face. "What story is this?" She glanced accusingly at Jeeves.

"About a dancing monkey," Narpat replied.

"You tell us that story a hundred times already."

"Then I have a hundred more times to tell it. Come, Kala and Sushilla," he shouted. When all his children had gathered around, he began. "Once there was a proud old rajah who owned a monkey trained to perform all kind of amazing tricks. Emperors and empresses and sultans come from all over the world just to see this monkey decorated with the finest jewels, dancing gracefully. One day while Mr. Monkey was performing, a mischievous courtier fling a handful of nuts on the stage. And guess what happen?"

"The monkey throw away it clothes and jewel and dive straight for the nuts," Jeeves told him. "It start behaving like a real monkey."

"I could go back to the kitchen to help Mammy now?" Chandra asked.

Narpat waved his hand.

Kala winked to Sushilla and said, "That is a nice story, Pappy. I think everybody in the family know it by heart now. Especially your three *big* daughters."

Jeeves noticed his mother arranging his schoolbooks on the table. "Tell me it again."

The two girls hurried away.

SEVENTEEN

*I*n 1964, the year after the land deeds were settled, B. J. Tiwary, the leader of the Sanatanist Hindus on the island, a strapping man who had made a fortune from trading with the Americans at the military base in Chaguaramas, died. On the day of his cremation, rain fell unendingly, and the pundits worried that his body would not be properly cremated at the Caroni river, but Hindu journalists marveled that "it seemed as if the heavens had opened up in tribute to the man who had changed the course of history." The cremation site was crowded with politicians, pundits, businessmen, and bemused Americans.

B.J., as he was known, was one of the few Indians on the island for whom Narpat had any time, and though the two men had almost come to blows at their only meeting more than two decades earlier during a public reading of the religious text the *Ramayana*, Narpat admired his brawny appearance, his brash, forthright manner of speaking, and the discipline that characterized his self-extrication from terrible poverty.

The mourners were all well dressed, and when Narpat showed up, his hair neatly groomed but with rumpled shirt and trousers, he stood out as he walked though the crowd sheltering beneath their umbrellas, and as he stood bareheaded in the downpour, listening to speech after speech. The orthodox Hindus who knew him from his public dissension with pundits conducting *Ramayanas* or *kathas*, glanced warily in his direction. The final speech was delivered by Isbitt Ramdeen, a Christian Indian who hoped to woo the Hindus in his campaign to replace the absentee leader of the opposition, Dr. Sohan Bhandara, who had resumed his job at Cambridge following his party's defeat. Ramdeen heaped praises on the local Hindus, citing their industriousness, thrift, introspection, family values, and religious devotion. Narpat moved closer to him.

"The Hindus are verily the bedrock of this island. They have brought with them and introduced to others centuries of finely honed dogmas and doctrines."

"And superstitious mumbo-jumbo."

A murmur went through the crowd. Some of the men glanced angrily at Narpat. Ramdeen adjusted his jacket and continued. "The Hindus are verily the envy of people all over the world because—"

"Because of what? Because it is the only religion that has not evolved properly? Because everything is a big pappyshow like this funeral here?"

"Sir, please have respect for the dead. This is not a time for needless arguments."

"Is not a time for making speech either. For campaigning and misleading these simple, stupid people here. Leave that for the street corner and the junction."

"Sir, I have been verily invited—"

"By who? The pundit? The *mahapatar*? The family? By special committee?"

"By me! I invite him."

Narpat recognized B.J.'s son, a husky young man who owned a racing pool in Tunapuna and who was often photographed in the newspapers with heavy gold chains draped around his neck. He gestured to the young man. "This is the Hindu you was talking about? Gambling and drinking? Centuries of civilization? Carrying around two hundred extra pounds?"

The young man rushed toward Narpat but was restrained by a group of mourners. "Leave me alone. Let me teach him a lesson. Coming in my own father funeral to cause confusion and *jhanjhat* like a blasted madman." He struggled with the men. "Your ass dark with me, you hear me. It dark with me." Unexpectedly, he began to cry. "In my own father funeral."

Narpat walked away, smiling. The crowd parted.

Later, there were several versions told of the disruption. The son had pulled out and pointed his revolver at Narpat. The dispute had later developed into a brawl at the roadside. The police had arrested both men. And at a hawk-and-spit bar, Mr. Doon heard that the Prime Minister, disguised as a woman, had also been to the funeral.

There were other, more visible dignitaries at the cremation. One of them was a stocky young man with a military crewcut and a carefully cultivated moustache. His name was Alvin Seegobin, and he was a former Member of Parliament who had resigned from the government after a humiliating junior placement in the Culture Ministry. He had been one of the few Indians in the ruling party, and following his resignation he developed a reputation as reckless and hotheaded. He eventually got a column in a local newspaper and wrote weekly of "plantation and colonial mentality." He advocated, in his columns, islandwide strikes of teachers, stevedores, and shopkeepers. When he was accused of "communist agitation" and threatened with jail, he turned his attention to reforms, and each week he resurrected some dormant group like the Poultry Owners Association, before he set his sights on the sugar industry and on the moribund Cane Farmers Association. He appeared suddenly in Debe and Penal and other cane-farming areas.

Eventually he came to Lengua. From Huzaifa, Narpat heard of the meeting. "Young fella. Fiery like hell. Say that cane farmers of the world have to arise. Talk 'bout Gandhi and the next creole fella too."

"I wonder if this Seegobin ever plant a single stalk of cane in his life."

"Educated in a big way. Had a nice briefcase load up with pamphlet. And manifesto too, some nearly three inch thick. Talk nonstop for nearly two hours."

"And that is all he will ever do. I wonder who invite him down here?"

Huzaifa clicked his nails nervously.

"These fellas just looking for a little fame. In ten months he will run to some new jhanjhat."

But Seegobin's campaign to dislodge the Cane Farmers Association took hold in Debe and Penal and Barrackpore. For years these farmers had complained of neglect by the government; now suddenly a former Member of Parliament, an ex-prisoner, and a journalist was paying them attention. Seegobin promised higher prices, increased subsidies, and a guaranteed tonnage. He waved glossy pamphlets describing the sugar industry in Cuba. He spoke of Castro as if they were old friends.

After each meeting he gathered endorsements, and one week he was able to write that he had collected more than a thousand signatures from frustrated farmers. The next week he announced his intention of forming the True and Noble Cane Farmers Association. Many of the farmers in

Lengua joined; Narpat's resolution of the land deeds was forgotten. During lunch breaks the farmers from the adjoining fields who congregated beneath the hogplum tree no longer gloated about their legal rights to the field but discussed Seegobin's innumerable proposals. Narpat thought of a class of unruly children promised some treat, but he said nothing. Soon these farmers stopped visiting his house, and at night he would untie the copper wire from the kitchen wall and spend much time reading and rereading the dietary stipulations and the quirky injunctions he had, over the years, stabbed onto the wire. His wife was confused by his uncharacteristic silence, but she was relieved that he was spending more time at home. In the children's presence she made mysterious Hindi jokes with him and chuckled. In the afternoons she cooked his favorite meal, sardine seasoned with lemon and turmeric and shadow beni, and after his meal she sat close to him on the Pavilion and closed her eyes.

Late in the night, when his wife was in the bedroom, Narpat untied the copper wire, and frequently Jeeves would be awakened by the rustling of paper. One night he heard his father mumbling, "We will see how this story will end."

"Story?" Jeeves asked sleepily.

His father did not reply immediately, and just as the boy was once more drifting to sleep, he heard, "Long, long time ago this mangy jackal fall inside a copper fullup with blue dye, and when it crawl out all the other animals begin to bow down before this strange new creature. They decide to replace the old lion, the ruler of the animals, with this jackal, and they build a nice throne with sip and tapano and poui and immortelle for it."

Jeeves had heard this story years ago, but because the resolution to his father's fables often changed, he asked, "And what the old lion decide to do?"

"To wait."

"For what?"

"For the beginning of rainy season."

"And then the dye wash away."

"Exactly."

"And the animals tear up the jackal and beg the lion to come back."

"Maybe. But the lion, while it was banished, had get used to the idea of wandering about the forest watching the sun rising every morning and the little animals running back to their hole in the night."

This was a new development. "So the old lion never come back?" Jeeves heard the rustling of paper once more and thought that his father was considering the question, but there was no response.

Narpat soon developed a routine. He left and returned to his house at the same time each day. His children came back from their television viewing at the Brahmin's house at seven-thirty. His daughters went either to the kitchen or to their bedroom. His son twisted and turned on his fiber mattress until he fell asleep. Each day Narpat carefully observed this pattern. He sat with his wife on the Pavilion for an hour and a half. She left for her room at ten-thirty. He unclasped the wire at eleven. He reordered the jottings and calculated the year and month he had written them. He went through the old bills and receipts, again carefully noting their dates. He assessed the time it took him to eat, shower, and get to the field. During the lunch break he no longer walked to the hogplum tree, but portioned, weighed, and carefully mixed his herbicides and fungicides. The old brass can that he slung on his back needed to be pumped sixty-five times before the chemical mixture ran out. In the afternoon, a pair of egrets flew to his field and poked about in the ravines. Cornbirds flapped out from the immortelle tree at the end of his field. Other birds— bananaquits and kiskidees and ground doves—waltzed and whistled overhead. Most birds looked alike: the ground dove he had seen yesterday could be the same bird he spotted today. On his way home he passed the same villagers at identical spots each day; and he thought: *To everything there is a pattern; everything is predictable.* The world was ordered by laws that, with careful observation, could be deciphered, their consequences anticipated. One night while his son was twisting on his mattress, Narpat mouthed the phrase he was recording: "There are no coincidences, only consequences."

The boy turned and asked sleepily, "What you mean by that?"

"Nothing, Carea. Go back and sleep."

Eleven months after Seegobin had announced the formation of his True and Noble Cane Farmers Association, he left for Rhodesia on a govern-

ment scholarship. Sending troublemakers abroad was an old ploy of the
government, but even before the scholarship Seegobin had grown frustrated with the association. The pamphlets from Cuba had described
neat little villages and orderly cooperatives and grateful farmers. The villagers he encountered were impatient, accusatory, and after a few drinks,
downright hostile. The villagers learned of his desertion from his last column, the title, "The Pleasures of Exile," stolen from a famous West Indian novel.

Narpat resumed his lunch breaks beneath the hogplum tree and listened to the farmers grumbling about Seegobin's abrupt departure. Some
had paid union dues; others had donated money for the importation of his
pamphlets. Once more they had been betrayed. From their energetic self-
pity and finally their lacerating resignation, Narpat detected all the old familiar patterns. Arguments he had heard year after year. *To everything
there is a pattern*, he thought.

One evening, after his work, he broke his routine by driving on his
tractor to Debe and Barrackpore. He used the company roads, which
were level and well maintained. On either side was cane, not broken into
two- or three-acre plots like the privately owned fields, but uninterrupted,
healthy, and majestic.

The following midday, when the farmers began their habitual litany of
neglect and treachery, he said, "We should be grateful that Tate and Lyle
even buying our cane." This was a new angle, and the farmers were surprised. "They have hundreds of acres of cane. They have their own factories to grind the cane. They make profit from rum and molasses. Why
they should study the farmers who in direct competition with them?"

"But we selling them cane for years."

"And one day they could decide that enough is enough."

"You think they could do that?"

"Look at the patterns. Look at the trends."

Every evening he drove through the company roads, choosing a different route each time, going farther too, to Siparia and Penal. And these
journeys became part of his routine, as were the farmers' recitations of
their woes. Every midday he offered the same enigmatic pronouncement
about trends and patterns. One day he told them, "Every year the company output getting bigger and the farmers' yield shrinking. In five years
the company will say they have no use for our cane again." He was speak-

ing slowly, as if he were choosing his words carefully. "Don't be surprised if they decide to shut down the factory too."

The farmers were disturbed. "What we will do?"

After a while Narpat said, "Build our own factory."

The following days he told them, "You all believe it can't be done because nobody ever think of it before. But a sugar mill no different from all the family-run sawmills all over Rio Claro and Tableland." He counted on his fingers. "Machines, workers, operation, product, and output. Exactly the same."

The farmers joked about the factory in the rumshops. "You ever hear a ordinary farmer build a factory in your born life? Factory that cost the British people hundreds of thousand of dollars to put down."

Huzaifa heard of the factory. He showed up at Narpat's house, wearing his white cotton shirt, white oversize trousers, and rough wooden shoes called *suputs*. He liked the crude frugality of the house and the absence of unnecessary decoration and furniture. He got to the point straightaway. "We could make our own bricks to build the factory. People in India does make them all the time using a stupid lil oven. For fuel we could use *goobar*. The best source of energy in the world." His communal instincts kicked in. "Get the farmers to go round the island and collect all the goobar they could find and make a big pile." He lowered his glasses and peered above the wire frame. "Own bricks. Own fuel. Own factory. That will show the British." How fitting, he thought, that Tate and Lyle was a British-owned factory.

But Narpat had everything already planned. The factory would be built with concrete, not clay bricks. It would be powered by a network of windmills, not goobar. "Wind free. Every other year a hurricane does be ramping through the island. Think of all the energy we could harness."

Huzaifa thoughtfully rubbed his hands together. Narpat called to Jeeves for a pencil and a sheet of paper. He sketched a box with a chimney stuck at the top and surrounded by windmills. Jeeves stared at the drawing and thought of huge butterflies circling a Popsicle stuck to the ground. Huzaifa murmured and gently flicked away a mosquito from his arm. "Go away, little insect, go away, please. I don't want to kill you. You is just a insect."

Narpat drew a series of intersecting lines beneath the box. "Water free too, if you know where to get it." Huzaifa was distracted by the mosquito, which landed once more on his arm, and as Narpat elaborated on the intricate subterranean plumbing, he tried to blow away the insect. "Building the factory could be the easiest thing if everybody cooperate. Sacrifice for the common good. If they think about the end result instead of the day-to-day problem. If they could behave like futurists."

Slap!

Huzaifa gazed at the mosquito flattened in a speck of blood on his skinny arm. He murmured, "You see, little insect? You see? You see when you don't listen how you does cause a peaceful man to turn into a savage beast?" Jeeves drew closer and strained to hear this strange-looking man's whispers.

Huzaifa returned to Narpat's house the next evening, and between these two men the factory gradually began to take shape, to acquire a vague form, with pulley, cranks, boilers, fermentation tanks, vacuum pans, gantry cranes, and windmills. Huzaifa was thrilled by the solemn consequence of these technical details, and he would listen intently before asking questions like "You think we should have the windmills in a line or facing each other? I think if they *face* each other, they will cancel out the wind. Two positive always hatch out a negative." Another evening he asked, "You think we should build the factory sloping like this house? So instead of the conveyor wasting energy, we could just throw in all the cane in one end and let it slide straight down to the other unit." He was dense as to the operation of any piece of machinery; to him they were batches of dead units clamped together and miraculously tickling each other to life. Sometimes he prepared his questions in advance. He began visiting every evening, his approach signaled by the slow knocking of his sapats on the pitch road.

Jeeves was fascinated by Huzaifa's strange stoop, his oversize clothing, and especially the way he crouched on his chair like a plucked helpless bat, but his sisters always seized on these conversations as opportunities to slip across to the Brahmin's house. Their father had recently threatened to put an end to these visits, and they were grateful for the distraction of Huzaifa every night promptly at seven.

Huzaifa also fancied himself as an informant—which he reconciled with Gandhian philosophy by concluding that in dire circumstances, *satyagraha* could be suspended. His information was usually harmless gossip he had picked up from his wife, but one night he told Narpat, "I get a bulletin. Premsingh and Soogrim and Janak and that nasty, maljeau-eye Manager say we ain't going to build no factory. They say is one setta old talk. And Kumkaran say all these crazy idea is a sign of Agra-mennon." He pronounced it as a Hindi word.

That weekend Narpat commanded Jeeves to the Farmall. "Where we going?" Jeeves asked.

"To look for something exceptional."

"Treasure?"

Narpat grinned. "Sorta."

When the tractor swerved into Toolia trace, the boy asked his father, "The treasure bury in your canefield?"

"It scatter all over."

"How I can't see any? It bury deep?"

"It all around. But first we have to build a mill."

"To grind it up?"

"Exactly." Narpat jumped down from the tractor and held out his hands, but at the last minute he stepped back and Jeeves fell, tumbling. "You have to learn to jump properly, boy. Someday it might save your life." While they were walking through the field, Narpat spoke mysteriously about shredding knives and crushing rollers. Jeeves gazed at the glinting melau pebbles in the ravines while his father spoke. "After you crush up the cane, you heat the juice and throw in some lime, which will cause all the dregs to sink to the bottom. Then you collect all the juice in evaporators." He clacked his tongue as if he were tasting it, and Jeeves giggled. "And finally you boil up all the juice in vacuum pans until you get something called massecuite, which is sugar crystals mix up in a thick syrup. When you spin and spin this mixture in tubs with hundreds of holes, the syrup leak out and leave the pure shining crystals."

"Treasure? The sugar is the treasure?"

"What you think we build the house with? And buy food and pay for electricity and all your schoolbooks?" They stopped walking. "But first we have to build a mill." He pointed to the field's edge. "Right here." He stamped the ground, and his boot collected a clump of mud. "Nice sticky mud. It mean that the ground reliable. It will never cave. It have a proper slope too, so all the water will run off in the drain instead of collecting under the ground. You see that immortelle tree across there? Look at how solid and tall it is. It standing on firm ground. You could always assess the state of the land from the type and quality of trees and plants."

On the way back Jeeves asked, "When you going to build the mill?"

"As soon as you ready to help me."

"Me?" Then the boy realized his father was joking. "You and Mammy then?"

"Your Mammy have other things to think about. This is man work."

"You and the bendup man then?"

"Which bendup man you talking about, boy?"

"The one with the wooden shoes."

Narpat climbed onto the tractor, chuckling.

Huzaifa was a bit offended that Narpat had not taken him along on this significant exploratory venture, but he soon got over it, and during the following weeks he discarded his sapats for tall tops, which reached to his thighs. He padded about awkwardly while Narpat surveyed, measured, and drove wooden stakes into the mud. They connected the stakes with a strong twine, *maling*, until they had boxed off four lots; then Narpat hoisted on his back a heavy brass can filled with the herbicide Grama-zone, pumped the handle a few times, and pointed the nozzle to the ground. Huzaifa stepped back and covered his mouth with his shirtsleeve.

For the next couple weeks, he mostly stood at the border of the desig-nated area and looked on while Narpat leveled and plowed with his trac-tor. He had always disliked manual labor and viewed himself more as a planner and troubleshooter.

After a month Narpat calculated that the land had been adequately prepared, and they shifted once more to an engineering and planning phase. Huzaifa brought construction manuals from YesRead, and while Narpat was poring over the manuals, he examined the set squares and protractors. Finally Narpat began to sketch his diagrams on a cardboard while discussing with his friend recent developments in the sugar indus-try and the period when sugar was king. "It had a time when eleven fac-tories was operating on this island. Two right next door in Craignish and Hindustan."

"Maybe was the war that cause all them to close. Heetlah. Real trou-blemaker." He had always been uncomfortable with Narpat's talk of the Aryans but he surmised that these Indian Aryans were good Aryans. The

German Aryans were bad Aryans. "I believe Gandhiji too was involve in the war." He tried to recall the connection.

"Gandhi was a jackass of the highest order."

"Eh?" Huzaifa almost slid down his chair, but he offered a strong defense. "Independence. Mighty British. Free India. Just one man."

"Not one man. Nehru. Tilak. Patel. Jinnah."

"Yes, Jinnah. President of Pakistan. Bookworm and aristocrat."

One night Narpat said, "I wonder what happen to all the machinery from the factories that close down in Reform and Hindustan?"

"Maybe people thief them out."

Narpat shook his head.

"You think they might still be there?"

"Most likely cover up in vine and lathro."

"Rusty units. Wouldn't work again."

"These old-time machinery build to last hundreds of years. A little fine-tuning and it good as new."

"But we can't just pick it up." Huzaifa viewed this development as an unnecessary complication to the pleasant nighttime conversations.

"It in the ground twenty years now. Nobody claim it so far."

"It might have some law or the other."

"Let them lock us up. It will give Partap son a nice little article. Cane farmers jailed for removing junk."

"Hmm. I see what you getting at. A sorta passive-resistance stealing. Yes, yes."

But on the appointed day Huzaifa did not show up, and the two workers Narpat usually hired during crop season uncovered the rusty engines from the rotted lumber and the swaths of vine, knocked off corroded exhaust and manifolds, attached ropes to flywheels, and dragged the engines along two planks sliding up the tractor. Three hours later they offloaded the junk beneath the Julie mango tree at the side of Narpat's house.

That night Huzaifa walked around the heap, occasionally tapping his sapats against a broken line or pipe. "Small, small engine. Wonder how they operate the mill with these little units."

"These is old bulldozer engines. That one is from a crane."

"Think we could run the factory with tractor engine?"

"If you link up all these small engine, you get the same power like a big engine. Like a tug-of-war with eight people pulling on one side."

Huzaifa gazed at the junk skeptically. "Maybe we could paint them over."

"Why? They good as new. Touch one pulley or camshaft by mistake, and the whole thing will start roaring and jumping up."

Huzaifa stepped back.

"We have to design a single ignition system so when you crank one engine, the rest must come to life too. A single fuel and electrical circuit. We have to be very precise with this." He walked around the engines. "You ever look inside a clock with all the cogwheels spinning against each other? This call for careful planning because one little fumble or misalignment could cause everything to malfunction."

"Yes, yes. Like a setta spinning jennies."

EIGHTEEN

During the next year and a half Jeeves grew accustomed to Huzaifa's daily visits. Narpat's tenure as a county councilor came to an end, and the money shrank once more. Dulari struggled with the grocery bills and her daughters' college expenses. Her debts to Bhola piled up, and she was forced to open an account at Lumchee's shop. Increasingly she grew frustrated for believing the intimacy she had recently shared with her husband would last. Whenever she complained, he would hold up one hand. "Cause." Then the other. "Effect."

She would shake her head in dismay.

"When you understand the connection between the two, then you will appreciate all the little patterns in this world. For instance, my county council job was part of a pattern. Now that it finish, is time for me to move on to a new stage."

"The only pattern I seeing is hardship and starvation."

"This is how short-termers always think."

She busied herself in the backyard garden till late in the night, planting and cleaning with a flambeau's dull light, as if fighting a battle against starvation. From the garden she would go to the kitchen, then to the bedroom, passing her husband on the Pavilion, his knees drawn up to his chest, his eyes closed.

Arguments spun from nowhere. One night while they were in the kitchen, her husband said, "Nothing of value ever get accomplish without sacrifices."

"You can't spend your whole life trying to prove everybody wrong."

"You know what the Aryans will say to that shortsighted attitude?"

"Aryans? I wonder if these Aryans will show up one morning and pay the grocery bills and buy clothes for the children."

"These fellas knew the value of sacrifice. That is how everything that important ever get done. By sacrifice."

"Yet everybody getting by without this so-call sacrifice. Everybody improving and getting more modern, while we sinking deeper and deeper in this hole."

"Modern? What is modern? The Brahmin house that build with donation and dachina? Nice modern house, but we will see how long it will last."

"It don't have a useless barrel sticking on top just waiting for a strong wind to send it crashing down on everybody. And no old junk in the yard either. All that useless engine that you pile up below the tree."

"Listen .... if you don't like it here, you free to pack up and go. Go to your crooked brother. Go to the Brahmin. The children does already spend half the evening there. He could put up a nice shed in the back for allyou. I could live here alone like a hermit. The best sort of life. No confusion, no commess, no jealously. No Puranic vices," he said, referring to a period in India named after a religious text, the *Puranas*.

The next morning Radhica told Dulari, "I don't know what to say about Ray father. Every day is some new flowers Ray father does be planting. Look at them. Marigold, *ixoras*, daisy, periwinkle. I don't even know the name of that one what does smell like shampoo. Shampoo-pampoo." She laughed tiredly. Dulari saw tidy flower beds arranged according to color, separated by shrubs and bordered at the far end by pendulous heliconia, rostrata, deep red ginger lilies, and wispy squirreltails. She saw butterflies flitting above the plants and smelled the fragrance of jasmine and nightshade. "Every evening I looking for him, looking for him, and guess where he does be hideaway?" She shook her head. "Walking between the flowers and reading his whole ton of books. I don't know what he intend to do with all this information he have pack up like jam inside his head. Just the other day he tell me"—this information necessitated several dramatic pauses— "he tell me—that—he going—to write—a Hindu—text. I could never ever understand these scholars and them," she added, pressing her orhni to her lips and giggling with prolonged snorts.

During the next argument with her husband, Dulari made the mistake of mentioning the Brahmin's interest in flowers and his intention of writing a Hindu text.

"Be careful he don't dig a cave soon. And start wearing tiger-skin clothes. Tell his wife to tie a strong rope around his foot before he start levitating all around the place." But a few minutes later he said, "What is the name of this text? How to propagate Puranic nonsense for your own benefit? How to be a Brahmin and a scamp at the same time? How to pretend to be a ascetic? How to corrode the lungs with cigarette? It have plenty 'how to' books a man like him could write. How to make neighbors' eye get long with material possession. How to create discord in a family." When Dulari went into the kitchen, he was still shouting suggestions.

She began to quarrel ceaselessly with her daughters, spinning her own fables of happy, carefree young women imprisoned by insufferable tyrants. With every one of her daughters she found a fault. She told Chandra, "Don't think that I not paying attention to how you does dress up every evening before you go to your little cinema across the road." Kala she told, "Every single thing you have a reply for. Always looking for an argument like a little hot mouth." She pushed her younger daughter to tears. "All day long you in your room looking at magazines and singing foolish song instead of helping the old slave." Frequently her arguments were nonspecific. "We have to see about the house. We have to cook, clean, and wash. We have to take care of the garden. Plant the garden. Buy the groceries. Worry about the money. Worry, worry all day long. And for what? Where the thanks?"

Which we? Jeeves wondered.

But later, after she had cooled down from fatigue, he heard her telling his sisters that while men ran about chasing down crazy dreams, the women were expected to stay at home and struggle to make ends meet. Jeeves wondered whether his exclusion from these conversations between mother and daughters was because he was just nine years old or because women ritually engaged in private, mysterious conferences. Invariably his father was occupied with Huzaifa, and the boy was left alone. Some evenings he wandered around the backyard and idled on the road. One day he walked farther, past the stretch of abandoned houses. A squirrel darted from one of the houses into the lathro. He ran after the animal, crawled through an opening between the net like vines, and brushed his legs against a cluster of stinging nettles. He looked up and saw before him an expanse of etiolated plants with weak pink flowers straining between the bamboo and older, taller trees. The ground was spongy with dried bamboo leaves and decaying bark. From the road the lathro suggested wild impenetrable bush, but the overlying vines and branches had blocked off the sunlight and formed a perfect bubble. When he glanced up, the sky seemed pitted with tiny holes. There were a few cocoa trees with crimson pods so glossy they could have been polished. A bird disappeared in a pod's hole, and a squirrel scampered along a bamboo. Some insects disturbed the dried leaves on the ground and disappeared. In the distance a parakeet screeched, the sound sharp and startling. Jeeves thought of Danny's magical forest behind the school and wondered whether his friend had been referring to this place all along. Danny had changed during the year, before he suddenly dropped out of school. He'd skipped classes for weeks, and he'd grown testy when asked about his absence. Occasionally he came to school with bruises on his arms.

"How you get these marks?" Jeeves had asked him one day.

"Mind your own business."

"You get in a fight?"

"If you don't stop asking these questions, I will cuff you in your mouth."

The following month he did not show up, and the teacher stopped calling his name during attendance. Rumors spread. Some of the students said he had been seen working in a lagoon. A standard-seven boy swore that Danny's father, recently released from prison, had pulled his son from school.

Each evening, while his father was chatting with Huzaifa, and his mother with his sisters, Jeeves came to the bubble, exploring a bit further each day. He discovered little ravines flowing between the trunks of the balata and toporite and, hidden in the cocoa trees, nests of dried grass and twigs. He saw a squirrel disappearing behind the loose bark of a *caimite* tree, and when he pried the bark loose, the animal gazed at him for a while before it darted up the tree. During the following days he wandered about, tugging at the loose barks, and behind each he discovered a trove of insects, some waving their mandibles threateningly. And he learned that each tree possessed a distinct fragrance and texture, from the clean, polished flakes of the guava to the damp, pungent immortelle. Occasionally a firefly, a *labay*, would flit overhead, its glowing tail leaving a minute trail of light. When he was bored with his explorations, he would lie against the trunk of the caimite tree and gaze at its lustrous purple leaves. Enclosed within the bubble, the squabbles between his sisters, his mother's sudden temper, and his father's moodiness seemed distant and inconsequential. But occasionally he dozed off and thought of Narpat's mysterious tests. His father had said years ago that these tests were like sticks on the ground waiting to be identified, and just before the boy returned to his house, he would walk around idly, gazing at the dislodged sticks and twigs, searching for some pattern. And while he was foraging about, he thought of his father's more recent talk about everyone possessing some special purpose. One day he came across Assevero digging for yams. He was surprised, but Assevero, alert to the sounds of the bush, pointed to his donkey and said, "Come, boy. The donkey didn't eat for two days." Jeeves fled.

The following day he walked along the lathro's edge and came across an elevation of new concrete houses, painted in bright colors. The next day he walked farther, past a broken-down bridge with salmon flowers floating in the muddy water. After about half an hour, the asphalt gave way to gravel, then to mud before the road dropped suddenly into what seemed from the distance a huge hole.

He stopped. Dogpatch. Where the feared Outsiders lived.

For two weeks he halted at the brink of the hole. Bare-backed men sometimes walked by, paying him no attention. On a drizzly evening, when the air was hot and sticky and little rivulets coursed their way along the road, he walked down the slope. The houses were of rickety boards and corrugated aluminum sheets and slabs of cardboard. There were no fruit trees in the yards and no children on the porches, though from some of the houses came the blast of calypsos. But for the calypsos, and the chickens digging about in the bare yards, and a few malnourished pothounds, the place could have been deserted. Then he came across a group of men playing dominoes beneath a *chenette* tree. They were very old, and they studied their blocks carefully before they made a move. Lower down, a man was stretched out on his porch, staring at his cigarette smoke. Across the road, another oldish man was sitting on a step, his head thrown back. A pothound was curled at his feet. Jeeves was astonished; he had expected surly men with machetes, and swearing children, and the confusion of ceaseless arguments, but the settlement of these dreaded Outsiders just seemed worn and derelict, and the inhabitants struck with some sort of malaise that made them sleepy and lethargic.

He wanted to tell his father that he was wrong about these people, and his mother that she had nothing to fear from them, but he guessed he would be rebuked for venturing there, so he said nothing. At school, when he revealed the details of his trip and the squalor he had seen to Quashie, the other boy scratched a circle on the sand with his foot and walked away. For the next few weeks he avoided Jeeves. From Quashie's reaction, he decided that his discovery would be his little secret, and from time to time, when his parents mentioned the Outsiders, he thought of the old men slowly playing dominoes and others lounging on their steps.

Another crop came and went. More canefields were abandoned, and the cane, refusing to die, grew tall and tangled, and when it was razed by bush fires, suckers sprouted from the barren land. The villagers continued their grumbling, but when Texaco announced that places like Barrackpore and Siparia and Lengua were rich in oil and natural gas, and conducted a series of explorations and dug wells and built derricks and installed pumps on state land, the villagers, fearing the oil would seep into their fields and destroy their crops, sabotaged the pumps one by one. The fires were a spectacle, shooting upward and seen for miles. The children peeped excitedly from their windows. The police received their bribes of rum and went away; the officials from Texaco were chased with cutlasses. Soon children began climbing onto the abandoned pumps and derricks in these villages that had rejected their one chance for prosperity. One evening in Lalbeharry trace, Kamini revealed that her father had already been engaged in negotiations for the use of his truck before the project was canceled. Mr. Doon's blossoming relationship with Kamini suffered because of his increasingly frequent visits to the rumshops. His novel had been revived by the inventive world he encountered nightly in the dirty hawk-and-spit joints, where tongues were loose and the rumors vibrant. He purchased rum for the reckless and encouraged them in gossip. He no longer winced at the Trinidadian habit of pinching and grabbing, and their circuitous manner of explaining every simple thing. At school, the other teachers who had heard of his bar-hopping noted his unkemptness and his haggard appearance. He paid them no attention, though; month by month his novel expanded; month by month his appearance deteriorated. His ties hung loosely from his collar, his once-neat shirts were soiled with sweat, his two-tone shoes caked with mud. During his liaisons with Kamini in Lalbeharry trace, he was silent and contemplative. She smelled the stale rum on his breath. One evening she asked him, "What eating you up, David?" He leaned his head on the backrest, looked up at the bamboo crisscrossing the sky like an errant painter's brush, and sighed. She followed his gaze. "I know you must be frustrated, David, but I not like other girls. I prefer to wait until"—she hesitated— "until I married."

Mr. Doon sighed once more. "How will it all end? As of now, I have not the faintest idea. I am eagerly awaiting the day when I can bring everything to a conclusion."

Kamini lowered her gaze and smiled knowingly. "Me too, David."

When he had completed eight hundred and fifty pages in longhand, which he calculated to be a respectable five hundred or so typed pages, he stopped. He tried to imagine the texture and the aroma and the heft of the finished book. On the day he finished his book, he wrote: *I have accomplished the unthinkable and I am released. Now I gaze back in wonder at the phenomenon. From whence did all this spring?*

It sprang mainly from an alcoholic fervor begun early in the evenings. Drunkenness added an edge to his writing; he discarded all his flowery descriptions and focused solely on the "grit and grime" of his characters. The novel centered on a tragic romance between a conscientious poet who had returned to the island from Canada, and the daughter of a corrupt official. The first few chapters traced the childhood of the doomed male, Harry: he was shy, awkward, and nervous ("shackled with an agitation that shattered his delicate frame"), and when in chapter six he suddenly mutated into a charming, confident, and cultured young man, tantalizing the residents of Ottawa with his poetry, no explanation was given. In chapter eight he returned to the island and was immediately pursued by all the village girls, but he had eyes only for the chaste, demure Virginia.

For two weeks Mr. Doon took his manuscript, bound with a silky red

ribbon, to the village bars. The other drunkards gazed suspiciously whenever he stroked the book and caressed the ribbon. They stopped their
chats to listen to his purring sounds. Then one afternoon he went to the
post office, and after a series of strident warnings to the postal clerks, he
released his manuscript.

That night in Lalbeharry trace, he revealed his accomplishment to
Kamini. He had always rebuffed her curiosity by saying, "Can't my dear,
until it is complete. Superstitious. My only vice."

"It have people in it?" she now asked.

"Incidental." *Mr. Mungas was a corpulent beast of a man bloated by a*
lifetime of iniquity.

"But it have any girls?" He had often referred to Kamini as his muse.

"Symbolic markers." He allowed a contemplative smile to soften his
seriousness.

Six months later he received a package from Penguin. He was impressed. Six months! The editors must have been smitten. He gently undid the string and read the two-sentence response.

In the Cocoyea apartment, he could barely contain his indignation.
He paced up and down the room shouting, "'A crude attempt at plagia-
rizing,' eh? 'Pretentious,' eh? 'Antiquated language,' eh? The bitches and
them. Kissmeass illiterate bitches." Gradually his rage settled. "Going to
show them. Going to put Penguin in they place. Going to send it to André Deutsch. Send it to a publisher with integrity. Penguin! What the ass
is a penguin? A damn stupid bird that can't even walk properly." Soon he
convinced himself that it was a blessing that Penguin had rejected his
manuscript. "Cheap, flimsy yellow paper. Ugly cover drawing. Fine little
print. Cheapness! Cheapness of the highest order."

For about a month or so, he asked his class questions like "What is the
ugliest bird in the world?" "Which stupid creature not sure whether is a
bird or a fish?" "What is the favorite meal of whales and sharks?" He developed a new affection for a talkative boy named André Mohan. But a
couple months later he would react with sudden savagery to André Mohan's minor transgressions. "A nice French name your father give you,
Monsieur André. He wanted you to be a wrestler? Or a illiterate kissmeass publisher?" For the first time he developed a taste for flogging.

One evening he stumbled into YesRead. "We get a batch of new dictionary," Huzaifa told him excitedly. "Some with nice drawings." Mr.

Doon surveyed the shelves sourly. "And just this morning we get fifty copy of this book. Hot off the press." He returned with a booklet. "Hotoffthe-press. By we very own writer." He gazed at the photograph of the Brahmin on the back cover. "Pundit Poochoon Sharma. Could barely recognize him with his dhoti and flowers around his neck. Make him look like a member of Congress. Like Ti-lak." He pronounced the word in two clicks. "The book only 'bout one-fifth of a inch thick, but plenty useful in-formation pack inside. Paper smelling nice too." He pressed his nose against the booklet.

That evening Radhica walked across purposefully, as if she had a lot on her mind. She was elaborately dressed and wore an additional gold bangle on each arm. "These mans and they ton of ideas."

Dulari, who was sprinkling ashes on her vegetables, stood up and dusted her palms. "He gone and write it! Ray father—gone—and write—the book." She partially covered her face with her orhni, as if this accom-plishment merited some bashfulness.

The thirty-five-page booklet, *Magical Mantras for Most Maladies*, sold out in a few weeks, and there was a brief review by Partap's son, who de-scribed it without irony as a "cure-all tome that should put half the doc-tors in Trinidad out of business. These quacks will doubtless be purple with envy to read of the mantric cures for diabetes, epilepsy, maljeau, fat blood, stale blood, bad blood, mad blood, slow blood." But the Brahmin's text was more precise, and there were also mantras for toothache, ear-ache, insect bites, blood clotting, and a host of other minor ailments.

Mr. Doon took his copy to Diablo bar, where he read intently, and if the other customers had not already written him off as half mad (for which there was also a cure), they would have been astonished at his agitated conversation over his empty table. Late in the night, in the Cocoyea apartment, he conducted a number of conversations with imaginary edi-tors. "Yes, yes, I see your point, Mr. Harcourt. My novel is too elegant, and my choice of language too ornate. Ahh, Mr. Fremlin, it's nice to see you again. And I must say that I agree completely with your observation that books like mine, scalded by anguish and innovative pain, are no longer de rigueur. Oh hello, Mr. Dungrey. I was just remarking to Mr. Fremlin about the local reading public."

His mother, with whom he shared the apartment, shook her head and walked slowly to the medicine cabinet, where she got out her bottle of bay rum. Then she went to her rocking chair. Long after she had fallen asleep, Mr. Doon read and reread the Brahmin's book. He wondered at the success of such a modest book. Early in the morning he startled his mother by screaming, "Eureka! I have the perfect recipe for these bitches." The following weekend, in Lalbeharry trace, he recited in a droll voice some of the mantras, before he asked Kamini, "Would you believe that there is also a mantra for preventing pregnancy?"

"Really? Oh, gee."

"Yes, it's right here." And he read the mantra.

After a while Kamini asked him, "You believe it? You think it will really work?"

Finally on New Year's Eve, their long affair was consummated. Three weeks later, just after the reopening of school, Mr. Doon stopped off at YesRead and bought a brand-new coilspring notebook with subject separators and a flap at the back cover for pens and pencils. Huzaifa was in a talkative mood, but Mr. Doon had other things on his mind.

NINETEEN

*D*uring his conversations with Narpat, Huzaifa tried to steer his friend back to the factory plans and away from the caste system—as a Muslim, he had a slight contempt for this classification—and particularly away from the Brahmin who, especially since the success of his book, featured frequently in Narpat's sermons. Occasionally, while he and Narpat were chatting on the porch, the Brahmin, garbed in his holy clothes, would appear in his gallery and settle on his lotus chair. Narpat would grow edgy and sullen and hectoring. Once when he was condemning the caste system, Huzaifa said, "Muslim don't have caste. Everybody equal."

"Muslim is a caste by themself. They can't get along with any other religion."

Huzaifa listened quietly, nibbling his nails. The next evening he did not show up. Now Narpat spent the evenings lecturing to his children. He distilled all the fables into simple statements. He repeated these statements slowly, as if speaking to himself. They should set clear goals; they should never be concerned with other people's views; they should always have a backup plan; they should be true to their beliefs. Occasionally, he forced them to listen to the calculations he had made for the coming crop season: the money that would be reinvested in labor, the percentage allotted to the home, and the sum he would put aside to start work on his factory. But he always came back to the Brahmin. He revealed that the *Upanishads* were first explicated by the Kshatriyas, and later hijacked by the Brahmins, who soon monopolized all forms of knowledge. He quoted excerpts from the *Mahabharata*, an epic poem of heroism and sacrifice. In time, his children sensed that he was comparing these heroic battles with his own struggles.

One morning Kala mentioned that the Brahmin had been receiving letters from all over the world. "That don't surprise me one bit. You know how much people he must be kill already? Right now it have some poor fella from St. Croix chanting away while diabetes eating away his body."

"I think the letters was from around the world."

"Summons! Summons to appear in their court. It have laws in these countries against frauds and charlatans. You know what a charlatan is, girl?"

Kala answered, "A swindler." Chandra piped in that she was going to say the same thing.

"Exactly. Snake oil."

"Snake oil?" Jeeves asked, interested now.

"Come, boy, it have a mantra especially for you."

Narpat's dietary prescriptions grew more stringent, almost as if they were a defense against the Brahmin's chicanery. Sugar and table salt were cut to a minimum. Oil and butter were halved. Vegetables like the bitter carailli, ochroe, melongene, and an assortment of wild spinach appeared at every dinner. The food, already tasteless, was boiled and steamed. Garlic, pepper, neem, cumin, *pudena*, and other herbs were tossed into the salads. The children ate slowly, fanning their mouths. Kala and Chandra grumbled.

"You notice how the pepper causing you to drink water? The best thing for digestion. Clear out all the circuits. Keep the engine from overheating. Prevent anger, jealousy, and deceit." The children were also introduced to a variety of beans, grains, and legumes, which swam in their plates like drowning insects. "Proteins. Fiber. Vitamins."

"Cockroach," Kala said.

Jeeves laughed.

The children heroically tolerated Narpat's dietary injunctions, including the sardine, which was soon incorporated into every meal. Chandra said that she vomited most nights. The taste remained in Jeeves's mouth for hours, and he constantly spat in class.

One night Radhica asked the children, who were watching *Lassie*, "What is that funny smell?"

Ray and Jag laughed.

"Sardine," Jeeves said.

Radhica opened the louvers. The Brahmin got up and walked to the gallery. The children watched the rest of the show with an awkward silence. When they were leaving, the Brahmin was in the gallery, his eyes closed, chanting. Without breaking his rhythm, he sang out, "Meat eaters—does born—back—as meat," as if it were part of his chant.

The children told their mother. Chandra was embarrassed, Kala furious, Sushilla ashamed. Jeeves tried to imitate Radhica, who had pushed out her lips and wrinkled her nose to stress her displeasure with the odor. Dulari forbade them from going across every evening. The strain between the two women tightened.

Each morning Radhica watered her husband's garden while across the road Dulari swept her yard. Both women performed their duties grimly, never once glancing at each other. Radhica soon appeared with a small bag of fertilizer, which she studiously applied to the flowers. Dulari jerked out the stubborn knot grass and deposited the pile at the back of the house. Radhica began smelling the flowers, pressing the petals against her face, inhaling deeply and standing a bit giddily. Dulari pruned her bougainvillea, wishing it would bloom as it had years ago, before it had been partially crushed by the tractor. Then Radhica began appearing each morning with heavy jewelry and expensive muslin dresses. Dulari rummaged her cupboard but could only come up with a light-green, pleated cotton dress that she usually wore during her visits to Princes Town.

Now the children received frequent warnings from her about socializing with the Brahmin's children. And when Kala protested, she said, "You want to bring shame to me now. You is a woman now? A hot force-ripe woman? Don't think that I don't notice them two locho boys sitting in they gallery and gazing across here, like if it have some big fashion show going on."

Narpat continued his lectures on the Aryans, and in the children's mind, these ancient Indians became a group of muddled tyrants, indecisive and brutal. He ate sparingly, and Dulari secretly added pinches of salt and butter and seasoning.

In the meantime the Brahmin prospered. He bought a new car, a Mazda, one of the Japanese models that had swept the island. The elder

of his sons, Ray, got his license and gunned the engine whenever he re-
versed from the garage. One morning a van from Kirpalanis, an Indian
store with a "buy one, get one free" gimmick, deposited a pair of oak
space-savers, a huge glass cabinet, and boxes of decorative lights. Radhica, outfitted in a beige dress, supervised the workmen carrying the
cabinet up the stairs. A few weeks later four men with shovels and spades
set about at the far end of the garden. In a week, they had built a small
concrete altar onto which each morning the Brahmin, in his holy clothes,
threw a lotah of water, closed his eyes, and chanted. He was followed by
Radhica in a sari.

The Indian ritual and the Indian clothing softened her expression
somewhat and gave her the idea that she was now beyond petty rivalries.
Soon she began shouting to her son, "Ray, stop gunning the car so. It have
other people living here, you know."

Dulari sensed this new mood—the magnanimity of the victor—and
was even more distraught. In the evenings before her husband arrived
from the field, she cautioned her daughters, "All of allyou, don't ever
make the mistake of marrying a cane farmer, because it will be hell for the
rest of allyou life."

"Me too?" Jeeves asked.

"You could marry whoever you want. You is a boy."

Kala tried to engage her mother on this topic, but Dulari was unwilling to elaborate. Chandra usually took her mother's side and pretended
annoyance at Kala's questioning. She and Kala got into little squabbles,
followed by bouts of silence and stiff, formal conversations. They usually
chose Jeeves as an intermediary.

"Jeeves, could you please remind Kala that she borrowed my bodice by
mistake."

"Jeeves, could you please tell Chandra that Mammy gave me the
bodice and to please not call me a thief."

"Jeeves, could you please tell your sister that I never call her a thief."

Sometimes he rebelled. "Tell her your ownself. She right here listening to you." He could not understand why, in the complicated aftermath
of these squabbles, he was singled out for flogging. He was almost eleven
years old, an awkward age, when the idea of bawling loudly and being
chased by his mother with her cocoyea broom embarrassed and offended
him. After each flogging he retreated to the engines piled beneath the

mango tree. He sat on the rusty seats and imagined the machinery to be new and shining and encased in a powerful vehicle. Sometimes when Narpat returned from the field, Jeeves would still be there, his tears now dried into sticky streaks. Narpat would dismount slowly from his tractor and walk to his son.

"You must always breeze off before you step in the house."

"To get clean?"

"To cool down. What you doing here every evening?"

Jeeves would be too embarrassed to say.

"In a short while all this will be yours."

"Me alone? Not Chandra and Kala and Sushilla?"

"They will get married off and go and live elsewhere. But you have to remain and see about the canefield. Run the factory. You have a big responsibility."

Jeeves grinned. "You still going to build the factory?"

"But of course, boy. I thinking about it all the time. Have to put aside a little money to get everything in first gear."

"Why nobody helping you?"

"Because people here can't see more than four footstep before them."

"I could help you then."

"You too small, Carea. Too small and weak." Jeeves would be stung, but his father would close his eyes and lay his head against the tree and say, "When the time come for you to help me, you alone will be able to sniff it out. You have a big, big task ahead of you, Carea."

TWENTY

On the surface Narpat's family resembled other families in the village: the father toiling in the field, the mother in and around the house, their combined effort enabling them to outpace deprivation. But as Narpat grew increasingly consumed by his factory, by his precise calculation of cause and effect, by the anomaly of the Brahmin's good fortune, his family was forced to acknowledge their dissimilarity from the other village folks. He developed puzzling new interests, like his obsession with time. He placed the wooden clock from his bedroom on the first shelf of Carnegie, and he would break from his sermons to gaze at the clock. "Time is the only thing that free." But on other days he would say, "Nothing ever happen before it appointed time."

One night Kala said, "Hocus-pocus."

His children kept hoping he was awaiting some opportune event that would wipe away his worries, but in 1966 Tate and Lyle announced it was decreasing sugar production because of low world prices. Cane farmers marched around government offices; politicians admitted they could not control international prices. In Lengua, a delegation of farmers whose land ownership Narpat had facilitated came to his house. They stood on his porch in their field clothes and talked about their debts. Narpat folded his arms against his chest and listened. The farmers blew smoke through their nostrils and fanned away the smoke with their hats. Jeeves, glancing up from his schoolwork on the table, felt that the farmers looked like sad, lonely ghosts. He heard his father telling them that the only solution lay in building their own factory. He saw the men donning their hats and hurrying down the front steps.

A few days later Jeeves was running an errand to Hakim's parlor when

Premsingh, one of the farmers he had seen on the porch, shouted, "Boy! You is Narpat son? Is not you I see in the house the other day?"

Jeeves slowed.

"Why you not helping your father build his factory?"

"Because is not time yet."

"What you say, boy? You making joke with me or what?"

"When the time reach, I will be able to sniff it out."

A group of young men loitering by the parlor's entrance laughed.

"You want me to walk across the road and put some good sniff out on your tail. Eh?"

Premsingh grimaced, and Jeeves watched his huge drooping whiskers. Without thinking, Jeeves spoke aloud the image forming in his mind, "You is a old ugly catfish."

Premsingh thrust out his hands as if he could grab Jeeves from across the road, then made a few lumbering steps.

Jeeves turned and bolted.

When he got home, he shut the front door and rushed to the kitchen. His mother noticed the money still in his hand. He told her what had happened, expecting a flogging, but she held his wrist, opened the door, and literally dragged him to the road. He felt his mother's nail digging into his wrist and wished he had kept his mouth shut. He was terrified of meeting Premsingh, but when they came to the parlor, there was just a single customer inside. Jeeves heard his mother questioning Hakim and the shopkeeper, a middle-aged man with an apologetic stoop and a shy, kind face, explaining that Premsingh was drunk and didn't mean anything by his threat. "The boy call him a catfish too." Hakim covered his mouth and smiled.

On the way back, Dulari quarreled about the bad influence of the lochos at Chin Lee's sawmill and threatened to put an end to Jeeves's visits there. Then she moved on to the cane farmers, who believed they could say anything when they were drunk.

Tate and Lyle's decision forced Narpat to postpone work on his factory. He began going to his field earlier, and in the late evenings, while his children were doing their schoolwork, they would hear the tractor's approach. A few minutes later they would see Narpat grasp the railing and lower himself onto the front step. His fatigue seemed to spread throughout the house, and Jeeves would hear his mother slowly turning the coals on the chulha, Chandra's tired scratches on her accounting notebook, and from the bedroom Sushilla's low humming. Kala sometimes tried to lighten the nighttime somberness in the house. She had recently coiffed her hair in plaits and weaves, and while her father was sitting on the porch step, she would glance up from her book and advise Chandra to cut her long hair. Once she drew a picture of a catfish on a sheet and pushed the sheet before Jeeves. And Jeeves saw his statement to Premsingh not as a mistake but as a funny observation.

One night Kala went to the porch and sat next to her father. She picked up his hat and fanned his face. Dulari watched from the kitchen's entrance. "Your face stain up with sweat, Pappy," Kala told him.

After a while he said, "One more year."

Dulari too began to work harder around the house and in the garden. Sometimes Jeeves would wander off to his bubble of lathro and bamboo, and when he returned, itching from stinging nettles, he would see his mother stooping and pulling out weeds in the garden. And in the kitchen, Chandra, her eyes shut, memorized definitions from a book in her hand. Chandra's final exams were just a few weeks away, and she frequently confided to Kala her doubts about passing. But she surprised everyone by scraping passes in four of her five subjects. Three months later she got a job as a postal clerk in Petite Café, a village half an hour from Lengua.

Narpat's only reaction to his daughter's job was a statement about being able to put aside more money for his factory. Dulari gave her daily advice about proper attire and her deportment at work and suggested she save half of her salary, but Chandra, following the village practice of young unmarried women, gave her mother a third of her salary at the end of each month.

One afternoon when Jeeves returned from school, he saw an old bulky Singer sewing machine squeezed between the table and the wall. On succeeding days he noticed new curtains and doilies of various colors beneath vases and lamps.

In the nights, he was constantly awakened by its whine and by his mother humming along with the machine as she pedaled. One afternoon Janak, who had transported the machine, brought his wife, a tiny woman with a huge mole on her chin. The woman withdrew a bundle of light-green cotton from a bag. Dulari spread the cloth on the table and fingered the material. She got out a tape from the machine's drawer and measured the woman's waist, legs, and hips. She wrote the measurements on the back of an old calendar. Other women came with parcels of cloth. Some brought little girls who glanced distastefully at Jeeves. A few days later new frilly blouses with fluffed collars and sleeves were replaced in the bags. Other doilies appeared beneath jugs and jars.

"Where you learn to sew these things?" Jeeves asked.

"At school."

"You went to school?"

Normally the question would have been greeted with either silence or frustration, but Dulari reflected at length on her school days and her circle of friends.

Friends? Jeeves thought.

While Dulari was sewing, she would note the richness of the material and the modern styles requested, and she would wonder at the private lives of these women. Some had even hinted they might soon leave the village. She pressed them in conversations, and when Narpat returned from the field, his cold food would be on the table and his wife chatting and laughing. For a few weeks he said nothing; then he began to complain about the neglected plants in the garden, the stale food, and the machine's whine. He stormed about the house, slamming books into their shelves and plates in the stand. The women shortened their visits; some did not return, and in the nights Jeeves was disturbed not by the pedaling and the humming but by the periods of silence before the sewing slowly resumed.

"Daddy don't like the machine?" he asked his mother one night.

"He don't like not being the center of attention."

Most nights the machine remained idle, and Dulari would sit before it and open and close the drawers and oil the pedals.

"Idleness is the cause of every single vice you could think about." Narpat was on the Pavilion, and he spoke carefully, as if he were reading from a book.

I wasn't idle before you manage to chase away everybody, she thought. She said nothing, though, because she knew it would just lead to argument after argument. For the first time she began to think of leaving. From the other women, she had glimpsed possibilities she had all but forgotten. She remembered specific conversations with her husband soon after their marriage and recalled how easily she had surrendered. Once Bhola had taken her to a residential area in Princes Town, and she had imagined a new house sitting on a corner lot. She had presented her husband with a design, snipped out from the *Guardian*, of a two-story house. It was then that Narpat had revealed his aversion to proprietors and businessmen and town dwellers. She had renewed her plea following the birth of each of her daughters, but by the time Jeeves came along, she had given up.

Seven months after Chandra began her work at the post office in Petite Café, the tail end of a storm swept through the island. Branches were wrenched off. Rivers burst their banks, and vegetable farmers in the low-lying areas counted their losses. And on Narpat's roof there was a gaping space where the hot-water contraption had been mounted. When Jeeves returned from school, he saw the smashed cupboard, the barrel on the floor, and flying ants circling the dislodged pots and pans. He ran to his parents' bedroom, and there he saw his mother sitting on the bed and staring at the wall. He asked her what had happened, but she was mumbling, over and over, "Enough, enough. I not going to die in this swamp." The next day she packed her children's clothes into a battered grip and hired Janak's car to go to her brother's house.

When the taxi pulled up at Bhola's house, it was raining heavily, and the children stood at the gate, drenched, silent, and somber.

Two days after his family's departure, Narpat balanced a ladder against the barrel, climbed to the roof, and covered the hole with a sheet of thick plastic fastened to the rafters with cutlass wire. Water ballooned downward, but the sheet held. The next day he rolled the barrel onto the junkpile.

Each morning he prepared a pot of tea before he left for the field. Some of the other farmers who knew of his situation offered portions of their food, but he refused testily and explained that periods of fasting were necessary for the body to repair itself. In the nights he boiled another pot of tea or occasionally a watery soup and sat on the couch, reading his Vedic texts and dreaming fitfully of ancient journeys and sacrifices.

Across the road, Radhica peeped at him leaving for work in his increasingly dirty and ragged clothing and, in the nights, walking about the house like a spirit. "Poor man," she said to her husband in an unsympathetic voice. "He bring it on himself. I wonder where his wife and children went?"

"Somewhere in Princes Town," Ray told her.

Normally she would have been suspicious of Ray's knowledge, but she was still caught in the role of the sympathetic neighbor. "Wouldn't surprise me if he go completely mad. Wouldn't surprise me one bit. A man that age shouldn't be living by himself." She thought for a while. "Ray, you think we will ever leave your father?"

Ray thought of the Mazda. "Nah."

"Jag, you think *we* will ever leave your father?" She interpreted his silence favorably. "Madness is a funny, funny thing. It does just creep up on you."

The Brahmin, listening to a religious song on his tape recorder, waved his hands and conducted his orchestra. He sang to the tune of the song: "As you—sow—so shall—you reap."

Narpat busied himself with tasks around the house. The heavy rains of the past weeks had left deep pools of water in the tractor ruts. He took out his spade, shovel, and fork from beneath the house and set about constructing drains on either side of the property. The moat he had promised his children so many years ago.

Radhica watched him, his body covered in mud, digging and piling the dirt on the banks. "Is a funny, funny thing." Three days later he abandoned the drains. Water seeped into the trenches and, because there were no outlets, settled in gummy, muddy pools. Mosquitoes laid their eggs. Frogs discovered the pools.

Next he turned to the cupboard. He straightened the crushed boards and loosely nailed the doors. Finally he hauled out two lengths of plank from beneath the house and fortified the counter. Radhica heard the pounding. "It does just creep up on you." But he soon abandoned the cupboard, so that one door was nailed shut and useless and the other hung from rubber hinges he had cut off an old tractor tire. With strips of tire, he also fastened the dangling electrical wires and wrapped the leaks in the plumbing.

In two weeks pliers and saws and hammers and nails and black smelly rubber lay all over the house, surrounded by half-repaired louvers, rafters,

and stools. One night he pried out all the books from Carnegie and applied a coat of old engine oil to the shelves. "Get rid of all the woodlice
and termites.for good," he muttered. The next morning he noted with satisfaction the dead moths and ants and flies stuck to the black oil, which
was too viscous to be completely absorbed into the wood. "Will wait till it
dry." The books remained on the floor with the tools. Heat from the aluminum roof softened the tire strips; the pipes trickled once more; and the
electrical wires sagged against their rubbery clamps. At night, he scribbled phrases about fate and duty. The phrases were short and precise, as
if these things could be weighed and measured. One night he wrote: *I am
alone. There are no distractions. I must make use of this.*

Each night Radhica peeped from behind her curtains to see what he
was up to. She was baffled when he began getting home later and later in
the evenings. Occasionally she fell asleep before his tractor pulled up.
She speculated wildly. It wasn't yet crop season, so what was he occupied
with? Too old to have an outside woman, but who could tell with a man
like him? Her sons were no help, and her husband, his eyes closed, conducted his orchestra.

Narpat had started his factory.

With the meager sum he had managed to put away, he hired his regular help, the two young men who worked in his field, to once more clean
and prepare the area. They leveled the land and dug drains. Every midday
Narpat offloaded about ten sacks of sand from his tractor, which they
sprinkled and leveled on the site. Sometimes he fetched buckets of grainy
mud from his field. "Good as sand," he told the skeptical workers. They
grumbled about the heavy work, the late hours, and Narpat's constant
quarreling whenever the work slowed. At the end of the first month they
collected their wages and did not return. Narpat continued alone. Rumors of the factory spread in the village. A few farmers turned up, but
really to confirm the rumors rather than help.

"It does just creep up on you," Radhica reminded her husband each
night.

Word of the factory reached St. Croix, then Princes Town. "It look like
your husband come a big factory owner," Bhola told Dulari. "I hear he
putting down factory like mad all over the village." That evening she
packed the battered grip.

"We going back?" Jeeves asked.

"Yes, child," she replied. For a while she had been looking for an excuse to return. Her children too were relieved; what had begun as an adventure, an excursion away from the village, had soon lengthened into an agonizing period of barrication in a small bedroom. The first day they had been taken to Bhola's cinema, where they sat transfixed, gazing at airplanes and tanks so huge and real and loud they seemed to be jumping off the screen. Then they were treated at Royal Castle, a recently built fast-food outlet. Bhola had pinched Jeeves and joked about his guests drowning their meals in ketchup. Jeeves and his sisters swore they would never return to Lengua, but at the end of the third day Bhola had fulfilled all his obligations to the family and there were no further extravagances. His wife and daughter, threatened by the invasion, expressed their displeasure both by formal silence and by pretending, during their conversations, that they were alone. Chandra, Sushilla, and especially Kala were annoyed at these exclusive conversations, but Dulari was more concerned about the reopening of school in a few weeks.

Bhola drove the family back and was once more the jolly joking uncle. As they approached Lengua, he stretched his neck out of the window. "Where all these factories? I not seeing any. Oho, it look like is underground factory allyou father building." He slowed by a pothole. "Anybody want to go and talk to him through that hole?"

In the house Dulari noted the mess, the unfinished repairs, the tools and rubber that had piled up during the month she'd been away. She told her children, "We will have to spend a few days cleaning up."

"Where Pappy? He not in the bedroom." Jeeves sped off to the engines.

"What everybody staring at? Allyou want to live in this cowpen?" They collected the tools, replaced the books on the shelves, and swept away the wood shavings. In the kitchen they restored the pots and pans to the nails, tried to close the swinging cupboard door, then wedged it shut with a wad of cardboard. Dulari took down the curtains and carried them to the washing tub at the back of the house. The children were surprised to hear her say, "All this mess. I don't think we could fix up this place before allyou father come home." The day the barrel crashed from the roof she had lamented her luck, her husband, the village, and the cane farmers and had vowed never to return.

Late in the night Radhica, peeping from behind her curtains, spotted

Narpat's approaching tractor. The children were all asleep when Dulari heard the rumbling. She got up from the couch, went to the front door, changed her mind, and walked instead to the kitchen. She heard his boots on the steps and the front door pushed open. There was a moment of silence before Narpat asked, "Everybody come back?"

"Yes. The children sleeping."

"How was the holidays?"

She bent over the kitchen sink, her back turned to him. "School going to open soon."

"In two weeks?"

"Yes, I believe so." She searched in vain for the anger that had forced her to leave the house the day the water barrel crashed onto the kitchen, for the frustration with his factory, for the desperation of her entire married life.

"All the mess clean up."

"The children clean it up. They didn't have anything to do for nearly a month." Now she was annoyed at how quickly and naturally her voice slipped back into its bare tiredness. She heard him leaving for the back door but still did not face him; then a tinkle of water dripped from the bathroom faucet. He came into the bedroom, unraveled a piece of foam his wife had bundled in the corner, rolled it on the floor, and almost immediately fell asleep, snoring loudly and erratically. Dulari lay awake late into the night.

After just an hour or so of sleep, she was awakened by the hissing of water in the kitchen. Narpat was in the kitchen boiling a pot of tea. "You want me to do that?"

"Is only water boiling."

"Here, let me strain it out." She took a *saphee*, an old rag, from a nail and removed the boiling water. Then her husband turned to face her, and the pot shook in her hands. His face was drawn, the veins stood out on his neck, and his cheekbones were accentuated by the loss of weight and by his shabby gray stubble. For the first time he looked his age, but his eyes, alert and piercing as ever, flashed over her in a swift, assessing glance. He finished his tea in three noisy gulps. "You going now?" she asked. He placed the cup on the table. She followed him to the door, searching for something to say. Inexplicably she blurted out, "I fix back the bed," and to cover her embarrassment, laughed softly.

"The foam good for my back."

And he left.

Dulari walked to the couch. She sat and passed her fingers through her hair, then leaned back and closed her eyes. A wave of exhaustion, sudden and almost dizzying, fell on her. She lay there for an hour, then got up unsteadily and prepared for the morning's routine. *This is what has preserved me,* she thought, as she got her broom from the corner. *This numbing ritual of sweeping, cooking, cleaning, and washing, this silencing of my mind.* She was still thinking of the unlikely benefit of her labor when Radhica shouted from across the road, "Didi, you come back?"

"Yes, sister. School opening in a little while. Besides the children was getting bored," she said, as if they had all gone on some annual vacation.

"Your home is your home, no matter what. The new curtains you put up looking pretty."

Dulari propped the broom against the ground. "The flowers in your garden springing up real pretty-pretty too. Especially the bunch where the pundit does say his prayers in the morning."

"Hawaiian torch," Radhica said tiredly. "Ray father insist he get that plant. He say the smell does help him meditate." She uttered a short dry cackle, an indication that this was another indulgence she barely tolerated. "These mans and they crazy ideas. Hawaiian torch-porch." She paused, then asked, "So the children father left already?"

"Yes, early in the morning. The pundit gone out too?"

"Every day is some puja or the other." She studied her bracelets. "Just yesterday morning he was looking at he *Lucy* and he tell me that the children might enjoy some of these new shows they have on the TV now. Some nonsense about a scientist talking to a ro-bat. Ro-bat, bo-bat," she cackled. "It does not compute."

That evening Jeeves and his three sisters walked tentatively across the road. The Brahmin almost imperceptibly adjusted his waving and gestured them inside.

Each evening, after Narpat had finished his work in the field, he hauled some new material on his tractor to the factory site and offloaded the equipment with the tight satisfaction that he had procured and salvaged everything at almost no cost: the bamboo, cut in lengths of about fifteen feet, he had dragged out from a grove surrounded by tall *balisier*; just beyond the balisier, he had located some young teak trees that would be ideal as braces. Planks and scantlings he had bought from Chin Lee's sawmill; bolts, nuts, and steel rods from scrapyards. In the night, in the flickering light of the flambeau, he drew his plans. At first he had decided on a tower built on steel posts and anchored by crisscrossing iron bars, but he soon decided that this frame would not be strong enough to hold the huge blades he envisaged. He knew that during storms the entire windmill could come crashing down.

The stone and brick windmill that he envisioned was closer in design to a lighthouse, and during his brief breaks, he imagined himself at the tower's top, surveying the idle villagers returning from the rumshops. He returned home late at night with his plans, and sometimes he would sit on the Pavilion for an hour or two, adjusting and modifying. He contemplated small innovations—flexible blades and furling vanes—and material he might substitute. He was surprised at how easy and uncomplicated everything seemed. On weekends his children heard him muttering over his designs, "The simplest thing in the world when you plan it properly. But you have to be a futurist to see it." Occasionally he would glance across the road and notice the smoke in the Brahmin's gallery. "Mumbo-jumbo. Living in the past. A make-up past. Usual rituals. Useless."

In this mood of inventiveness, he bought an old arc iron set from Neck's scrapyard, and for two weeks he welded together an assortment of impractical items: a weathervane, a lopsided baker's shelf, a rotating clothesline, a crude can opener, and two corner shelves from a car rim he had cut in half. "Building everything, Mammy. In a little while we will have a nice little castle here."

"Scrapyard," Dulari said. Later she collected all his unfinished projects and pushed them beneath the house.

Finally after all the planning, he was ready to begin construction of his tower. First he dug a trench, twelve feet across and six feet deep. Into the hole he poured boulders, gravel, sand, and cement, tamping the mixture so that it settled properly. In twenty-eight days his foundation was complete, and he now set about laying a ring of concrete bricks. In two months his tower was knee-high, and in four months it reached his waist. He returned to the brick factory in Tableland, selecting the best blocks, smashing those he deemed defective against the floor to verify to the startled owner that he was cheating on the mixture.

He built a rough platform with cedar and mora scantlings, and late in the evenings he hauled up the bricks and the cement in an aluminum pail. When he arrived home, his body was sandy and streaked with cement. His wife noticed the bruises and abrasions on his arms and legs, but when she came with an old rag and a bottle of iodine, he waved her away. "Look at the sign on the bottle. Poison. Destroy the thyroids in no time." He explained he had daubed the injuries with pitchoil, which was fast-drying and worked only on the body's surface.

The bruises did not heal as easily as before, and eventually he was forced to apply poultices of neem and saffron and turmeric to the afflicted areas. Sometimes in the mornings he left without his icy-hot, and Dulari had to run after him with his meal before he pulled off in his tractor. All day long while she was cooking and washing, she worried about the money he was wasting on his crazy dream, and when she glanced across the road, she imagined what they could have done with the dwindling money. She concocted lines of argument to dissuade him, but she knew her husband too well and could anticipate all his irrational reasoning. Sometimes, though, she tried. "How long this factory going to take to finish?"

"It going to build before this old man dead, Mammy."

"You think farmers will drag their cane to a factory in the middle of the bush?"

"They don't have to drag it far. Where you think most of the cane in this country situated? Right in the bush."

"How much people you will need to run this factory? And what you will pay them with?"

"These same idlers, these lochos, who running from rumshop to rumshop, will be glad for a regular work. They don't have the brains to initiate anything but show them a honest day work, and they won't let you down."

"How much time they already let you down?"

He changed the topic. "This factory wouldn't belong to you or me but to the entire village. Run like a cooperative with a rotating board of directors."

"One week you, then the next week Huzaifa, and the next Sookdeo. You could get Dev Anand and Assevero and Sybil to sit on the board too."

Narpat laughed at this, but his eyes were serious. "What wrong with

these people? You think they any different from the directors in Tate and
Lyle and the other companies? Lining their pocket with money they thief
out. Drinking rum like it going out of style."

"So you going to have a few training seminars for them? Train
them to—"

"The only thing I have to teach them is how to survive. How to be a futurist. How not to depend on the government for anything. Teach them to
fish rather than give them a carite."

As usual, she relented whenever his voice slipped into a lecturing
mode. "So when you going to bring home the first bucket of fish?"

"I will take it over to the Brahmin. He is a ideal fish seller, with that
conch he does be blowing."

The following day, recalling the argument, she was irritated at how
easily she had resigned herself.

Sometimes the other farmers, cutting their cane and slicing the tops from
the stalks, paused to look at the tower, rising higher and higher each
week. The younger ones joked and laughed. "It look like that Narpat fella
building a nice little castle."

"Like the tall one where this woman use to let down her hair for these
scamp to climb up on."

"Maybe is a lighthouse to guide all the bison in the night."

"I wonder how far up he will go."

"Take care a airplane don't crash in it."

"You think it will be so tall?"

"Why you don't ask him?"

"Not me, sah."

Late one night the Manager came in his rickety truck. He parked at the
side of the road and walked toward the tower. In the moonlight he saw
bags of cement covered with a tarpaulin, and bricks scattered about. He
considered stealing the cement but was frozen by the image of Narpat
lurking about in the bush, suddenly jumping on him. He ran to his truck,
cursing.

Part Three

*N*arpat's windmill was destroyed before its completion by one of the tropical storms that yearly razed the island. The storm had spawned swirling gusts that flattened the canefields. He did not reveal the destruction to his family, but on the Saturday following the storm, he beckoned Jeeves to his tractor.

When they arrived at the canefield, Jeeves asked his father, "That is the factory?" He gazed disappointedly at the pile of debris.

"That was just the tower."

"What happen to it?"

"It was no match for the storm."

"And the cane too? That is why they so flat?"

"They just sleeping, boy. In a week or two they will spring up good as new."

"And the tower?"

"The tower." He walked around the rubble with his son. "This is nature telling me that the design was faulty. Look at that immortelle tree. What you notice?"

"The flowers looking like little birds."

"If you watch carefully, you will see the wind direction. That tell me that the windmill blades should face the east, not the south as before." He mentioned other technical flaws and stressed that each error could be remedied with intelligence and foresight. Jeeves grew bored and wandered off to collect the orange immortelle flowers scattered on the ground.

On Sunday, when Jeeves heard the tractor's engine, he ran out, but Narpat told him, "Not today, Carea. I have to concentrate real hard. Is me against nature, boy."

For a week or so Narpat contemplated building the windmill piece-meal at his house and hauling the sections to the site, but it would not be the same: the solitude of the field, working without interruption, the cool night breeze on his back as he shoveled and set up his bricks one by one.

He suspected that in his original design the towers were too narrow and the sails too stout. The base of his new tower would have to be wider and sturdier. On his cardboard he designed new shutter sails that could be opened and closed like venetian blinds, and that could be rotated to face the eye of the wind. Finally he discarded the design, dismantled the old blades, and narrowed the tips with his cutlass. He checked the bearings and, not satisfied, replaced them to minimize vibration. Only when he was reassured did he begin his labor in earnest. He remained at the site sometimes past midnight. The villagers gave up on him once more, because from this craziness they knew that there was no pulling back. In the village rumshops, descriptions of him grew more colorful: both sinner and saint, a man to be avoided at all costs. The next day they might spot him driving on his tractor, his eyes staring straight ahead, and they would turn away or look to the ground.

Three months after the storm Narpat walked past a group of farmers clustered outside the small agricultural depot in Princes Town, complaining about the late payment and the meager sum they had received from the government's Agricultural Emergency Fund. These farmers who had not seen him for a while noted that although he was noticeably thinner, and his hair longer and now speckled with gray, he still walked with the loose confident stride of a young man. Narpat picked up his check and walked away, not bothering to chat. One of the farmers said, "Like Narpat diet acting good on his body."

Another replied, "But bad on his mind."

The farmers laughed.

In the rumshops, Mr. Doon heard the farmers' gossip and felt a strange affinity with this misunderstood man. He contemplated his own life. In the year and a half since Narpat had begun his factory, Mr. Doon had made mistake after mistake; the first, his running off with Kamini, and the most recent, the birth of miserable twins who seemed to conspire with their mother. He recalled the hostile reception of his manuscript and thought that just like the old man he had been energized by ridicule and doubt.

Unlikely inspiration had come from the success of the Brahmin's ridiculously simple booklet. One night he rushed to his untidy bookcase and plucked out book after book until he located Samuel Pepys's *Diary*. He read with growing excitement, and two days later, on the last page, he was certain that a diary was the appropriate form for the island's tumult. As usual when he was excited, he shouted at the wall bisecting his mother's apartment, which he had constructed soon after Kamini's arrival. "'Inventions,' eh? 'Silly,' eh? 'Implausible,' eh? We will see what these publisher bitches will say when I present my diary to them."

He filled notebook after notebook. The diary also provided an excuse for his nightly visits to the rumshops, and whenever Kamini quarreled, he would tell her, "No one really understands the writer's plight. We are a breed apart."

"A rum-drinking breed."

"We are driven." He had been surprised at Kamini's transformation from a shy, obliging girl into a nagging, troublesome woman immediately after the birth of the twins.

"All this talk about going back to Canada to live."

"In due course. My work must be completed first. I must return on my own terms. As a bona-fide writer."

"The only thing bona-fide about you is your drinking."

"You cannot get to my sensitive soul, woman. It's encased in an armor of—of brood and mull." He was frustrated at his tendency to slip into rumshop parlance when he was angry, and he would cap off each argument by banging on the wall and shouting at his mother on the other side, "Eavesdropping is condemned by every single religion."

One night Kamini told him, "Could you please stop banging like that, David? You are disturbing Dolly and Tolly."

Oh, god. Bitches. They climbing on me like ants, he thought to himself. But he replied calmly, "The children's names are Tolstoy and Dostoevsky."

"I am not going to call them any funny names."

"Very well. I hope you take responsibility for the neuroses he will suffer when he grow up and everyone still calling him Dolly."

"The only thing I hope is that when they grow up, they don't follow some wasteful profession." Her admiration of her husband's writing ambition had long since waned. "Going to the rumshop every single night. Pretending they is some nineteenth-century ghost writer."

"I am simply collecting material." He used his familiar excuse.

"All you are collecting is debts. And a big beer belly. You are looking just like Sad Sack nowadays. A skinny man with a big soft belly." The comparison always infuriated him into a spluttering silence. "Oh, sorry. Pardon me, I forget is Samlal Pepsi."

"Samuel Pepys," he shouted. "My model." His wife, and his mother on the other side of the wall, simultaneously groaned.

Bitches!

"And you really expect people to buy a diary?"

"I am simply resurrecting a forgotten form to its rightful state of grandeur. Replacing it on the mantle."

"When you decide to put some food in the mantle instead, let me know." She turned to her babies. "Hush, Tolly. Hush, Dolly." But Mr. Doon imagined he held a trump card. Occasionally while Kamini was changing her twins' diapers or feeding them, she would say in a deceptively casual voice, "I talk to Daddy this morning. And he ask me when we going to get a proper house."

"There is nothing wrong with this apartment."

"Nothing? It have a big Berlin wall in the middle with all the doors nailed shut."

"Privacy. The prime prerogative of the artist is the right to tranquility."

"From who? From your poor sick mother who you say does be eavesdropping 'bout everything we say? I see the poor woman about three times, and she could barely get up from her rocker."

"A masterful thespian."

"Anyways, as I was saying, Daddy was asking when we going to finally get married legal and proper?"

"An antiquated custom."

"I could just imagine the rumors."

"Water off a duck's back. The next time you bounce up one of these gossip-mongers, tell them, please, that true artists are bohemians. *Bohemians*. Remember that word good." He pulled the skin on his chin and squeezed. "We could name the next baby accordingly."

"What next baby? Are you crazy? You can't even support these two that we have here. All that talk about poetry and foreign magazine chasing you down. I wonder where all that poetry gone?"

"To market to market to buy a fat pig. Fuckaway fuckaway jiggety jig."

"You have no shame."

"Then I fit in perfectly in this boat."

Kamini turned to the twins. "Once upon a time there were four rats living in a little hole. A drunkard father rat, a mother rat, and two little baby rat. No, I think was five rats. A poor, sick grandmother rat too."

We will see, he thought, as he prepared to leave for the bars. *We will see. After almost two years of perseverence, a forgotten form is about to be revived. A quaint and touching diary.*

She held her twins in both arms. "Come, baby rats. Tell your daddy rat goodbye. He going to the rumshop again. Bye-bye, Daddy Rat."

He turned to leave, then went instead to the wall and banged loudly. "Mind your own business please, you thespian."

Occasionally he would stumble from Diablo to the bookstore and gaze sourly at the local books, mostly shameless autobiographies. He rarely purchased anything, and whenever Huzaifa approached, he would mumble, "Wouldn't waste a tuppence on this self-published trash, old man."

Once Huzaifa asked him, "Like you writing something yourself?"

"A diary."

"A diary?" Huzaifa was disappointed. "How thick? Half-inch?"

Mr. Doon, who was quite drunk, laughed loudly, startling Huzaifa. "No less than seven hundred pages. Measure that!"

One evening Huzaifa showed up at the factory site. Almost two years had passed since he had left his friend's house vowing never to return. In the interim, he frequently surprised and infuriated his wife by bad-mouthing the Indian independence movement. "Damn rogues and scamps. All of them." He pretended he received secret bulletins that proved that Gandhi was an avid meat-eater and that Nehru had a harem of Turkish prostitutes. When Salima asked where he had heard this, he would nibble his nail and mutter, "Inside info. Bulletin."

Once he told her, "Latest count is that Nehru had close to one hundred outside children. All caste. All race. Kaffir."

Mostly his wife just ignored him.

"Gandhi favorite meal was tandoori chicken. Wouldn't surprise me if he was a pork-eater too. Pork vindaloo. Will try to get a bulletin on it."

Sometimes his wife reacted. "Huzaifa, you know, for a little dry-up

piece of a man, you does talk real big. Why you don't go outside and pile
up all the rubbish instead of chooking up inside the house all day like a
pregnant woman?"

At these times he would reach for his radio, turn the dial carefully,
press his ear against the squawking speaker, and pretend he was tuning in
to some Pakistani station. "Going to get it one of these days. Nearly-nearly
get through a few nights ago. They was talking about some cricket match
or the other."

"You ever hold a cricket bat in your life, Huzaifa?"

"Ever hold a cricket bat?" He attempted to laugh cynically. "I nearly
get pick for the county team. Was the best opening bat in the whole
south."

"Huzaifa, the only thing you could open is your mouth. And one day
that will land you in big trouble."

One midday after she had returned tired and sweating from cutlassing
the backyard, she snatched the radio and flung it against the wall.

"Aah, aah," was all Huzaifa could say.

"Is my luck to end up with the laziest, sickliest man on the face of the
earth."

"Nearly pick up Pakistan." He collected the radio from the floor. The
cardboard back was hanging by two red and white wires from the trans-
mitter. He stared inside the box and was impressed by the tiny wires, the
transponder, the broken speakers, and the precision of their placement.
"Look at all these unit inside here. Never know a small simple little radio
could have all this machinery hide away inside here. Aah, aah."

"How come you never pick up any inside bulletin about your friend
who building the factory? Take the radio to him. Allyou could build a generator."

A few days later he showed up at the factory site. He walked around
the paved area, surprised and touched by the materialization of the plans
drawn on the ends of cardboard boxes. For a brief moment he saw the
factory rising up from its foundation. He heard the whirring of windmills
and smelled the aroma of cane sugar. When he opened his eyes, Narpat,
gaunt and unreal as the brief illusion, was standing before him. Huzaifa
was overcome with guilt and timidity. He struggled for words.

"I going to put the boilers on that end. And the centrifugal tank across
there."

"Yes."

"The windows will be all around there."

"The units in a nice little line. What about the engines?"

"I will have to tune them up first. That will take careful planning."

"On cardboard? I have one setta boxes at home. Useless. Just laying around. Just the other day I was telling Salima that these box what looking so useless is the perfect thing for drawing plans." For the next hour he listened to Narpat's engineering projection.

Every evening after his work at the bookstore, Huzaifa ate his meal hurriedly and headed for the factory site. He never helped in any way; instead he sat on one of the platforms and waited for a break in the other man's labor. Narpat was usually too tired for any prolonged conversation, and now it was Huzaifa who did most of the talking. "It wouldn't surprise me one bit if Tate and Lyle have spies in all them bush watching this secret project. Just like how the British was spying on Gandhi and Nehru. And Jinnah."

He was in awe of the tower, and frequently he nodded off from staring at the slowly spinning blades. After a few months he visualized himself sitting on the platform as a professional sentinel, and he would grow alert whenever the breeze ruffled the nearby cane stalks. He carved out a solid poui walking stick. *A nice little weapon*, he thought. *Perfect sentinel missile.*

"Ay-ay, the Muslim Gandhi come back," Salima wife told him. "I wonder where he was all this time? Now he have a crook stick."

Occasionally he left the platform and pointed his stick menacingly at the fluttering cane, but he was careful not to stray too far. He muttered, "Allyou come on. Come on. Is Huzaifa allyou will have to pass through. Hide as much as you want, but Huzaifa, master spy and sentinel, will prize out every last man that hiding in the bush." Sometimes he added, "Bookworm and aristocrat."

One evening he almost suffered a heart attack. From the waving stalks, three muscular black men emerged, walking slowly and purposefully. One of them was sucking an orange. Huzaifa fled to Narpat, shrieking. Narpat was about to offload a barrow of cement over some boulders. The three men walked up to him, taking their time. Huzaifa stepped behind him.

"Evening, boss," the man who was sucking the orange said. "Me and

Kimbo and Wonders hear that you building this factory by yourself and decide to drop in. To tell the truth, boss, was in the back of my head for a while." He glanced with astonishment at the windmill. "I hear 'bout this, but seeing it for the first time . . ."

Narpat offloaded the cement and smoothened the mound with his boot.

"Wouldn't have believe it if I didn't see it with my two own eyes. Eh, Wonders? Eh, Kimbo?"

"I still can't believe it." Wonders spoke with a slight stutter.

Kimbo made the sign of the cross.

Huzaifa was surprised by and suspicious of their respectful tone. He calculated that Ashton, at forty or so, the oldest of the group, was the ringleader. Wonders was probably his henchman, and the feebleminded Kimbo did the cleaning up. He eyed the distance between himself and the tractor, his only means of escape. He had little stomach for running through the canefield with its hidden ravines and sleeping snakes.

Wonders stepped forward. "So how big the building going to be, boss?"

Narpat walked to the middle of the plot. The three men followed him. Huzaifa trailed some distance behind. "From this end to that end."

"These factories and them does have a open entrance, not so?" Ashton asked.

"The main entrance will be big enough for a Farmall to drive through."

"Rooms or one big unit?" Ashton asked.

"A complex."

"Yes, yes, a complex," Huzaifa repeated timidly. "Multipurpose."

"A complex, you say, eh?" Ashton turned to Wonders. "That don't remind you of the big macco wholesale grocery we build for Ramlogan in Torrib trace?"

"Steel beams. First-grade bricks. Aluzinc roofing. One-seventy by twofifty. Big, big building. Yes, yes, exactly like Ramlogan place. They say that Indian money does dip low but doesn't run out." Kimbo laughed with a deep exhalation at Wonders's joke.

"So where allyou fellas from?" Narpat asked seriously.

"We originally from Les Effort, boss, but work was tight on that side, so we push down here. Is a nice little village, not so, Wonders?"

"Can't complain, Ashton. Can't complain at all."

Outsiders, Huzaifa thought. *Enemies. Interlopers.* He had heard Narpat himself voice this opinion so many times. He waited for the explosion.

Ashton continued. "Is the sort of place where honest hardworking people could make a good living."

"A dying breed, though," Wonders said. "Skilled tradesmen. Carpenter. Mason. Bricklayer. Now any and everybody picking up the trade."

"Yes, *picking up*," Ashton said sarcastically. All three men laughed. "So you do all this by yourself, boss? The foundation and the tower? Never see a windmill before, to tell the truth."

Huzaifa stepped from behind Narpat.

"What so hard about doing this? You could do anything if you set your mind to it. Once you understand the purpose."

"Might finish faster with some help," Ashton said.

"Skilled help. Dying breed."

"Dying because work so tight nowadays. You might surprise to know that me and Kimbo and Wonders does work for twenty dollars a day. Kimbo don't mind taking home fifteen if the situation"—he said *situation*—"demand it." Kimbo shrugged as if it was okay. Ashton noted that Narpat made no attempt at haggling. "You know, boss, I seeing this with my own two eye, but I can't believe that is one man who build this windmill by himself." His admiration was genuine. He glanced at Narpat's now-gaunt but still-muscular body, so different from the other Indians in the village.

"Let me warn you one time. If you looking for easy work, you better go elsewhere."

"We not looking for easy work, boss," Ashton said. "You just tell we what you want, and we will build it."

"Plans," Huzaifa said shyly. "We have plans for everything."

Ashton ignored Huzaifa. "Okay, boss, we will see you tomorrow morning. You have any extra wheelbarrows and spades?"

"I have a extra wheelbarrow park up behind my house," Wonders said. "A little rusty, but it should work."

"Bring it. At six o'clock sharp. If you can't make it by six, don't bother to come. I don't tolerate slackers."

"Don't worry, boss. I will leave a hour before my boy who going to the Lengua government school. I will time myself good and proper."

Jeeves, now almost twelve years old, was in standard five, a few months away from the dreaded Common Entrance exams. There was nothing at school to mark him as special or different; he was never embarrassed because nothing was demanded of him. He formed temporary friendships with other ordinary awkward boys, quarreled about trivial things, and promised never to speak with them again. He missed Danny and his incredible stories. Sometimes Jeeves would think of his friend when he was in the school library, a cupboardlike room that had once housed the school's agricultural supplies and that still smelled of insecticide. In the library, he chose the books on Greek and Indian mythologies—children's versions of the *Odyssey* and the *Mahabharata*—only because his father had given him a taste for quests and sacrifices. He read fitfully, never more than a few pages at one sitting, because fragments of his father's fables would creep into the stories; and he would close the book and envision a hero not as a young handsome man but as someone struggling with endless sacrifices. The mood would remain with him while he was walking from school, and he would imagine that his father's factory was a special secret. During play, he would wonder if each of the other boys possessed their own secrets. And though he was never singled out for praise and never received much attention, he felt that this special secret was a strength that set him apart.

He spent his weekends on the junkpile, closing his eyes and pretending to drive the rusty engines, clearing everything in his path. Occasionally he would stare at one of his father's drawings and try to make sense of it by mentally redrawing some of the lines and adjusting the angles. After a while this became a little game. He rarely saw his father during the week and was happy when Narpat came to him on Sunday mornings. These conversations, though enjoyable, were brief, because Huzaifa invariably showed up a short while later. At school some of the other students had taunted Jeeves about the factory, but that was now stale news and he no longer expected to be heckled about "the crazy windmill man." So he was surprised when Quashie asked about the factory.

"This damn mill you father building . . . is really true?"

"True no ass." Jeeves tried to imitate Quashie's breezy recklessness.

"You mean all this assness people mouthing off about is no joke, man?"

"The assness is no joke, man."

"So what he going to do with the blinking factory when he finish with it?"

"Make blinking sugar, man."

"Where he getting all this shitting money from? I hear allyou Indian does have money hide away inside every hole in the yard."

"Shitting true, man."

For the next few evenings Dulari quarreled with Jeeves about digging up the yard and crawling beneath the house. "Damn holes around the house so big you could hide for days," he confessed to Quashie.

"So frigging deep?"

During the following days Jeeves was astonished that Quashie, who had now been in Lengua for close to six years, had learned so little of the village. He was still suspicious of the religious rituals, the many gods and goddesses, and the Hindi songs that blared from the newer houses. "Is true that allyou Indian does pray to rat and goat and monkey?"

"All the damn time, man."

"Your own father too?"

"Nah. He don't believe in them thing."

"How come?"

Jeeves thought for a while. He recalled his father's conversations about ancient Aryans and horse sacrifices. "He prefer horse."

"What? He does worship them?"

"Don't talk shit, man. He does eat them."

"That is why he so stiff and strong?"

Jeeves was pleased by this comment from the athletic boy, but he asked, "Who tell you that?"

"My stepfather." He added quickly, "Town does talk, man."

"You mean tongue?"

"Town. *Tong.*"

From Quashie, Jeeves learned of the carnival fights and the steelband wars and badjohns in Morvant and Laventille who carried switchblades instead of cutlasses. He spoke of nightclubs where there was dancing late in the night, and other kinds of clubs where mysterious women carried men upstairs to dark, smoky rooms. He mentioned the calypso tents where the Mighty Sparrow and Lord Kitchener belted out their tunes before drunk, cheering crowds. "Going to head to Porspain," he said, abbreviating the nation's capital. "For the carnival. To see real mas, not these jackassy blue devil and jab jab it does have down here."

Jeeves recalled the first time he had spotted a masquerader, disguised in horns and tail and covered with a blue dye. He was about four then and had run screaming into the house. "This is just Sidney, boy. What you bawling so for?" But Jeeves was also afraid of Sidney, and when the man twisted up his eyelids, Jeeves had burst into another wail. He couldn't understand why his mother and sisters were laughing.

"Bands with hundreds of people," Quashie said. "Soldier, sailor, Red Indian, Viking, Zulu. All kinda kissmeass warrior. Women from the States and Germany jumping up too like if they listening to this music all they life." But always during these conversations he came back to the factory. A few days later he told Jeeves, "It look like you old man start putting up the wall." Whenever Jeeves asked about his sources, he would strike a laconic pose and say, "Town does talk, man."

But for Narpat's children, the year dragged on. They grew accustomed to his unpredictable moodiness and their mother's retreat into an unyielding silence. She had changed since her return from Bhola, and Kala and Chandra wondered whether her listlessness was because of guilt or helplessness. She met each problem by saying, "We have everything we need right here. What you complaining about?"

The children realized that this was partially true: now that Chandra was working, they were better off than many of the villagers, and although there were adjustments in their food—some of these by Narpat's decree—they never went hungry. Also, every other week a solitary woman would come to Dulari with a parcel of cloth and leave swiftly.

At school Quashie's admiration of Narpat endured, and it was from his friend that Jeeves learned of the factory's progress. "They dragging one macco setta bamboo for the wall. I believe they put up the steel beam for the foundation already. It look like the factory will be bigger than this kissmeass school."

"I see the shitting plans, man. I know that already."

"What? You joking. You see the plan?"

"Yeah, man. Hundreds and hundred of them. A big blinking book."

"Your father does draw these plan himself?"

"Whole night he drawing plan."

"I could see them."

"Wouldn't make sense. Nobody else could understand them."

"They in code?"

"It have a lotta people who will be glad to get they hand on them."

Quashie's suspicions of the villagers was roused. "To do what?"

Jeeves thought for a while. "To build they own blinking factory. Not any and everybody could draw plan, you know."

Quashie whistled. Then he asked, "It have a ugly little man who does be with him sometimes. He know 'bout these plans?"

Jeeves recalled Huzaifa's solemnly furtive manner while he listened to Narpat on the porch. "He is a spirit."

"A what!"

"A sorta watchman spirit."

"A *lagahoo*?"

Worse, man. A prate. A *baccoo*. I think he does sleep inside a bottle. Right on top of the plans."

"He . . . he dangerous?"

"He eat a lotta children already. Prefer them to chicken."

Jeeves was surprised at this imaginative burst and the reaction it generated from his friend. He repeated his story to Sushilla.

That evening he received a spectacular flogging from his mother. It was as if all her energy buried under layers of despair had been released. "Spreading rumors about people, eh?" She slapped him hard on his back. "Innocent people who didn't do you anything." She aimed at his face. "How you will like if people start saying that your father crazy? That this factory bring a madness to his head? That he dragging his whole family to the poorhouse?" She was shouting now. Jeeves had flinched at the first few blows; now he stood his ground. He tried to focus on the pain on his face and back and wondered why the pain was so localized, why it didn't diffuse throughout his body. Blow after blow fell on him. He concentrated on the sound of the blows, and from the sound he began to count. Fifteen, sixteen, seventeen. Seventeen was an unusual number. Why didn't she round it off to twenty? He became dimly aware of his mother's drained, expressionless face, of his sisters staring down at him. He looked away, not wanting to see their concern, and he noticed his trembling knees. Why were they trembling? He closed his eyes and tensed his arms and legs, to force his body into immobility. He heard other sounds, as if someone was talking from a great distance. He could not distinguish the words, but the voice was warm and soft. He smelled his mother's clothing, and for the first time he realized that she had a distinct odor: cooking oil, burnt milk, and the vague aroma of some pungent vegetable. The familiarity of these mingled odors both comforted and enraged him. He walked away. His mother tried to hold his arm, but he brushed it away. "Leave me alone. Don't touch me."

He ran to the junkpile and covered his face with his hands. He heard a nightbird's hoot, maybe a jumbie bird. He imagined the bird to be as black as ink with sharp, retractable claws. The breeze bothered the branches, and a bat flew out and hovered at the house's eave. Why couldn't his father come and sit with him? He closed his eyes and tried to imagine this man who Quashie so admired, sitting at his side. He pictured, in the distance, the musical sound of the windmills, like a flute whistling in the breeze. He got up and walked to the road, caught by the flush of the sinking sun on the trees and the clouds. The Brahmin's heliconias looked like kindling birds. He bolted down the road. He passed Hakim's parlor and, at Four Roads junction, stopped to catch his breath. He tried to recall the direction his father had taken during their trips to the canefield, and as the sun disappeared behind the immortelle and cedar trees and the palmiste, he realized that, in the shadows, a mistake could lead him to the forest, where he might be lost for days. He had heard stories of partially eaten bodies found in the midst of some thicket. He imagined wild pigs and ocelots and huilles, their massive heads on the water's surface scanning for a prey. When the road was straight, he closed his eyes so he wouldn't see the black bamboo and the teak patches where, he'd heard, there were lagahoos, *mama diglous*, *la diablesses*, *soucouyants*, and a host of other spirits prowling about. He sped down Crappo Patch, and by the time he reached Toolia trace, he was breathless. But he was calmed by the fragrance of rotting hogplums. He stopped to catch his breath and heard the hum of crickets and the squawk of a bird above him. Then he heard the windmill, a faint muted whirring, and he spotted the tower rising from the bush like an ancient watchman forgotten by everyone but still guarding his territory. As he got closer, he tried to see his father in the faint moonlight. He crossed to the other side of an incomplete wall. He could not see his father, but the tractor was parked just before the tower. He glanced up at the whirring blades, and when he looked down, he noticed a flickering light coming from the tower's door, a narrow slit.

He drew close, peeped inside, and saw his father, sitting on a rough bench, hunched close to a flambeau. He was writing and drawing on a piece of brown paper. Now for the first time Jeeves thought of how his father would respond to his recklessness. But he was scared of returning through the forested stretch by himself. Briefly he contemplated hiding in the tractor. His father looked up. "I need a special kind of brick for the fermentation tank."

The boy was surprised at his father's casual statement, as if he expected his son to appear suddenly before him, alone, at this time of the night. He took a few tentative steps, then sat next to his father. "That is what you drawing?"

"No. These are boilers." And his father explained, as to an adult, the entire process, explained the purpose of his kilns and tanks and coppers. Finally he asked Jeeves, as if the notion had just occurred, "What you doing here this time of the night, boy?"

Jeeves hesitated. "I come to look for you."

Narpat packed away his plans, but his eyes were on his son. When he was finished, he said, "Time to go. Come here." He guided Jeeves through the track. "Might have coral snake hiding in the grass, Carea." His voice was as gentle as Jeeves could remember.

"Why you spending so much time with this factory?"

"You think so?" He hoisted Jeeves onto the seat. "Because I can't give up. Is a pledge. A perfect pledge."

"What is that?"

Narpat was about to turn the key, but he hesitated as if he were thinking of the question. "Is when you willing to make any sacrifice to fulfill a promise you spent your whole life preparing for. Something that only you could do."

When Narpat parked the tractor in the yard, the entire family was in the porch. Jeeves noticed his mother's annoyance. She said nothing when Narpat swung him up the porch steps. She remained serious when he said, "This flour bag getting heavy, Mammy." Later his lightheartedness put his family at ease somewhat, but Chandra, every now and again, looked reproachfully at Jeeves.

TWENTY-TWO

*D*ulari did not mention Jeeves's reckless trip to the factory site until two weeks later, when she heard bamboo creaking and popping in the distance. From the kitchen window she watched the dark cloud of smoke and, in the night, sparks scattering in the air. "All that bamboo that burning is right at the side of the road. The same road that you take on your little adventure. When the fire out, you will see all the burnup skeleton of dog and cat." His mother continued scolding, but Jeeves was thinking of the animals frantically trying to escape.

When Narpat came home in the night, he said, "You could hear the fire barking like dogs. Yap yap yap."

"I think is real dogs," Jeeves said. "You think they get burn up?"

"Every single thing get burn up, boy." Narpat explained that the fires were unusually strong this year. He blamed the other cane farmers for not properly clearing their fields before they set them afire in preparation for harvest, he blamed the unruly bush, the lathro that had been allowed to flourish in the adjacent fields, and he blamed the villagers for the rubbish they routinely piled around their houses. "One little piece of burning leaf could blow about and set fire to all these people who don't properly dispose of rubbish." His family realized that he was referring to the Brahmin, whose flower garden had been ruined by a pile of bamboo just beyond the fence.

A few of the old wooden houses were ruined, and there were rumors that the small flimsy shacks of the Outsiders had been destroyed. The villagers filled buckets and pails and lined them on porches and landings. Each morning the Manager kept his truck idling and waited in the gallery for the straggle of men who wanted barrels of water transported to their houses. In the night he counted the day's takings, moistening his thumb and piling the bills.

Narpat's house was one of the few in the village untouched by the fire. The flames had crept steadily through the dried bull grass and paragrass, getting closer and closer. Narpat had stood on his porch staring grimly at the fire's approach. His wife was worried, his daughters terrified, and Jeeves secretly excited.

"We should full up some bucket," Dulari said.

Kala ran to the kitchen and returned with a pot of water

"Boil corn, boil corn," Narpat said in the singsong tone of a vendor.

The fire advanced. Jeeves thought of an army of commandos inching forward. Then it stopped. "What happen?" Jeeves could barely contain his disappointment.

"What suppose to happen. What always suppose to happen when you prepared."

"The drain that you build?"

"Not a drain. A firewall." The fire had been cut off by the drain filled with stagnant water and teeming with keewees. "The same firewall that everybody complain about. Pok, pok, pok." He bunched his fingers and shook his hand as if it were a puppet. The children laughed anxiously and wondered how long this mood would last. The next Sunday morning, as he was preparing to visit the factory site, he glanced up at the plastic sheet he had tacked onto the roof. "Sunlight. Free vitamins, Mammy. Could grow all sort of plants right here in the kitchen. Just like people in these other country. Vines with bell and star flowers creeping up these nails, and little pale bamboo sprouting by the wall, and these desert plants dressing up the cupboard." Reluctantly the children joined in the fantasy and imagined this exotic arrangement.

During the week he found hidden benefits to all the incomplete renovations. The misaligned louvers that had to be forced noisily into place were a deterrent to thieves; the engine oil on Carnegie would forever keep away insects; the cupboard with its perpetually open door would discourage rats and cockroaches, which roosted in dark musty places. Each boast was accompanied by an oblique condemnation of the Brahmin. "Flower garden? What is the use of flowers when you could plant vegetables instead?" The next day he said, "People who like to paint their house in all these bright, show-offy color just asking for trouble." The Brahmin's bright green walls had been blackened with soot. "A simple thing like a proper drain could solve some people a lot of problem. But they don't think about tomorrow. Only today. And they believe they could protect themselves with magic. Chanting. Superstition. Hocus-pocus. Cat."

One morning Radhica complained to Dulari. "When Ray father get a idea in his head, it does take the devil to drive it away." The idea became clearer during the following days. The concrete balusters in the front steps were knocked down and replaced with fancy twirling steel cantilevers. They were painted a bright green. The steps themselves were painted in bright red. The fence that had been ruined by the fire was toppled, and a wall of decorative red bricks rose in its place. A hammock with a canopy was slung between two fruit trees.

"Colors," Narpat said. "The sign of a primitive people." But as the Brahmin's renovations proceeded, as the house recovered from the tarnish of the fire, as chelas descended on the property volunteering their labor, he began to sink once more into his fretful, sour mood. "They helping out the god with free labor. Guaranteeing a nice position in their next life." During the following nights, he observed the space taken by the sewing machine, his children's books scattered on the table, the wedge of wood beneath Carnegie, and the cobwebs on the rafters, and although he was responsible for the house's size and many of its defects, for each flaw he blamed some member of his family. Now the place was too noisy, he complained. One evening he slammed his book on the Pavilion and walked out of the house when Sushilla began to cough. He imagined the period when his family had gone to Bhola and he had been left alone as a time of freedom and release. He got down his pile of papers from the kitchen wall and wrote: *Great deeds are only accomplished by great sacrifices.* He scratched out *great* and replaced it with *noble.*

He got back from the factory site later and later each night and fell asleep on the Pavilion rather than on the foam, where he had continued sleeping since his family's return from Bhola. His wife listened to him twisting and turning, and from long experience, she knew he was simmering on the edge of a rage that would soon explode for the unlikeliest reason. She guessed that the money set aside for the factory was running out once again. She warned her daughters to keep away from their father, and when they questioned her, she grew exasperated. "I don't have to explain every single thing to allyou." In the mornings, she saw him flinching at the conch's wail and the chelas' greetings.

"Changing a ordinary man into a god. Throwing money after him. Giving him free labor. Refusing to lift a finger to help in the factory. Something that will benefit everybody. Savages! Blasted savages!" One night he flung a cup of milk against the wall. "What is this? Milk and sandfly? A nice meal." He kicked the cup. Jeeves rubbed his eyes sleepily. His father shouted out the names of diseases. And the children realized that the period of calm had passed.

"This is what you wake up everybody for, Pappy?"

"What!" He turned to Kala. "You arguing with me like a big woman? Come here right now."

Kala stepped forward.

"Clean up this mess right now." He pointed to the spilled milk.

"Go back and sleep, Kala. I will do it."

"No! No! Let the big woman do it."

"Is okay, Mammy." Kala took the saphee from her mother, who was standing at the kitchen's entrance, and bent to her knees. She wiped the floor, went to the sink, wrung the rag, and returned to the soiled area.

"Is okay, Kala. It clean enough."

The girl continued wiping.

"Kala."

Her mother's voice was gentle, but the girl said, "It not clean. You can't see that."

Narpat went into the bedroom and slammed the door. Dulari took the saphee from her daughter. "Go to sleep. You have school tomorrow. And stop crying, Sushilla."

Jeeves remained awake for half the night listening to the hushed conversation in his sisters' room and the sound of his father pacing around. When Narpat emerged from his bedroom, Jeeves pulled the cover over his head and pretended he was asleep. He heard his father's footsteps in the kitchen, then the creak of the back door. The boy removed the covers and strained to hear other sounds. After a while he drifted off to sleep. When he awoke a short time later and saw a shadowy figure on his mattress next to him, he thought it was a dream, but when he turned, he saw his father sitting hunched, his arms encircling his knees. In the dim light his face appeared even more gaunt and his eyes, empty sockets. When he felt his father's rough hands ruffling his hair and smoothing his forehead, he closed his eyes tightly. His father got up and walked slowly to the porch. He left the door open, and the boy heard him muttering, "This man is inactive. The biggest vice of all. Others do work for him. But he is prospering. Why is this so?"

In the morning Jeeves wondered whether it had all been a dream. That day in school he avoided Quashie, and when he returned home, he changed his clothes, ate hurriedly, and rushed over to the Brahmin. Throughout the evening his sisters were silent, not laughing at the antics of Lucy, not rolling their eyes when Radhica interrupted with, "Ro-bat, bo-bat." Soon the woman grew speculative, and she gazed suspiciously at their faces. When there was a long interlude of advertisements, she asked her son, "Ray, if anything ever bothering you, is a promise you will tell me?"

Ray looked at her blankly.

"Jag, if anything ever bothering you, is a promise you will tell me?"

"Yes, yes. Now stop bothering me."

"Thanks, beta." She usually slipped into Hindi to signal she was over-wrought.

A few nights later, as Jeeves and his sisters were leaving, Radhica called out to Jeeves, "Just you, beta. The rest of allyou could go home." She waited till Chandra and Kala and Sushilla were safely across the road, before she asked him, "How your father going, beta? I does hardly see him these days. It look like he does come home real late. He okay?" She placed a hand on his shoulder. "He does beat you?" Jeeves, liking the sympathy, almost said yes. "You could tell me, you know. I is like a *poowa*, a auntie."

"No, he don't beat me."

She removed her hand from his shoulder. "What about your Mammy? He does beat she?"

"I don't know what does happen in their room."

Abruptly her hands slipped down once more to his shoulder, and in a rough tug she whirled the boy and hugged him tightly. "Is okay, beta. Your poowa understand." Jeeves struggled to disentangle himself from her stiff embrace. He noticed Kala and Chandra watching him from the porch. Finally he wriggled free and ran across the road.

"What she wanted?" Kala asked suspiciously.

"Nothing. She wanted to know if Pappy does beat Mammy."

"She too damn fast." She looked at him suspiciously. "What you tell her?"

"Nothing. That I don't know."

"Don't tell anybody about this. Especially Mammy. And if Auntie Radhica ask you any questions again, don't answer. Is none of her damn business."

"So is true then?"

"What?"

"What she ask?"

"You stupid or something?"

"But he does get vex all the time for nothing. And he make you clean up the whole floor."

"He was just in a bad mood."

"Because of the factory? My friend in school does talk about him and the factory. He say Pappy strong and brave and different from the other village people."

"He say that?" She bit her lower lip. "Okay, you could talk to this friend. But not to Auntie Radhica."

Jeeves took Kala's advice, but he noticed that Quashie was now avoiding him. He no longer talked about Narpat or the factory, and whenever Jeeves raised the subject, his friend would grow uncomfortable and make some excuse to leave. At first he said he couldn't waste time because the Common Entrance was just five months away; then he mentioned his cricket and football matches; and finally he cited Carnival, just one week away. And Quashie was not being totally evasive, because soon the class was deluged with extra lessons and homework. Jeeves now spent most of the evenings puzzling over mysterious formulae and dates and intricate vocabulary exercises. His mother supervised his work, but occasionally she would call Sushilla to take over. All of this was very frustrating to Jeeves, and although he enjoyed the glasses of eggnog and orange juice, he missed his freedom. When he was barred from watching television, he protested and stomped his feet but eventually gave in. One day at school he told Quashie, "I fed up with this blasted exam."

"Then why you don't go and build some damn factory with your father? All that big plan and no money to finish it. Why he don't go to Barclay's and borrow money like everybody else? Go with your father, man."

Jeeves was astonished, but he managed to say, "I thinking about doing exactly that. And this weekend we going to a Carnival show."

"I don't believe you."

"Believe what you want, man."

For the entire weekend, Narpat railed against the island's penchant for fetes and limes. His children were uncertain whether this concentrated fury was because of the heavy rains that had forced him from the field, or because of the villagers who were swarming to the rumshops, or because of some unspecified problem with his factory. Dulari walked around the house with a worried look before she sent them to the Brahmin, from where they peeped out whenever they heard their father quarreling.

The Brahmin smoked and read as if he were immune to the shouting, but his wife examined her visitors' faces one by one, hoping for some confession. On the Sunday night prior to the two days of celebration, while the calypso competitions and the Dimanche Gras were taking place in the towns, Narpat walked out of his house and headed for the road. Jeeves, who was sitting on the junkpile, thinking of the Carnival stories told by Quashie, asked, "Where you going, Pappy?"

"To the Scale."

"I could come?" Since Narpat did not reply, the boy followed him. "Why we not going on the tractor?"

"I need some fresh air to clear out my head."

"From what?" Once more Narpat did not answer, and Jeeves walked faster to keep up with him. In twenty minutes he was breathless. Only when they heard the distant drums did the old man slow. "What is that?"

"We will find out in a little while."

The drumming grew louder, the rhythm loose and sustained, different from the familiar tassa beat. A circle of flambeaus illuminated the weighing area where the tractors and bull carts lined up. The flambeaus were held aloft by men swaying in a slow circular dance. They seemed consumed by some spectacle in their midst. Then Jeeves heard a low unfamiliar chant and felt a thrill of excitement at its strangeness.

"This is what happen when you show weakness. The Outsiders take over. Feting in a place that sacred to every single farmer." He pushed past the men until he was in the inner rim of the circle.

Two men in the center of the circle, the *gayelle*, armed with taut solid

sticks, were dancing around each other. Suddenly one of the men lunged
forward with his poui *bois*. The blow was taken and returned. The drums'
tempo increased; the combatants seemed almost in thrall to their rhythm
as they danced and leaped and threw blows from all angles and directions. Unfamiliar aromas swum through the air, of sweat, and pudding
and souse from pitchoil drums. Jeeves was mesmerized. Then one of the
combatants, a barefooted, sinewy coco panyol unleashed a range of blows
so swiftly, his opponent was forced back. Whack! Whack! Jeeves squeezed
through the crowd until he was in front of his father and saw the wiry
man twisting his body like a snake, perhaps to frighten his opponent,
feinting and jabbing, transferring the bois's weight from one hand to the
other. The crowd, as if sensing drama, lowered their chants. Jeeves thought
of a medley of secrets relayed from man to man. He strained to hear the
words. They were saying "Beat the keg, boy," teasing and encouraging the
fighters, altering the fight into the sort of grand battle Jeeves had read of
in his schoolbooks. He jumped back against his father when the coco panyol threw three blows in quick succession, one at the head and two on the
shoulder of his opponent, each finding its mark. The coco panyol held his
bois loosely, relaxing only when the other man stumbled up and shook
himself like a dog, transforming his pain into play. The chanting ceased.
"Give Hangman a drink," someone shouted, gesturing to the victor. A flask
of Puncheon rum was passed to Hangman, still in the center of the gayelle.
He tipped back his head and stylishly tossed a drink into his mouth. He
wiped his lips, tossed the empty bottle into the crowd, and grinned.
"Okay, who next?" Jeeves felt his father's hand heavy on his shoulder.

A drunken young man was pushed into the circle by his friends.
Hangman played with him for a while before he unleashed a barrage of
blows. The young man dropped his bois and ran to his friends. He was
followed by much laughter and hooting. Two men followed, one lasting as
long as the young man, the other—defensive and cautious, as if he had
prepared for the fight—enduring for five minutes. Hangman was now
sweating profusely. After each victory he took a drink, collected the
money thrown into the gayelle, and grinned at the crowd.

"Take a rest, Hangman. Nobody want to deal with that bois of yours."
The crowd laughed.

"Is Spanish prayers that mount this bois," Hangman replied. "I have
enough magic to last 'bout three more fight." He held the bois above his

head and twisted and flexed. "What happen? It have no man left in this village? Allyou blood turn to lagoon water?" He spat and said with mock exasperation, "Look, look, gimme another drink."

"Hold back on that drink." When Narpat stepped forward and picked up the bois discarded by the young man, Hangman seemed surprised. His taunt was part of the play, the interaction with the spectators heightening the drama. He was tired and had not expected another competitor. Besides, he had never seen this man before. The stick fighters all knew each other, and after their battles in Tabaquite and Rio Claro, they drank together in old dirty rumshops. The man who was confronting him, who held his bois as he would a machete, seemed in his sixties, a good twenty years older than most stick fighters. And he was not dancing around. He seemed to be waiting. Hangman wondered at the magic with which he had armored himself. The crowd too was thrown off guard. The drumming slowed, the chanters lost their rhythm. Hangman circled Narpat, trying to read his immobility and wondering at his techniques and tricks. Narpat shifted from foot to foot and turned to meet Hangman's cautious circling. In an attempt to feel him out, Hangman flicked his bois with his wrist and caught Narpat on the face, but before he could aim another blow, the old man's stick cracked against his head. For a few minutes the fight continued in this fashion: Hangman circling, waiting for an opening, striking swiftly from his wrist, and recoiling to meet the counterblow. The chanters tried to gauge the rhythm of the fight, and the spectators who had congregated around the pudding and souse vendors now pushed into the audience. The crowd—the villagers' Outsiders—did not take sides; they encouraged both men, and when Narpat broke the rhythm of the fight with a solid blow to Hangman's waist, they cheered him on. Jeeves, constantly pushed aside by the spectators, watched the fight with disbelief. He thought of his father's talk of ancient tests and ceremonial sacrifices. His hand went to his mouth when his father took a glancing blow on his arm and another on his chest.

These ricocheting blows were supposed to soften his opponent, and Hangman couldn't understand why the old man's face was locked in a grim, almost ghastly grin. He tried to match his opponent's air of amused indifference. The bois swished the air, barely missing Hangman's head, and he cursed and leaped back. Now he retreated to the edge of the gayelle, attacking swiftly and retreating to the shadow. The crowd had seen this strategy before, and they knew the fight would soon be over. So they were shocked when Hangman, emerging from the darkness, was met with a blow to the abdomen and another to his waist that left him doubled over. Hangman began to fight from a distance, began to understand that his opponent's strength was his determination, not any special technique. He crouched and bounced away to the gayelle's edge until he saw the old man finally losing patience with the cat-and-mouse strategy. And the first blow of the fight that drew blood fell plumb on Narpat's forehead. Another blow cut open his mouth. After each blow Hangman retreated and prowled about in the shadow. Again and again his blows landed, and each time he waited, offering the opportunity for a graceful withdrawal. Someone in the crowd shouted, "Throw down your bois, old man. You last longer against Hangman than anybody else."

And that was the truth. Not since a duel with the well-known Lopez in Erin village had a fight lasted so long. Hangman was beginning to lose patience. He glanced at the crowd as if he expected their silence to signal to his opponent the battle should be ended. And when a solid blow landed once more on Narpat's head, the blood trickling over his eye, Hangman tossed his bois from hand to hand. For this he was rocked with a sturdy clap to his ear that drew his own blood. He grew relentless, as if he sensed there would only be one conclusion to the fight. He fought his frustration and his fatigue and his respect at the sight of the old man's swollen face and bloodied shirt.

Jeeves was horrified. He watched in a daze and when the crowd pleaded, he shouted hoarsely, "Come back, Pappy. Let us go home now." He wanted to run into the gayelle and pull away his father. A blow brought Narpat to his knees. He rose slowly, and another landed on the same spot. He lashed out blindly, not bothering with defense, and one of his wild chops caught Hangman on the side of his face and opened his cheek. Now, from the flailing, the other man spotted an opening and finally, leaping in the air and using all his strength, slammed his stick on Narpat's head, just above the temple. The seasoned men in the crowd gasped. Hangman uttered an old Spanish prayer. Narpat fell to his hands and knees, attempted to rise, and collapsed. Three men rushed to him. One called for rum, another for water. Jeeves wanted to go to his father, but his legs were heavy and leaden. He heard one of the men saying, "Oh god, boss, why you do this to youself?"

"You understand what I tell you about this fella, Kimbo? You understand now?"

Two of the men carried Narpat from the gayelle and laid him on the weigh bridge. They were followed by a solemn procession holding their flambeaus above their heads.

"Make a bed with some of that cane trash, Kimbo. This bridge too hard."

Kimbo scooped up the dried leaves and spread them over the bridge. They eased Narpat onto the rough bed. Kimbo produced a handkerchief and wiped the blood from Narpat's forehead. "Why, boss? Why?"

"It look like he might have a 'cussion."

"We should carry him to a doctor."

"Where the ass you will find a doctor this time of the night? And in Lengua too."

Advice was given freely: his head should be propped, his knees elevated, his arms crossed over his chest.

"Check his pulse," someone said.

"Where is that?"

"You know this old man, Kimbo?"

"Yes, yes, man. Me and Wonders and Ashton was working for him till the money run out. He is the factory fella."

"Oh, shit."

The crowd, mostly black men from the periphery of the village and coco panyols from Monkeytown and Moruga, had heard rumors of the factory. Now they gazed at him with renewed awe.

"You know where he living?"

Kimbo shook his head.

"He come alone?"

"I dunno."

A stocky bald man with walrus whiskers shouted, "Anybody know where this Indian fella living?"

Jeeves pushed through the crowd and knelt at his father's side. He passed his finger over the bumps and bruises and was surprised at their softness. Blood was trickling from his father's nose and ears. "He . . . still living?"

They gazed at the sobbing boy and at his father as if they had not thought of this before. Finally Kimbo said, "His chest still moving."

Hangman, somber and shaken, said, "Pour a few drop of rum in his mouth." The stocky man passed a bottle to Kimbo, who sprinkled a few drops into Narpat's slightly open mouth. His eyelids fluttered, and he tried to shift his head. "Easy, easy, boss."

"What he saying? He trying to say something?"

The crowd pressed forward

Kimbo bent over Narpat's face. "Something 'bout poison."

"He still in a state of shock," the stocky man said. "Better we get him to his home fast." He shouted, "Anybody have a car?" And to Jeeves, "Boy, you know the direction to your house?"

A little distance away, a car started.

"Make way, make way, everybody." Hangman and Kimbo lifted him. The crowd parted. Jeeves felt a hand on his shoulder. He turned and saw Quashie. "Come, boy. We carrying your father home," the stocky man said.

TWENTY-THREE

*D*uring the two days of Carnival in February, from the J'ouvert of Monday morning to the Las' Lap of Tuesday night, Narpat lay on the foam sinking in and out of consciousness. During public holidays doctors were unavailable, and Dulari tended to his cuts and bruises with iodine and rubbed his arms and legs with Bengue's Balsam. She fed him porridge and green tea and, when his eyes closed, spoke softly to him. On Ash Wednesday, when the tired revelers were flocking to the island's beaches, Huzaifa came and gazed at his friend reverentially. "Hear about it last night." He peered at Narpat. "It look like he trancing." After a few minutes he sensed the family's impatience. "Is better I go now. Let him trance for a while. I wonder what he thinking about."

During those three days away from school, Jeeves fled to the lathro, away from his sisters' accusatory looks and his mother's questions. He sat against a cocoa tree and gazed at the insects climbing along the vines. After a while the activity in the lathro blurred, the sounds of the birds and the crickets seeming to come from a distance, and Jeeves, his head against the trunk, saw his father refusing to buckle, laid on the bridge, brought home in a stranger's car, whispering incoherently about cane and his factory and the Outsiders. He saw the shock on his mother's face and the horror of his sisters. He saw the three strangers laying his father on the foam mattress and, in the room, the calendars on the wall, the raised varnish on the dresser, the floral pattern on the rumpled sheet.

When school reopened, Quashie came to him shyly and talked about the impending exam but did not mention the stick fight, and Jeeves wondered whether he had imagined his friend's presence in the crowd.

A week after the fight he returned home and heard his father, in a thin voice, reciting a poem, "The Burial of the Sea King." On the following days Narpat combined stanzas from other poems like "The Lost Doll," "The Sands o' Dee," and Sunday school hymns and *bhajans* he had previously mocked. The next night Jeeves bolted up and pressed his ear against the wall. His father was reciting, in the low mournful tone of the chanters, something about his factory. The boy rushed back to his fiber mattress when his mother emerged from the room to boil a pot of tea.

Each night he listened carefully, but though other poems and strange Hindi verses were sung, he heard nothing more of the factory. One afternoon Jeeves saw Narpat staggering around the house, his trousers so slack they had to be fastened with twine. On another evening he stumbled to the Pavilion and related a story about a family of birds. "During this terrible drought, a poor old father bird went out searching for food for his family. As he was flying over the edge of the forest, he notice a tree fullup with bright red and yellow fruits. But hiding in the branches was Mr. Nagee, a hungry snake waiting to swallow anything that come near. Mr. Nagee snatch the father bird and begin to coil around him tighter and tighter. 'Please spare my life,' the father bird begin to beg. 'I have a starving family waiting for me to return with something to eat.' 'That is not my problem,' Mr. Nagee tell him. 'I starving too.' 'If you let me go, I promise I will return to you. That way my family will get their food and you will get yours.' 'You think I stupid?' Mr. Nagee ask him. 'No sir, I think you very smart. And you have my word of honor I will return to this very spot.' Finally the snake say, 'If you don't come back before nightfall, I will come and gobble up your whole family.' And he allow the bird to take a plump pommecythere to his family. The father bird wait until the smallest baby bird had finished eating. Then he say, 'I better go and see if I could get some more food.' And he fly away to the edge of the forest, to Mr. Nagee, who was waiting for him."

Sometimes it would be a family of squirrels or lambs or fishes, but the story would always be the same: a father promising to return to his fate after taking food to his family. He gazed carefully at his children's faces, one by one, while he was relating his story. Sometimes his glance lingered on Jeeves. In other stories, he referred to his own father and to his uncle, confusing his children. One of his recurring stories was of a father on his deathbed apologizing to his two children about his illness and about not fulfilling his promises to them. At the end of this story, the father transferred his broken promise to his son and cautioned the boy, not yet twelve, about showing weakness. Many of his fables now were of pledges and covenants, but they were all sad and unsatisfactory: the covenants unfulfilled, the pledges broken. One night he brought out one of his yellow books. On the cover there was a mystical symbol and the name Rumi. Narpat read aloud, "'At the twilight, a moon appeared in the sky; then it landed on earth to look at me . . . That moon stole me and rushed back into the sky. I looked at myself. I did not see me anymore.'"

"Where you went?" Jeeves asked.

His father turned to his book and read silently, not answering his son.

Another afternoon he told Jeeves, "Run to Carnegie and bring all the books that start with A."

Jeeves rummaged through the shelves, wiping the sticky grease from his fingers. Kala stood at his side. "Here, take this."

A few hours later Narpat ordered his son to bring all the books beginning with B. By midafternoon the foam was an untidy mess of old classics and texts passed down from child to child, and tracts and booklets on sugar production and yellow powdery Hindi tomes. "You going to read all these books?" Jeeves asked him.

"Every single one. I not going to stop till I finish. And you going to help me."

"Me?"

"Yes. You going to help me. Now sit down here." Narpat propped a pillow against the wall and shifted into a sitting position. Sometimes he read just the first paragraph of a chapter, and at other times just the first line of a page. He created looping conjoined narratives that both confused and bored his son, who soon fell asleep. When he awoke, the room was dim, but his father, squinting and holding a book close to his eyes, was still reading. He glanced at his son. "Later I going to test you on all this, so pay careful attention."

"But I can't understand Hindi."

"Is the same as English. The same root. Sanskrit. If you close your eye and concentrate, it will sound the same." He rattled off a complex Hindi paragraph. "You see? Exactly the same." When the boy got up and went by the light switch, his father shouted, "Leave it off. It will strengthen all the blood vessels in the eyes so that after a while you could see in the pitch black."

"Really?" Jeeves grabbed the diversion. "So what it have underneath the bed then?"

His father closed the book. "One dead rat, a fat crappo, a nest of cockroach, and a nasty bat. You want to peep and see?" Jeeves shook his head. "And outside it have insects with hundred of eyes watching each other, and a night bird that nobody see before, and a snake hanging from branches and swinging from side to side." He thought for a moment. "And four men with machete tiptoeing through the lathro. Outsiders."

"Where they going?"

"Nowhere. They just waiting."

"For what?"

"For something to happen."

"Maybe they will get fed up and go home."

But his father did not reply. Jeeves looked at his closed eyes and sneaked out of the room. "What Pappy was telling you?" Chandra asked.

"'Bout four men tiptoeing outside."

"Close the louvers now," Dulari said. She herself locked the back door. When she returned, she told Jeeves, "You don't have any studies for your exams?"

"I too tired."

"Tired doing what?"

"Listening to Pappy."

She exhaled. "Then go to sleep. All of allyou."

The next day's routine was similar. Narpat lay on the foam for the entire morning, reading to an increasingly frustrated Jeeves, who wondered how long this new hobby was going to last. He was briefly interested when he was asked to fetch the *National Geographic* magazines, but instead of focusing on the pictures, Narpat spoke of fertile lands converted into cities and farmers forced into starvation.

Jeeves tried to steer him to the animals and the snow-capped mountains and the erupting volcanoes and the horrible microscopic creatures with fearsome mandibles and pincers. "These things look real bad and dangerous. They might eat up everything on the way." His father punched the air, snapping his fingers. Suddenly his hand closed into a fist. "What you have in there?" Jeeves recalled the games they had played years ago. "I could see it?"

Narpat raised one finger and peered inside. "It sleeping."

"How you know that?"

"Listen carefully, and you will hear it snoring." He placed his palm against his son's ear.

Jeeves warmed to the game. "It making a funny sound. Like a baby bird."

"Yes, yes. You really hearing it."

"I think it trying to escape."

His father asked him seriously, "You really think so?"

Jeeves nodded. "It want to go back to it family."

Narpat glanced around. "You might be right. I think I spot a few of the family flying around and looking for the father."

Jeeves giggled. "Let it go then."

Narpat slapped his hand against his chest. "No. It hiding from them. You hear how quiet it keeping. Not a sound."

"Why it hiding from them?"

"Shh. It don't want them to find it."

After a while the boy repeated the question.

"Because it going to change into something else. Another bug," he whispered. "A *katimal*. It don't want to frighten them."

"Frighten them because it so ugly?"

"No. Not that."

"Why then?"

"Because it have to die first to change into something better." He wriggled his fingers. "I think it beginning to change."

"Is true. I think it getting bigger." Jeeves chortled. "Careful or it will bite you."

Narpat flung out his hand, shaking his fingers.

Jeeves laughed.

"Get away from the mattress fast." He pushed his son off the foam, rolled up a *National Geographic*, and slapped the wall and the foam. "It getting away. Oh, god." His family ran into the room. "Get out from here. All of allyou. Run away fast." His daughters' horror was muted by Jeeves's laughter. "It growing bigger." He lashed his body with the magazine. Spittle caught in his beard.

"Jeeves, come here this very minute."

The boy could not understand his mother's concern.

"Now!"

"Oh, god. Bigger, bigger—"

"Jeeves!"

"Open the louvers fast. Hurry!"

As Jeeves moved to the louvers, his father dashed to the door, knocking down the boy. He bent down, grabbed his son's collar, and dragged him from the room. "Close the door fast."

When Narpat released his son and went to the porch, stooping and crouching and peeping through the railing, Dulari shouted, "Jeeves, come here now." She pulled him into the kitchen. "Every time you and your father alone, something bad does happen." She flogged him with a controlled energy, as if she were calculating the energy expended with each blow, pacing herself so she would not tire. "You will eat up this whole family with your blightness. Destroy every single one of us." She looked at him in horror. "You is a snake. I minding a little snake in this house."

During the month before his exam, while his father recovered sufficiently to complain about the food's taste, Jeeves thought of his mother's accusation. He pushed aside the bowls of porridge, and whenever she sat by the table, he took his books to the porch. And when the results of the exam were published in *The Guardian* and his name was not in the list of successful students, his mother, who normally would have flogged him for his failure, went to her sewing machine and oiled and adjusted the knobs and levers.

The other failures were not as fortunate. Those whose parents had feted the teachers and had boasted in the rumshops about their children's marked improvement were flogged remorselessly. Some of the parents carried their frustration into the school, cursing and threatening. The Manager noted these altercations from his gallery, and although he amiably greeted the disconsolate, furious parents and even offered an obligatory defense of the school, he could barely contain his glee. He had not been so energized since Kamini had deserted him.

On the last day of school a function was held to honor the successful students. Quashie, who had passed for Fyzabad Composite, came up to Jeeves. "I going to get a transfer to a school in Laventille. What about you?"

"I don't know."

"You will help your father with the factory?" When Jeeves did not reply, he said, "My stepfather and uncle was helping him build it."

Jeeves was surprised. Quashie pushed his hands into his pockets and stared at the couteyah's dome, and Jeeves felt that his friend was divesting himself of the village and preparing for his new life in the town. He felt sad at the loss of this friend who knew his future. "See you later, man. And take care of your father." Quashie walked away.

While Jeeves was walking home, he thought of the successful students' excitement during the function, of Quashie's revelation, and about his mother's accusation. Perhaps she was right; it would be best if he avoided his father.

Seven weeks into the holiday, during the brief *petite carême*, when the dry season was broken by a week of thunderstorms, he was poking about in the lathro, avoiding his mother and his sisters. When he arrived home, a persistent drizzle had soaked his clothes. His father was chatting with Huzaifa on the porch. Jeeves sprinted up the steps.

"Take off your shoes and put it on the step," his father told him.

"In the rain?"

"Rainwater is the purest thing on the face of the earth."

Huzaifa nodded. He placed his fingers against his mouth and emitted a small nibbling giggle as Narpat got up from his chair, took three long strides, and spread his arms. Water sprinkled down his bare chest and drenched his pajamas. He closed his eyes and stood still like a scarecrow. Normally Jeeves would have laughed at the spectacle, but his memory of the last few months warned him that this display could lead to some unexpected drama. He hurried inside, puzzled by Huzaifa's amusement.

He usually remained in the bedroom until either Sushilla or Kala returned from school, and then he was chased off, but he heard his father talking loudly. He sprinted to the kitchen, opened the window, threw his clothes into the tub, and ran to the porch. His father was now dancing outside and reciting, "Long ago people used to celebrate the first rainfall of the season by celebrating and preparing a big feast." He noticed Jeeves lurking around the living room and shouted, "Go and tell your mother, boy. Tell her to prepare a big feast and invite the whole village. Milk and honey and the finest grains. Fruits of all size and shape. Pears. Apricots. Dates. Sapodillas. Plums. Mangoes. Soursops. Pommecythere." Huzaifa cackled after each fruit named.

The rain ebbed, then strengthened, blowing into the porch. The winds tossed the branches of the mango tree. Sushilla came home, fol-

lowed a few minutes later by Kala. Both were drenched, and when Kala
saw her father dancing farther away from the house, she said, "Come inside, Pappy. You will catch a bad cold. You not well as yet. Your head injury still—"

"Catch a cold? Where it? Tell me fast?"

Huzaifa's laughter was cut short by a rumbling burst of thunder.

"Careful of the lightning, Pappy. Where you going?" Kala followed him.

"Going to inspect the moat. Make sure it filling up properly."

Lightning lit up the sky, and Kala covered her face with her hands.
When she looked again, her father was at the drain's bank staring down at
the swirling muddy water. "The wind will—" But she didn't complete her
warning because Narpat turned to her and, in the same motion, slipped
and fell backward. His hands spun in the air as if trying to clutch something, and he disappeared into the water. Kala dove in after him. Jeeves
ran after her and tried to brake, but in the slippery mud his momentum
sent him headfirst into the hole. His face brushed a mud-filled can at the
bottom. A tangle of wet, clinging weeds wrapped around his neck. The
weeds, soft and squirming, seemed alive. He opened his mouth to scream
and swallowed the acrid water. He felt something grab his legs. He tried
to scream again, but now, propelled to the surface, he gulped in a lungful
of air. He was slammed onto his back on the muddy bank. He saw Huzaifa and Sushilla above him, and when he raised his head, he spotted his
mother on her knees, clutching Kala's hand as the girl climbed out of the
drain. Narpat was behind her, pushing. Kala tumbled onto the bank but
got up immediately. "Pappy."

There were clumps of mud on his shoulders and chest and a crown of
dripping water grass on his head. His beard was brown and stiff with silt.
"Okay, everybody inside. The inspection complete. The moat working
properly." He seemed to be smiling.

"Complete, complete! This is the second time." Dulari placed her
arms around Kala's waist. "The second time." Her husband raised his
hands and shook off the mud. His pajamas slipped down. The hair beneath his waist was matted with mud. "Oh god, man. Oh god."

"Don't call god name in vain, woman."

"Kala and Sushilla, get inside right now."

"I was born naked, and I will die naked." Huzaifa laughed as if Narpat
had said something funny. "Is only people who have nonsense in their

head does feel ashamed of the body." But he bent down and pulled his pajama, drawing it up to his chest. Huzaifa pressed his hands against his mouth.

"Look at you. Look at how everybody laughing at you."

"The first principle in life is to never care what other people think. Gossip and slander is like ballast drawing you down to the bottom."

She glanced at Radhica staring from her gallery. "That is why you making the whole family shame? Dragging us down, one by one with your madness. One crazy idea after the next since I know you. While everybody else progressing, you still living in all your useless dream. Everybody laughing at your foolishness. Your uselessness." Her voice was softer now as if she were ashamed of this public argument. "Getting in fight like a ordinary peong. I don't know what you trying to prove."

"You don't know? Then get out. Get out right now. Everybody." He raised a hand and pointed to the road. "Now!" Dulari pulled her children toward the house. "Go somewhere you wouldn't be ashamed. Go somewhere else and live like a hypocrite. I will survive. I was born alone and will die alone. I don't need anybody. Get out." He was still outside screaming when Chandra came home, when Dulari packed away her children's clothes in the cardboard suitcase, when Huzaifa decided he had had enough. But Narpat was not finished. He barged into the house. "Allyou still here? Eh?" He raised the table off its leg and smashed it against the wall. Then he toppled Dulari's sewing machine, the drawers slamming open and bobbins of thread and bits of cloth spilling out. On the other side of the wall, dishes loosened from their nails crashed to the floor.

Jeeves had never seen his father like this. Usually the violence came and went quickly, but now his father's fury seemed uncontrollable. Narpat ran to the bookcase and began pulling off the books and throwing them at his family. A hardcover edition of *Lorna Doone* whizzed by his head, and his mother pulled him into the room where Sushilla was cowering on the bed. Kala tried to restrain her father, but he threw her off. She fell on the couch. Chandra pulled her to the porch. They fled across the road. Jeeves and Sushilla and their mother ran through the back door. Behind them was more screaming, more crashing. The lights went off, one by one, but the screaming continued.

From the road Jeeves saw the house dark and desolate; but for the shouting it could have been abandoned. He saw the Brahmin emerging from his flower garden, smoking, his face reposed, his manner suggesting a man at peace; and his wife offering sympathy and concern but annoyed at her husband's offer of his car. He saw his mother and sisters hurrying to the vehicle. And Dulari calling out to him while Kala held the door open. "Jeeves! Hurry up."

"Jeeves!" Chandra was screaming.

"Leave the boy." He heard his father's voice but could not see him.

Jeeves listened to Sushilla and his mother calling from the car, their voices seeming far away.

"Leave him here. He staying." Other words were shouted in Hindi, the unfamiliar cadence seeming to thicken the resonant anger.

He saw Radhica watching from the gallery and shouting to Ray. The car inching forward. His mother looking out of the window. Chandra still screaming. He wanted to run out of the yard, but his feet felt rooted like in a dream many years past when a huille was slithering ponderously up to him and he couldn't move. He was still frozen when the car slowly disappeared

"Come, boy."

He pretended he had not heard, but the command was shouted louder.

Narpat was sitting on the Pavilion, staring at the ground. Around him were the overturned chairs and the machine, a tangle of threads hanging from the drawer like entrails. His father did not look up, and Jeeves fled into the kitchen. He picked up the cups and plates and gingerly replaced them on the nails. From the other side of the wall, he heard, "The story end, the wire bend . . ."

TWENTY-FOUR

𝒯hat night for the first time in seven years he slept in his sisters'
room, and in the faint fluorescent lamp he saw their clothes strung
along an iron tubing, and on the dresser brushes, combs, and bowclips. As he tossed about on the bed, he remembered when his mother
had draped an old plastic tablecloth beneath the sheet and Chandra's annoyance at his thumbsucking and his clapping of mosquitoes. He wondered where they were sleeping, all of them. He was sure Sushilla was
crying and Kala was attempting to console his mother. But maybe Bhola
had taken them to Royal Castle or to his cinema.

During the entire journey to her brother's place, Dulari had gazed out of
the car while Ray whistled a Hindi movie song and tapped the steering.

When they approached the town, Ray had turned down the volume
and asked, "Lothians road, you say, Auntie?"

"What you say, son?"

"Is a big house on the hill opposite the cinema," Chandra told him.

"Yes, I think I know it. It does have a Leyland park up in the garage
sometimes." He offered an explanation. "I does pass there on the way to
the cinema."

"Yes, son. They own the cinema."

"You want me to drop any message . . . any message back home?"

The offer was simply a reflex of his sudden importance, but Dulari
didn't know what to say. "Come and tell me if anything happen to Jeeves.
Don't forget." Her daughters now wondered whether they would ever return.

"Okay, everybody, we reach." Ray got out of the car first. Dulari hugged him, and he stiffened in embarrassment. Kala raised the iron clasp on the gate and banged it down. A German shepherd ran out barking from the darkness. The dog snarled and raised a paw against the gate. Ray came up and snapped a finger playfully at the dog but recoiled swiftly when the animal tried to push its snout through the iron railing. "I don't think is a pure Alsatian. Look like it have some pothound in it."

Voices drifted from the house, and the children recognized Bhola's high-pitched singsong voice. "Who the ass is that at this time of the night?" Then he appeared on the porch, his smooth belly glistening in the dim light. Behind him the curtain shifted. When he spotted the family, he bellowed, "Ay-ay, is allyou," as if he were expecting them all along. "Let me tie Napoleon before he bite out somebody foot." He laughed, the sound blending with the clap of his rubber slippers as he came down the stairs.

During the previous visit the family had been herded into an upstairs room; now they were taken downstairs by an unsmiling Babsy to a small cubicle beside the garage.

The walls were painted in an evanescent blue, which had peeled off in miniature butterfly wings at the ends of the cracked boards and around the nail dents, making the room gloomy and austere. The furniture—two chairs, a deeply varnished stumpy table, and an old sofa that might have been a bus seat—was piled in the corner, beneath a cobwebby narrow ledge that ran along the length of the room. On the ledge were three pennies and a cent stuck in a turpentine deposit. A few insects had also been trapped by the residue, and they were preserved like polished mummies. At the opposite end was a stack of old dusty cardboard boxes, arranged to form a squat table. A bed was set in the center of the room, and when Dulari straightened the sheet with a sudden flap, a cloud of dust rose to her face. She replaced the sheets, tucking the ends beneath a two-inch foam mattress. The bed, she saw, was another box. In the night, the sharp odor of diesel and burnt oil seeped through the cracks on the wall. While Dulari was unrolling a fiber mattress on the floor, she worried about how her son was managing.

Early the next morning Narpat awakened his son. "Never sleep past sunrise, otherwise the organs will operate only at half throttle." The boy rubbed his eyes and pondered whether the events of the previous day had been a dream. "When you change your clothes, I want you to run down to Hakim and get two sardine sandwich and something to drink." Jeeves took the shilling and escaped from the house. After his purchase of the sandwiches and two bottles of grapefruit juice, he considered lingering at the parlor but guessed this would further aggravate his father, so reluctantly he headed back to the house. His father was waiting on the porch, and Jeeves gave him the paper bag. "Come with me." Jeeves followed him to the table. "Bring a plate." The boy watched as Narpat opened a sandwich and spilled its contents onto the plate. He wanted to ask his father what he was looking for but decided to remain silent.

"One piece of rotten onion." He placed it aside and continued probing. "A different sorta meat here. Most likely sea snake. The machine does grind up every single thing. A slice of beef too. This tell me that Hakim does use the same utensil for everything. And right here . . ." He extracted a small globular piece of meat. Jeeves leaned forward, some of his trepidation of the previous day evaporating. "A cockroach egg." Narpat pushed aside the plate and took the two bottles of juice to the window. When he placed them on the ledge, the sunlight illumined the contents, and Jeeves saw the sediments swimming at the bottom. "Sugar water. The perfect poison. Okay, start eating." Jeeves gazed at the meal in consternation until his father began to laugh. Later he heard his father still chuckling in his bedroom.

He ran outside to the junkpile, but within half an hour, driven by hunger, he returned gingerly to the house. The sandwiches were gone. He poked around in the garbage bin and concluded his father had thrown them away in the back garden. In the fridge were two huge plastic containers with rice pelau. He ate greedily. For the rest of the day he wandered in and out of the house trying to avoid his father, but in the late evening Narpat summoned him to the Pavilion. "Go to the porch and tell me what the Brahmin doing."

Jeeves peeped from the front door. "He in the garden."

"I didn't ask you that. Tell me what he doing there."

"He walking among the flowers."

"Anything else?"

"He picking some of the flowers. And either smelling them or eating them."

"Eating! Eating! That is what he doing. Munching the flowers like a goat. Tonight if you listen carefully, you will hear him baa-ing at top speed." Jeeves wanted to laugh, but the memory of the previous evening was still fresh in his mind. "What you eat today? Some flowers too?"

"Pelau from the fridge."

"Good. It have enough to last for four days at two meals per day. Now go and eat."

The next morning Narpat gave him a shilling once more. "Buy a different type of meal today. And a copy of *The Guardian*." Jeeves returned with the newspaper and a brown paper bag with phoolories. His father spread the saffron balls on the table. Jeeves looked on interestedly; he had chosen this delicacy because it seemed impervious to cockroach eggs and rotting onions. "What wrong with this meal you bring back here?"

"It mightn't be enough," he volunteered.

"That is an advantage. Now look carefully." Narpat reached for a phoolorie, closed his fingers around it, and squeezed. A drop of oil fell onto the table. "The perfect grease for axle. For oiling *poinyants* and machetes. Could work in the Farmall too. Take it outside and throw it in the engine." His father flicked open the newspaper and left the boy puzzled.

Later in the day he noticed Radhica staring at him from the gallery. She called, "Beta," and gestured to him. When he went across, she said sternly, "This time you remain with him. You eat?"

He nodded. "Mammy leave food in the fridge."

"She leave food behind?" Her eyelids narrowed. "She was expecting to leave then?"

"She always leave food."

"When they coming back?"

"I . . ." He remembered Kala's caution about revealing too much to Radhica, but the woman misunderstood and hugged him tightly.

"Don't worry, beta. You poowa understand. Is a whole ton of worries on top of you little head. Wouldn't surprise me if you go mad too in a little while. Better you stay and watch some television." Jeeves had never come across this early, and that evening he watched serials like *Ivanhoe* and *Robin Hood*.

During that week he was awakened by his father each morning and sent to Hakim for a meal and a copy of *The Guardian*. He brought home cheese sandwiches and doubles and potato pies and *sohina*, a blend of

split peas and spinach. While Narpat was dissecting the meals, the boy
wondered at the waste of a shilling each day and concluded that his father was attempting to teach him about toxins and diseases.

In the late afternoons Jeeves went across to the Brahmin and watched
the serials. He realized that a melancholy silence to Radhica's prying usually made her sympathetic and ended the questioning. Occasionally she
conversed in a low voice with her husband, and Jeeves wondered whether
they were discussing his family. One evening he saw Radhica in the
kitchen applying dye to her husband's hair with a toothbrush. A towel was
strung on her shoulder, and she carefully and tenderly wiped away the
residue rolling down his neck. He was surprised at the couple's intimacy.
Jag was rarely around in the day, and whenever Ray returned from his
work, he'd eat and disappear. Jeeves noticed that he avoided his parents,
and once when Radhica and the Brahmin were in the garden, Ray sat
next to the boy in the couch and Jeeves smelled a strange aromatic fragrance. "You sister send this." Ray held out a dollar.

"Who?"

"Chandra. I meet her in the town. You better take it, or I will shub it
back in my pocket." Jeeves wanted to ask him about his sister, but Ray
rushed out of the house.

At night when the boy returned, his father would be on the Pavilion,
lost in his drawing and designing. Sometimes Narpat would hear the footsteps and without looking up would say, "You ever notice that the sky
always have a speck of cloud?" or "You ever pay attention to how the crickets outside sounding as if they clicking out a Morse code?" One rainy
night Jeeves saw him on the porch looking at the water tumbling from the
aluminum roofing onto his tractor. "You ever realize that anything that rest
too long does become useless?"

The next morning Jeeves met his classmate Balack in Hakim's parlor.
The other boy asked why he had not returned to school. Jeeves had completely forgotten about the reopening of school, but he said that he had
been helping his father. He repeated this excuse the following day to the
other boys in standard six, but there was no need because in this class
were placed the Common Entrance failures. Ignored by the teachers,
these thirteen-year-old students idled there until their parents plucked
them out for the field, a trade, or if they were lucky, a private school.
There were eleven students this year, and their only instruction was when

the Headmaster strolled by with a copy of either *The Students Compan-ion* or *Words at Work* and, following a confusing lecture about character, wrote on the board some adage. Since attendance was not taken, most of the boys left after the morning recess and loitered in the playground. One midday, following a brief stint in class and another at Hakim's, Jeeves spotted his father on the porch staring at the Brahmin. "Where you disappearing to these days, boy?"

"I went to school."

"Why? You already fail your exam." He gazed at his son. "I never write any exam, you know. Too busy making a living." He leaned over the railing. "Come here, let me tell you a little story." Jeeves sat forward on a chair and watched his father's loose merino flapping against the railing's bar. "In a jungle far-far away, there was a proud fox living with other animals. One evening Mr. Fox get his foot hook up in a trap while he was hunting. He was beginning to panic because he know that with nightfall the hunter would come to check his traps. But just at that time, Miss Fox pass by and hear him bawling. She return with a stick and unclasp the trap and lead away the limping animal. During the next few days she massage his injure leg with all sorta herbs that grow in the jungle until he get just as new. But Mr. Fox was a vain fella and he soon start boasting about how brave he was to endure the pain of the trap and how quickly he recover and how smart he was. Miss Fox continue living with him even though she was getting fed up of all his boasting. In two years they had two little baby fox. And all this time"—he bunched his finger and made a puppet—"pok pok pok."

Jeeves laughed.

"One night Mr. Fox return to the cave in a panic. When his wife ask him why he was so frighten, he tell her that a lion was heading their way. 'What we will do?' he begin to bawl. 'He will gobble up all of us.' 'But you so brave and smart. I sure you will find a way. Not so?' She smile as she went to the oldest of the children and begin to beat him up. 'What you doing?' Mr. Fox ask. But she just continue beating the child and then she turn to other one. 'No lion meat for allyou tonight,' she begin to shout loud-loud. 'Where you expect me to find a lion tonight?' She gone mad, Mr. Fox thought, but outside the cave the lion was listening carefully to the commotion. And when Miss Fox scream out, 'All right, I going to see if I could find a lion,' the fella outside take off like a bullet. 'They ain't going to eat me,' he say as he run like mad to the other side of the jungle. 'Not me and them damn crazy fox again.' And he never ever bother them again." Narpat glanced at the Brahmin in his lotus-shaped chair and smiled grimly. "Nothing could ever beat common sense. Always remember that. Is simple common sense that give me the idea of the factory and simple common sense that going to send me back to finish it. First, though, I have to build a shed for the Farmall. All that rain will seize up the engine."

But the story had reminded Jeeves of his mother, and that night in bed he speculated about when she might return with his sisters.

Each morning Dulari, aware of the imposition on Bhola's family, swept the house, dusted the furniture and the pictures on the wall, washed the wares, and cooked. In the evening when Chandra returned from her work and Kala and Sushilla from school, she listened to their complaints in the little room before she took them for a stroll in the town. And momentarily she would brighten up as she walked through the Syrian and Indian stores and fingered the fine cotton and silk bales or when they went into Woolworth and she gazed at the silver bracelets and the delicate necklaces in their glass cases.

Following her trip she would go immediately to the kitchen to scour and scrub. When Bhola returned, he would say in his singsong voice, "Take it easy. Take it easy. It don't have no fussy husband around here, you know." Both Babsy and her daughter would exchange glances when Dulari was spooning out their food or when she was chatting with her brother. In the nights she would listen to Sushilla coughing and rise from the mattress on the ground where she slept with Chandra and pat her daughter's back until the coughing stopped.

One night she heard Kala, next to Sushilla, grumbling, "I can't take this no more."

"Shh." She stroked her daughter's head until the girl was asleep.

The next evening when they were in Woolworth, Kala said, "Four of us pack away in that little room like criminals while Lady Lalloo and Princess Lalloo sleeping upstairs in their throne. And the minute we get back there Sushilla will begin to cough. She getting asthma from all that dust." Dulari said nothing because she knew that her daughter was right.

"I going back," Kala said suddenly.

"Going back to what, Kala?" She was staring intently at a brooch with tiny butterfly wings.

"To my own house."

"Here nearer to your school and to my job," Chandra said.

Kala glared at her but said nothing.

Sometimes the girls noticed their mother talking to Bhola, and they wondered whether she was making arrangements for their permanent stay. Some nights Kala thought of leaving a note in the room stating she had returned to Lengua, and at other times she considered taking Sushilla with her. She got into hushed squabbles with Chandra, and Dulari would say, "I will always be surrounded by quarreling. I will never escape from it." The sisters would look at their mother's disheartened face and retreat to the corners of the cramped room, sulking and determined never to speak to each other again. But one afternoon Chandra returned early from her work crying out to Kala and her mother. Kala was not yet at home, and the girl rushed up the stairs. "A message. A message from Ray." She was breathless.

Her mother carefully draped the saphee on the railing and stared at her daughter's frightened face before she asked, "What happen?"

"Pappy."

Dulari slowly dusted the flour from her hands, pushed a streak of hair behind her ear, and sat. "What happen to him?"

"We have to go back now."

"Stop crying and tell me what happen."

"I not sure. A accident. We have to go back."

The accident had happened in the shed Narpat was building for his tractor. He was nailing a corrugated aluminum sheet onto a wooden canopy attached to four iron posts when he fell face first, his chest crashing against the steering column and his feet slamming against the metal seat. When he tried to lever his body into a sitting position, his leg would not move. A lancing pain shot through his chest. He squirmed and pushed until he was able to swivel onto his back. He saw how narrowly he had missed being impaled on the exhaust. Blood was pouring from his nose, so he struggled to a sitting position, his back braced against the steering wheel. With both hands, he pulled his legs until he was able to undo the laces and slip off his boots. Blood was dripping from an awkwardly twisted ankle, and he knew it was broken. He pulled up the pants fold and saw a deep gash on his calf, almost to the bone. When he tried to straighten the leg, the pain was so sharp that he clenched his teeth and pitched back against the steering. He remained in that position for about fifteen minutes, but he was weakening from the loss of blood, so he grasped the seat and forced his body forward. With both hands pressed against the seat, he swung his injured leg onto the tractor's running board, but as he transferred his weight, the leg crumpled and he fell onto the spiked gravel. The pain slammed into his chest, radiated to his back and shoulders, and briefly ebbed into a raw numbness before it returned to hammer his body. Inch by inch he crawled and dragged to the front step. He heaved himself up the steps and struggled to the couch, where he laid his head and tried to shut off the pain. When Jeeves returned from school more than an hour after the accident, at first he thought his father was resting but then he saw the blood. He shook him, and Narpat said weakly, "Stop shaking me like that or you will drain out all my blood. Now make a tourniquet."

"What is that?"

"Get something to tie my foot. Hurry!" The boy glanced around and pulled a doily from beneath a vase. The vase tumbled onto the floor. He recoiled from the deep gash and the blood and the white flesh. "Tie it tighter."

"It . . . it still bleeding. I going to get something else." He tore down a curtain and stripped the sheer material. He wrapped the curtain around his father's leg and knotted the ends.

"Bring a pillow."

When Jeeves returned with the pillow, he said, "Put it below my foot." Jeeves stood over him, and Narpat closed his eyes. After a while he asked, "Where Mammy?"

"Mammy? She by Uncle Bhola. I thought you—"

"Okay, let me rest."

Jeeves stood by the couch until he heard Ray's car approaching. He ran across the road.

————

Throughout the entire journey back to Lengua, Dulari sat impassively in Ray's car, fighting her horror of what she would soon see: the house that had trapped her for close to forty years, the inevitable improvements to the building opposite, her husband recovering only to bring more trouble. When the car stopped before the house, she fought her rising concern for the man who, since she had known him, moved from one battle to the next. As she entered the house, she felt anger at having to return; anger at the sudden affection for the figure lying on the couch.

TWENTY-FIVE

*T*he anger remained with her throughout the night as she cleaned and bandaged her husband's injuries. The next morning she noticed her daughters' despair as they got dressed. A few hours later she was turned down by doctor after doctor in Princes Town. Janak was surprised to hear this quiet, shy-looking woman quarreling with such gusto. "Money-sucking leeches."

"I drive out a few of them. You would surprise to know how they does suck rum. It have nothing they could do that Doodoon can't do."

"He is another doctor?"

"Sort of." After a while he said, "He does make false teeth. Living just half a mile from me. You want to try him out?"

"Leeches, leeches."

When Doodoon emerged from his rickety office in his soiled coat, Dulari was too desperate to be skeptical. He was a short, chubby man with bushy hair jumbled around his ears. His open mouth and huge sunken eyes gave him the appearance of being perpetually surprised, but once he arrived at the house, he got busy and efficient. "Foot break."

"It will heal?" Dulari asked.

"Everything does heal. In it own way. If you give it time." He spoke in abrupt snaps.

"He cough up blood last night."

"Bad sign."

"What it mean?"

"Lung. Belly. Throat. Foot."

"You could fix him up?" Janak asked.

"Everything could fix up. If it want to fix up. It could go this way. Or that."

"So what you going to do?" Dulari asked.

"Plaster Paris. Have a lump somewhere in my office."

The next day he arrived with a bag of plaster of Paris, a basin, and a bent long-handle spoon. Narpat gazed dully as Doodoon mixed and stirred and applied the paste to a piece of gauze, which he wrapped around the injured ankle. But when he returned two days later to examine Narpat's chest, his patient, slightly more alert, told him, "Just a minor bruise."

"You will put a cast on it?" Dulari asked.

"Can't cast chest. Chest does breathe. Plaster does crack. My job finish."

"Mammy." Dulari went to Narpat. "Ask the doctor how much people he kill this year?" And when Doodoon had left in a huff, Narpat twisted his head on the pillow and grinned; and his wife wondered how he could so easily have forgotten that less than a month ago he had stormed through the house, pulling down the furniture and evicting his family. She avoided looking at him when she passed the couch on the way to the kitchen; tried to ignore his lighthearted banter too, until one morning she realized that though he spoke of the unfinished tent and his tractor soaking in the rain and the weeds sprouting in his field and his factory, he had not uttered a single word about his injury. She walked over to him and wiped away the scabs and the plaster residue from his foot. Her daughters sometimes came across this scene and retreated swiftly to their room, but Jeeves, forced once more to sleep on the fiber mattress, listened to his father saying that when his foot was healed and the cast removed, he would have to work harder than ever in the field. Maybe he would buy another tractor.

One week after the accident Huzaifa appeared with a walking stick. "Just hear the bulletin this morning. Ray tell Janak and Janak tell Poolchan and Poolchan tell Kumkaran. And the minute I hear the news, I see this walking stick looking at me from below the table." He tried to spin the stick like a baton twirler. "Was looking for it months and months. Never find it. Then braps! I see it looking at me from below the table." He thrust out his hands. "Good solid guava. Have it for years. Was a sentinel stick."

Narpat practiced walking in a little circle. He found that by slightly dragging the injured leg and half-hopping with the other, he was able to move from kitchen to porch. When his three daughters returned in the evening, he joked about the cast while he practiced: "Trip trap trip trap, went the hooves of the old Billy Goat Gruff as he tripped trapped over the wooden floor." As word of the accident spread, he was visited by several villagers who had not been impressed with his feats in the gayelle nor with his previous moodiness—mental problems were seen as self-indulgent— but who now offered genuine sympathy. Soogrim and Assevero and Premsingh and James each asked about the fall and each tapped the cast and contended Doodoon had done a splendid job. Kumkaran came too, sprouting cryptic religious epithets. "Man propose and god compose and woman oppose and animal dispose." Huzaifa became a regular fixture in the house and to each visitor he remarked on the walking stick that had miraculously appeared beneath the table. He was thrilled when Kumkaran referred to the stick as a staff. Narpat enjoyed the visits and all the attention. He asked Dulari to boil tea, and while the guests sipped slowly, he remarked that his swift recovery was due to his diet. "I flush out the toxins years ago." He tapped his chest. "Inside here is like a field of ice. Any germs that try to enter will get frozen instantly. And even if they get in, the general here"—he pointed to his head—"will outflank them. Out-think them."

During the mornings he got out a thick brown book titled *Virology* and read intently of diseases and remedies. He underlined and made notes at the sides of the pages.

He gave Chandra a list of topics: diseases, herbal remedies, nutrition, and virology. She joined the Princes Town library and returned with stacks of books. Sushilla brought simpler children's books from her school library. Narpat read and reread each, and frequently he would surprise his guest with a detailed history of some disease and its remedy. He told them of eugenics, which recommended sterilization or worse for the disabled, of leeches sucking away at the infirm, of bloodletting and colonic irrigation.

He instructed his daughters to borrow books on ancient poultices and elixirs, and was surprised at the practicality of the ancient remedies prescribed by the Chinese and those found in the ayurvedic texts. These prescriptions whetted his appetite for the ancient Aryans, and Huzaifa, the bestower of many of the health books, was disturbed by the reappearance of this old obsession. But Narpat now read his Vedic books as carefully as he had studied those on medicine. He contemplated the appropriation of Sanskrit symbols like the swastika and reflected on the debate about whether the Aryans had invaded India or were indigenous to the area. Every weekend he held lengthy discussions with Kala and was pleased to note her developing cynicism of ritual and tradition. "A ritual serve a time and a purpose, and once that time pass, the ritual get useless and dangerous. A man with seven or eight wife nowadays is just a vice. Facing a particular direction when praying is just stupidness. Making a set of noise with a conch shell is just inconsiderate. You know what is the biggest vice in the world? Superstition. Honey flowing out from picture. Milk springing out from stone. Angel flying all over the place. Every day people seeing spirit and ghost, Mammy."

"Why people still believe in these thing?" Jeeves asked seriously.

"Because they don't want to be smart."

"Why?"

Narpat answered quickly. "Because is a pain. The superstition just like this cast here. It preventing me from seeing the cut and the pus and the scab. The worm."

Kala told him, "You could open your own office right here, Pappy."

"Across the road from the Brahmin. One man selling magic, the next man selling science." He smiled, pleased with the image. He glanced at the Brahmin smoking and rocking gently and wondered why the pundit had not visited him nor offered a word of sympathy. *That man don't have peace in his mind,* he concluded. *He is a troubled man.* The notion strengthened him, and frequently he brought out his books to the porch, and with his cane against the railing, and the Brahmin singing and waving opposite, he read intently, paying attention to all he had previously ignored or trivialized. He read that the universe's origin was an act not of creation but of organization. Every single act of creation, of initiative, was a campaign against chaos. When he came across a passage from the *Bhagavad Gita,* he read aloud, his voice drifting across the road. "'No one can destroy this unchanging reality. It is not born; it does not die. Unborn, enduring, constant and primordial, it is not killed when the body is killed.'"

The Brahmin stopped his waving.

"'Every single thing is in a state of flux,'" Narpat repeated to his family. And in this mood he convinced himself that his infirmity, like his problems with the factory, his haze following the battle in the gayelle, and the Brahmin's successes were each a chaotic strand that would soon be organized into an understandable pattern. The world would synchronize itself. He just had to wait. One night he told his wife, "The real difference between the advanced mind and the savages is that one could see far in the future and the other could only see what going to happen tomorrow. All we have to do, Mammy, is to wait."

She paused in her rekindling of the fire before she threw in some fresh wood. Sparks scattered above the chulha and fell onto the pot of milk, blemishing the surface with gray dust. The following morning, while Narpat was chatting with Huzaifa and Soogrim, Jeeves asked her, "Pappy get back better now?"

"Only as long as he have these people here listening to him. Just wait till they get fed up and stop coming."

TWENTY-SIX

*T*wo years into her marriage, when she was just nineteen, Dulari's father had told her, "The man above know exactly how much weight we could bear, and he always make sure that he don't give us a pound extra. Now go back to your husband and try and live a good life." He was a small, quiet man who approached most problems with a disarming amiability. Dulari had been disappointed with his benign fatalism; now, so many years later, at a time when she was frustrated at how easily she had reverted to the position of dutiful wife, alarmed by the accumulation of debts to her brother, and worried about her daughters' futures, her dead father's advice seemed to bear fruit. Kala was awarded a government scholarship. Although she had not won the gold medal, she had earned one of the three open scholarships offered to the students with the highest advanced-level grades in the island. It was only the fourth time a student from the south had won a scholarship and a first for St. Stephen's. Her picture was plastered on page three of the *Trinidad Guardian*, Partap's son wrote a glowing tribute in the *Evening News*, and several teachers from the Lengua government school visited to offer their congratulations. Bhola visited too, with a new scientific calculator in a leather case, and while his family sulked behind him, he said, "Pick it up in Woolworth. All these damn numbers and buttons. I prefer my finger and toe. Using them since I small." Prutti muttered something about leaked exams and pouted her way to the car. Her mother followed her.

Suddenly Dulari began fussing once more about the meager furniture. She cut out the articles, framed and hung them on the wall, and read a line or two each time she walked across the living room. She began to talk of a new dining room set, a proper desk, a varnished bookcase, and a space saver to separate the living and dining rooms. She calculated size, position, and model for each piece of furniture. She hinted at these proposed renovations to Radhica. "I think is time we put up another room. Just a library with books and a desk and a table."

Radhica inhaled deeply. "Sometimes I does sorry we living in such a big-big house. Is a whole ton of headache to clean out these rooms. Time after time I tell Ray father we should have move to a smaller place, and time after time he tell me that this house is not for me or him or the children but for the chelas." A few days later she said, "Ray father does really get on my nerves, yes." She fingered her bracelet. "Whole night he inside this room he call a den writing his next book. Den-pen." Her lips formed a smile. But she could not sustain her mirth, because now Dulari refused to play the supporting role. Soon Radhica began shouting to her sons, "Ray, how much time I talk to you about knocking about in the car for no rhyme and reason? Jag, how much time I tell you that your father willing to teach you Hindi, if you find the time? To come a famous pundit and book writer just like him. He didn't win any scholarship, you know. He went through the proper channels."

One morning Dulari shocked her. "Leave the boys alone, sister. Education is not everything." Dulari had spoken sincerely, but Radhica was aghast. She stopped her roadside conversations. She shouted vulgar insults at her sons in the house. The Brahmin conducted his meditation farther afield, walking down the road, the cigarette smoke trailing after him.

"Why Auntie Radhica behaving so?" Sushilla asked her mother.

"Everybody have their own worries." She brightened up. "But it always go away."

Narpat's enthusiasm was more restrained, and when the visitors remarked on his daughter's achievement, he said, "We need people to work the land, not win scholarship." But later in the night Jeeves noticed him reading the articles Dulari had pasted on the wall. He murmured some of the phrases: "'The first student from the southern counties' . . . 'intelligent and beautiful' . . . 'daughter of a well-known cane farmer.'" Dulari, who had avoided him during the last month, now tried to engage him in conversation about Kala's accomplishment and about the area she should choose. One evening he said half-jocularly, "What she should study is how to properly treat broko foot people. Develop a cure for hop-and-drop in her university."

University. Such an important word. Following the visits from the village women, who had dropped in to offer their congratulations and complain about their own duncy-head children, Dulari would sneak up to one of her daughters and hug her and giggle mysteriously.

One evening Chandra returned from her work with a small white box that she placed on the table. Dulari opened the box, removed the crepe paper, withdrew a new flannel pajama, and walked into the bedroom. Fifteen minutes later Narpat emerged in the new pajama, followed by his wife. "Look what your mammy buy for me. A brand-new pajama. Good for hospital people and invalids." He placed his cane on the table and gripped the edge. "Where the ambulance? Anybody hearing it?" The children laughed uneasily.

In the evening Jeeves asked him, "Why you does read these thing on the wall all the time?"

"Is my walking I practicing." He grinned and limped to the window. "Listen."

Jeeves went to him. "To what?"

"If you listen carefully, it have music all around us. In the tree and field and the road. If you concentrate hard, you could hear the electricity humming through the wires. Even when it completely quiet, we carry the music here." He tapped his head.

"You hearing music now?" Jeeves asked.

"A whole orchestra."

From Chandra's expression, Jeeves gathered that his sister did not want him to pursue this conversation. He heard her whispering to Kala and Sushilla in the night, but when he approached, they grew silent. "Be careful," he said. "The wall have ears." But he was annoyed at their secretiveness. A few days later Chandra walked into the house, straining with a huge box. From its size, Jeeves knew it did not contain pajamas or shoes. He followed Chandra inside.

"What is this now?" Dulari asked with exaggerated amusement.

"Open it," Chandra told her.

"Who it is for?" Jeeves asked.

"For everybody," Chandra said.

Finally his mother undid all the staples and opened the cover. Jeeves peeped inside. "Is a gramophone."

"Careful, Jeeves," his mother cautioned. "These things have a lot of parts to spoil. Ay-ay, what is this here?"

"Speakers." Kala removed the speakers from their foam padding and plugged the cord into the player.

"And records too? How much you pay for this, girl?"

"Not much, Mammy. It was old stock in Pereira shop. And the records was free. They come with the player."

Dulari removed the records and laid them on the table. "What is this? Man-to-vani? Who is him?"

Everyone laughed.

"Orchestra blues. Goodness." She pressed her palms flat against her cheeks.

"You want to hear it?" Kala asked.

"Let me wash my hands first."

"Hurry up, Mammy," Jeeves shouted impatiently when, after five minutes, his mother was still in her room.

She emerged in a new dress, her hair combed, a smattering of powder on her cheeks. She dusted the couch, sat forward, and placed her hands on her lap. "Okay, play it now."

Kala slipped the head over the record, and the sound of violins and flutes and oboes and pianos floated from the speakers. Dulari closed her eyes and sat back. She imagined beautiful birds and crystal lakes and handsome men and women in strange costumes. Momentarily, her tiredness seemed to take wing and float away with the music into the air and out of the house.

Across the road the Brahmin strained to hear the song. He pulled up his feet onto his lotus-shaped chair and waved his hands like a conductor. Radhica broke the spell: "This was such a quiet place when we first move here." Not satisfied, she added, "I don't understand how some people could listen to music without any words. And foreign do-re-me-fa-so music, to boot." She glanced disapprovingly at her husband. "This is the sorta vice that could spread if you not careful." She harangued her sons into promises that their taste would not stray from Indian movie songs, as she gazed at Narpat hobbling from the back garden.

When Narpat came in from the kitchen, he stared at the gramophone. "What is this?"

"A gramophone."

"Is for you, Pappy," Chandra said.

"For me?" he asked testily.

"For you to listen to while your foot healing."

"You think this will heal my foot?"

"Don't argue, Pappy. Just listen to it." The other children were surprised at how boldly Kala had spoken to their father.

He limped to the Pavilion and gazed at his wife and children, one by one. He waited until the song was over. "Instead of listening to other people play music, we should learn to play it ourself. This is what wrong with people in this place. We good at follow-fashioning, but if anybody ask us to make up something on our own, we will bawl and run as fast as a horse. It easy to teach us tricks. To give us a idea to hold for a while. To play with."

The following day, he emerged from his room just before noon and turned on the gramophone. When the song ended, he replayed it. He did this each day before he got out his stack of drawings or his books on ayurvedic remedies. Chandra brought other records; old songs that were inexpensive because they were no longer popular. Nat King Cole. Jim Reeves. Doris Day.

Radhica continued her complaints about foreign music and extracted annoyed promises from her sons, but three weeks after the first burst of music from across the road, she bought a record player of her own and several LPs of pundits chanting the *Ramayana*.

"Superstition. Hocus-pocus. *Simi-dimi*," said Narpat.

Sometimes the children felt that their father's unexpected affection for these American singers was a kind of talisman, his own simi-dimi, protecting him from the hocus-pocus across the road. From listening to the songs so often, he memorized several verses, and occasionally he would sing aloud. Both Kala and Chandra encouraged him, and Sushilla sang along with him.

Jeeves was surprised at how well his two eldest sisters got along. He had imagined that Chandra would be offended at the attention thrown Kala's way since the scholarship, but she seemed as proud of her sister's achievement as everyone else. She grew serious when Kala asked her advice about the choice of university. Dulari frequently came from the kitchen and joined their conversations. She listened quietly before she added her own suggestion. She felt her daughter should opt for medicine or law and mentioned the packed Princes Town offices of several doctors and lawyers. She grew expansive and spoke knowledgeably about professions and salaries as if she had reflected on those issues all her life. In the reflective lulls, she explained that her marriage had taken place when educated women were seen as strange and threatening. Women were expected to stay at home and tend to their families. Sometimes she placed her arm on her eldest daughter's shoulder and said that even though things had improved, sacrifices were still necessary. She might have been speaking of herself or Chandra, and both women shook their heads with sadness and satisfaction.

When their father joined the conversations, Kala, perhaps remembering her father's aversion to doctors and lawyers, mentioned strange courses in philosophy and psychology and anthropology. Occasionally she surprised Jeeves with her knowledge of ancient Greeks and Romans and Aryans, and when he mentioned facts he had gleaned from the books in the meager school library, she explained that these myths, told from a Christian perspective, were not historically accurate. Jeeves was disappointed at this revelation, but Narpat always agreed with his daughter. "The people who win the war always get to tell the story."

"That is why they used to fight?"

Kala was about to reply, but Narpat said, "Exactly."

Usually Jeeves grew bored with the conversations and went outside, and when he returned after an hour or so, father and daughter were still chatting. Mostly they ignored him, or Kala spoke to him as to a child. He began staying the entire day at school and hung around at Hakim's parlor for an extra hour. One afternoon he heard Kala stating that she had set her sights on agriculture. Dulari told her daughter, "Is your choice," but questioned her repeatedly about job prospects. The next day she seemed more determined, more prepared. Agriculture was a trap. Farmers were backward and stubborn. They resisted advice. They felt they were always right. They operated by unflinching codes. Their children were wisely moving away from farming. When Kala explained that the proposed degree would enable her to be a government consultant or a researcher rather than a farmer, her mother repeated what Narpat had said so often: The government always turned a blind eye to farmers. Access roads were never repaired, drains never cleared, subsidies always rejected. Kala listened patiently to her mother and said it was her intention to remedy these problems. She mentioned the spillages from the foreign oil companies that were ruining fertile lands.

Her mother sighed. "Remedy. You know how much people try to remedy these things before you? The village council, the local councilors"— she hesitated, then said—"your father spend his whole life fighting and fighting. And for what? What is the difference? What is the improvement? Show me."

Jeeves assumed that this conversation signaled the end of the peace and cooperation in the house, but a few days later he learned that his mother had hired Janak to take the family to the St. Augustine campus. On the morning of the trip, she said, "We have to make sure you renting in a good place. I don't trust these areas by the university. Tunapuna. San Juan. Curepe. All sort of crime and drug-taking does go on there."

"How you know that?" Jeeves asked, surprised.

She hustled him into the car. "Because I pay attention to what happening."

"You getting like Pappy then?"

Jeeves felt he had made a funny observation, but Kala said quickly, "I will be staying in the campus, Mammy."

Campus. The word sounded foreign and important to Jeeves.

As the car was pulling out, Narpat limped from the porch. "Stop putting this fear in the girl head, Mammy. People who frighten every step of the way never get anything done. She will be as safe there as anywhere else. This is a good field you choose," he shouted. "When you graduate, me and you will fix up these touts who running the cane farmers unions. Me and you together. Age and youth. Experience and energy."

Across the road Radhica noticed the family pulling out and the old man shouting at the car weaving around the potholes. "That family," she muttered a bit hopefully. "Upside down today. Downside up tomorrow. Updown side the next day."

Throughout the trip Dulari warned Kala about crime and drugs and offered sensible advice on food and laundry and proper budgeting. Jeeves stared out the window at the change of country to town and back to country, and settlements that were neither but seemed to have dropped plump from the sky. The landscape shifted so swiftly that it was difficult for him to process the transformation. Highways gave way to narrow, potholey roads, plains to hills, and hills to swamp. The hills were littered with awkwardly sloping shacks, the plains with sugarcane, and the swamp with mangrove and lilies sitting on stagnant basins. At the sides of the road, muddy boys shook their strings of cascadoo and cascarob whenever a vehicle approached.

They passed settlements of identical prefabricated houses and older concrete houses with decorative frescoes like those Jeeves had spotted in the couteyah. In the yards of some of the older houses were *deyas* and other bits of pottery enclosed in wire mesh cages. Lower down he saw vegetable stalls barely an inch from the speeding traffic. He tried to simplify the landscape by counting colors. He counted the gray and cream of the older houses; the red, pink, and turquoise of the newer buildings; the dirty brown of the hills; the silvery blue swamp water; and several shades of green. He glanced up at the billowy clouds. Though almost every color was represented, he felt that if an artist—like Constable from his *West Indian Reader*—were to depict the scenery, the canvas would be a jumbled quilt of blurs and blots. Nevertheless, he was stunned at how different all this seemed from the places he knew, and during the trip he developed a new appreciation of the island. His respect increased when they entered the university compound and he spotted the poui and flowering shrubs planted at the sides of the huge concrete buildings. "'Faculty of Arts,'" Dulari read from a sign. "All these big buildings. Where your building, Kala?"

"Look it there!" Jeeves shouted.

"Department of Agriculture. Ay-ay, where all the flowers and plants and vegetables?"

The children knew their mother was joking, and they all smiled before Janak said that the plants were in a glass house. Finally they came to the girls' residence, and Kala took her mother and sisters to the main office, which was closed, and along the spotless corridor. They came across a guard patrolling, and when he greeted the family politely, Dulari said, "It have watchman and thing. Goodness! And look how white and clean everything is. With lights on everywhere. Who paying for all this?" She read all the signs in a lilting voice and pressed her hand against her mouth as if she had said something funny. How it so empty? How the place so big? Where the bathrooms and toilets? Kala interrupted Janak's responses to provide accurate answers. "Drive around the place a little bit," Dulari said when they returned to the car. "I want to see where these girls from the village does come to take degree."

Janak drove through the campus slowly, bringing his car to a complete stop at each speed-bump. On the way back, Dulari chatted excitedly and directed Janak to slow at a big deserted house in Charlieville. "That is where I used to live."

"In that old house?"

"It wasn't old at the time, son. It was new and spotless, just like the university place. With a nice balcony full of flowers and a big yard where we used to play games. There was a swing on that dead chenette tree." She said excitedly, "You smelling it? The curry and spice and masala. We used to smell that from the curry factory when we was swinging."

The children smelled the spices from the nearby factory and gazed with their mother at the old abandoned house. Dulari remained silent for the remainder of the trip, but every now and again she would shake her head slowly and mutter, "Hmm."

Less than a week later Kala moved into the residence, and the house in Lengua felt empty. Gone were the sisters' lively discussions, gone their father's lectures on agriculture and ayurvedic remedies. Jeeves couldn't understand why the absence of just one person could make such a huge difference, but he too was caught by the mood.

One night while Jeeves was lying on the fiber mattress, his father said, "The light out." He walked to the gramophone. "Look at this nice gift Kala buy for me."

"Was Chandra."

"But who used to sing with me?"

"Sushilla."

"And talk about long-ago things?"

"Mammy."

The old man seemed slightly frustrated. "But of all the children, who you think take after me?"

"Everybody."

"And who you think will never neglect me?"

"Nobody."

Surprisingly his father lightened up. "Okay, mister politician, you have a nice lil answer for every question I ask. A plaster for every sore." But he was not able to sustain this levity, and Jeeves noticed that he was spending more time in his room. Occasionally he listened listlessly to a record. When Dulari tried to engage him in conversation, he would perk up for a while before he lapsed into a tired silence. Chandra bought him Kepler, a sweet, viscous tonic, and Sanatogen Nerves Tonic, and Bemax, a powdery cereal, and read the ingredients and their purported healing qualities. "All these thing you could find right in the backyard," he said, grimacing as he read the fine print. "You just have to know where to look." While he was stirring the mixture of Bemax and Kepler and slowly chewing the paste, he mumbled, "Processed weed and stalk and vine. Horse food. When I die, allyou could send me to the glue factory and melt me down. A hop-and-drop horse."

Dulari guessed what was bothering him. "Stop talking nonsense, Pappy. Just now the cast will be remove, and you will be able to go back to the field. And Kala will come on the month-end."

TWENTY-SEVEN

Four months after Narpat's accident, the cast was removed. Doo-doon appeared suddenly one evening with a hacksaw blade and a chipping hammer. As he sawed away, he said, "Good cast. Good material. But the trick is the mixing."

"What so hard about making a cast? Is just like mixing flour for a roti."

After he left, Narpat got up and wiped away the dust and flakes from his foot. He flexed his thigh muscles and noticed the atrophied state of the injured leg. "Have to get you back in action with some good exercise," he murmured. But when he attempted to stand on the leg, he fell imme-diately. He tried once more and fell again. When he sat and examined the leg, he saw that the ankle, twisted to the right, had not been set properly. He reached for his cane and experimented with the amount of pressure he could place on the leg, but after a while the effort both tired and frus-trated him. He flung the cane against the louvers. "The blasted quack!" Dulari appeared from the kitchen. "A little thing like setting a bone he couldn't do properly. Damn stupid chamar."

She picked up the cane and placed it next to him. She had never heard him use the term disparagingly. "It will take time."

"Time? How much time? One year? Ten? Look how twistup the ankle is." He straightened his leg. "The only way to fix this is to break it and set it again." He grabbed his cane and whacked it against his ankle.

"Don't!"

Holding the cane with both hands, he brought it down on his instep. "I have to break it first. Get it in a state of flux."

"No! Don't do that." She tried to wrench away the cane. "Why you do-ing this? It going to make it worse."

"How it could be worse?" He stamped his heel on the floor, again and again. The pain shot through his ankle and up his leg.

"Look at how you behaving like a child."

He gazed up at her, annoyed and astonished. Finally he looked away and whispered, "Like a cripple, not a child."

"You is not a cripple. And you just making it worse by pounding it on the floor. It will heal. Everything does heal. Give it time."

"I was just getting back the circulation."

She smiled bleakly. "I think it get back enough circulation. Now put it up and let me rub it with some Tiger Balm."

He closed his eyes, but every now and again his eyelids would flutter as he watched his wife applying the ointment to his ankle and massaging in a circular motion. "The pain passing," he said quietly. "I think it went to the other foot." He placed his other leg on her lap.

When Chandra returned from work, she saw her father lying on the couch, his feet on his wife's lap. She was about to ask who had removed the cast but decided to leave them alone. She went into the kitchen. A pot of milk was boiling on the chulha. She pulled out a burning log. On the cupboard were sliced vegetables: eggplant, tomato, and carailli. She poured some oil into a saucepan and threw in the vegetables. Half an hour later Sushilla returned from school and asked her, "You cooking this evening? Mammy and Pappy looking nice sleeping together on the couch." She giggled, then said seriously, "Go and change in your home clothes. I will finish this."

"Make sure you don't put too much salt or you will upset Pappy. And don't burn the roti."

Sushilla placed her hands on her waist and pretended she was annoyed. "Okay, madam, I will try my utmost not to burn anything." She playfully pushed away her sister from the kitchen. "You already get a oil stain on your dress. Now go."

"Shh, you will wake them."

"Romeo and Juliet, man."

A worried look crossed Chandra's face. She seemed set to say something, but when Sushilla began humming the song from *Love Story* and danced around the kitchen as if she were playing a flute, Chandra smiled tiredly and placed a finger against her lip. "Shh."

———

Narpat continued practicing with his cane. He realized he could hop for only three or four steps without support. When he grew tired, he would sit on the couch or on the Pavilion and wonder how he would manage with crop season just two months away. His factory, once more, would be neglected. He hid this worry from his family and joked about his infirmity. "Make way for the crappo," he said when dinner was served. "What is this? Rice and vegetables and sardine? Where the flies?" He flicked out his tongue as if he were catching invisible insects. "I need a parrot," he told Jeeves one weekend. "Yo ho ho and a bottle of rum. You know who say that?"

"Long John Silver."

"Then you better start calling me Captain *Langra*."

"Lengua?"

"Langra." He spelled the word. "It mean broko-foot."

"Like this?" Jeeves hopped around the living room.

"Jeeves!" Chandra glared at him.

But Narpat got up and placed his hand on his son's shoulder. "You have to teach me how to hop, boy. You doing it better than me." On evenings he hopped around with Jeeves and recited poems about cripples. He told his son of an amputee mechanic who dragged on a box cart, and of an artist who drew with his feet. But as crop season approached, Narpat's simmering worry increased. He asked the few visitors about hiring labor, but they all knew of his impatience, and although they promised to look around, most never returned. Jeeves noticed his growing reluctance to engage in stories about crippled men and women. The boy gauged his father's silence. "You think is a test? Like the kind of test you used to tell me when I was small and was afraid to sleep alone?"

"What?"

"Like the tests these old-time Indians used to take?"

"You have a good memory, boy."

The compliment pleased Jeeves. "I even remember the part about your uncle mashing up the room and how you save and save to buy a canefield. And how your mother stop talking. And the promises your father make you listen to."

After a while Narpat said, "A test must have some result. You can't keep on taking test after test after test." His voice faded as if he were talking to himself.

At the beginning of the crop season, he stood on the porch watching the tractors and bisons plodding to the fields. He noticed the chatter and animation of the farmers, and he knew they enjoyed these five months of hard work because they had grown up in the canefield with their families and friends; he knew that the wielding of the cutlasses, the clearing of the fields, lighting the mounds, and gazing at the crackling sparks shooting up to the sky were like a ritual of purification conducted for centuries by men and women who saw no shame in honest work. He recalled his discussions with Kala and felt that the old plantation owners—or anyone not connected with cane farming, for that matter—misunderstood the singing and the dancing at the end of the crop season. In his frustration at being stuck helplessly in the house, he forgot his own criticisms of this merriment.

One evening Huzaifa told him, "I making a little study of all these new machinery which does be machining out these days. It have something call a combined harvester, for example. Just jump in, throw in a gear, and it level the field in no time. Cut, bundle, and transport. Like a little factory." He nibbled his nails. "I have to do some more research to see if it could squeeze out the juice and dry it up to make sugar. Yes, yes, a nice little factory. Portable."

Sometimes he brought along books with photographs of other machines that cleared, fertilized, dropped seeds, and harvested. He liked the fact that his friend was silent during these conversations, but one evening Narpat told him, "You notice all these fields in the book, flat?"

"Is true."

"You put a machine like this anywhere in Lengua, and it will roll over in the first hour."

"Hmm. Maybe it have another unit to pound down the land and make it flat. Have to check into that." But his research revealed no such contraption, and gradually his enthusiasm for this sort of technology dwindled. He noticed too that Narpat's silence was not a sign of acquiescence but rather a brooding. Occasionally he heard his friend muttering mysteriously about flux and chaos.

Early in the mornings, when the leaves and the grass were wet and turgid from the dew, Narpat hobbled to the backyard garden and gazed at the variety of leaves, some serrated as if they had been torn away and others smooth and heart-shaped. He noticed their textures and the different shades of green. Hidden were fruits too tiny or too well camouflaged to be noticeable. He flicked away aphids and caterpillars and mealybugs with his cane. Dulari looked at him from the kitchen and occasionally joined him outside and chatted about the freshness of the tomatoes or the purple sheen of the eggplants, but he never responded to her comments. One morning she repeated an old statement of his: The backyard garden was better than any freezer or fridge because the vegetables were always crisp. She also mentioned the money they were saving.

He remained silent, but when he returned to the porch to watch the farmers going to the fields, he said, "We saving a few pennies here and losing hundreds in the canefield."

"It have anybody you could hire to cut the cane? It not too late." He stared at the tractors chugging along, and Dulari realized he must have asked the farmers about hired help and that the cessation of their visits was possibly because they had made excuses or promises they would never fulfill.

One evening the Manager showed up. Narpat was chatting with Huzaifa at the time. "Ay-ay, Huzzie, you still living? I didn't see you for a long time. I thought you get sick like your cousin Haroon or you drop dead or something. He still writing them stupid letters?"

Huzaifa bared his yellow teeth and said, "Aah, aah," with muted menace.

The Manager turned to Narpat. "Sorry I couldn't make it before, but your accident was resting heavy on me heart. Just last night I was talking to meself, and I say, 'You know something, Manager? Is full time you pick up yourself and visit Narpat insteada worrying about it whole day.' So said, so done." He peered at the ankle. "It still twist a little. That is the thing with ankles. You could never know which way they will twist. Is like they have they own mind. You walking and thing?"

"With this mister here." Narpat tapped his cane on the floor.

"It must be so painful. Tsk, tsk." His eyes clouded. "I could never understand why these things does happen to good people for. What is the purpose?" He said *pupposs*. "Just last night when I was talking to meself, I say, 'You better be careful, Manager, because you might be next.' Tsk, tsk."

All Narpat's revulsion for the Manager rose, but he held his peace.

"You could never anticipate these things, that is the problem. They does happen in good time and bad time, in crop season and outta crop season." He glanced at Narpat. "Just the other day I was dropping off some material for Poolchan, and I pass by your field." He stared at his boots. "Tsk, tsk. Cane standing up straight but dry as hell. Weed all over the place."

"It have unit that could—"

The Manager cut Huzaifa short. "It hurt me heart to see all that waste." He pounded his chest. "It hurt me so bad because I don't like to see anything go to waste."

"It wouldn't waste. The field will still be there next year," Narpat told him.

"Yes, yes, it will still be there, but in what condition? Soil done get hard like cement. Suckers done dead out. Weed done take over." He shook his head sadly. "Is things like this that does make a big man cry." He wiped the bags beneath his eyes. "In my stupid opinion you should sell it out while it still looking halfway respectable."

"I see. You think is a good idea to sell it out? Who will buy it?" Narpat grasped his cane tightly.

"I always say that in time of distress neighbor suppose to help neighbor. Is they pupposs."

Huzaifa looked at the Manager in horror.

"A 'bandon field like that wouldn't bring much cash, but something better than nothing."

"I tending that field for close to forty years. It send all my children to school. Buy food and clothes. You think I will give it up just so?"

"But it useless now." He laughed wet and congested. "When a donkey get old and useless, you have no choice but to put a good kick in he tail and send him on he way."

"Get out."

"Eh?" The Manager's smile was still frozen on his face.

"Get out from here now." Narpat's voice was calm and steady.

"Get out from your house? The chamar not good enough to offer sympathy?"

"And don't ever let your shadow cross this yard again." Narpat raised his cane.

The Manager got up. "I going. And I wring me ears that this is the last time I ever help out hardup people again. From now on I will leave every single cripple alone."

"Get out, you chamar. Everybody who come to this house want something."

"I wring me ears. I wring it a thousand time. Everybody feel they could just 'buse the Manager and insult he dreamsanhope just because he have a soft heart, but all that come to a end." He stormed out, but before he climbed onto his truck, he shouted, "I have a little prabble for you. You listening? A dog that taking kick in he ass whole day does turn 'round one day and put he mouth where he ass was, and drop some good bite on the kicker. Remember that prabble good. The Manager might look stupid, but he don't forget."

Huzaifa left soon after, walking slowly to his house.

Narpat's gloom deepened following the Manager's visit.

One morning Dulari saw him clubbing the marigolds and daisies and the poinsettia at the side of the front step. "Flowers, flowers. What is the use of flowers? It good to eat?" The milky sap from the poinsettia stained the wet leaves and coated Narpat's cane. "Just good for superstitious people. Hocus-pocus. Simi-dimi."

Across the road, the Brahmin exhaled his cigarette smoke in little gusts.

In the evening Narpat flung his cane against Carnegie. He fell to his knees. "What you doing?" he asked Dulari, who had rushed to help him up. "You never see a cripple drag before?" He climbed onto the couch. "Run across the road and tell your friend to come and watch too. A nice cinema show."

Later in the morning Jeeves noticed the old man trying to climb onto the tractor. "You want me to help you, Pappy?"

"You think you could help?"

"Tell me what to do."

"I want you to drive this Farmall to the canefield and reap all the cane."

"I can't do that."

"Why?" his father snapped. "How old you is now? Thirteen? Fourteen? When I was your age, I work in the field from morning to night."

"But I going to school."

"They teaching you how to solve problems in school, not so?"

"All the time. Hard arithmetic and—"

"Okay, see if you could help me out with this." He sat on the running board and rested both hands on his cane. "It have this old fella who had an accident and can't work again. What you think this old fella should do?"

"Wait till it heal."

"The injury permanent."

"He should ask his friends to help him."

"His so-called friends refuse."

"His family then."

"His family say they too busy with school."

"Then he should find another job."

"It have nothing else for him. He doing that job all his life. Now tell me this." He stared across the road at the Brahmin's flower garden. "You don't think that when people become useless, then is time for them to go?"

"No, I—"

"You disagreeing because you don't understand how this world operate. When an animal get old and sickly, the rest of the animals leave it behind because that animal have nothing to contribute to the herd again. It become a liability."

"People different from animals."

In the night, the boy asked him, "What happen to the old fella in the story you was telling me?"

"He leave everything to fate. *Jon hoi, ton hoi.*" His father was staring at him with a taunting half smile, as if the statement were a challenge.

Part Four

*J*eeves believed that their conversations were somehow responsible for his father's return to the canefield, and on that first day the boy stood by the tractor with his mother watching nervously as Narpat hooked his cane onto the steering and pulled himself up. When he started the engine, his voice lost in the roar, Dulari said, "Why you don't get somebody to drive the Farmall for you?"

"Why? I still have one good foot." He glanced at Jeeves. "And a mahout to help me out. Hop aboard, Sabu." Jeeves climbed aboard before his mother could object. Throughout the trip, Narpat shouted to his son about how faithful the Farmall was, how easily it had started after months of being parked. "Like a elephant ready to pull out big-big tree in the jungle."

Jeeves was amazed at his father's change of mood. "Why you driving so slow?"

"I can't change the gears, boy." As they approached the field, he said, "Put your foot on that metal plate and press. Not so hard, not so hard." The tractor shuddered to a stop.

Jeeves went with his father four times that week, and although Narpat just limped through the field and gazed at the paragrass enveloping the suckers, and at the spindly weeds growing in the ravine, the boy enjoyed this break from school. He noticed, though, his mother's disapproval whenever they returned. "You enjoying the cane work?" she asked him one evening.

"I like to ride on the tractor with Pappy. I does help him to hold the brakes."

"You have a few weeks of school again. You will go to the field every day then?"

Now Dulari made her own inquiries about hired help. She badgered Janak, and during her visit to Lumchee's grocery, she spoke to the young men idling outside the dingy rumshop. One afternoon Jeeves saw two skinny boys sitting beneath the hogplum tree. They followed the tractor to the field. In the night, when Narpat mentioned that he had gotten some help and spoke about the lochos who were not entirely useless, Dulari said, "Now that you get workmen, you have no use for Jeeves again."

"This is his inheritance. Is time he begin to learn the value of the land. It will never let him down."

"How much you getting for one ton of cane now?" she asked quietly.

"We farmers have the means to put a end to that. I already strike the first blow. When the factory finish—"

"And in the meantime?" Dulari got up and walked to the chulha. In the morning she went to her brother. That month Jeeves was awakened several times by loud conversations between his parents. He heard his name being mentioned in the stream of Hindi.

He guessed that the determination to send him to Bally's—a private school at the back of Naparima college and housed in a huge wooden two-story building, a former boardinghouse for Presbyterian missionaries from Nova Scotia and New Brunswick—had been made during those conversations. He was annoyed at the arrangement sprung so suddenly on him, until his mother's patient explanation that in order to repay Bhola for the tuition fees, he would be allowed to work in the cinema after school. And during a visit to Bhola, his uncle sweetened the pot. "Free cinema show just for cleaning and sweeping the place. Better than carhooting with them ignurrent cane farmer in the bush."

When school reopened and many of his friends from standard six moved to their fathers' fields, or sat listlessly by vegetable stalls before their small houses, Jeeves journeyed with his mother to Bhola's place in Lothians. She unpacked the cardboard suitcase in the small downstairs room where she and her daughters had been squeezed, strung his clothes on the racks, warned him about the idlers in Princes Town, and cautioned that he should always obey his aunt and uncle.

Each morning he walked to a small Chinese snackette at the side of Woolworth and took the crowded bus to the wharf in San Fernando, then made a half-hour walk along the shore to his school. In the afternoons he hurried to the wharf and joined the bustling chaotic line at the Princes Town terminal. The line dissolved in a mad rush when the bus approached, and once it was full, the driver pulled off, scattering those who were still trying to climb aboard. Once in a while Jeeves had to wait a half-hour for the next bus. He paid his ten cents, collected his ticket, and squeezed in with the other schoolchildren at the back. Market vendors and an assortment of drunk grumbling men took the front seats. The one-hour trip was lengthened by an additional twenty minutes, because the driver always pulled up at a rumshop in Matilda, where he and the conductor and some of the drunkards filed out and leisurely consumed a flask of Puncheon rum. By the time Jeeves arrived at Bhola's place, his school uniform was dirty with grime and sweat. Occasionally he spotted his cousin Prutti dismounting from a taxi by Woolworth, but she never acknowledged him.

She didn't speak with him during dinner either, and Jeeves noticed her exchanging contemptuous glances with Samdaye, whom he had never seen before. She was a distant relative of Babsy's who functioned as some kind of maid. Bhola was hardly ever at the dinner table, and late in the nights Jeeves would be awakened by the truck's arrival and, a few minutes later, by Bhola lumbering up the steps and humming an advertising jingle. Sometimes he heard quarreling upstairs and doors being slammed.

Jeeves arrived at Bhola's house at five p.m. and left for the cinema at six, which allowed him a half-hour glimpse of the end of the four-thirty matinee. Then he walked through the rows, collecting beer bottles, snack boxes, and crumbled paper bags. After he had deposited the litter into a barrel just outside the cinema, he returned with a broom and a scoop and swept the cigarette butts, peanut shells, and pieces of chicken from the floor. Frequently he stumbled upon unusual items: an empty shoe filled with vomit, a clotted handkerchief, a brush with a smooth handle, a brassiere with some sort of internal wire skein. He kneaded and probed the brassiere before he finally discarded it.

The work was not difficult, but he blanched at the puddles of spit and vomit on the floor, and the cockroaches that scurried from beneath the seats. Once in a while he avoided entire rows. Yet none of this mattered while he was watching the end of the previous matinee, usually the climactic action scene of a western or a gladiator movie. The audience booed, catcalled, and hissed. Bits of dialogue from other movies were memorized and became a part of the strange interaction between actor and audience. Jeeves soon realized that the crowd held a preference for strong, steely-eyed men and contempt for dandies and primping women. They admired Sean Connery, Katharine Hepburn, Pam Grier, Bruce Lee, Charles Bronson, Clint Eastwood, and from the Indian movies, Dharmendra and Dilip Kumar. They despised anyone with a nasal British accent. The half-hour fragment whetted his appetite for more, and he began leaving Bhola's house earlier and hanging around the cinema till nine, entitling him to a half-hour of the eight-thirty showing too.

Jeeves was excited to be out so late at nights. In the village, doors and windows were always open and people who had lived alongside one another for a generation or more knew the details of their neighbors' lives. But in the town there were sturdy cube-shaped buildings, their louvers and doors shuttered at nights. Beneath some of the stores he would see couples embracing and, on the pavements, solitary men who seemed to be sleeping. He saw vendors, their pitchoil tins yellowish from the dull glow of the streetlight, and as he passed the vendors, he would catch a whiff of some strange meaty odor. Sometimes he would see a car parked at an intersection and its driver looking through its window. He imagined Princes Town as a place of secrets; and returning from the movies to Bhola's place, Jeeves would color the scenes of the embracing couples and the vendors and the waiting drivers. For the first time he felt like an adult, independent of his family in Lengua.

He practiced this new independence on the ticket collector, a short dark man with curly hair packed to one side of his head and a gold tooth peeping from a scrubby moustache. One night the ticket collector asked, "You watchmanning who and who or what?"

"What you mean?"

"You is a spy or what?"

Jeeves recalled a Bronson movie. "Whatever you say, buddy."

The collector pulled up his jersey and scratched his belly.

Soon snatches of movie dialogue seeped into Jeeves's speech, and at school he was seen as strange and comical. The reputation was unwittingly enhanced by his unusual responses to questions in class. One morning Bassarat, the literature teacher, instructed him to recite Wordsworth's "The Daffodils," which the class had memorized during the week. Jeeves demurred, grinned, and scratched his elbows. After he was thumped on his back with a text and sent to his desk, he whispered to his seatmate, "I allergic to flowers." He hated the school, the old wooden rooms with photographs of stern wrinkled men, the subjects, the cranky old teachers, and the long bus trips. He couldn't wait to get to the cinema.

And gradually his anger at being palmed off to Bhola, his discomfort in the presence of the family and the maid, and the confusion and guilt about his father were displaced by his excitement for the movies. He never saw them from beginning to end and speculated wildly about the unseen segments. At school he wondered how the soft-spoken Clint Eastwood character had developed into a snarling, trigger-happy lunatic; and during his weekend trips to Lengua, he tried to draw Chandra, who picked him up at Woolworth, into his excitement. On Sundays, before he returned to Princes Town, he stared out from the porch, hoping he would spot an old schoolmate to chat with about these movies. One night in Lengua he offended Radhica when he complained about the constant television commercials, and a few minutes later when he said, "This TV Tarzan don't know how to bawl properly. And he don't hold the rope the correct way. The Tarzan from the cinema does swim with a knife in his mouth."

Radhica took a deep breath. "Ray and Jag is a promise that allyou wouldn't get proud and force-ripe after spending a couple months in the town?" As usual, they ignored her. For the rest of the night, she cackled appreciatively at each commercial. "Fun-rose dog hot sausages." And later, "Klim is really the best milk, yes. Strong bones and teeth. These advertisements does teach you a whole ton of learning"—she grew stern—"if—you—willing—to—pay—attention."

Chandra was annoyed by Jeeves's new show-offiness, Sushilla confused, and Kala, when she came from university, delighted. And it was from Kala that he heard of his father's gradual reestablishment of a harvest routine. He was confused, though, at the changes he noticed in his mother each weekend. It seemed as if her fatigue had sunk too deep to register on anything but her blank little smiles as she bustled around the house. During Sushilla's and Chandra's trivial arguments, she stood apart and remote, as if she were beyond the raised voices. Even her inquiries about Jeeves's new school and his interaction with Bhola's family were asked with a formality that puzzled and offended the boy. When he returned from the sawmill after searching for his friends, she did not quarrel as before but merely reminded him he should use the weekends to catch up on his schoolwork. Gradually, Jeeves saw the benefits to his mother's new remoteness and was relieved that he was no longer singled out for punishment.

He did not entirely escape rebuke, though. As his mother grew more aloof, he noticed that Chandra was stepping in the older woman's shoes, and frequently his sister would complain about his clothes strewn on the floor, the trail of sawdust he left behind, and his habit of not removing his cup and plate from the table. "Who you expect to clean up after you? This is not Uncle Bhola palace, you know. We don't have any servants here." She was beginning to resemble her mother too, with the same round face and broad hips and her hair tied in a bun.

One month-end while she was complaining, Jeeves fixed her with what he hoped was a menacing Bronson scowl, spat on the plate, and wiped his mouth with the back of his palm. She raised a hand, and Jeeves said, "Touch me and you dead." Her hand froze in midair, and when Kala began to giggle, Chandra glanced hatefully at her.

"Cinema babu," Kala cried. "Big starboy now. Draw your gun, hombre."

"Bam bam," Jeeves shouted. "Pu-jing, pu-jing."

Chandra slammed her plate on the table and strode off. In the night, Jeeves heard her singing a sad movie song while she was helping her mother wash the dishes. Kala came up to him. "Go tell her you sorry."

"For what?"

"Just tell her."

He contemplated his sister's request. "Starboy don't beg."

For the entire weekend, Kala called him Starboy and laughed mischievously.

The following week at school Jeeves submitted an assignment on which he'd written at the top, "Starboy Dubay." The geography teacher, a rumpled man with long legs and a short torso that looked as if it had been compressed in a vise, giving him a tall man's stoop, peered at Jeeves above his glasses rim. The class waited expectantly; the teacher was nicknamed General Gee because he pronounced his j's as hard g's when he was flustered. "Who give you permission to change your name from Geevan to Starboy? The police? The GP? Geesus Christ?"

Jeeves narrowed his eyes like Trinity from the western series. "Starboy is still muh name."

"Is so? Is so? You could make a nice little gail for this fraud. You little gackass."

Jeeves was flogged by the principal, a contemplative oldish man who sighed sadly before each stroke. Soon the class began calling Jeeves Starboy, and he was surprised at this felicitous new image, acquired so smoothly, so naturally, that he soon felt that it was his life in Lengua that was a fake; and when he reflected on the shy, bumbling boy who was not known for anything special or different, who was flogged whenever his mother was in a bad mood, he imagined that all that had happened previously was a preparation for this new role. Starboy. Able to shift from one personality to the other. Gangster, cop, vigilante, owlhoot. Occasionally he wished he could spot some of his old schoolmates in the cinema and shock them into admiration. He conducted a keen lookout. And one day he saw Mr. Doon, his head bowed, hurrying into the cinema. Jeeves followed him and saw him peering around in the dark before slipping into the sixth row, next to a woman with a huge round bob. A horror movie was playing, a Hammer production popular with the Princes Town crowd because they all featured Christopher Lee, Peter Cushing, and Vincent Price, and in each there was a pivotal scene of a woman in a skimpy white dress being pursued through the English countryside, her blouse buffeted by shrubs until her breasts were finally free.

About twenty minutes into the movie Jeeves squeezed his way through a group of grumbling men in the seventh row, tapped the teacher's shoulder, and whispered into his ear, "Mr. Doon."

The teacher uttered a soft squawk, bolted up, and fled from the cinema. A few minutes later the woman with the bob, a plumpish Chinese, followed him.

As Jeeves was about to leave, the ticket collector ambled up to him. "Against policy to bother customers. Rules and regulations."

"That was Mr. Doon, my teacher."

"Who? He is a teacher? You sure?"

"Yeah. From Lengua. You know him?"

"Regular customer. He come in here often. Drunk as a fish. I don't know how his madam does put up with him."

"That wasn't his madam." Jeeves was surprised that this had not registered before. "His madam is a monitor from the old school. They run away together."

"That is a good one." His gold tooth glittered dimly in the dark. "You want to hear something special? I have a dossier"—he said *dusseya*—"on every manjack in Princes Town. They could fool who and who, but not this mister here." He laughed again in abrupt, hollow rasps. Jeeves puzzled over his amusement. During the following days he fleshed out these mysterious *whos*, and Jeeves soon began thinking of him as Dr. Who.

From Dr. Who, Jeeves learned that Princes Town was teeming with swindlers and drunkards. One night he pointed to a squat man with bloody overalls. "Butcher fella. Does cut up anything that get in his way. Nobody does mess with Alibocus."

"That sounding like a magic-man name. What you think he will do if I shout out 'Hocus-pocus Alibocus'?"

"He will take off you hand or foot." He glanced around. "But don't think is only scamps in here, eh. We have doctor and lawyer too." He motioned to a figure crouched in the front row. "That fair-skin fella is Dr. Mukerji. Use to work as a cleaner in Dr. Sampath office. One Easter Dr. Sampath take a week off and tell Mukerji to clean out the office for him. But Mukerji sit down in the doctor chair and start injecting up patient from a side. They thought he was a new doctor with a modern way of prescribing tablets according to color. Green for flu, blue for dog bite and infection, and red for madness."

Jeeves was confused. "So he is not a real doctor then?"

"Dr. Mukerji? Some people did prefer him to Dr. Sampath 'cause he was cheaper." One night Dr. Who grew serious and asked Jeeves, "You sure Bhola didn't put you here as a watchman? I don't trust any who and who, but you look like a quarter percent decent lil fella."

"Nah, man. We don't pull." Jeeves thrilled at the grown-up phrase and repeated it.

About a month later he discovered the reason for Dr. Who's suspicion: some of the customers got in by passing two shillings instead of a ticket.

"Nice move," Jeeves told him.

Dr. Who pulled up his jersey and scratched. His fingers crept lower. At the end of the week he gave Jeeves a shilling. "This is just between me and you."

"Is not any who and who business, man."

With the shilling, Jeeves was able to buy from the snackette in Princes Town tough biscuit cakes, spongy bellyfulls, watery grapefruit juice, and when he felt like splurging, foamy peanut punch from a fountain machine. The shilling also gave him the opportunity to loiter in the small cafés owned by old, harassed-looking Chinese with huge spectacles. Sometimes he went into Woolworth and spent the entire shilling on a pair of sunglasses or a miniature ashtray. He kept these treasures hidden downstairs. In one month he had added a plastic cowboy hat and a ship encased in a glass bubble and in two months a stainless-steel pennant and a flashlight-pen. Each evening he walked through the crowded, dusty stores with their wares displayed deliciously on movable wooden crates.

Jeeves had usually glimpsed Princes Town while squeezed in Janak's slow-moving taxi; and sweating and uncomfortable in the car, he had seen a dirty, disorganized town cluttered with vehicles and idlers. Now, waiting for the bus in the mornings, and sipping his peanut punch in the evenings, he saw patterns to the disorganization: the idlers descended at specific times on the same liming spots; the traffic grew busy at the same time each day; and the young office women each had a favorite café. These young women were different from the village girls who wore long skirts and walked tiredly and blushed whenever they were heckled. The town girls wore short skirts and trousers and returned the idlers' frank stares. They were confident and pretty, and Jeeves wondered whether Kala had picked up these characteristics from the town.

At school, the weekly shilling bought him friends, and periodically he would buy from a vending machine at the nearby teachers' college Solo sweet drinks—Apple J and Grape and Banana—which he shared with the other boys.

After dismissal, a group of them would loiter by Flatrock on the way to the wharf, walking along the narrow concrete embankment and sometimes jumping on the grimy sand to collect a shell or pausing to gaze at a junked ship about a mile into the ocean. One afternoon Jeeves said seriously, "It have a lotta treasure in that ship."

"Nah, man. Thief clean out all that."

"Government seize it already."

"They wouldn't find the chest." Jeeves pelted a coral in the direction of the ship. "And even if they do, they will have to deal with Captain Morgan ghost."

"Captain who?"

"Morgan, man. Use to hang out with Bluebeard and Richard Burton and Oliver Reed and Peter O'Toole."

"The actor fellas?"

"Who else."

The boys laughed.

He sometimes wished he could spring his Starboy act on Bhola's family during dinner, but in the face of Prutti's and Samdaye's hostility, he was frozen into a shy discomfort. They glared at all his little mistakes: chewing too noisily, slurping his soup, and scattering breadcrumbs on the tablecloth. Once he heard Samdaye saying to Prutti, "Some people does behave as if they still living in a lagoon." He was relieved whenever Bhola returned early, because he transformed dinner into a clumsy affair with his crude jokes and slurred comments. Later Jeeves discovered that Babsy's irritation and Prutti's discomfort were because Bhola was usually drunk. Most mornings he left when it was still dark and Jeeves would be awakened by the truck pulling out. Frequently he could not get back to sleep and would lie on his bed for an hour or so contemplating some recent movie before he got out his flashlight and pennants from beneath the bed. Then he steeled himself for another day at school.

Before he took the bus at Woolworth, he bought a bellyfull from the snackette, and during the bumpy trip to San Fernando, he felt the spongy cake stirring around in his stomach. Sometimes he worried that he might vomit in the bus, but the nausea always passed while he was walking along the shore to school. He began skipping dinner with the family. In a small snackette he bought, for five cents, a crusty hops bread with a tiny wedge of cheese. He wandered around the town during dinnertime, and one evening he walked into the Princes Town market, congested with buyers arguing and haggling with the vendors. At the far end was the abattoir, with slabs of beef and pork and, suspended from wires, animals' heads, their eyes still open. He looked up, expecting the lifeless ears to suddenly flap away at the flies swarming around the congealed blood. Just outside the door he spotted Alibocus caressing a pig with one hand. In his other hand was a pointed knife, and Jeeves jumped when the knife plunged into the pig's throat. Alibocus was muttering into the ears while he twisted the knife. Jeeves was frozen, but when Alibocus glanced at him, he fled. He kept a nervous lookout for the butcher in the cinema, and one night he noticed Samdaye walking past Dr. Who into the cinema. When the movie began, he came up to the ticket collector. "Samdaye didn't pay?"

"She don't have to pay. She is some kinda family."

"Some kinda spy too."

Dr. Who said, "Hmm," and tapped his gold tooth.

"I living in the same house. I does hear talk. You better put it in your dusseya."

Dr. Who dipped into his pocket and gave Jeeves a shilling. "Keep your ears open, and if you hear anything, let me know. She playing with who and who. I will fix she good and proper. People who living in glass house shouldn't throw glass."

Jeeves repeated a line of movie dialogue. "You really can't trust quiet people. Still waters run deep."

The extra shilling enabled Jeeves to enhance his dinner at the snackette, but more significantly, he felt he had learned an important lesson: If you waited long enough, things automatically remedied themselves; good people were rewarded, sly ones punished. He spotted this in the movies too, with murderers and rustlers surprised years after their crimes and gunned down in saloons. One night he told Dr. Who, "Them fellas what went inside that tomb and steal out all the gold, get in accident, one by one. You think is coincidence?"

"Coincidence? Don't gimme that." Dr. Who seemed almost angry. "It ain't have no coincidence. Every little thing that you do does jump back on your ass later on."

"What you mean?"

He leaned toward Jeeves. "When I was growing up in Manzanilla, I use to see things."

Jeeves was caught by his taut whisper. He tried to match it. "What you see?"

"Soucouyant. Lagahoo. Douen. Mama Diglou. La Jablesse."

"You see all that?"

"The place was crowded with them, but they use to only come out in the night. It had this old fella call Amos who nobody ever see in the daytime. But it had a big macco dog roaming 'bout in his property all day. One morning a fella leggo a stone behind the dog." He paused. "And that very said night self, Amos appear with a nasty limp."

"Amos was the dog?"

Dr. Who took a deep breath. "A next night I was coming home from catching crab, and as I pass by a lonely teak patch, I see this pretty lady walking out from the bush. I jump down from my bike to ask her if she lost or something. Then I see it."

Jeeves waited.

"One of her foot wasn't human. She had a cow foot. I never ride so fast in my entire life. I see plenty things." During the following nights he interrupted Jeeves with slices of what he called his "bush life." He had grown up with seven brothers and three sisters. Their house was on the brink of a canal that led to a lagoon, and each day he and his brothers would cast a seine into the muddy canal for cascadoo or catfish. When he was eight, his father slipped from the canal's bamboo bridge and drowned. In the morning, they found him just in front of the house, facedown in the water, surrounded by lilies and wild dasheen.

Dr. Who had never been to school and never learned to read or write. He spent his teenage years working in the lagoons and at nights hunting for agouti, lappe, manicou, and sloth. He told Jeeves of encounters with anacondas sleeping slyly in the rivers and caimans jumping out from the dried bullgrass. Dr. Who's stories merged with the fantasy of the movies and gave an authenticity to the vengeful acts and the unlikely deliverance Jeeves glimpsed on the screen. While he was walking to Bhola's place, the dingy little shops with cheap wares would be transformed into a delightful bazaar, and on the bus the incomplete houses balanced on uneven stilts would be replaced by some memorable movie landscape. When he closed his eyes, he saw tumbleweed rolling about in a deserted town, and a saloon's door opening and closing slowly. Three years earlier he had wandered into his primary school's library and had visualized what a hero might look like. Now he saw himself in some majestic setting, a snow-capped mountain or a vast plain, riding off to a valiant mission that would transform him from a boy into a man.

TWENTY-NINE

As Jeeves fell into the routine of school and cinema, increasingly Lengua felt remote and distant. Each Friday he waited beneath the snackette for Chandra. Frequently she did not show up at the appointed time, and he loitered outside the stores.

One evening she arrived at the snackette more than an hour late. Jeeves was some distance away, staring at a display of aluminum vessels and a cast-iron mill. Surprisingly, Chandra was smiling timidly, and a few minutes later Jeeves discovered the reason for her nervousness. Ray was waiting for them in the Brahmin's Mazda. During the entire trip neither Ray, Chandra, nor Jeeves said a word to one another. When Ray slowed at Four Roads junction and Chandra got out, Jeeves asked his sister, "Why he drop the two of us out here to walk home? Ain't he going right across the road?"

She did not reply.

"I know why." Jeeves was both thrilled and disgusted. For the rest of the year he rode with his sister and Ray to Four Roads junction and pretended not to notice their increasing boldness.

He was always unsettled by the journey to the village. Beneath the disorganization of Princes Town he had seen small patterns, but in Lengua everything seemed disconnected. The lagoons, the canefields, the tumbledown houses in Crappo Patch, a block of newer concrete houses— each could have sprung from a different movie. In the dry season the lagoons became basins of crumbling mud, and the canefields expanses of ash and burnt stalks. So coming from Princes Town, where the streets were shaded by tall buildings, Jeeves began to see Lengua as a place of unrelenting heat.

The minute he arrived at his own parents' house and was confronted by the smallness of the rooms, the old walls covered with dusty calendars, and passepartout pictures of animals, the electrical wires snaking and dangling loosely from the ceiling, the buzzing fluorescent lamp that never lit properly, transforming the house into a gloomy, dusty cubicle, he wanted to return to the city. He could not properly splice in movie land-scapes here, because everything was too familiar, and because he was too connected with the droning quarrels. He disliked the squabbles between Chandra and Sushilla and their unwieldy attempts to still cast him as an infant; and more and more he grew uncomfortable with his moth-er's strained cheerfulness. The entire village seemed caught in one of the slow-motion sequences he had seen in horror movies. The trees fluttered faintly, people on the roads drifted lazily, even the dogs and goats and chickens seemed sick and lethargic. The television shows at the Brah-min's house no longer appealed.

Occasionally he would hear his mother or Chandra singing melan-choly Indian songs, and he would hurry away from the house, offended by their thin, cloying renditions. He knew that a house this size, in spite of the holes and cracks, retained the stale odors of cooked food, worn clothes, and sweat. He began to hate the aroma, then the taste of herbs, curry, and sizzling oil. He would walk to Hakim's parlor and return with a bag of salted prunes, strolling slowly along the road, spitting the seeds into the drain, and watching the tiny black fishes scatter in the muddy water. Fre-quently he finished the bag on the junkpile, and gazing at the Brahmin rocking on his chair, he would drift into a brief sleep, awakening tired, sweaty, and miserable from the mosquitoes. Sometimes he disappeared into the lathro and watched battalions of leaf cutters advancing along the branches, and he poked around in the ground for more interesting insects.

His sisters noted these changes and put it down to the pretentious-ness of a country boy who had moved to the town. They also assumed that he got along with Bhola's family. Sushilla took the most offense, and one Saturday, when Jeeves brushed off her attempts at conversation, she mimicked Prutti's shifting accent and asked if he was missing Royal Cas-tle. After these little arguments Sushilla would retreat to the bedroom and Chandra would emerge from the kitchen with her hands on her hips and glare at Jeeves. Chandra had grown stouter, with dots of pimples on her face, but Sushilla seemed no different from the girl who had walked with him to school. She still had the same delicate features and the same long wavy hair. Jeeves, who was now as tall as Sushilla, sometimes forgot she was three years older than he was.

One of his biggest fears was that during a weekend visit he would witness—or worse, be caught in—one of his father's arguments, but when Narpat returned from the field, he was usually too tired to complain. Most nights he went straight to his drawing and designing. One night Jeeves noticed him scratching a boil on his ankle. The boil was red, and when the old man raked his nails over the swelling and squeezed, pus spilled out and ran down his heel. Jeeves imagined he could smell the infected blood. He was revolted and wanted to run away. Within the revulsion, a thought clear and precise came to the boy: his father was being punished; without some overriding pattern of fairness, the injury, the sores, the fluctuating moods were pointless. He recalled movies like *The Ten Commandments* and *King of Kings* and Indian religious epics, where proud, strong men were struck down by some unseen force.

The heaviness left him as soon as he returned to Princes Town. The situation with Bhola's family had not improved; if anything, it had grown worse, but he found the direct hostility easier to deal with than the awkwardness with his sisters. It was easier, he discovered, to operate in an arena where the hostility was beyond propitiation; easier to just wait. He knew that Prutti disliked him deeply, but Samdaye's loathing was more difficult to comprehend. She followed him around, alert and cagey, and once when he pressed his fingers lightly on Prutti's piano, she reported the infraction to Babsy, who berated him for interfering with other people's property.

One morning Jeeves threw the washrag into the sink rather than replacing it across the tap. He was about to restore it when he felt a painful pinch on his ear. He spun around and saw Samdaye. He felt like swearing, but her thick arms and legs, her square face, and her protruding front teeth gave her a menacing, unhinged look. "I don't know why you come here for. You stupid little country bookie."

"You should know."

"What you say? Who you think you talking to? One of your stupid sisters?" Her lip tightened above her teeth.

A damn manicou, he thought, and hurried away.

That evening, after the requisite lecture from Babsy about uncouth lagoon behavior, he told Dr. Who in the cinema, "I don't know why who and
who like to run their mouth all the time for."

Instantly Dr. Who grew alert. "Who you talking about?"

"Bothering poor Bhola head with all her spying."

"Oho. I see. I will put a good spokes in her wheel."

A few days later Bhola appeared at the dinner table disheveled, his
face swollen, a sure sign he was drunk. He pulled a chair roughly, stumbled into it, and tapped the table. "Samdaye!" Everyone jumped. Samdaye
came from the kitchen, wiping her hands on her dress. "Sit down here."
He kicked an empty chair toward her. When she sat, he bellowed, "What
assness I hearing about you and taxi driver Nanan. Blasted Nanan with a
wife and seven children." She continued wiping her hands on her dress,
stretching and yanking the material. This seemed to infuriate Bhola even
more. "You think the kissmeass cinema is your bedroom? You think your
old half-dead father will be happy to know that you carrying on like a
damn *jagabat* with that damn taxi driver?" He turned to his wife. "The
whole family. All of them is the same thing."

"Daddoes!"

"You and all keep your ass easy." He turned once more to Samdaye.
"Now bring my blasted food. And make sure you wash your hands clean
and proper." Jeeves was quivering with excitement at this retribution. He
felt even more pleasure at Prutti's look of betrayal.

During the following week Samdaye sat listlessly at the table, wiping
her hands and glancing down at her food. No looks were exchanged with
Prutti, and whenever Bhola appeared, she made an excuse and withdrew
to the kitchen. Surprisingly, Bhola seemed to have put his drunken out-
burst behind him and would ask jovially, "Ay-ay, where the hot woman going? Come, eat your food, girl." Samdaye would take a deep breath, her
blouse tightening, her lips shuddering as she exhaled. Bhola would reach
across and massage her shoulder roughly with one hand, the other dipping into his huge bowl.

Jeeves tried to mask his amusement, but one evening he blabbed,
"The last taxi driver from Princes Town pulling out. Straight trip. Hop
aboard, hop aboard." Bhola cuffed Jeeves playfully and roared with laughter, his cheeks smothering his eyes. The table shook. It was only after
Bhola's hilarity had subsided that Jeeves was able to gauge the effect of

his joke. Both Babsy and Prutti were frozen stiff. Samdaye was spinning her spoon over her plate. She inhaled and, in the delayed release, let loose a horrible wail. The effect was startling. Prutti ran into her room. Babsy walked slowly into the kitchen. Bhola was still smiling, but his eyes were somber and calculating. Jeeves wanted to leave, but he was caught by the hatred on Samdaye's face. Bhola kicked the chair until he was behind the girl. He hugged her, his palms flat against her breasts. "Take it easy. Take it easy." He hugged and squeezed.

She let loose another wail.

Jeeves fled.

He developed a slight fear of Samdaye. She was blocky and strong-looking, and the new air of menace she now carried around made her seem slyly dangerous. However, she no longer followed him, and gradually he began to feel guilty about his role in her distress. So when Dr. Who asked about any further acts of spying, Jeeves said, "Who and who learn their lesson good. No more problems in that department."

"Hoo hoo hoo." After a while he asked, "So what Bhola is to you?"

"My uncle."

"Father brother?"

"Mother."

"Your family from 'round here?"

"A lil distance away."

"Main road?"

"Lengua."

"I know it good. People from there does come to the cinema regular to see Indian pictures. So who is your father?"

"A caneman. You wouldn't know him."

"What is his name?"

"Narpat."

"Don't make joke! The troublemaker fella?"

Jeeves glanced around the cinema, thinking of how he could change the topic. "He mostly in the factory these days."

"He own a factory?"

"Still building it."

"That don't surprise me. That fella always up to something." He spoke as if he knew Narpat well, but when Jeeves asked him, he said, "I just see him a few time when I was working as a smallboy on Bhola truck. He was

always quarreling and giving advice for every little thing. All the workers
was 'fraid of him." He whispered, "Bhola too. Everybody in them days
used to call him *Jhanjhat*, a troublemaker. You know what he tell me one
day? You wouldn't believe it. I was a lil boy then, washing truck and
sweeping out the yard. Jhanjhat take one look at me and say he sure I
have a hammock in the house. Never figure out how he know that. Just
one look. Like if he could see straight inside my mind. So how he doing
these days?"

"Reading a lot in the room. Drawing plans for the factory. So what picture showing today?"

After a while Dr. Who said, "Some damn love story. Is Thursday."

"Boring, eh?"

"Not up in the balcony. These sorta pictures does encourage all sorta
slackness."

Before Jeeves left for the night, he climbed the stairs to the balcony,
but in the darkness he couldn't distinguish any carnal acts.

At school he invented stories of strange proceedings in the cinema.

One afternoon while he was eating a cheese sandwich in the snackette
and slyly appraising the female clerks ordering peanut punch and the bitter mauby-bark beverage, he spotted a brawny man wearing a tight shirt,
the sleeves rolled to his shoulders. The man glanced at Jeeves and seemed
set to cross the road but came instead into the snackette. He looked familiar, and Jeeves wondered whether he was a regular cinema patron.

"Jeeves?"

Jeeves looked up from his sandwich to the man. His hair was cut short
at the sides but curled at the top into a funnel that fell over his forehead.
He appeared to be smiling, but the curve of his moustache also suggested
a scowl.

"What you doing here?" the man asked.

"Taking a bite before I go to the cinema." Jeeves tried to place the
man's face and voice.

"So you move out from Lengua. That is a good move, man. Take it
from me." He hawked and jettisoned the phlegm neatly onto the pavement. "You remember the creole fella from class? When me and he had a
scramble and I put a good licking on him? And that fat nasty one who use
to always eat snat. The Skrattel." Jeeves couldn't believe how much his

old friend had changed. It was Danny, and he was hard and tough, a man rather than a boy. And watching him clasp the biceps of one hand with his other hand, he felt as timid and juvenile as he had years ago, watching Danny somersault on the mango tree and listening to his talk of papa bois and secret gardens with bizarre animals. He wanted to slip into his Star-boy role. "Hardly ever see these fella again, man. Busy with the cinema."

"You working there?"

"Yeah, man. A sorta junior ticket collector. Uncle cinema. So what you doing these days?"

Danny looked away, at a well-dressed woman, rouge plastered on her dark face, slapping a child, and Jeeves felt he saw some of his friend's old evasiveness. "I working on a project. We will bounce up later."

Less than a week later Jeeves saw him at the cinema's booth, glancing around. Jeeves hurried into the stockroom with his broom and scoop. When he emerged, Danny was already in the cinema. From then Jeeves started his cleaning routine earlier, prompting Dr. Who to remark approvingly, "Like Jhanjhat train you well, boy. But I hope you don't come out like him in the quarreling department."

Jeeves poured a scoopful of bottle caps into a bag. "What you mean?"

"Complaining all the time." He thought for a while and added, "But so far you look like a quarter percent decent lil fella. Not like some of these other smallboy who use to work here before. Most of them barely last a month. And you here how long now? Eight months?"

"Nine."

"Time does fly, eh. In a short while you will take over my job here as a ticket collector. So it is. I have two boys in school. One five, the next one six. Every evening the madam does sit them down and correct their schoolwork. And if I around, I does straighten their tail anytime they fall short. School was my enemy, but I going to make them like it, even if I have to drop pie-pie on them every day." Jeeves felt this was funny, but Dr. Who was serious. "I hear they drilling for oil all across Mayaro and Manzanilla. This will be a rich place if they find any. Good work for allyou youngboys."

At school, Jeeves told his friends about oil rigs and platforms on the east coast and, borrowing from old episodes of *Beverly Hillbillies*, of dirt-poor farmers and fishermen suddenly transformed into millionaires. "If I not mistaken, oil use to be leaking out from all these holes in my father property." He had a vision of his father driving an old jalopy with the entire family swinging from side to side in the car. The mood remained while he was traveling home in the bus, and he felt a brief, sudden affection for the village of his childhood and the little house where four children had laughed and clapped as their father danced around.

CHAPTER THIRTY

*D*uring that year, unknown to Jeeves, his father, with the help of the two boys, managed to harvest some of the crop and, with Huzaifa, made a few perfunctory forays to the factory site. They had gazed at the vines trailing from the windmill and anchoring the blades to the ground, and at the two weatherbeaten walls, discolored with snatches of moss and lichen. Huzaifa marveled they had not toppled onto each other. "One good dose of Roundup will get rid of all these parasites," Narpat had said. He had glanced at the absence of weeds at the tower's base. "Pure high-grade melau and sharp sand."

"It looking like the factory just taking a little rest," Huzaifa murmured.

On other days they discussed the practicability of the site and the precise planning. "Cut down them nasty vine, and the blade will start spinning like a airplane propeller."

One afternoon Narpat brought along his machete and, resting his body against the cane, hacked away at the vines, some as thick as ropes. He pulled down the tangle, and the blades rotated, creaking and grumbling. Huzaifa puffed his cheeks and blew at the windmill. "It a little rusty," Narpat said. "Once the kinks go away, it will pick up speed." The blades, as if in agreement, turned a bit faster. A rat jumped off the pulley. Another vaulted from a blade, then a family of black cockroaches, as big as bats.

"Careful it don't have snakes," Huzaifa warned.

Narpat and Huzaifa journeyed twice a week to the site and discussed the depressed price for sugar, the corruption of the cane farmers union, and the uselessness of the government, but they avoided any direct reference to the factory itself. Huzaifa suspected the factory would never be

completed; the biweekly visits were attempts to escape his wife and avoid
the list of chores she routinely assigned to him. Soon they began to chat
about the offshore exploration conducted by Amoco and Texaco and the
migration of some of the young men to the coast of Mayaro. Among the
migrants were Narpat's hired help, and during the following planting season most of the old cane remained on the ground, crowding and swallow-
ing the suckers. In the nights, while Narpat vowed to plow the field and
harvest the cane single-handedly during the next crop season, Dulari calculated her increasing debt to her brother. That year too the Brahmin
published his sequel, *More Magical Mantras for Most Maladies*, which like
his first booklet was a best-seller. During her roadside conversations Radhica now mentioned strange ailments from her husband's tract. Soon
she herself, she claimed, was plagued with abrupt vertigo; tingling in one
ear; temporary loss of smell and phantom odors; hot, cold, and intermediate flashes; and the inexplicable urge for wood. Her husband's mantras
cured all these ailments, and frequently during her conversations she
would wince and flutter her eyes and groan lowly. A steady stream of visitors descended on the Brahmin's house. A tarpaulin-covered shed with
three plastic chairs was set up to accommodate the visitors. "All these
chelas who coming every minute of the day. You would think that Ray father is the only pundit in the island," Radhica said. The Brahmin betrayed
neither excitement nor gratification, and he continued smoking in the
gallery and wandering about in the garden.

Narpat surveyed these additions darkly. "Toys. The sign of an undeveloped mind. The kind of mind that will invent a simi-dimi for every occasion." One weekend Jeeves heard him saying, "These vagabonds who
only smart enough to repeat things that write down thousands of years
ago is the most dangerous people on the face of the earth."

"Why?" Jeeves asked. He couldn't imagine the Brahmin as dangerous.

"Because they chelas does take everything they say as the word of god.
All the centuries of invention and progress pass them straight."

Dulari recognized his mood and attempted to shift the dialogue to
Kala and to Sushilla, who would soon write her advanced levels. She in-
structed Chandra to buy other records, which she played continuously.
She wished for the vacation when all her children would be around.
When it arrived, Narpat was briefly energized. He went with his tractor to
the field and on his return chatted with Kala and Chandra, sang with

Sushilla, and elaborated on the properties of common herbs to Jeeves. "If people know that it have a cure for everything right in they backyard, they wouldn't waste time chanting every time their big toe start paining." Then the vacation ended, and Kala returned to St. Augustine, Jeeves to Princes Town, and Sushilla to her examination routine.

Ten months later the results of the exams were published in the *Trinidad Guardian*. Sushilla had passed all her subjects, but her grades did not qualify for a scholarship; if she were to attend university, the family would have to pay for rent, tuition, and books. Once it was established this was not possible, she set about the dreary task of finding a job. Jeeves was alarmed when his mother suggested an accounting position at the cinema, but Sushilla deferred. Letters were sent off to government offices and ministries and schools. Eventually she was offered a position at the Poole government school, about twenty minutes from Rio Claro and an hour and a half from Lengua. She left at six-thirty in the mornings and returned at six-thirty in the evenings.

Radhica told Dulari, "I getting the feelings again. Look at how simple Ray father does be meditating in his flowers garden. You would never know that he turn down a whole ton of teaching job at St. Stephen's and Presentation and Naparima. Naparima-paparima."

Dulari listened silently, but with Sushilla's salary she was soon able to rewire the house, varnish the inner walls, replace the plain railings on the porch with decorative balusters, and buy a new pro gas stove, which she set next to the chulha. Suddenly the worry about money disappeared, and from long years of deprivation and fanciful planning, she was almost bewildered at this new independence. She repaid some of her debt to Bhola, and on a Friday evening Jeeves was surprised to see her at her brother's house. She took the boy to the Syrian stores and bought new trousers and shirts and a pair of leather shoes. He was astonished at his mother's brief exuberance, and he grasped this opportunity to ask her, "You and Pappy must be happy now because Kala get a scholarship and Sushilla get a teaching job?"

"In all the years that you know your father, how long he remain pleased with anything?" She unfolded a pair of serge pants and looked at the price tag. "He believe happiness is a sign of weakness." After she had paid for her purchases, she told her son, "But *I* happy that allyou move out from Lengua."

In the cinema Jeeves began to pay attention to the sweeping epics of honor and redemption, particularly the Indian mythological dramas, crudely produced, improbable and overacted. And in these dramas like the *Mahabharata* and the *Ramayana*, he saw men whose proud inflexibility matched his father's. But the movies didn't offer much hope because the contentious patriarchs were always saved by some unlikely act, like sparing an animal or offering charity to a god disguised as a beggar. Gods were everywhere, spying and keeping count; they were not above trickery.

These movies reminded Jeeves of the animal fables told by his father many years before. On the bus he gazed at the new well-kept churches, and the older colorful couteyahs, and for the first time he noted the prevalence of places of worship.

One Saturday night he followed Chandra across the road. She glanced at him suspiciously. "I thought you didn't like television shows again."

"I want to check out the new shows."

"It don't have any."

"The commercials then."

"Look who come to watch we small stupid television, Ray." Jeeves felt Radhica's eyes on him during every commercial, and when, at the end of an *Invisible Man* rerun, he followed the Brahmin to the gallery, she shifted the curtain to peep. The Brahmin sat on his settee and lit a cigarette. Jeeves wondered how to start a conversation. Halfway through the Brahmin's cigarette, he asked, "God must be just like that invisible man?"

The Brahmin replied immediately, as if he were thinking of the same thing. "God is invisible and visible. He is everywhere and nowhere." He spoke in a singsong voice as if he were chanting from a holy book.

"How that is possible?"

"Everything is possible."

"So everything always turn out right in the end?"

The Brahmin clasped his hands. "God is dreaming."

"What?"

"And when he wake up the universe will come to an end."

Jeeves was growing frustrated with the Brahmin's enigmatic replies.

He saw both Chandra and Radhica staring at him. He was about to return inside when he noticed the Brahmin's rare smile. He didn't suspect that his neighbor had suddenly hit on his next book: *Interpreting the Signs. A Conversation between a Guru and an Acolyte*. "That don't make sense," he told the Brahmin.

"Everything make sense if you adjust the angle."

"I think I should go inside now and watch TV." Later Jeeves heard him chortling and offering advice to Lucy.

While they were walking across the road, Chandra asked him, "What the two of you was talking about?"

"Some nonsense about angle."

"What angle?"

"You have to ask Ray father that. Only he could see them." When he noticed her worried look, he added, "So you better be careful."

"I should let you travel home alone on Fridays."

"So you will have more time with Ray?"

"You don't know what you talking about."

"I know very well. I does see the two of allyou holding hands in the front seat. Mammy and Auntie Radhica know?"

"Shh." They were now on the porch, and as the dim fluorescent light cast its flickering glow on Chandra's face, Jeeves was shocked by her fear and dread. His father was stretched out on the couch, asleep with his mouth open.

During the end of the school year, when Kala returned, Jeeves got a better idea of Chandra's apprehension, which was transferred to Kala after several lengthy conversations, and finally to their mother. Dulari walked through the house and to her backyard garden, heavy with anger. "I expected all sort of shame in my life. All sort of hardship. But not this. Not this. I was prepared for anything else." When Kala and Sushilla went to console her, she stormed away. "All of allyou will do the same thing. Chandra set a good example. Leave me alone. I need some time by myself."

"What going to happen?" Sushilla asked Kala. Jeeves strained to hear her response.

That vacation was a jumble of secret conversations and intervals of strained silence broken only by Dulari's recriminations. Chandra was never a participant, because she retreated to her room immediately after work. There were lengthy, hand-wringing chats between Radhica and Dulari and soon afterward mysterious preparations. In spite of his best effort, Jeeves was kept in the dark, but he heard Kala and Dulari discussing how best to break the news to Narpat.

"Let me tell him," Kala said.

"No. Is my daughter. Is my responsibility." In the night Jeeves tiptoed to his parents' room and pressed his ear against the door. From Kala's concern, he had expected violent quarreling and objects flung to the floor, but all he heard was his mother's voice, low and muffled.

In the morning he asked Kala, "What going on?"

She walked to the porch. Jeeves followed her. "Chandra getting married."

"So what is the fuss about?"

"She have to get married quickly." She hesitated and added, "Before the holidays finish."

"Pappy know?"

She chewed her nails. "Yes. About the wedding."

For two days Narpat refused to speak with anyone, not even with Kala. His expression betrayed no emotion. He stared at the walls as if he were thinking and calculating. When Radhica visited, he remained impassive, not bothering to acknowledge her.

This was her first visit to the house, and after a brief, assessing glance at the furniture, she dusted the couch and sat. *"Sita Ram,"* she greeted Narpat, who was on the Pavilion.

Narpat did not turn to her. Dulari came from the kitchen and pretended surprise. "Is nice of you to visit, sister. You want some tea?"

"No, didi. I just had a cup of Ovaltine. I have one every morning as a rule." She sighed. Midway through, the sigh evaporated into a brief, fluttering laugh. "So we is family now?"

"Yes, sister. We is family."

"I did always consider your family as my family and my family as your family." She studied her bracelets and inexplicably tittered once more. "Modern children nowadays. They have their own way. Just the other day Ray father was telling me that whether we like it or not, the world have to turn. Modern children nowadays don't like a whole ton of fuss. A small little tent. A couple family. And Ray father chelas."

Now Narpat turned to her. One of his eyes was closed; the other fixed its gaze on her. "We having no tent, no guests, and no ritual."

"But . . ." She was disconcerted by Narpat's staring eye.

"No hocus-pocus and no simi-dimi. And I have a list of obligations for both the bride and the groom."

Radhica flinched at the English terms. "The *doolaha* and the *doolahin* already—"

Narpat got out a sheet of paper from his pocket and waved it to Dulari. "Give this to your didi."

Radhica skimmed the sheet, then reread it more carefully. "The bride will promise to support, encourage, and defend the groom. The groom will promise to treat the bride as an equal in all matters." She frowned and mumbled other stipulations. "No poison, drugs, tobacco, and alcohol must find a place in the household. Both bride and groom will promise to abstain from superstition, magic, and idol worship." Radhica took a deep breath and played with the sheet on her knees as if she were preparing to leave.

"Both parties must sign that contract before any wedding take place."

Radhica got up and walked out of the house. Dulari followed her. Jeeves saw both women talking by the roadside, and from the way Radhica was continuously adjusting her orhni, he guessed she was upset.

Later, he heard his father telling his mother, "Absolutely no ceremony and no guests. Is a marriage between two people, not a pappyshow for the entire village." He limped behind his wife to the kitchen and to her garden, explaining the backwardness of ritual and ceremony. Jeeves felt he was enjoying this show of power.

Throughout, the Brahmin smoked in his gallery as if he were unconcerned, but one night after Kala had persuaded Jeeves to visit with her, he asked the boy, "All the questions dry up? No questions about why the doolahin family must always give dowry? Eh?" Although his voice was sharp, his face still held its indeterminate formality.

During the following days there were numerous roadside conversations between Dulari and Radhica and lengthy lectures from Narpat. Occasionally Dulari and Kala whispered to each other in the kitchen.

"That sheet that he calling a contract . . ."

"Is just routine promises, Mammy."

"Routine? What routine about—"

"Pappy just simplifying some of the old laws. And leaving out others. Is fairer to Chandra."

"You always defending him. On top of everything, he can't do any wrong in your eye. You think anybody will sign that piece of paper? What man in his right mind will ever sign something like that?"

"Pappy just trying to protect Chandra. He don't want her to end up like"—she saw the spasm in her mother's face—"like the other women in this village."

In spite of his mother's warnings, Ray grinned and signed the contract. "Just a stupid sheet of paper a crazy man write."

"You read it, Ray? You read the part about no dowry?" Her voice began to drag. "And no ceremony and no invited guests either. What kind of wedding is that? But you already had you little wedding, not so? You couldn't wait. You let a hot little girl trap you like a semp."

Ray laughed scandalously as though it were a big joke.

Narpat held firm to his stipulations, angering both Dulari and Radhica. Occasionally both women put aside their sparring and turned against him. "My first child. I always dream that we would have a big wedding. My first son."

"My first daughter."

"All these chelas will be so disappointed."

Having no chelas, Dulari said, "All the relatives."

And it was at Bhola's house that the marriage took place. There was a small ceremony conducted by the Brahmin, and Ray and Chandra walked around the fire and recited Hindi vows. Bhola enjoyed the whole affair. He pinched Jeeves. "Just now will be your turn, little Dubay. A sexy little craft from Lengua. Or a town chick with tight pants and T-shirt. Eh, Samdaye?"

Samdaye was busy during the rituals as she brought camphor ball and pitchpine wedges and mango leaves and small pellets of turmeric and *hing* and ghee. Prutti and Babsy, both in saris with sliver sparkles, stood apart, affronted and unsmiling. Prutti had received the results of her exams during the vacation. She had passed just three subjects and was consigned to the repeater class. Both she and her mother had fulminated against exam leaks, favoritism, and unfair questions. They exchanged pained glances whenever Sushilla or Kala performed a ritual. They had speculated on the hasty marriage and had been satisfied with Bhola's tipsy assessment: "These young girls nowadays does open they leg anytime they close they mouth. Skin too tight. It have to open somewhere. Not so, Samdaye?"

Occasionally mother and daughter glanced at Radhica, noticed her dry, fatigued look—a sure sign she was wealthy—her multitude of bracelets, and her expensive sari. And Radhica, for her part, was surprised at the size of Bhola's house, at the modernity of the furniture, at the carpeted living room, at the truck outside, at the cinema across the road. She regretted their acquiescence to Narpat's no-dowry provision.

Jeeves was thrilled by his sister's wedding and by the hint of scandal. It broke the monotony of Lengua, and he wondered whether Chandra would continue living in the old house and visit Ray at nights or vice versa. He rehearsed what he might tell his friends at school. He was disappointed, first of all, by his friends' reaction—many of whom claimed sisters who had eloped, divorced, or borne children out of wedlock—and then by the developing situation in Lengua. When Chandra returned from work, she stayed at her parents' house until the night, and in the morning she came across for a few minutes before Ray took her to the post office. The only marked difference to Jeeves was the size of his sister's belly.

Unknown to him, Chandra was regularly harangued by both mother and mother-in-law, one advising her to move with her husband into a place of their own, the other furious because the girl refused to help her in the kitchen. Radhica took her complaint to the Brahmin. "I not saying she should work like a slave. All I asking is that she wash a couple pot and pan and dry out some clothes." She turned to Ray. "Son, I want to give you some advice." She slipped into her fatigued pose. "If you spoil women, then you shouldn't surprise if they swing back on you and *ramajay* you up good and proper. Look at your own father. Even though he appear to be so quiet now, he use to put me in my place whenever I step outta line." The Brahmin rolled his palms against each other and nodded almost imperceptibly. "That is why I am like this now." She studied her bracelets. "You have to start this training in the beginning before it get too late."

Finally she complained to Dulari, who quietly defended her daughter. "Things different nowadays. The girl working from eight to five. What she could do when she come home? Besides, this is her first child." Occasionally she managed to shift the blame to Ray.

Radhica felt isolated and persecuted. What was the use of a daughter-in-law, she thought, who refused her duty to cook and wash? The frustration bubbled into a barely controlled rage. She adjusted her orhni violently whenever Chandra was around. She walked with heavy, stamping footsteps. She dropped abruptly onto the couch. She groaned for no reason and cleared her throat with a violent clatter. She aimed her belches like weapons. And when she spotted Chandra at her parents' home, she uttered puzzling aphorisms. "A inch does bring a whole foot. A whole foot does bring only idleness. Idleness does only bring long-eye."

Soon she began telling Chandra, "You could hand me that saphee, please?" She asked for cups, towels, spoons, and plates. Chandra noticed that the items were always within reach of her mother-in-law. Late one night Radhica asked her, "You could just switch off the lights in the hall, please."

Chandra was in the living room. "But it right by your finger."

"You back-chatting with me, child? That is what happening in this house now?" She raised her voice. "You know what would have happen to me if I did back-chat with Ray father? He would have put a good slap on me."

"Well, I is not you, and Ray is not his father."

"Oh god! Oh god!"

Ray rushed out of his room. "What going on?"

Radhica was slapping her forehead with her open palm. He repeated the question. Finally she sobbed out, "Ask your wife, don't ask me. Ask she." Chandra glared at her and brushed past Ray to the bedroom. "You walking out on me? I tell you that you could walk out on me?" Chandra slammed the door. "You see what going on in my own blasted house," she shrieked. "Oh god, oh god." When Ray walked past his father smoking in the gallery, she was still fuming.

Across the road, Narpat said to his worried wife, "The fish market open. I hope you teaching your daughter to catch fish." He had no idea of Chandra's predicament because she always took her problems to her mother.

One morning Dulari told Radhica, "Chandra seven months now."

"I work like a mule till two weeks before I drop child. I didn't have anybody to wait on me, hand and foot. I didn't get spoil."

The constant complaints depressed Dulari. She renewed her pleas to her daughter. "You working in the post office, and Ray working as a driver in Sharma grocery. If the two of allyou combine, allyou could build a nice little house."

"I not going anywhere until the child come, Mammy. You right across the road."

During the following weekends, Jeeves felt a mixture of fascination and revulsion at his sister's distended belly, at her manner of sitting, and at her now-puffy face, which made her look much older. He gave his friends a running commentary and in turn was surprised to learn in graphic detail of water bags and navel strings and afterbirths. One of the boys said, "Women in this stage interested in only two things. Food and sex." Jeeves's revulsion grew.

The baby girl was born on December 24, 1971. Jeeves had fled the moment he heard his sister's painful groans. When he returned, the midwife, reeking of parched ginger, roasted cumin, and cucumber stems, was lightly massaging his sister's legs. Radhica was cradling the slimy little baby. "It looking like a fish with close-up eyes," Jeeves said.

The midwife fixed him with an evil stare. "You think you did look any different?" She wiped her hands on her dress and retrieved a *zoot*, a cigarette end, that she tapped against the wall. "I pull you out in this same room." She cackled and pointed to Sushilla and Kala. "All of allyou. Even the boy who didn't make it." She cupped her hand and lit her zoot.

"Which boy?" Jeeves asked.

"In this village, for every child that born, another dead. Now go outside and play." The midwife pointed to the door. "How much man you see in this room?"

Jeeves tried to return the midwife's stare before he went into the kitchen. His father was at the back door looking out. "What is that smell?" Jeeves asked him.

"Saffron and ginger and Guinness. To purge and strengthen the mother," his father said.

Radhica came with the baby. She was surprisingly chirpy. "You don't want to hold your granddaughter?"

"This hand too old and hard to hold a baby."

"Look at how she trying to smile." She tickled the baby's chin. "Coochy coochy coo."

"The baby belong with it mother. It need her smell right now. Take it away."

Radhica returned to the room with her baby talk.

"You don't like it?"

Narpat turned to his son. "Is just a little ball of flesh right now. We don't know how it will turn out. What sort of household it will grow up in. Who will properly instruct it." Jeeves felt this was a harsh assessment until he noticed his father's smile. "Only time will tell whether it will grow up as a futurist like me and Kala or a believer in Puranic nonsense."

"I don't believe in that nonsense too." Jeeves wished he could explain to his father that he was no longer the little boy who believed everything told to him. "I don't believe the nonsense Ray father does talk either."

"I see. And what you believe? The nonsense that Bhola and his family does talk about?"

Jeeves wondered if he would ever please his father. He thought of what he should say; eventually he told Narpat, "I think Auntie Radhica like the baby."

"We will see how long that will last. It don't pose a threat to her right now."

THIRTY-ONE

*D*uring each weekend he was home from school, Jeeves imagined he spotted some change in the baby, and he was surprised at its transformation, in less than a year, from a quivering, squealing lump into a smiling, gurgling girl who paddled her feet into the air, rolled over, and clenched his finger with her fist. He liked the fresh baby smell mingled with Johnson's Baby Powder and the manner she would crinkle her round face so that she resembled the Chinese grocer, Lumchee. The first time he tried to hold her, she was so tiny and soft, he felt she would slip through his hands.

One month-end Kala saw him playing with the baby. "So you is not the baby in the family again, Jeeves? You lose your place?"

He felt embarrassed. "What baby you talking 'bout?"

"You right, boy. I think your voice beginning to change. And what is this here?" She tried to pull the sprinkle of fine hair on his chin and laughed when he stepped back. "You better give me the baby."

Narpat also developed a belated affection for the baby. He had been furious when he learned the Brahmin had named her Kalawattie. "A nice little Puranic name. The superstition start early." He'd refused to touch her. "Take her to the fish market. Teach her to sell baby fish."

"Hold her, Pappy. Look at how cute she is, looking at you."

He glared at Sushilla. "Cute what? With all that *kaajaar* paste on to her eye. And that *sindoor* in the forehead? And jumbie beads around the wrist? What century we living in?"

"She making eyes at you, Pappy."

"All that protection they stick up on her. They make her look so ugly." He couldn't resist for long, though, and he finally hit on the idea of giving her a proper Vedic name. He consulted his old yellow Hindi books and listed and crossed out names. "Mala," he told his daughter one evening. "It mean a garland. From now on that is the baby name in this house." His children soon learned he was serious about this injunction, and whenever he heard the name Kalawattie, he quarreled and said, "Take it to the fish market to sell baby fish." Soon everyone pretended that Mala was her real name, and for the rest of his life Narpat used no other name for his granddaughter. Once this was established, he grew into a doting grand-father, creeping around the floor with his Mala, bouncing her on his healthy leg and speaking to her as to an adult.

"Why Pappy talking nonsense to the baby for?"

"Is not nonsense," Sushilla told Jeeves. "If you listen carefully."

"You think a little baby could understand the reason for idol worship and protection from evil spirit and all that simi-dimi?"

"It making Pappy happy, and that is a good sign."

"You think is a sign?"

She looked at her brother in confusion. "Yes."

This was intriguing, but Jeeves was skeptical of Sushilla's disclosure, especially since she was developing some strange ideas of her own. She had recently discovered the benefits of vegetarianism and spoke often of living in an ashram in far-off Benares. Jeeves began to pay attention to the interaction between grandfather and granddaughter. Once when Narpat was lecturing to the baby about the devolution of the caste system and the Brahmins' monopoly of knowledge, Jeeves asked the old man, "You think she could understand all this history?"

"She understanding every single word. Look at how carefully she lis-tening." The baby's eyes were closed. "Everything sinking in her brains." She opened her eyes and looked at Jeeves.

At the Brahmin's house, the old sourness between Chandra and Ra-dhica reemerged. Radhica complained to Ray. "She with Kalawattie all the time. You don't think she could spare a few minutes to wash some cup or plate or dry some clothes?" She took her grievances to Dulari and was exasperated when the other woman offered no sympathy.

Every evening Dulari told Chandra, "A daughter-in-law who stay in her mother-in-law house just looking for trouble." She mentioned lots that were going cheap in Debe and Matilda and Monkeytown. "Two–three thousand for the land, and a next two–three thousand to build."

"You think it so easy, Mammy?" Chandra felt helpless and frustrated. "Is like you trying to get rid of me." Sometimes she broke down in tears, and Dulari would feel guilty about haranguing her daughter. But one evening Chandra and Ray returned later than usual. "We went to look at a lot in Petite Café." She didn't mention the brutal argument with Radhica the previous night. Radhica had called her a snake who was poisoning the relationship between mother and son.

"That is a very good place. Is only twenty minutes from here and about ten minutes from Princes Town. It convenient for you and Ray."

The shouting across the road grew more frenzied, and when Dulari listened, she heard Radhica screaming about entire families of snakes.

"The fish market doing good business these days." But Narpat too was disturbed by the screaming, and each evening he limped to the tractor and started the engine. That infuriated Radhica even more.

One night during the commotion, Dulari told Narpat of Ray's and Chandra's purchase of a lot in Petite Café. Surprisingly, he offered no denunciations. During the following evenings, while the baby played at his feet, he sketched designs on cardboard ends. In two weeks he presented his family with the design. "Modern plan. Split level. Concrete outer wall and cedar inner wall. Flat roof." His family peered skeptically at the design with its familiar slant. "Bamboo instead of boxing board. Small posts. It not building in a swamp. Simple and cheap. This plan will save a thousand dollars at the very least." His family, pleased with his enthusiasm, humored him, expecting that by the time construction began, after the rain, he would have forgotten. But when the rain ended and the farmers rode on their bisons and tractors to their fields, Narpat drove with Janak to Petite Café. Despite her mother's misgivings, Sushilla paid Janak each weekend. "It will get him out of the house, Mammy. And what harm he could do with his bad foot?"

At first the builders treated him with an amused deference because of his disability, but as he got in their way more often, shouting suggestions about using untreated lumber because it was not coated with toxic material, or mixing clay with the cement to increase porosity and insulation, their lightness faded. "You have to prepare for everything when you building a house. This place long overdue for a earthquake, and the only thing to prevent the houses from crashing down is by tying the crossbeam loosely. So it will rock." When they didn't take his advice, he said, "The day the earthquake come, half this island will get wipe out. The government will blame the contractors and the contractors will blame the government. The newspapers people will suddenly discover all the defects in planning. The pundits will say we paying for our sin, and the stupid people will bawl about bad luck. It have a easy way to prevent all that." Another day he told them, "If you use carat leaf instead of aluminum to cover the kitchen, all the bad odors will float out."

"Carat easy to catch fire."

"Only if you careless. Everything is a hazard, if you careless. In that case, you might as well build a iron box."

Ray just grinned when they complained.

Narpat was in his element. After his frustration with the factory and his injury and with the Brahmin's intolerable successes, he felt reinvigorated. He had hoped to complete his factory with the cane's profit, but since his accident the portion of harvested area had shrunk with each crop season. His old inventiveness returned. He stood at the side of the masons while they set up the bricks for the outer walls and behind the carpenters while they hammered the crossbeams into place. He confused them with talk of tension and torque pressure and auger depth. When he felt the builders were not following his directions, he drew alternate designs on waxy drafting paper. The builders stared at the design of a skeletal house with a tilted floor, a round roof, and walls that seemed to be suspended from the ceiling. "You must never disturb the natural shape of the land. Instead of cutting and carving, you must use the natural topography to your advantage." As the construction progressed, he drew other sketches detailing the electrical wiring and the plumbing.

"It not easier to install a straight pipe instead of one that twisting and turning all over the house?"

"You not thinking like a futurist." He explained that because of its lengthy passage, the water would be warm by the time it reached the tap. When they complained about the placement of the electrical switches and outlets, he said, "Is not a hospital allyou building here. Every task should involve some bending and stretching."

The builders had begun calling him Crackpot, though never to his face because their frustration was mixed with a slight trepidation of the old man. In spite of his injury, he spoke as if he expected to be obeyed.

And because of his relatively proper English, they guessed he was educated. They speculated on his former profession.

"He look like a old schoolteacher."

"He strike me as one of them lawyer fellas who get in trouble with the
magistrate and get throw out from the court."

"I have a feeling he is some sorta seerman. Telling the future and reading hand and that kinda thing."

"Maybe he use to work in the hospital because he always talking 'bout
poison and drugs and complaining about smoking and rum drinking."

"It too early to idle." Narpat limped up to the chatting builders. "If you
don't start the day with a proper attitude, then nothing will turn out right.
Everything will be incomplete and defective."

One afternoon an official from Town and Country Planning came to
inspect the building. He glanced at the structure and at the realms of
designs Narpat had sketched. "Who design this?" he asked angrily. The
builders sensed it would be a mistake to identify Narpat, who was tapping
his cane against the beam of the front door. "What exactly you all design
here? A house or a rocket or a submarine?"

Narpat heard. "Mister, what is the difference between a house or a
rocket or a submarine?" He limped toward the official. "They all serve the
same purpose. To protect the inhabitants and provide an escape hatch in
case of emergency."

The official, who was from Barrackpore, studied the old man. "You is
not the fella who was building the factory?"

"Not *was* building. Still building."

The official had heard idle talk of Narpat's stubbornness during his
routine inspections. "Still building?" he asked timidly now.

"Just allowing the building to take a rest. To settle. When I return, I
will notice all the structural faults. But I don't expect to see any because
I make sure everything was properly designed. Anything you don't prepare
for, does come up and bite you straight on your bottom."

The builders laughed, relieved now.

The official scrutinized the plans and glanced up suddenly. "I could
see the factory? It not in my jurisdiction, but I never ever witness a factory before. Studied them in drafting school though."

"Drafting school is a waste of time. You must have imagination to design a proper building. You have to anticipate every obstacle that might come up and remember where every single nut and bolt went. You can't put aside your building for a minute. You have to think about it day and night. You can't stop until the job is complete. They can't teach you these things in drafting school. You either born with it, or it get cement in your head when you still a child."

The official recalled his own discomfort at the drafting school, and his disappointment at the dry, tiresome designs he was forced to study each week. He remembered his frustration with the chain of bribes and kick-backs in the construction industry. He was a neat, slim, mixed-race man in his mid-thirties with huge black-rimmed glasses that made the rest of his face irrelevant. He was neatly dressed but for his shoes, the tongue of which flapped out from his pants hem. A white plastic packet in his shirt pocket contained an assortment of pens and a wooden ruler. "So I could visit the factory?"

When Narpat agreed, the builders were overjoyed. But Narpat had been thinking more and more of the factory. The design of the house was too simple, and he yearned for the challenge and complexity of the factory. A house was just a ceiling and a roof with a few walls. Anyone could build that. A factory was different.

The official, Rupert Guerra, was in a testy mood on the day he was to visit the factory. He had received conflicting directions about the site from the villagers; it was now late in the day, and he was just about ready to give up. He was disappointed too at his first glimpse of the structure, with the vines and lathro and waist-high bull grass. He walked around the tower and gazed at the dried vines at the tower's base and the shoots that had miraculously sprung from the dead mass to the blades. *The damn old man make me come all the way from Barrackpore*, he thought. Idly, he tugged at a liana, and the blades creaked an inch or two. He heard a rustling from within the tower and thought suddenly of snakes and wild dogs.

"I thought you wasn't coming again."

"Oh, lord!"

Narpat emerged from the tower with a cardboard box.

"You give me a real scare." Guerra wiped his face with his handker-chief. "I didn't realize you was hiding in there all the time. I didn't hear a single sound."

"I wasn't hiding. And you didn't hear a sound because you wasn't paying attention."

"What you have in that box?"

"Come inside." He turned with his box.

"In the tower?"

"You not coming?" Narpat's voice echoed from the tower.

"Yes . . . yes." He entered gingerly. In the dim light, he saw a bench and a rough table and a stool shaped from a tree stump. "We will be able to see in here?"

"The human body design for adjustment. Just be patient." He dropped the box onto the table.

For the entire evening, Narpat explained the rationale behind the graphs and the diagrams. Occasionally, his face serious and intent, he pointed with his cane to some aspect of his sketch. *This man with his bad foot, standing for two hours without shifting his position,* Guerra thought. *Talking nonstop with no sign of tiredness. And every single explanation make a kind of crazy sense.* His own back was aching from crouching on the small wooden stool. He looked at his watch and stood up. Narpat continued his commentary.

Guerra coughed and said apologetically, "I think this is enough for one day."

Narpat was surprised. "You will come back?" he asked, his normally firm voice soft and uncertain. He looked away, tapped his cane on the ground, and waited for this weakness to pass. He tried to recall all the times he had been disappointed.

"Next Wednesday. I finish work early on Wednesdays."

Narpat placed the box beneath the bench and limped to the trace. Guerra followed him. "You want a lift?" Narpat nodded and got in the car. On the way to Kanhai trace, Guerra asked, "How you get to the factory?"

"I get a lift halfway. I walk the rest."

"With your cane? It must be take you a while."

"Nothing wrong with a little exercise. The country air is the most purifying agent in the world. Pull in to that trace."

"I think I better pick you up next Wednesday."

"Why? That house on your left."

"Because it—it along the way."

"Where you from?"

The car stopped by the house. "Barrackpore. About half a mile from—"

"Barrackpore is not along the way. It will take you twenty minutes to drive here and another twenty minutes to the factory."

"So you don't want me to give you a lift then?"

"I didn't say that. I just explaining the inconvenience. Once you understand that, the decision is yours." He closed the door, not waiting for a response. Guerra looked at his watch. Eighteen and a half minutes from the factory. The old man's calculations weren't too far off.

When Narpat entered the house, he went straightaway to his plans. Late in the night Dulari took his untouched food from the table and threw the plate's contents into the garbage bin.

$\mathcal{T}$he house was completed in three months. Chandra moved out from Lengua, and on many weekends Jeeves found his mother at home alone. His sisters' absence seemed to stretch from room to room, and the silence, which was once a relief from the arguments, now seemed embedded to the walls and the furniture like dusty, unsprung traps. He was startled by the splash of water from the kitchen sink and by the sharp hiss of the stove. He wandered listlessly through the house, noting the small improvements. The simple decorations managed through Sushilla's salary would once have made her fussy and possessive, and it occurred to Jeeves that perhaps she still felt this way. So to break the silence, he would say, "This is a nice tea set," or "The new curtains match the couch," or "The plate rack in the kitchen looking real strong." His mother would smile, and a few minutes later, as if the comment had just registered, she would say, "Yes, it nice and strong." Two years ago she had taken him to a Syrian store and bought him new clothes. She had mentioned her happiness at her children's escape from the village. Now he wondered whether the old men and women he saw staring dully from their porches were similarly beset by regret at the loss of their children. Occasionally he went to the backyard garden, scrutinizing the medicinal plants his father had identified, breaking off the leaf and tasting the bitter sap. He poked around for insects and frogs and, when he was bored, went to the tractor and counted the rust spots forming on the exhaust and on the steering column. Pools of water and dried mango leaves had collected in the exposed cylinder heads. Spindly water grass sprouted from between the twisted metal. There were clumps of moss and lichen on the gas tanks. Rats somehow managed to build their nests beneath the hoses

and pipes. The oil had leaked into the grass, creating a barren brown border. By the time Sushilla returned in the night, about half an hour before
Narpat, Jeeves, fatigued by lethargy, was often fast asleep on the couch.

Sushilla left early on Sunday mornings for an ashram in Rio Claro,
where she had been spending much of her time. When Jeeves asked
whether their father knew, she shrugged and said she wasn't sure. And
Jeeves, perhaps because he was out of touch with the more subtle
changes in the family, was surprised at her nonchalance.

Both Kala and Chandra visited on the last Sunday of each month, and
Jeeves, who had noted his mother's fixed smile and her silence, was
struck by her brief energy during this one day. She prepared an elaborate
dinner, asked about their lives, gave advice, spoke about the prices of furniture, and fussed about the new kitchen utensils and the pro gas stove.

Then Kala graduated from university and was offered a job in the Ministry of Agriculture in Port of Spain, where she would work for two and a
half years before she applied for and was granted a CIDA scholarship to
study forestry at the University of North Carolina.

When she got the job, everyone was excited and congratulatory. Dulari
hugged her and spoke about the heavy traffic in the city and the best areas to rent, and Narpat limped around saying this was not a time for road-
blocks and fear and that Kala would be able to help him form his cane
farmers union. Just in time too, because the factory construction was going at top speed. He turned to Jeeves. "You hear that, Carea? This family
going to put back sugar on the map."

But Jeeves, noticing Chandra's and his mother's restraint, and recalling how fleeting and misleading these moments were, could not be drawn
into his father's mood. And once Kala left for her apartment in Aranguez,
close to Port of Spain, the oppressive silence enclosed the house once
more.

During the following weekends, he renewed his efforts to chat with
his mother. He noticed how much she was affected by the bleak after-
maths of these successes, as if she too knew that these moments would
pass, that the changes would not lead to lasting happiness. Sometimes
he glanced at her expressionless and spent smile and wondered whether
all parents fell into this kind of stupor. Yet his father was different; he
bounced back from all his mishaps with more maniacal energy.

While his mother was in the kitchen, he contemplated the strangeness of having parents who were almost as old as his friends' grandparents. The months of movies had given him an eye for detail, and in the little house he had lived for most of his life, he now noticed the play of light as the day progressed: the amber tint of dawn on the louvers and the rusty shadows of dusk on the furniture. He saw what he'd taken for granted in his mother's face: the sad pretty eyes, the round chin now weakened by age, and the tiny wrinkles on the thin upper lip, which from years of signaling resignation and amusement now seemed to signify both.

He awoke abruptly in the nights and saw his father on the Pavilion reading from a book held close to his face. On some nights the roof exploded with sudden thunderstorms, and long after the rain had subsided, he would hear the water falling from the gutter into the copper. Throughout, his father read as if he had not noticed the rain and the drip of water.

After a storm Jeeves would open the louvers to allow entrance to the cool night breeze. Rain flies and moths fluttered against the curtains and dropped to the floor. Only then would his father stir from his reading. "Careful these insects get in your ear." Whenever his father spoke, he would hear muffled sounds in his parents' room, the creak of the bed, and sometimes soft footsteps.

One night the thunderstorm came and went, the louvers were opened, the insects tumbled in. His father continued his reading. His parents' room was still. The place was so quiet that Jeeves felt like coughing loudly or kicking the vase on the coffee table just to break the silence. He imagined the sharp, pleasant sound of glass splintering and the relief of his father's inquiries. All at once he thought: a house this quiet is not normal; someone is going to die here soon. He winced at the notion and curled up on the couch, but the idea could not be dislodged. He lay awake staring at the dried, thorny shrubs his father had hung on the rafters and stuffed into the eaves to keep the bats away, until he finally fell asleep. He dreamed of a field of rotting fruits, the bright colors spotted with decay, and on the horizon a man and a women walking slowly away. He ran to catch the couple, but their distance from him remained the same. Suddenly the field was awash with vaguely familiar faces: regulars from Princes Town, movie characters, and laughing, chatting children. He searched for the man and the woman, but they had disappeared.

The dream stuck in his mind, and he repeated it to Dr. Who, who immediately grew worried. "You hear a jumbie bird bawling on the night of the dream? Or a dog howling?" Jeeves shook his head. "But it had children running around and crying, you say?"

"Just running around."

"Any music like this, boom boom taroom taroom?"

"No music."

"I don't like it. Something going to happen."

At the end of the week, Jeeves learned that now that he had written and failed his GCE exams and was no longer in school, his mother's arrangement with Bhola had run its course. The news was broken as suddenly as was the decision to relocate him, and during his last dinner at the table he focused on his uncle's hearty laughter, which did not soften his small cagey eyes. He saw Babsy's relief, which made her statements of regret so ridiculous. He noted Prutti's elaborate makeup and was astonished at how adult she seemed. When Samdaye hugged him, he felt her large firm breasts, and when she looked at him although her eyes were wet, he was transfixed by her broad mouth and protruding teeth. Her nostrils flared with each sniffle, and he recoiled and tried to push her away.

Downstairs he stuffed his clothes into the faded cardboard grip with which he had arrived. There was no place for his books, so he placed them on the table. Then he remembered the trinkets he had purchased from the old stores in Princes Town. He reopened his grip, and all at once, he was seized with a great fear. He had failed his exams. He was out of a job. The dreary futility of Lengua with its incomplete houses and canefields and old tractors and dingy rumshops stretched before him. When Bhola came down the steps, Jeeves leaned over the grip and pretended he was arranging his clothes.

"The cleaning job in the cinema is still yours if you want it." Jeeves wiped his eyes and looked up, grateful to this crude man. "But you will have to travel to Lengua. It mightn't make much sense."

Jeeves said swiftly, "I still want it."

"How much it will cost to travel by bus?"

The bus didn't go all the way to Lengua, but Jeeves lied desperately. "Fifty cents."

"That is a dollar two ways. I will throw in a extra dollar."

"Two dollars?" It seemed a fortune to Jeeves.

"You does drive a hard bargain, little Dubay. Just like you damn father."

He exploded in laughter. "All right, three dollars but don't push it." When Jeeves was hefting his grip up the stairs, Bhola grabbed a chunk of flesh and twisted. "Working man now. Just now we will have to fix you up with a lil craft."

On his way to Lengua, Jeeves was amazed at how easily the fear had been quelled. He tried to convince himself that the desolation of his parents' house had been exaggerated by his boredom, but the minute he saw the place, his old fears resurfaced. Now that he was once more lodged in the little house, he felt trapped by his mother's soft smile, and he began to avoid her. He wondered whether Sushilla had made the same decision. He could no longer stand his father's fixation on the factory either, and between both parents, between blasé optimism and resignation, he felt like a swimmer whose legs were caught in a tangle of weeds. He was relieved that he now worked on weekends because Chandra's visits grew more infrequent and Kala no longer returned each month-end. He wished he could remain in the cinema till the end of the eight-thirty showing, but the last taxi to Lengua left at nine.

While he was waiting for his taxi, he attempted to distract himself from the dread of returning to the village by inventing a game in which he transformed familiar faces into actors. The fat menacing clerk at Woolworth became Shelley Winters; the bony pharmacist at Easeright pharmacy, Peter Cushing; the mean-looking cripple dragging himself atop a box cart, Lee Van Cleef. Occasionally he fabricated flimsy movie plots, but in the mouths of the local characters, dialogue faltered. One night he noticed a lanky young man with a flapping unbuttoned shirt stumbling from Maggie's rumshop. *One of the hoodlums from an Indian movie*, he thought, but as the man approached, he saw it was Ray.

Ray almost passed by before he asked, "You is not Chandra brother? What you doing here so late in the night?"

"I just come from the cinema."

"What picture you watch?" Jeeves smelled the peculiar aromatic fragrance he had noticed once before.

"I working there."

"Nah, man, you joking. And all the time me and Chandra going to Metro in San Fernando and paying all sort of"—he paused for a word—"hifalutin money. That is why you never visit? You get too big?" He was speaking in the loud manner of a drunk unable to pitch his voice properly. "You forget me? You forget your own sister?" Suddenly he brightened up. "Come on. I park right by the library. I carrying you to visit your sister."

"I waiting for a taxi to get home."

"Taxi?" He frowned as if he didn't understand. "I tell you I carrying you to visit your sister." He held on to Jeeves's collar. "You too big to visit us? Eh? What you worried about? I tell you I will drop you home."

Jeeves went with him, not because he wanted to see his sister but because Ray was pulling his collar and shouting. Jeeves had been there during a few hurried visits, and he had usually remained outside staring at a neighbor's birdcage while his mother chatted inside with Chandra. Ray drove slowly, bumping in and out of potholes and singing Indian movie songs and waving an arm as if he'd forgotten Jeeves was in the car.

The house was more spacious than its outside appearance suggested. It was a three-bedroom wooden flat on a concrete foundation, with an expansive porch and decorative fretwork. It was built in the modern hodgepodge style that borrowed from the old cozy Port of Spain cottages, the small Spanish villas in places like St. Augustine and Arima, and the gaudy country mansions built by the newly rich. On each inside wall there were decorative mirrors enclosed by circular tiled designs. Plastic covers had been placed over the living room table and on the lowest rack of a scrolling corner shelf, on which were set glass figurines of angels, flowers, dancing women, and miniature palaces. Inside a space saver were china wares and a huge, ugly ceramic baby.

"Chandra! Ay, girl!" Ray rapped a wall. "Come and see who I bring." From the other side of the wall, the baby began to cry. "Shut your little tail, Kalawattie. I not talking to you." Jeeves felt that this forced playfulness was meant to impress him, but he felt uncomfortable. "Ay, girl!"

"You and your blasted liming. Look at the time of the night that you return from work. Take out your own food."

"I bring somebody to meet you." He grabbed Jeeves's collar, pulled him closer, and whispered conspiratorially, "You see how she does talk to me." He shouted once more. "To see Kalawattie."

"I don't want any of your *rangotango* friends touching the baby."

Ray put his fingers against his lips, winked, and suppressed a laugh. Jeeves struggled away, and Ray almost fell. "Kalawattie. Come, baby. Don't study your mother. I have a visitor here." Chandra, hearing the commotion, emerged from the room cradling the baby. She seemed set to say something when she saw Jeeves. Ray doubled up and choked with laughter. "You don't want the baby to see her own uncle?" He straightened and turned to Jeeves. "You see how she does treat me?"

Jeeves felt even more uncomfortable in this domestic setting. Chandra was wearing a black nightie, and in his embarrassment Jeeves looked at Ray while he said, "I just step in for a few minutes. Ray say he will drop me home."

"He in no condition to drop anybody home." Her mood changed. "You want something to eat? I could heat up some chicken and rice."

"And nothing for me?" Ray asked in an amused voice. "You see how she does treat me?"

"Take Kalawattie." She thrust the baby into Ray's arms. "And don't drop her again."

"Ay! I didn't drop no baby. I was just teaching her to jump."

Now Chandra rolled her eyes, and Jeeves wondered how the scene would have played if he had not been present. His sister stood over him while he was eating, asking if the food was warm enough, if the rice was soft, if the chicken had the right amount of salt. When he was finished, she encouraged him to a second helping. Ray disappeared with the baby into a room. She asked Jeeves where he had met Ray and what he was doing out so late, and when Jeeves said he was still working in the cinema, she inquired about their parents. He didn't want to worry her about Sushilla's prolonged absence or his mother's constant silence, so he said nothing. She sat down and idly dusted the crumbs on the table like their mother.

"I should go now."

"Ray went to sleep."

He got up and went into the kitchen. There were plate racks above the vinyl-covered cupboard. The fruits on the brown vinyl matched those on the cream wallpaper. The floor was spotless, and in the narrow space between the fridge and the wall, there were scoops, mops, and a broom. While he was washing his hands, he said loudly, "I could get a taxi here?" He didn't catch her response, which was muffled by the water. When he returned to the living room, he saw his sister arranging a blanket across the couch.

He awoke the next morning, confused by the Celotex ceiling and the pictures on the wall and the fragrance of boiling milk and cassava pone, a sweet wet cake. He got up immediately. Chandra came from the kitchen. "You had a good sleep? The baby disturb you?"

He slipped on his shoes. "I better go home before I go to work. Mammy must be worried."

"Ray will give you a lift. Is an hour before he start work. I take leave from the post office to see about Kalawattie." She glanced toward the bathroom. "Ray!" He emerged from the bathroom, a towel around his waist. "You better give him a lift to Lengua, Ray. He a little worried." Ray nodded shyly, and Jeeves was struck at how different he now seemed. He barely spoke during the journey.

"Thanks, Ray." Jeeves rushed out of the car wondering what he would say to his parents. His mother was in the kitchen looking out the back window. "I stayed by Chandra for the night."

Without turning she asked, "You eat there?" When he said yes, she seemed satisfied and Jeeves didn't know whether he should be relieved, disappointed, or offended. His father was still in his room. *Neither of them missed me*, he thought. *I could disappear for a week and they would not notice.*

"You had a good time there."

"Yes."

"You like the house."

"It nice and clean."

Jeeves wasn't sure whether these were questions or statements. He brushed his teeth hurriedly, washed his face, and combed away his hair from his forehead. As he was leaving, his mother asked or stated, "You staying there tonight."

"You prefer if I stay there, Mammy?"

"It closer to your work, son."

Jeeves felt that his mother meant: *It further from Lengua.*

Chandra betrayed no surprise when he showed up that night. "You want something to eat?" Without waiting for a response, she went into the kitchen and returned with a plate of rice and pigeon peas. While he was eating, she dusted the crumbs. "I will fix up the last room for you tonight. Jag does stay there on weekends when he get tired of Lengua." She uttered a tired little laugh that Jeeves could not interpret.

"Ray home?"

"Is only nine-thirty. He and his friends still have a joint or two to smoke out."

He said, "I feeling tired. I better get to sleep." He followed her into the room. He fell asleep before Ray's arrival, but he was awakened late in the night by sounds from his sister's room, the bed creaking slowly, the bedpost tapping against the wall, and low mournful groans. He pushed his head beneath the pillow. In the morning he smelled the hot cocoa and homemade bread.

Ray greeted him cordially, and Jeeves wondered whether his brother-in-law thought this was just a random visit. On his way to the cinema he felt guilty about his unannounced imposition, but later in the day he thought: *This could be the last time I ever visit my sister. Nothing was arranged. This evening I could go straight back to Lengua.*

He stayed there for eighteen months. During that time Kala left for North Carolina, Chandra gave birth to another daughter, and the Brahmin died suddenly, but Jeeves, secure and happy in his sister's house, felt distant from all these occurrences. He stood apart from the brief fuss surrounding Kala's departure and the mourning in the Brahmin's house. When Radhica hugged him and shrieked, "He gone, boy," and when she added inexplicably, "You alone now, boy," he noticed the hairless pudginess of her arms and her eyes vibrant with grief, but he felt no sympathy. For the first time in his life he felt strong and isolated. He imagined his little room as a sanctuary.

THIRTY-THREE

$\mathcal{J}$eeves quickly grew used to the familiar patterns in his sister's home: the nightly arguments between husband and wife, the creaking of the bed and the low groans, and the quiet domesticity of the mornings, as if the arguments of the previous night had not occurred. It was this familiarity that gave him comfort, and because he was involved in neither quarrel nor reconciliation, he felt safe and removed. In the mornings he played with Kalawattie and the baby Gomuti while his sister was in the kitchen, and frequently Kalawattie would slip into his room while her parents were arguing. Ray hardly spoke with him other than to comment, "The baby take a liking to you."

Jeeves soon fell into a routine—another comfort—leaving for work at precisely the same time, returning at nine-thirty, and spending half an hour eating and playing with Kalawattie. Because this routine fell into a pattern that was predictable and over which he wielded some control, his weekend visits to Lengua grew more tolerable. Occasionally he rifled through a box of comics and muscle magazines Jag had placed on a short mahogany bookcase and stared at the photographs of the Mr. Olympias and Mr. Universes, with their inhuman vascularity and bulging muscles. One night a picture hidden in a muscle magazine fell on the bed. Jeeves took one look at the photograph and locked the door. On one side of the page, a woman on a stool had her hand down her unzipped jeans, a sprinkle of short thick hair between her spread fingers. On the other side, the woman was lying on a bed, her knees slightly raised, her fingers in the same position. Her back was slightly arched and her eyes were partially closed. A caption at the bottom of the page mentioned she was a starlet.

Jeeves hurriedly replaced the page, but three times that night he returned to it.

The starlet reminded him of a woman he'd often seen chatting with Dr. Who. The woman was in her thirties, he guessed, and she wore tight pants and jerseys that showcased her huge breasts and fleshy hips. She walked slowly, her hair and breasts bouncing with each step, to the back row, where she sat alone. A few times he heard her low, hoarse laughter and speculated she might be a prostitute, but he never asked Dr. Who because he and the woman chatted as old friends. There were other women who had briefly drawn his curiosity, but the older women seemed unapproachable, and the younger ones reminded him of Prutti and he imagined they were snobbish and pretentious.

When he was at Bally's, the other boys had often boasted of their jocking techniques and frequency. Some of the quieter boys had claimed they were able to jock ten times a day. Jeeves's little circle of friends had frequently mentioned their girlfriends and had hinted at salacious private acts. Jeeves, having no girlfriend, invented a cute, vivacious, composite woman from a variety of movies.

"What this craft name?" one of the boys had asked skeptically.

"I dunno."

"You dunno your own girlfriend name?"

"Not really."

"You never ask her."

"We have better things to do."

"You could introduce me to this craft?" a boy with flat, sneering nostrils asked.

"She like her privacy."

The boys had roared with laughter, but two years later Jeeves met just such a girl.

The first time he saw her was at the Thursday four-thirty matinee, and though he kept watch, she didn't show up until the following Thursday. And every Thursday after that. Jeeves might not have paid her much attention if on the first Thursday she had not glanced at him with sudden interest, her eyes widening, her upper lip skirting up as if she were about to smile. But apart from that hurried bit of attention, she subsequently ignored Jeeves, which both excited and intrigued him. From her eyes and mouth, he began to notice other features, like her poised walk, her indifference—which was at once shy and confident—her smallish breasts, which in the boy's eyes set her apart from the starlet and the woman he felt was a prostitute.

Jeeves dreamed up myriad gallant opening lines but at the last minute always backed out. He tried to distract himself with the comics and the muscle magazines. The comics with their simple plots and overblown dialogue had at once seemed silly, but their brevity and simplicity provided a temporary distraction. This went on for almost two months before Jeeves progressed or rather blundered into the next stage. He was tempted to ask Dr. Who if the girl was mentioned in his dusseya, but he was nervous about what he might hear. One evening as he sat behind her while a Hammer production, a vampire movie, was playing, he felt that her nervous hair-fondling suggested a ripeness for contact. He fiddled nervously with the cold Coke in his hand. The vampire charmed, seduced, and sucked away at scores of white-dressed women. Finally Jeeves could bear it no longer. He had no idea what he would say when she turned around with her shy eyes and just-smiling lip, when he abruptly placed the Coke between his legs and touched her neck with his cold fingers. She shook her shoulders shudderingly as if trying to dislodge a horrible insect, bolted up, and without looking back rushed to the row just before the screen. She left ten minutes later, before the movie was finished. His mind was in a frenzy that night. *Could you hold my civilian clothes while I whirl swiftly from my gawky human identity into the man of steel. There's no phone booth around I'm afraid.*

During the following days Jeeves expected that she had reported him to the police or would bring along some hot-tempered brother or father or, worse, would not turn up at all. But when she did, Jeeves was so ashamed of his mistake, he kept away. So he was surprised when one evening as she gave Dr. Who her ticket, she glanced at him and smiled, both the smile and the glance so fleeting that he wondered whether it was just his imagination. The next Thursday, during a showing of *The Graduate*, she did the same, but her more lingering glance suggested curiosity and her just-smile, interest. Jeeves hovered at the exit at the end of the movie. As usual, she left after the unruly crowd had thinned. As she passed by, he blurted, "I don't understand what Dustin see in that old lady."

Without stopping or looking at him, almost as if she were talking to herself, she said, "I can see."

In the night Jeeves puzzled over her response. *I can see*. What did it mean? What special insight did she possess? And what exactly did she see? He was frustrated because the Thursday features were usually boring, enigmatic movies like *The Great Gatsby* and *Mahogany* and *Hello, Dolly!* He blamed these movies because he knew he could have impressed her easily with his broad knowledge of buccaneers pillaging some Caribbean island, or Eastwood calmly taking a town apart, or Steve McQueen, stoic and assured in a leper colony. One Thursday there was a rerun of *The Sound of Music*. Prutti came with her girlfriends. Her hair was elaborately woven and her cheeks nursed an unnatural redness. When the movie was over, Prutti paused and said, "I chuss vove dese Churmans." There was no friendliness in her voice, and Jeeves suspected she had spoken just to practice her strange German accent. The girl, waiting in the aisle, glanced at Prutti and her friends. When she came up, Jeeves discarded his prepared phrase and said, "I just hate these Germans."

"They are no different from anyone else."

Jeeves had seen enough movies to know this was untrue. "They think they are better than everyone. That's the problem."

She hesitated. Her hands went to her hair. "Really?"

"It's made them cruel . . . to their families."

"Really? To their families?"

He was on a roll. He repeated one of his father's expressions. "The strong learn from their mistakes. The weak blame their fault on others." She looked at him with a long, assessing gaze. Her lips parted. Jeeves held his breath. She walked away. The next Thursday he was hidden in the dark, but he noticed her gazing around before she walked to a seat. He followed her swiftly before her eyes adjusted to the gloom. The phrase *under the cover of darkness* popped in his mind as he sat next to her. She shifted away. He cleared his throat. "Oh, it's you," she said. He couldn't catch her expression, but she drew closer. "The cinema is empty tonight."

"People don't like this sort of movie."

"You do?"

"Sure," he lied. "My favorite type." He reeled off a list of actors he hated: Dustin Hoffman, Ingrid Bergman, Woody Allen, Glenda Jackson, anyone who'd acted in a Neil Simon movie.

"I agree with you. They have a strong inner coil."

He waited for an explanation, but she shifted closer. He felt her shoulders against his. They remained like that, barely touching each other, for about twenty minutes. He peeped from the corner of his eyes at her shapely legs. He lost track of the movie. She crossed her legs toward him, and before he knew what he was doing, his hand dropped on her thigh. She uttered a tiny birdlike sound as if she were quietly clearing her throat. Her shoulder stiffened, and he guessed she was looking at him. His palm was sweating, and he considered removing it to wipe away the sweat but that would be a kind of retreat. After a while his hand felt so numb that he imagined it would be impossible to remove. His shoulder too grew numb. He clenched his fingers to test its feeling. She jumped and shifted away her leg and in the same motion held his hand. She didn't release it, and for the rest of the movie, she squeezed his fingers. Later, Jeeves debated whether that was a sign of affection or an immobilizing tactic.

The following Thursday he placed his hand on her shoulder, but she reached up, grasped his fingers, and squeezed tightly. He leaned over to plead for release, and she turned at the same time and brushed her lips against his. He felt dizzy, caught in a room of apricots and ripe mangoes. The fragrance of her lips remained with him in the taxi.

The next Thursday the brief brush grew into a lingering kiss. She sucked in his tongue and licked and bit gently. Mandarins. Pears. Passion fruits. To Jeeves the kiss lasted a small lifetime, as long as his stay at Bally's, as long as the months at his sister's place. Time lengthened, compressed, and warped as in the comics. He felt sick with joy and excitement. Whatever her coil was, he knew he possessed it. He was in a daze. On Friday, Dr. Who told him, "I notice you and your craft making some heavy movement last night."

"Yeah, man," he replied, wanting and not wanting Dr. Who to say something more.

"She does only come here one day of the week?"

"On Thursday. She like these classics."

"And you too?"

"Yeah, man. They a little slow and hardly have any action, but the dialogue real deep. Deep, man. These fellas have coil." He felt suddenly grown up.

Dr. Who frowned. "So you like her?"

Jeeves blushed. "She is quarter percent decent lil craft, man."

"Hmm." Dr. Who raised his jersey.

Jeeves blamed *The Exorcist*, and the projectionist who had hurriedly substituted that movie, for the calamity. She had sat taut and immobile like a tree during the movie, and when Jeeves removed his hand from her shoulder and slipped it between her legs, she didn't flinch, but when he snaked his fingers into her silky panties, she snapped her legs together. Jeeves removed his hand hurriedly and watched her get up and walk away. He jumped when he saw the butcher, Alibocus, seated directly behind him. On the screen, Linda Blair spun her head right around.

Jeeves walked through the dank crowded cinema the entire week and was surprised at how empty it felt, as if the chattering audience were just shadows or wraiths from another dimension, soon to dematerialize to the Phantom Zone. On Thursday, when Dr. Who asked, "Like you and the craft had a falling-out?" he shrugged and said, "You know how women design. They like you to chase them. Play hard to get." But he was weak with grief and disappointment. He had listened skeptically to the boys at Bally's whispering about *tabanca*, an extreme love sickness that left the victim languid and listless, wandering around like a zombie, uninterested in food, friends, or family. Now he felt every one of these symptoms. He searched for her at night while he was waiting for a taxi, his heart quickening whenever he spotted a woman who from a distance held some whiff of familiarity. He did not know her name, and this compounded his sense of loss. He was startled and embarrassed when one night Ray said, "What happen to you now? Like you get a good dose of tabanca." Jeeves had no idea the affliction was so visible. He didn't seem any different in the mirror, but just to be safe he avoided Ray and his sister.

He began leaving Princes Town later than usual, hoping he would spot her. One night he saw Danny standing over the Lee Van Cleef vagrant. Jeeves moved into the shadow of a store. Danny leaned over and threw something to the vagrant. The scene was repeated the following night, and from the vagrant's gestures, he seemed to be angry. Danny said something and walked away. The vagrant tried to grab his feet.

Jeeves, not wanting to meet Danny, resumed his normal hours.

One Friday just when he was about to give up hope, he saw her. At first he wasn't sure because she was walking with a young man whose hands brushed hers with every step, and even when she hesitated before she tugged the young man's arm, he still couldn't believe it was her.

The young man was an inch or so taller than Jeeves and even skinnier. His lush moustache seemed transplanted onto his bony face. Jeeves was offended by his sinister, drooping eyes, the ridge on his nose, and the loose lips that pulled his mouth into a polished leer. *Damn hypocrite*, he thought, *with all that talk about inner coil.*

In the night he rolled out the crude dumbbells from beneath the bed and stared at the rusted iron locks. He got out Jag's exercise strands from the dresser and pulled, but the cables rolled and twisted like a row of snakes snapping at his shirt.

In his bed, he pushed aside the comics and stared at the muscular men in the magazines. Frank Zane. Dave Drape. Franco Columbo. He focused on their vascularity and definition, which had once seemed grotesque. He noticed the tautness of the skin, the ridges between the sinews, the striations on the chest, the diamonds on the calves, the balls between the arms. In repose, they stood with bowed head and the muscles softened. They were like superheroes. Outfitted in blue capes and cowls and gloves and shining boots, they could all be gathered in some atrium awaiting an urgent call from the president. *How different they are,* he thought, *from the soft, needy, coilless sallowness of Woody and Dustin and Richard.*

Jeeves decided to hang around until Saturday morning, when Jag usually came to share his room. Jeeves stated his interest. Jag grew serious. He asked Jeeves to remove his shirt and tapped, pinched, and kneaded. Finally he said, "We will have to start from scratch. Like bringing back a old, defective car." He removed his own shirt and flexed into poses Jeeves had seen in the magazines. "You have to train like a mule to get wings like these," he said proudly as he tensed his lats. Jeeves was surprised at the long, lean muscles. Jag replaced his shirt and told Jeeves of protein bars and amino acid drinks and glucose cocktails and egg shakes that jolted the muscles into growth. All the powerful bodies that seemed as if they had been drawn by Steve Ditko and Jack Kirby were actually within reach. He imagined slabs of muscles on his arms and shoulders.

"We have to work on the split system," Jag told him the next weekend. "Arms and legs one day, and chest and back the next. Then we will move on to the Heavy Duty system that get startup by a fella name Mike Mentzer." He removed two strands from the unit. "Try pulling this for a few weeks. It will awaken the muscles and get them ready for the iron."

He showed Jeeves some of the exercises. "Keep your chin up. Don't bend your back like that." Jeeves struggled with the single cable. "Imagine you is a old gladiator fighting a lion. Aha! You like that. Careful, careful, we don't want to massacre the lion so bad." He laughed as Jeeves frantically stretched the cable. Then he grew serious. "Is time for you to clear out from the room now. My shift here start."

"I will try the strands again on Monday."

"Yeah, yeah." He got up from the bed and went to the window. "You probably hear plenty in this house."

"I mostly drop asleep as soon as I reach here. I hardly notice the quarreling."

"So they does quarrel, eh?"

Jeeves tried to backpedal. "Only now and then. They does patch up in the morning."

"And in the night too, I sure." He laughed humorlessly. "You ever hear them quarreling about me?"

"Nah. I don't think so."

"You sure?"

"The argument does be mostly about Ray liming."

"Some of them fellas on steroids."

"What?"

He turned from the window. "How you think they so big. You ever see the creole fella, Sergio Olivia?"

"Yeah." Jeeves pondered the sudden shift in the conversation.

"He and Arnold does be duking it out in every competition. The two of them start out just like you too. Weak-looking. Long, skinny hand and foot. Like crab with all the flesh inside." He rolled up a muscle magazine. "Take this. It have some good articles for beginners." As Jeeves was leaving, he said, "And if you hear any talk, let me know."

That Saturday Jeeves hung around the town, browsing the new muscle magazines in Woolworth and gazing at the protein shakes in Easeright pharmacy. A little after midday he walked by Maggie's rumshop and bought two doubles from a vendor. The midday weekend crowd seemed more relaxed, better dressed, he thought. There was more noise too, with the constant screech of traffic and the loud conversations and idlers catcalling passing women. Then he heard a more concentrated sound, a quarrel in progress across the road. Danny and the Lee Van Cleef vagrant were arguing loudly. Drunkards from the bar peeped out, happy with the bacchanal. Danny's shirt collar was up in the style of badjohns, and he was rapping his fist against his palm and screaming, but when he tried to walk away, the vagrant managed to grab his leg. He struggled for a while. The vagrant's long white hair was tossed over his face, so he might not have seen the first kick, which caught him flush on his forehead, nor the second, which rocked him backward. But he held on, and Danny began to kick him about his body, savagely and unrelenting. Some of the drunkards rushed across the road. A few of them managed to pull Danny away, but he broke free and lunged once more at the vagrant. Finally he was subdued. He left screaming and cursing. The crowd dispersed. The drunkards returned to Maggie's. The vagrant flopped forward, his face hidden by his hair.

"I know that would have happen one day."

"It happen already. I was in this very said bar at the time."

"Sancho look for he kick. He think he is still a badjohn instead of a damn cripple."

"Is that same nonsense that cause his leg to get chop off."

"He should be thankful for the couple cents he does get every few days. He always want more."

"Who is the boy to him?"

"You dunno? Is his son. He is a big drug pusher. He make some time already."

"Is just a matter of time before one of them kill the other. Sancho does have a knife hideaway under his clothes."

"I wonder why the boy so mad with him."

"Don't wonder so hard. He just naturally mad. Just like he crazy father."

The drunkards laughed. Already the incident was transformed into a joke, already the tragedy was trivialized, but Jeeves could not be so flippant. He recalled the boy who had somersaulted up the mango tree and told stories of hidden gardens and fish-eating rainbows and sadhus floating on cardboard clouds.

Jeeves had been flogged often and severely both at school and at home, but he had never witnessed brutality so without purpose. From habit, he tried to frame the assault within a movie, but he also wanted it to be unreal and impermanent. What had happened to his friend, he wondered, that would drive him to such ferocity? Maybe he had always been like this. He scanned the faces of the young men walking past the rumshop and tried to assess how many of these peaceful-looking men routinely beat their infirm parents. A taxi pulled up, and he ran to it, brushing aside a young couple. The driver turned around. "Make allyou self small before Pangay reach." One of the men in the front seat gestured, and the driver saw the policeman. "Oh god father, is trouble in me ass today." He straightened. "Good day, Mr. Pangay. I just giving some of me cousin a squeeze in the taxi."

"How much cousin you have in this town? Every time I see you, is some cousin you helping out." He was a thickset man with heavy folds beneath his eyes and at the sides of his mouth. He seemed to be perpetually smiling, but he was the torment of the Princes Town taxi drivers.

"This one dropping right 'round the corner." He pointed to Jeeves.

Pangay pushed his head into the car. His thick lips trembled as he counted silently. "Twelve in all. Serious overloading. Lemme see your insurance."

The driver sighed and opened the glove compartment. He pulled out a clump of papers strung with a rubber band.

"Insurance up too."

"I was just about to renew it, Mr. Pangay. Look, I have the money right here." He reached into his shirt pocket and withdrew two twenty-dollar bills.

Pangay took the money. His lips trembled. He returned the clump of paper.

The driver pulled off. "That nasty mothersass take every cent I work for today. Always digging in we ass for bribe. I wonder where he was when the fight was going on?"

"Right below Bata shoestore. Watching everything," a passenger said.

For the rest of the trip the driver quarreled, but Jeeves was thinking of Danny. Later he felt that witnessing the sudden violence, the brutality of son to father, and the transformation of a friend into a hoodlum marked a turning point in his life. More than all his father's lectures and fables about backbone and resilience, the assault, he felt, emphasized the value of independence and inviolability as the greatest of strengths.

When he arrived in Lengua, he sat on the porch and looked at Radhica, her head bowed slightly. He had never particularly liked her, but now, gazing at her moving slowly in the gallery, he realized that since the Brahmin's death she was alone in the house on most weekends. He recalled the evening he'd seen her tenderly dyeing his hair in the kitchen, and he wondered how she now spent her time. Did she enclose herself in a fortifying fatalism like his mother, or was she moody and erratic like his father? He considered the burdens of age: not the infirmities or the forgetfulness but the loneliness. Perhaps these old people looked forward to death as a release from pain and neglect and isolation. He wondered whether Radhica occasionally contemplated her younger happier days; maybe her dreams were filled with these memories. He had never previously reflected on the daily routine of his own parents. What did each expect of the other? Did they actually speak with each other? After dinner, alone at the table, he took his plate into the kitchen. "The food taste real good, Mammy."

His mother turned on the tap. "Is rice and lentil and cabbage and potato," she recited, the words almost lost in the drip of water.

"You get any letter from Kala?"

"Not this month."

"She must be busy." When his mother did not reply he added, "Where Pappy?"

A sharp fleeting frown crossed her face as she turned off the tap. "Who?"

"Pappy."

"He building his factory." Once that statement would have been uttered with a sprightly annoyance, but now the words were just words, flat and mechanical.

"You wish he was home more often?"

She shook her wet hands. "I don't wish again." She went to the stove and turned off the burner. The blue flame gasped and crackled and died.

THIRTY-FOUR

*T*he factory was built carefully now. The remaining walls went up slowly, the bricks positioned and pounded on their beds of cement with an attention that infuriated Narpat. The mortar was mixed unhurriedly by a silent man with a broad face the color of worn leather, Guerra's contribution to the factory. Guerra was careful to a fault, and while Narpat argued about cost cutting and the substitution of native material and the advent of the rainy season and pretentious draftsmen, Guerra weighed and measured and scribbled calculations on one of his gray writing pads. Sometimes he argued with Narpat and grew frustrated and impatient and promised silently never to return to the factory and to the miserable, opinionated man who was tolerable in small doses but confounding in close quarters for three hours every day.

But he came straight to the factory after his work, Narpat already there, hobbling around the walls, pinching at the mortar with a sour look. In spite of everything, Guerra was still impressed by Narpat's devotion. Compared with the crooked contractors he encountered daily, Narpat's forthrightness was invigorating. Guerra made jokes to lessen the old man's protests but was roundly chastised for his flippancy. One evening he was surprised that a light comment about Narpat getting an old motorbike was taken seriously.

"It will cut down my dependence on other people."

"Is no trouble dropping you back," Guerra said uneasily.

"Is a trouble for me. One day you will decide to collect this debt."

"It might be difficult to learn to ride a motorbike."

"I drive and operate every single kind of machinery it have on this island."

"I mean—"

"You mean my bad leg? If you look carefully, you will see that motor-bikes design for people like me. All the controls on the handle."

"It might be expensive."

"Young fellas like you always looking for a roadblock."

"I just trying to be practical."

"What impractical about me getting some independence." He turned to the workman. "You think you could manage by yourself for a hour?" The workman glanced at Guerra. "We still have time to get to Neck's scrapyard before closing time."

On the way to the scrapyard Guerra, sensing disaster, renewed his objections. Neck's was known for selling defective machinery. The bike, if there was one, would be a trap. Parts would be impossible to get. Repairs hopeless. Narpat made his puppet, aggravating Guerra. "Pok pok pok."

And at the scrapyard they found an old scooter that, though battered and rusty, was whole. Guerra paid twenty dollars, Narpat promised to repay him the next day, and the scooter was lodged in the trunk. Narpat spent a week dismantling, cleaning, and reassembling the scooter. He whistled and hummed songs and shouted his satisfaction to his absent children. And Guerra, who felt he had accomplished a remarkable amount of work during Narpat's absence, was surprised to see him driving up to the site one evening. The workman glanced from Guerra to Narpat.

"Allyou never see a man on a scooter before? You shouldn't let a little thing like this provide a excuse for idleness." They soon realized that Narpat's sudden rejuvenation was a calamity. He grew more preachy. He got in their way more often. He insisted with renewed energy on specific modifications. He spoke of perseverence and fortitude. "Allyou young fellas think that this broko-foot make me a cripple, not so? That I should give up and swing from a hammock all day and wait for death." He tapped his ankle with his cane. "This is just a roadblock. A minor inconvenience. A test to see if I will give up. But this old man never going to surrender. Too much people waiting like corbeau for me to chuck everything. That is my strength." Guerra flinched when he added, "I going to be here until my last day."

He grew more talkative at home too, explaining there was a familiar pattern to his life; that the world was reordering itself. He lectured about fluxes and circles. The single worker he had managed to hire in the canefield was paid from Sushilla's salary. The profits from the cane were spent on the factory. And one day the factory would provide enough revenue to support the entire village. Dulari, who from years of practice often reflected her husband's shifting mood, found herself slipping into her old fussiness, her meager optimism kindled by Narpat's enthusiasm. She surprised Sushilla by murmuring she spent too much time in the commune, and Jeeves, by displaying an interest in the length of his hair and in his tight clothes, which showcased his new modest muscles. And when she complained about the blurriness of her vision, her constant fatigue, and the swelling in her hands and feet, her children took these as signs she had emerged from her silence, like a woman freed from darkness suddenly rediscovering the whisper of light. Unknown to her children, there were more serious symptoms: she fainted one evening and recovered late in the night alone at home. From then on, whenever she felt dizzy, she would brace against the wall to the sofa. Some mornings she was too weak with nausea to prepare her husband's meals, and he would stare silently at the bare table before he went to his scooter. In the night, he noted the cold food, the unmade bed, the unswept floor; the house almost as he had left it in the morning. Occasionally he glanced swiftly at his wife and noted with abhorrence how the puffiness had added a softness to her arms and a weakness to her face. He sermonized loudly about sloth and the effect on the body of inactivity. Perhaps she was too tired to care, or maybe her weakness opened some window of compassion and alerted her to what she had missed before, because she responded to his complaints by cautioning him about his alliance with the young draftsman and the money spent on the factory. She developed a sudden sympathy for Radhica.

All of this confounded Narpat, and he saw in his wife the image of another weak woman more than fifty years earlier. He recoiled when she said between breaths, her voice ebbing to a dolorous wheeze, "The poor old woman have no one to talk with, Pappy. Who will know if she get sick in that house? Who will call the doctor?"

"No need to call any doctor. The Brahmin leave a few hundred mantras for any complaints."

"The poor old woman, Pappy."

He couldn't stand this. "She paying for her deeds. Karma."

"Don't say that. You don't know what going on inside her mind."

One morning after Narpat had left on his scooter, she walked tiredly across the road. Radhica glanced at Dulari climbing the stairs slowly and came down to meet the other woman halfway. They sat side by side, staring out and not saying anything. Then Radhica pressed her head against her orhni and, as if excited by the warm drop of tears, began to sob, panting loudly into her orhni. "He gone so sudden, didi. He never give any sign to prepare me. Gone like a breeze. Here today, gone tomorrow. When you live with somebody for fifty-six years, you expect them to be still near to you in the gallery smoking or watching flowers." Her sobbing relaxed into guttural cackles. "He and his Lucy."

Dulari came across every morning and comforted her by listening. Soon it emerged that the Brahmin had not really departed like a breeze. He had left a multitude of signs. He had mentioned dreams of the Himalayas and the Ganges. In other dreams—visions, Radhica called them—deities had complimented him on his good work. His left eye had been nictitating steadily for weeks. Black cats crossed his path as if waiting especially for him. Two days before he died Geronimo, one of his favorite chelas' dog, began howling for no reason. An episode of *I Love Lucy* had mentioned funerals.

When Dulari grew too weak to walk across the road, Radhica still sat on the step and looked out.

Apart from Jeeves, none of Dulari's children were aware of her slide into feebleness. One weekend he noticed the inflammation around her eyes and the gray pallor to her skin. When she spoke, he saw the lustrous sheen to her pupils as if she were seeing either deep inside him or not seeing at all. She asked with long pauses about Chandra and Sushilla and her grandchildren, and when he mentioned the babies' new skills, she patted her knees and smiled blankly.

The following day he confessed his concerns to Chandra and suggested his sister pay a visit with the babies. Chandra pushed out her lower lip and in the half-bantering voice she used with Ray in the mornings, she complained about her husband's liming and the lateness of his return every night. "You think he in any condition to drive to Lengua in the night?" she fussed.

"Maybe on weekends."

"And these two little devil here don't give me any spare time." She cooed at her babies. "Eh? Not so?"

The next weekend Jeeves delayed his stay in Lengua till late in the night. When Sushilla returned from her ashram, he told her, "I think Mammy not feeling well."

"She told you that?"

Jeeves noticed the pitch of her voice and the little smile fixed on her face. "She didn't have to mention anything. She look . . . different."

"That is the gift of god, Jeeves. Old people develop a nice peacefulness."

Who is this woman? Jeeves thought. He recalled their conspiracy during a distant Christmas and walking with her to school and sharing seasoned mangoes on a crumbled brown paper. "They develop some nice diseases too."

"Boy, you talking just like Pappy. Look at you." She came up to him. "You beginning to look like him too when he was younger. With all these muscles you growing, Every Saturday night I docs hear you clanging away in the back of the house with the weights you build from Pappy junkpile. Take care you don't start building your own—"

"Maybe we should take her to see a doctor."

She pretended surprise. "That is not Pappy talking now." When she finally saw his irritation, she said, "Doctors can't cure what in the mind. Leave Mammy alone. She had a hard life, and now she getting closer to her maker." She began to hum a melodious *bhajan* and, perhaps for her brother's benefit, sang a stanza in English. "'When you walk in my shadow, no harm shall come to you. Put aside thy worries and seek the bliss of my name.'"

"No blasted body care about anything again." Immediately he regretted the statement, and he ran out of the house, stung by the hurt in his sister's eyes. What right had he to complain? His parents were actually surviving on Sushilla's salary, just as he himself was subsisting on Chandra's hospitality. His weekly salary was twenty-one dollars. From Dr. Who he received another nine dollars in "hush money." From the grand total of thirty dollars, he spent twenty dollars each week on food and snacks and protein drinks. When he recalled the bread and egg and the chicken roti and the currant rolls and the slices of doughy cakes he purchased most middays, he was surprised at the extravagance. One dollar could provide three doubles, an entire meal.

When he returned to Chandra's place, he withdrew thirty dollars from his wallet, money he'd been saving to purchase a huge tin of Joe Weider's bulking-up formula, and laid the bills on the table.

"What is this?" Chandra asked. Jeeves was suddenly embarrassed. He didn't know if he had offended his sister. She noticed him squirming and broke into a grin. "Look, boy, put back this in your wallet."

Ray came to the room. "Gimme it. I could put it to good use."

"Waste it on ganja, you mean."

Jeeves sensed another of their ribbing arguments.

"Ay! I talking 'bout buying booties for the babies." He made a playful snatch for the money. "And some good baby food. Not that nonsense you does mashup and stuff them with."

Chandra walked over to Jeeves and pushed the money into his pocket. "Keep this. You will need it later. Maybe I will borrow it when that druggie get fired from his job."

"Ay! Who going to fire me?" He winked at Jeeves. "We will talk later."

"Leave him alone, Ray. He not interested in your vices."

"Then why I does see him in Maggie rumshop hiding and drinking Carib?"

"That is not true. I—" He stopped short, offended and embarrassed by the couple's loud laughter.

Ray withdrew a bunch of keys from his pocket and dangled it before Kalawattie. "I will see you in a little while. I have some matters to fix up."

"Which backroom these matters in?"

"I gone." He bolted from the house.

"He going to come back home high like a kite." Jeeves noticed her nasal singsong voice, a sign that her irritation was moderated by some private joke (or worse, Jeeves thought, some undisclosed intimacy). He wanted to talk of his mother, but his sister was still half-complaining about Ray. When she said, "Don't mind all the smoking, he don't get involve in anybody business," he couldn't understand what she was talking about.

But at the end of the week he saw a different side to his brother-in-law. The argument was already in progress when he arrived at the house. Ray and his brother, Jag, were on the porch shouting and swearing at each other, and Chandra, holding the babies, was staring out from the doorway. An old couple from across the road was gazing with muted interest at the spectacle.

Jeeves's path to the house was blocked by the quarreling men, and he felt it was inappropriate to leave his sister, so he stood rooted at the front gate. The argument developed into a minor scuffle, pushing and shoving at first, and then suddenly, as if a scene from a violent movie had been spliced into the raillery, Ray slapped his brother with such force that he staggered back, his momentum stopped only by the railing. Then they were at each other's necks, clawing and cuffing. Jag the bodybuilder was stronger, and soon he floored his brother, but when he hoisted a potted plant from its stand, Chandra put down her babies and flew at him. He fell backward, rolling down the steps, the plant still in his hands, globs of manure spilling on his face. He howled and cursed.

Now Ray rose up and grabbed the stand and flung it at his brother, the wrought iron shattering the clay pot, the dislodged dracaena falling in its clump upright onto Jag's face as if it had been planted there. He got up like a wild beast, rubbing his eyes and shaking his head, the manure flying from his hair. Ray jumped to the second step and attempted to kick his brother's chest, but he fell on the stair, his arms spread like a dancer's.

Jeeves, transfixed, realized that his sister had been screaming all along, her voice erased by the violence. When Jag snatched a white-washed stone from a circle decorating a dwarf palm, Chandra knocked away the stone from his hand, and Jag, perhaps because he was blinded by the dirt or maybe because he no longer cared, struck her across the face, the blow drawing blood immediately. Ray got up groggily from the step and saw the blood on his wife's face. "You nasty, shameless bitch. Hitting a woman!" He pushed his wife before his brother. "Hit her again. What you fucking waiting on? Hit her again, I say." For a moment it seemed as if Jag would take his brother's advice, but he lowered his head.

Ray was now incoherent, cursing and crying and bawling. "You fucking little dog. Hitting my wife in front my own face." Suddenly he pushed away Chandra and launched at the other man. They both tumbled on the ground, rolling on the graveled pathway, striking each other with short, snapping jabs.

"Kill each other." The words—uttered without malice, without emotion, more an observation than a taunt—had come from the old woman. For some reason it broke Jeeves's spell, and he ran to the fighting men and pulled up Jag, surprised at how easily he came up, how easily the clasp around his brother's throat was broken. And when Ray, seizing the respite, attempted to rush at his brother, Jeeves stepped before him and finally managed to hold both his flailing hands.

"Leave me alone, man. Don't interfere. This is between brothers. Me and that fucking thieving brother."

Jeeves heard Chandra's voice, "Jag, you better go now," speaking softly as if a normal visit had come to an end.

"Yes, get your ass out. Get out and don't let me see your face in this place again. You nasty fucking snake." He struggled against Jeeves's clasp before his body slumped. "Go, go. Go and spend all the money." His voice was softer and weaker now, like a man regaining consciousness.

Jeeves heard a van's engine, the sound seeming to come from a distance. He released Ray's hands.

"Jeeves, take away the keys!"

But Ray pushed back the keys into his pocket and said tiredly, "I going to sleep. Wake me up when Pink Panther and the aardvark start."

"Yes, go and sleep," his wife said. When he took up the crying babies from the porch and disappeared into the house, she added, "Boy, is a good thing you was here today, or one of them would have kill the other for sure."

And Jeeves, who had often fantasized about being thrust into some heroic act, shrugged and said, "I didn't do anything."

"Stop talking like Pappy." She squeezed his arm and looked up at his face. "Look at you, boy. So handsome. Where that skinny little boy gone? You get Pappy strong face and Mammy nice soft eyes. You lucky, boy. Lucky boy." Her voice began to drag like her mother-in-law's, but her eyes were wet.

"You better go and wash out the blood from around your mouth," Jeeves told her.

Chandra brushed the back of her palm against her lip and examined the blood. Then she sat and, in one long burst, explained the source of the quarrel, speaking quickly as if she wanted to get this off her chest. Kalawattie came from the room. "I best go and see if Ray okay." She got up. "I think I hearing him snoring already."

Jeeves lay awake later than usual that night, and he was surprised when, just after midnight, he heard the familiar creaking and groaning. But tonight there were whispers and a subdued conversation. He guessed they were talking about the fight and about Jag's unexpected decision to sell the property at Kanhai road to the Manager. Although Chandra had not directly mentioned this, both she and her husband had felt it was unnatural for the property to be given to Jag instead of the eldest son. Chandra had hinted to Jeeves that Radhica, who disliked her, must have played some part in this aspect of the Brahmin's will. Now the old woman was without a place in which to live, and for that, Ray was enraged.

Jeeves guessed the time had passed to talk about his mother.

The following weeks were no better. In the nights, Jeeves heard the whispers thickening into subdued arguments, and sometimes there were no intimate sounds. He mused over his sister's testy mood while he was exercising in the evenings and when he awoke to the aroma of cocoa and freshly baked bread. One morning, as he was about to leave, Chandra slapped Kalawattie across the cheek, and when the girl began to cry, she hugged and pacified her with baby noises and fed her syrupy Quaker Oats. Two weeks later Jeeves discovered the reason for his sister's glumness.

Jag removed his mother's bulging suitcase from the van but stopped short at the front gate. "Come and collect this," he shouted cheerfully to Jeeves, who was in the front porch. "It heavier than all these weights you lifting. Like you exercising hands down, mister. How it going?" But he did not wait for a response. The van sped off with a screech.

"Take this inside for me, beta." Radhica's face seemed sliced by two deep diagonal furrows pressing against her mouth and pushing out her lower lip. Her nose seemed more bulbous too, and when Jeeves grasped the suitcase, he noticed the scatter of blackheads on her cheeks and the curly hair sprouting from a mole on her chin.

"Take it to your room, Jeeves." Chandra seemed set to add something, but as Jeeves heaved the suitcase to his room, he felt there was no need for an explanation. The room itself was cleaned, and his clothes were pressed into a small wedge of the closet. He heard his sister in the living room saying without feeling, "The room straighten out for you. Jeeves use to sleep there." There was a pause as if she expected some response, before she said roughly, "You want anything to eat?"

"No, beti. I okay." Jeeves emerged and saw Radhica attempting to hug Chandra. When Chandra led her stiffly to the room, she wiped her eyes. "It so nice and small."

Chandra removed the other woman's hand from her own. "I will leave you to unpack." She went to Jeeves in the porch. "So you lose your room, boy?"

"Is no problem. I think is a good idea for somebody to stay with Mammy. And it have plenty taxi in Lengua these days."

"You remember when the only taxi was Janak," she said suddenly. "And when Pappy squeeze in all of us with Janak children in the old Austin for Ramleela?"

"His boys have their own car now."

"Things does change so much." Her mood changed with the statement. "You never know what going to happen."

"Is okay." He felt she was going to begin an unnecessary apology.

The old woman called out her name from the bedroom. "No, is not okay," Chandra said to her brother. "You will sleep on the couch."

"I really prefer—"

"Me and Ray discuss it already." The old woman emerged from the bedroom. "In any case you accustom sleeping in living rooms. And it don't have any bats here to bite your neck." She uttered a short laugh. The old woman looked at both, and she too began to laugh, a low drumming cackle.

After a week Jeeves knew he could not stay for long at his sister's place. Radhica followed Chandra around, her soft slippers registering no sound. Frequently she squatted on the floor and said she was developing *gookools*, painful warts. Once he awoke with a start from the couch and saw the old woman sitting before him on the floor, her feet stretched abjectly. "I couldn't sleep, beta. The *rumatism* does walk up from my foot straight to my neck." She bunched and raised the hair from the back of her neck. "Right here. Squeeze right here." Jeeves was disgusted at the oily skin, and the soft flesh giving way in his hands, and the blackheads and moles so alike in appearance and texture as to be indistinguishable, and the satisfied, crooning sounds coming from the old woman. "I have to get to work now," he lied, rushing to the bathroom.

The relationship between Chandra and her husband changed too, and Ray's normal silly expression was now masked by a vigilant anger. One evening Jeeves heard him telling his wife, "She is a old woman. What you want me to do? Put her out? That will make you happy? If I get just like Jag?"

Radhica, with the oblique slyness of the old, offered comments about her son's and her granddaughter's thinness. "Like you is the only one eating in this place, beti?" Chandra could never respond to these criticisms, because the old woman would thrust her neck this side and that like a turkey alert to danger and groan about her rumatism and her gookools. Occasionally she picked up bits of fluff from the floor and hid them in her hand until her son's arrival. "I find this on the floor. It was just waiting there for one of the children to choke on. Is a good thing I spot it in time."

On some mornings Jeeves heard Chandra banging the dishes in the kitchen sink as his mother had done.

"You will mashup the plate, beti. Move aside and let me do it for you." But she stood before the sink twisting her neck and complaining about the pain. "When I was your age, I used to wash four times this amount, but I can't manage again." She broke into sobs.

Jeeves recalled an old and typically cold statement of his father: Never trust a man or a woman who does cry for every single thing, because behind every drop of tears it have a scheme forming. And that was how he viewed the old woman, as a schemer hiding behind her tears. Late in the nights he thought of his mother's silence about her own condition.

He realized that his lengthened presence at Chandra's place was meant to convey to the old woman that her stay was temporary, but after three weeks of sleeping on the couch, he informed his sister he was moving back to Lengua.

"The room is yours the minute it get free," she told him.

"Beti. Beta. What allyou whispering about? Why allyou leaving me out?" She twisted her neck. Jeeves hurried away.

Part Five

When Jeeves returned to Lengua, the Manager had already moved into the Brahmin's old house. The flower garden had been paved over and converted into a garage for his rickety truck and his straightening business. Haphazard renovations were already under way in the house itself. The Brahmin had created a sense of order to the property, with the color of the outer walls matching the paint on the roof, and the arrangement of his garden on one side of his house balancing the empty lawned area on the other. He had surrounded the house with a variety of hybrids—plums, mangoes, cherries, pommecytheres—and under each were anthuriums with broad fan-shaped leaves and crimson heart-shaped flowers. Bird feeders had been strung to attract bananaquits. All had been destroyed or mutilated to make way for the vehicles. And Narpat, who had criticized the Brahmin's horticultural pursuit as idleness, said, "You take a monkey from the zoo and you put it in a proper house, and he will start destroying everything in no time."

He had been annoyed at the Brahmin's impassiveness, which he had seen as caste-pretentiousness, but the Manager, loud, vulgar, and intrusive—in every way the opposite of the Brahmin—drove Narpat to a fury. The Manager was a repository of diseases, bad food, sloth, and malice; the Brahmin had represented superciliousness, the Manager promised only chaos. When Guerra had finally had enough of Narpat and stormed off from the project, rueing the months he had wasted, taking his workman with him, Narpat parked his scooter against the tractor and each morning gazed at the Manager's belly hanging over the railing while he brushed his teeth and spat at the goat wandering around and swore at the boys pounding and straightening the wrecks brought weekly to his place.

Narpat recoiled from the Manager's easy familiarity, calling out to him as if they were old friends, shouting out his name so readily it seemed a taunt.

Everyone on whom he depended had betrayed him. He limped around the porch, knocking the floor with his cane. The world resisted improvement; decay and instability were its natural states. Everything he had fought for was in vain because he was going against the natural order of things; in spite of him, everything would revert to chaos. Progress was a trick, an illusion that encouraged, then shattered hope. He could see the disintegration in his own house. The passepartout pictures on the wall were discolored with mildew. The electrical wires sagged against their bindings. He could punch his finger in portions of the wall where woodlice had hollowed the boards.

Outside the engines lay rusted and useless, the parts seized together. The drains at the front and at the sides of the house were filled with slime. The trees beyond the back garden were plagued with scabs and epiphytes. For most of his adult life, he had believed that toughness was the only buffer against dissipation, but now he felt that parasites were better equipped for survival. He thought of the cane farmers union, his uncle, the politicians, the proprietors, and right across the road, the Manager. They were all successful. But they were parasites. Soon the Outsiders would displace the few remaining farmers.

He hobbled to the road, tapping his cane so rapidly that a few times he almost lost his balance. He stopped before each house, and when its startled occupant emerged to shout a greeting, he moved on. Some of the neighbors remained in their galleries and gazed at Narpat repeating the act before each house. But he was not interested in socializing. After a fleeting glance at the occupants, many already smitten with diabetes, his gaze shifted to the junk. Chaos, he muttered, over and over, as he noticed the old radiators, the rusted truck rims, the overturned barrels, the empty paint containers, the rotting ladders, the sagging clotheslines, the battered aluminum doors, the discarded bee boxes, the old bed frames, the broken bottles, the slumping tiger wire, the drains stuffed with cans and slimy clothing. Chaos!

Having no one on whom to vent his rage, he turned as usual on his wife. And in the two months before she died—vomiting in oily black globs, carried to the hospital too late, dying in Ray's car—during those two months Narpat's argumentative nature thinned into a precise, lacerating cruelty, as if he had been blunting away every bit of compassion, discovering and practicing how to hurt; waiting especially for this time.

On some days Narpat stormed through the house, his cane a weapon, striking down books and plates and vases, and when his wife had replaced each item in its proper place, wiping and cleaning as if she had discovered some new flaw, he would repeat the destruction. Occasionally he saw her squinting before the Singer, patching the holes in his pants and darning socks and shirts. He listened to the slow pedal of the machine and her barely decipherable humming. He blamed her for his disability, for the Manager's presence across the road, for the treachery of Guerra, for the standstill in the factory, for the absence of his daughters. The quiet pain in her eyes and her compliant smile sent him into an uncontrollable frenzy, and one morning while she was stooping to retrieve a vase, he lashed out blindly with his cane, the tip striking her on the temple.

She whimpered in a small gust and looked up at him wonderingly. "You hit me?"

He glared at her, seething in hatred.

"Why you hit me?" The question was asked with genuine confusion, like a child seeking an answer to some puzzle. Her eyes filled with tears. The vase dropped. She stretched her hand toward him, hoping he would help her up, admit his mistake, but he stormed away. In the night when Jeeves returned from his work, she was on the sofa, her hand against her forehead.

"What wrong, Mammy?"

She opened her eyes slowly but kept her hand on her forehead. "I fall down." She raised her head slightly and looked around. "Where Pappy?"

"I dunno. Maybe in the factory, but where—"

"He don't be there much since the other people leave."

He heard the pain in her voice. "Where you fall?"

"In the kitchen."

"You hurt your head?"

"A small lash. It will get better."

"How long you here on the couch, Mammy?"

"A few minutes." She attempted to get up. "Let me get your—"

"No, no. You rest, Mammy." When he was spooning out his dinner from the pots on the stove, she came up behind him. "Go back to the couch." He now saw the gash on her forehead and led her to the couch. "How you fall?" he asked when she had settled her head on the pillow.

"I was feeling dizzy." She closed her eyes.

"You want to go to the doctor? I could get Janak to take you."

Her head ruffled the pillow as she turned away. "I just need a little rest."

"You sure?"

"Mmm-hmm."

Jeeves felt in his bones that his father was in some way responsible, and for the two and a half weeks, the seventeen days, before his mother died, he avoided his father, afraid of what he might see in the old man's eyes, afraid of his own feelings. One night he dreamed that he and his father were fighting in the canefield. He awoke in a sweat, the details of the dream still vivid. The canefield was familiar, with its blowing tassels and guppies swimming between mossy rocks and the aroma of cane mingled with that of rotting hogplums. In the dream his father had knocked him down with a spade and was dancing before him, leaping and gibbering, his arms long and loose, dangling at his side, his shoulder hunched squarely.

The house felt hot and airless, the weight of the blanket suffocating. He got up. The door to the room where he had slept till he had been ousted to the living room was open. Sushilla was away at her ashram, chanting and praying. He opened the front door and walked to the porch. Across the road he saw a small glow wobbling in a small circle, leaving a dull trail of light. In the distance a dog howled, the sound ebbing in the night breeze. A stir of disquiet ruffled his body, and as the rustling branches murmured a medley of wails, he felt the night was suddenly colder than usual. Then he heard a muffled cough and saw the door of the Brahmin's house opening and closing.

In the morning he strengthened himself by remembering his father as a playful, witty man before he told him, "I think something wrong with Mammy." When he saw the sharp hostility in the old man's eyes, he almost turned away. "I think she should visit a doctor, but she wouldn't listen to me."

Narpat looked from his son to his leg with the same grim expression. "We have the ability to get rid of any handicap by ourself if we choose to. If your mother want to get better, she will get better. You feeling sorry for her?"

Jeeves noticed his father was now staring at him, his eyes running down his shoulders and arms and chest. At another time he would have been proud that his father had finally noticed the firmness of his body, but now he felt only weakness dusted with disgust. "What I feeling not so important, Pappy. I just think—"

"Think what? That anytime you show sympathy it will create a cure? That weakness could treat weakness?"

Jeeves saw his mother emerging from her room to the kitchen. She opened her mouth, perhaps asking a question, but Jeeves was unable to distinguish the words.

He glanced from his mother to his father, incapable of answering either.

Three days later she died, her body lodged in the funeral home, the cremation delayed until Kala's return. The cause of death written in block letters on a light cream certificate was "heart failure."

And the family who had refused to acknowledge the woman's illness, who had all immunized themselves from concern by conceiving their own problems, now performed their duties. A tent was constructed in the front yard, folding wooden chairs rented, coffee and biscuits prepared and served. In the night Chandra and Jeeves and Sushilla huddled together in their parents' bedroom and stared at their mother's nightie slung on a chair, her brush and baby powder on the dresser next to a small tin of Bengue's Balsam, at the swollen varnish on the dresser. Every now and again, Chandra would glance at one of her mother's modest possessions, shake her head, and cover her face with her hands. Sushilla would lean across and pat her on the shoulder. Distant relatives filed in and out of the room, old men and woman and young rouged girls. The relatives the children had never seen before hugged them forcefully, offered their tears, and reluctantly left. The villagers, under no such obligation, were more restrained. They stared at the children, played awkwardly with the brims of their hats and their orhnis, and walked away to the card games, Wappie and All Fours, being played under the tent.

Narpat hobbled between the rows of chairs, his face alert, his eyes bright, brushing aside expressions of sympathy and forcing an uneasy admiration from the mourners. "What you sorry about? If you not sorry when someone born, then you shouldn't be sorry when they die. That pattern is as simple as the day that going to come tomorrow. The world is in a state of flux."

"But how you will manage?"

"The same way I managing all my life." Some of the men who knew

Narpat well suspected he was enjoying this role. "Is only when you rid yourself from attachment that you finally free." He delivered the same dry lecture on the different stages of a person's life to each group.

The body was brought out from the hearse on a wheeled stretcher and placed on a table. Chandra burst into tears. She ran down the step from the porch and pressed her head onto her mother's chest. Sushilla followed her with a sad smile. Kala, unable to get an early flight, arrived from North Carolina on the day of the funeral. When she arrived in a taxi, the old women from the village leaned over to one another and whispered. She went straight to the body, the mourners parting.

From the porch Jeeves heard a low piercing wail, the sound silencing the murmuring crowd. Those at the back straightened in their chairs to get a better view. The cry had come from Chandra, who had seen Kala's approach. Kala, formally dressed and rankled by the flight, seemed out of place in the gathering. Her eyes swept over the mourners, perhaps looking for familiar faces, pausing momentarily on Jeeves, widening in confusion. She whispered into Chandra's ear, and Sushilla gestured with her finger to Jeeves.

Reluctantly, he came down the stairs, averting his gaze from the body, glancing instead at his father chatting with a sprinkle of men at the tent's perimeter, villagers he recalled from his childhood, Kumkaran, Dev Anand, Assevero, Sidney; and closer, Chandra, her face swollen beneath her scattered hair; at Sushilla in a simple cotton dress, her emotions closed up and hidden by her fixed smile; and at Kala, fairer than he remembered, chewing her lips and trying to process this sudden death.

"Jeeves, I almost didn't recognize you." She placed her hand on his cheek. "Look at how you've changed." And all at once, too sudden for Jeeves to pinpoint the transformation, her composure dissolved. Jeeves stiffened away from her clasp and for the first time looked at his mother's body. She seemed as peaceful as she'd ever been. Her hair had been combed and swept back, and some sort of powdery substance had been applied to her face, giving her a luminous, matte tinge. He traced his finger over her forehead, the curve of her nose, her cold hands. His eyes burned and seemed to swell, but no tears came.

Sushilla came to his side and whispered, "Is okay to cry, Jeeves. It will get the pain out."

The statement angered him, the anger attaching to the mourners, to his father acting out his strong, inviolable role, to his sisters, to his peaceful-looking mother, to himself. He walked back slowly to the porch. From there he saw the pundit, a diminutive man with huge tufts of hair sprouting from his ears, walking around the body and sprinkling flowers from a small basket and water from a lotah. When he began chanting, Kala walked up to Jeeves. "Where's Pappy?"

"In the crowd somewhere." After a while he added, "You not going to meet him?"

"Later. Did she suffer?"

He didn't know how he should answer the question. He saw his father walking toward the pundit. "She was old."

"Yes, I know that, Jeeves," she said impatiently.

"Well, I don't know what you want me to say."

She glanced up at him, and he realized that the impatience in his voice had matched hers. The pundit cleared his throat, rocked onto his toes, and said in a voice surprisingly resonant for such a small man, "Before we go down to the creek for the cremation, I will now recite a few *dohas* from the *Ramayana*. About Sita, the virtuous wife."

"No! This is a funeral, not a *Ramayana*. No chanting, no simi-dimi nonsense." Narpat glanced at the mourners, implicating them in the pundit's travesty. He saw Kala. Without missing a beat, he said, "My daughter didn't come all the way from America to witness this primitive nonsense. She didn't come for a pappyshow." He pointed his cane at the pundit. "Proceed. We have an early appointment at the creek."

There was one more surprise in store for the mourners before the procession left for the creek. Soon after the body was wheeled onto the hearse, the Manager, who had been staring gloomily from his gallery, rushed down the stairs. "O god *maharajin*, how you could just pull out and leave like this? I only recently come to live in this house, and you gone and dead." He ran to the hearse, grasping the startled driver's hand, beating at the roof and, when the driver pulled off, attempting to hold on to the rear mirror.

Jeeves followed the procession in Bhola's car, sitting next to his uncle, who for once was quiet and somber. His wife and daughter were in the rear seat. Jeeves's sisters left with Ray and his father with Janak.

After the cremation, Jeeves wandered past the mourners, who were already leaving in their vehicles. About a mile away on the other side of the promontory, the hospital and the wharf were faintly visible through the haze of smoke and fog. Seagulls floated above the ocean in an even trajectory, not dipping into the water. The waves, heavy with silt, rolled lazily. He tried to distinguish Flatrock, where he had walked for half an hour twice a day. He wondered whether his mother had been finally trapped by her illness in the house in Lengua at the same time he was discovering a new world that offered the make-believe of the cinema not as fantasy but as substitute. He had been almost fourteen then, and the four years he had spent in Princes Town trying to shake off his attachment to the village seemed a world away.

He had blamed his sisters—even today he'd felt annoyance at Kala, who appeared late, uselessly—but he himself was no better. In the year of his return to Lengua, he had seen what he wanted to see and, until it was too late, had viewed his mother as a dependable piece of furniture that would always be there. Now the tears held back since her death came, swept by the breeze and cold against his face. He spotted Kala and Sushilla coming toward him, and he walked away, along the edge of the small cliff. He noticed the huge chunks of mud that had caved onto the shore littered with gnarled stumps and dirty gray corals. A discarded jhandi, the cloth torn into strips, was washed alongside a dead fish. Jeeves smelled the rotting fishes and the mud and another odor, strong and overpowering, a combination of the burnt pitchpine and the stagnation in the ocean. He wondered whether some of the corals were really human bones.

Beyond the cremation site was a small fruit grove partially enclosed by bamboo, their fibrous roots holding the soil together so that the grove jutted like a small peninsula. As he entered, he saw Chinese coconut trees, several varieties of guavas, and taller, spherical samaan, their crimson flowers softened by the wispy fog rising from the water and soaking through the bamboo's tiny leaves, as defined as those in a careful painting.

The scene reminded him of paintings he had seen in his *West Indian Reader*. The artist's name was John E. Millais, and one of his representations was of Ophelia, wreathed by flowers, floating faceup in a stream. The wind fluting through the hollow bamboo stalks blurred the dead, heavy sound of the ocean. An iridescent hummingbird zoomed away from a ripe guava, and he noticed a harmless green horsewhip snake curled around the sleek trunk.

When he emerged, the mourners had all left.

In the distance, someone was poking around in the ashes where his mother's body had been cremated. As he drew closer, he saw that what he had mistaken for a wizened vagrant was Radhica. She held the stick in her hand like a claw, stirring the ashes and the live coals, gazing intently at the residue. He walked to her, wanting her to stop but curious at the sacrilege. She continued prodding with her claw. Her face and hair were dusty with ash.

"What you looking for?"

"For *she*."

The stick dislodged what looked like a white cylindrical shell. She froze. Her slack lower lip fell on her chin. She tapped the stick on the shell and murmured, the sound low in her throat.

Jeeves walked down the hill, where there were still three cars parked at the side of the road.

Two days later a small memorial was held in the tarpaulin tent for the family. Huzaifa showed up, and a little later, Janak. Just before Narpat emerged from the house, dressed in a white shirt and khaki pants, a small depressed-looking woman of about seventy, walking with a slight stoop, and a younger woman with huge oval glasses emerged from a car. Bhola whispered to Babsy and turned to Jeeves. "You not going to meet your father sister and your cousin?"

"Who? I never see them before," he whispered.

"That surprise you?"

Narpat passed the visitors straight, acknowledging neither.

When Narpat was seated, Sushilla got up and said her mother was already in heaven, "twinkling like a star." She looked up at the tarpaulin, and Jeeves wondered whether her ashram also explored Christian beliefs. Kala made an impressive speech about the sacrifices of women of her mother's generation and said she hoped those sacrifices would be recorded for posterity. Chandra got up, burst into tears, and sat down. Everyone looked at Jeeves. He didn't know what to say. He remembered Radhica poking around the embers. "I don't think Mammy really gone. She leave a little bit of herself." Sushilla smiled and nodded. "In each of us."

Babsy pushed Bhola. He stood up and tugged at his jersey. "I had one sister in this world," he began in a rehearsed voice. "She was the kindest, gentlest person you could ever know. I never hear her say a bad word about anyone." Then the rehearsed voice slipped away. "Not against any-body. She might have seem to be a simple woman, but she had her dreams. Is not for me to say whether she achieve these dreams." He looked at the house. "She die here where she live for fifty-odd years. Right here." He pointed to the house.

Narpat got up. He spoke of his early life, housed in a cardboard room beneath his uncle's place. He mentioned the scene where his uncle had smashed the room and his move with his mother and sister to a shack de-serted by a Portuguese shopkeeper. He described the one-room shack in minute detail: the draft at the side of the clay oven, the flapping alu-minum sheets on the roof, the floor of mud mixed with cattle dung, the bench that served as a bed. His sister, whom the family had never seen before, listened impassively, as if this description evoked no memory. He did not mention her. He moved on to the years of frugality that had en-abled him to buy one, then five acres. He had married late because of this goal. He paused, and his children felt he would talk of their mother, shed some light on their romance, if there was any, and of the first years of their marriage. But he diverted to the factory. No one believed it would be pos-sible. The villagers were too busy drinking and swinging from their ham-mocks. Only his wife understood, he said, staring at the little group as if challenging them to dispute this.

He fiddled with his cane and then placed it against a chair. Because of her loyalty, he was going to dedicate the factory to her. When it was com-plete, he would erect a statue bearing her likeness. He also had plans to build a boarding school for girls at the site. His wife would have wanted that. Kala leaned forward and rested her chin on her clasped fingers.

No one should feel sorry for him, he said. His wife's death had finally freed him from attachment.

Jeeves thought: *But what about the factory?*

His life was following a pattern repeated for thousands of years. He spoke of his Aryans, his warriors, his philosophers and hermits. The an-cient books prescribed all the stages of a true Aryan's life. They advised— he changed the word—they *stipulated* the necessity of a man whose wife had passed away finding a suitable companion. A woman who had passed the childbearing stage.

It took a while before this sank into the gathering of family. Bhola said lowly, "That blasted man."

His wife told him, "Shh. That is the madness talking."

"Is that what you intend to do, Pappy?" Kala asked him

"Trying to replace Mammy less than a week after she die," Chandra said.

For once Sushilla's meditative composure melted. "I don't believe he really saying this."

"I am not trying to replace anyone. I said a companion. Someone to talk with."

Huzaifa sensed the children's hurt. "You could talk with me."

"It must be a woman. If the balance is not maintained, then the mind will go."

"It look like your blasted mind gone already." Bhola got up. "And I gone too." He realized he'd just made a joke. He laughed harshly as he walked away. The woman with the cream dress and her daughter followed him.

Chandra pulled at Ray's sleeve, and when they got up, so did Kala and Sushilla. All four walked through the rows of chairs to the road.

"Get out! Get out and don't come back. All of allyou. The wickedness in your mind not mine. Undeveloped brains. Like monkey." He grasped his cane. "Get out and don't let me see any of allyou here again."

Kala paused. "You don't have to worry about that, Pappy. It's not like before. We each have a home now."

But Jeeves didn't. He sat on a wooden folding chair while his father screamed, "Useless savages. Primitive and backward just like everybody else." He saw Jeeves. "What you still doing here? You don't have a home too?"

Jeeves stared at the old man, his body whittled down to skin and bone, and he thought: *It would take ten seconds to reach him. One minute to break his neck. If he resisted, perhaps another two or three minutes.* He was surprised at the calmness of his thoughts, as if he were calculating the cost of lunch at the Chinese snackette.

He went into the house.

Kala stayed by Chandra for the five days before her return to America. During the trip to the airport, she told Chandra, "Don't bother to call when our father pass away. One funeral is enough for me."

Sushilla moved to the ashram.

All three sisters vowed never to return to the house in Lengua; all three fulfilled their vows.

THIRTY-SIX

*D*uring the next several months the house in Lengua took on the appearance of an abandoned property. The bougainvillea at the side of the porch grew thick and knotted and braided into the railings. Paragrass climbed up the copper. Jack Spaniard's nests hung like clay udders from the eaves. Because the doors and windows were usually shut, the house smelled of woodlice, dust, and a sharp, sweet odor—which, Jeeves realized one night, came from the oil his mother had applied to her sewing machine.

During this time too the ownership of the sugar factory, Tate and Lyle, passed to Caroni, a local company that immediately announced it was phasing out sugar production within the decade; the Manager finally won the county council election by bribing almost everyone in the village; and Mr. Doon, Kamini, and the twins moved into the downstairs apartment of the Manager's house. At one time these changes would have drawn some scathing comment from Narpat, but each night when Jeeves returned from work, he would see his father clad in pajamas on the Pavilion with a book in his hand. As Jeeves hurried to his room, he would sense the old man's eyes following him. Sometimes he felt that Narpat's quietness was his way of dealing with grief, but his silence seemed alert and cagey. Jeeves wondered what private battle his father was now locked into.

Narpat never spoke directly to his son nor inquired about his daughters. Sushilla had not returned since the funeral, and whenever Jeeves visited Chandra, his eldest sister spoke only of their mother. Once, cradling Gomuti to her breast, she had said, "I know how Mammy suffer. *I* know what she was going through."

Jeeves thought: *But you refused to listen whenever I mentioned her ill-*

ness. He said nothing, though, because he saw how his sister drew comfort from her grief. Before he left, Chandra would give him a container with rice and pigeon peas and slices of plantain. He ate from the container in the night and placed the remainder in the fridge. Most mornings the container would be on the stand, empty. Before he left for work, he boiled himself a pot of cocoa or green tea, and when there was time, he gathered provisions—pumpkin and ochro and chives and shadow beni—from the backyard garden and made a leafy soup. In the night the remainder of the soup would be consumed, as would the jug of protein drink.

Yet his father never spoke with him.

Jeeves wondered how someone who had lived with a spouse for most of his life could so avoid the slightest reference to that person, and yet three months after the funeral, when his father for the first time mentioned his mother, the boy was enraged.

"She didn't complete her task. She give up."

"What task? Seeing about everybody problem but her own?"

"That was her duty. You take away her duty, and she had nothing else."

"And what was your duty?"

"My duty isn't to a single person or to a single family. Some people get placed on this earth for a very specific purpose."

Jeeves walked away.

From then on the old man seemed to be baiting his son, uttering statements about duty and foresight. Perhaps it was because of Jeeves's silence, or maybe he was working his way toward this stage—the boy was not sure—but one day he said suddenly, "I going to put up that statue of her. Right next to the tower." And another day: "The girls' boarding school will save all these young women in the village. And every one of them will see Mammy face when they enter and leave. The face of a saint."

This infuriated Jeeves more than the previous oblique condemnation. But the belated acknowledgment of his wife seemed to remind the old man of his family. He began visiting Chandra and from her learned the location of Sushilla's ashram. Although Jeeves was relieved by the move, Chandra began to complain about his interference and his constant sermonizing. She mentioned Sushilla's annoyance too at his prolonged visits to the ashram, where he criticized the meals, the chanting, the idol worship, and the guru.

On successive weeks Chandra mentioned specific infractions: he re-

fused to flush the toilet, he quarreled with Ray and with Radhica, he
barged into the bedroom at inappropriate times, he was putting nonsense
in the children's heads. Finally she suggested he return to Lengua. He
told her a story of a woman. The woman, each morning, carried her parents on her back across a river, where they pounded stones for a living.
She never complained because it was her duty, as it had been their duty
to raise the young woman. But the story failed. Narpat could not recall
the exact conclusion. He suggested that the girl drowned her parents, and
at other times he insisted the girl took her parents' dead bodies across the
river. The daughter may have been a saint, a murderer, or a lunatic. Chandra wondered whether she had missed this disorder in the stories told
by her father years ago. She grew uninterested. But Narpat, striving for
meaning, became angry and frustrated. His calmness disappeared. He
called her a neemakaram who was just waiting for his death. He accused
her of poisoning his food. He stormed out, striking the ground with his
cane. In the road he shouted that she need not worry about him being a
burden because he would never cross her doorstep again.

Two nights later Ray stumbled on him on the porch, his head on a
peerha. Ray called his wife, who looked at Narpat's shivering body and
asked him to come inside. He said he was comfortable. The hard floor
firmed his back, the splinters improved his circulation, the peerha relieved the pressure on his neck. His chakras were enjoying this exercise.
She brought him a blanket. He began another story. Midway through she
returned inside. He continued the story in a loud voice. This story was
about a god wandering the earth as a beggar and discovering generosity
and cruelty in unexpected situations. It was the kind of story Narpat had
mocked as Puranic nonsense.

For the next two weeks his father did not show up in Lengua.

From then on the old man shuttled between Chandra's place, the
ashram, and the house in Lengua, showing up unexpectedly and leaving
without notice. The boarding school idea revitalized him, as had the factory for so many years. But now he was frail and even more cantankerous,
and his muddled plans drew annoyance from his children and frustration
from strangers. He accused his children of turning their backs on him,
and strangers, of stupidity and weakness.

At the ashram, he resurrected his notion of futurists and dancing monkeys. The chanters, imitating rituals they could not understand, were gibbering chimpanzees; the guru, a slightly stooped, bearded man, was an ape. "All this meditation no different from the sort of trance an animal will go into when it facing some crisis. Instead of spending five hours every day like zombies, why you all don't do something beneficial. Like build a boarding school." He criticized the diet during every meal. "Starch and sugar and oil. Is not real meditation that going on here. Is the body shutting down. The organs going one by one."

The members of the ashram, who chanted "peace and love fill my heart" daily, struggled with their hatred. Avoiding direct criticism, they spoke of his negative aura. During a meal Sushilla told him he was "disturbing the vibrations of the ashram."

"Vibrations? What vibrations you could get in a place where everybody does fall in a trance anytime a bhajan begin?"

"If this ashram don't agree with you, brother, may you find peace in another." The guru tried to hide his annoyance.

"All these sects is the same. Creating zombies and fanatics."

"May you find peace in another, brother." The guru's voice was slightly higher.

"You all don't want any disputation. Just blind loyalty."

"We try to avoid discord, brother."

"In the ancient days, a ashram like this was a place for discussion. Everyone was free to voice their opinion. And there wasn't any chanting either. And none of this sugar and starch allyou serve here every day. In those days the members would go to the forest each morning and collect nuts and grains and fruits."

Sushilla got up. Some of the other members followed her. The guru closed his eyes and chanted. Narpat stormed off, limping along the mud road for almost three hours until he came to the bus stop. The driver glanced at him and contemplated driving on.

He took his boarding school idea to Chandra, and when she mentioned Ray's late hours and her preoccupation with her daughters, he told her, "These same daughters will benefit from the school. They will learn the value of fasting and penance, and they will do exercises to strengthen the mind and body. Real tests instead of stupid games." Chandra gazed at her daughters playing with a stuffed rabbit and said she was in no posi-

tion to help. He reminded her that the school would be dedicated to her
mother and accused her of selfishness.

He went to Huzaifa, who was briefly excited by the image of industri-
ous little girls operating spinning jennies in a humming room, but whose
experience with the factory alerted him to all the dangers of this new project. When Narpat departed, Salima said, "He building school for his dead
wife now. Why he didn't do all that when she was still living?"

"Dedication. Posthumous." Huzaifa still felt obligated to defend Narpat
to his wife.

"I see. Dedication. Posthumous. You will dedicate anything to me
when I go." He thought: *You wouldn't go, Salima. Some people get put in
this earth to create hardship.* "Allyou mans and allyou crazy idea. Don't let
me catch you with that blasted crazy man again, you hear. Allyou mans!"

Narpat went to each of the cane farmers whose land ownership he
had facilitated, and each spoke of their problems and wished him luck.
Finally, he hobbled across the road to the Manager, who was brushing his
teeth in the gallery. The Manager looked at his approach warily at first,
then with growing apprehension. He swallowed, flicked his toothbrush
against his pants, and placed it in his pocket. His weak smile was made
maniacal by the toothpaste foaming down his chin. He gazed at Narpat
struggling up the stairs. "Life is a funny thing when you think of it. Just
last night I tell meself, 'You know something, Manager? You living here
nearly a year now, and you never visit Narpat as yet.' And look how you appear right here in front of me."

"I didn't appear. I walk across the road."

"Is just a prabble I was prabbling. So how everything?" His wariness
increased as he spotted the stern expression on the old man's face.

"Everything is how we make it. Is up to us to perform our duty. My
duty is to build a boarding school for girls in the memory of my dead wife,
and . . ."

The Manager had heard the rumors. "That is a very good dreamsanhope."

". . . And your duty, as the elected councilor, is to assist in worthwhile
ventures."

"Worthwhile?" He fiddled with the concept, searching for an escape.
"What is worthwhile and what is not worthwhile? Who is to decide? One
day something is worthwhile, and the next day it come worthwhileless."

He thought of Narpat's descent from a leader in the village who had facilitated the important land deeds and had won the county council elections, to a miserable old man. "The villagers, my loyal constituents and stakeholders, is really the one to judge the Manager." He used a phrase from a political speech. "They is the holders, I is only the stake. Is for them to decide."

"The school could be completed in two months. Before rainy season."

"Just the other night I was telling meself, 'You know something, Manager? We have one of the best school in the island right here in Lengua.'"

"A school just for girls."

"The modern saying is that girls no different from boys. They cut from the same cloth."

"The only one of its kind in Trinidad."

"What is good for the goose is good sauce." He was fast running out of prabbles and felt increasingly irritated.

"You could cut the ribbon at the ceremony."

"Eh? Ribbon? Ceremony?" He was sorely tempted, but he knew Narpat too well. He remembered the humiliation of his previous election defeat and then being chased away by Narpat when he'd come with his land purchase proposal. He recalled all the lectures to which he'd been subjected. He decided to cut the conversation short. "The best I could offer is this offer. You build the school, and I will 'ganize the ceremony. Half a loaf is just as good as teaching a man to fish."

"I must do the dog-work while you collect the fame?"

"Fame? What is fame? Is like a light that—"

"I not interested in hearing any of that illiterate nonsense. Will you, Sookdeo, help or not?"

"Illiterate?" The Manager fought his rising temper. "This same illiterate chamar in front of you does sit in big-big committee and decide who getting water and 'lectricity, who—"

"Who fulling your wallet."

"Eh? You insulting me in my own doorstep?" He spoke loudly, attracting the attention of the workers downstairs.

"Trained monkey. Can't see more than a few step before you." He grasped the step's railing and lowered himself.

"I glad that I is a monkey. I glad that I, the elected councilor, who does sit in big-big committee, suddenly come a ugly monkey and a scrapegoat."

The workers gazed up at him. "Get to ass back to work, allyou sickly little jackass. Is I, the Manager, the so-call monkey and chamar, who ordering allyou back to work." He pounded the railing, then withdrew his toothbrush and flung it at the goat. He was frustrated at the return of his self-pity, and unnerved that an old invalid still possessed the ability to pry out his old weaknesses.

Just before Narpat crossed the road, he uttered a statement that would have surprised his family. "You living in a house that had some values at one time. But none of that rub off on you."

For the rest of the day, the Manager quarreled with his workers and his goat.

The hurt lingered. In the night, after his son-in-law had left for the rumshop, the Manager walked down the inside steps to the Brahmin's stockroom. He noted the books on the shelves and in the cardboard box beneath the table. When his daughter asked why he was grumbling, he said testily, "I just trying to get some dreamsanhope." The Hindi texts were useless. Then he saw a book, its green cover inscribed with a playful, squiggly circle. He pried out the book and took it upstairs. "*Open Spirit*, by Boros. No pictures, but nice, simple title and nice ball on the cover." During the following nights he read, underlined, and half-memorized a variety of sentences. At the next committee meeting the other members were stunned to hear him quoting from Dante and Socrates. (He kept away from Nietzsche and Teilhard, whose names were too difficult to pronounce.) He also practiced on his son-in-law, who in turn told his wife, "The bitches never cease to amaze me."

"Hush, Tolly. Hush, Dolly. The house will be quiet in a little while. Is almost six o'clock."

Occasionally the Manager would ask his daughter to read from *Open Spirit*, and with cigarette smoke drifting to her sons perched on her knees, she would read until one of her boys fell asleep. Her father would say with genuine wonder, "I never know it had fellas who could prabble so good. Read over one or two for me." Frequently she was forced to read till late into the night.

THIRTY-SEVEN

*L*ate one night Jeeves was awakened by loud knocking on the door of his sisters' room, where he now slept. He got up sleepily, and in the dull glow of the fluorescent he saw his father at the doorway. "I want you to read this for me."

"Now?" Jeeves rubbed his eyes.

His father did not answer but entered the room, and with the tip of his cane he tapped the bulb. "This light no good again. The life nearly gone out from it." He sat on the bed, and Jeeves pulled up his feet and propped his back against the bedstead. His father gave him the sheet. "Read it aloud."

Dear Kala,

I have not contacted you since the funeral but as you know I have been busy trying to get the boarding school dedicated to Mammy off the ground. As I quite expected, nobody is willing to help. They make excuses left right and center because they don't have the vision to see what few people could see. I am one and you are another. I propose that you return to Trinidad and help supervise the construction. Your reward apart from knowing the school will be dedicated to your mother will be principalship. I believe you have all the qualities to make an excellent principal. There will be a few issues to be discussed but those can be done when the school is completed.

I regret to inform you that none of the family has been of much help. Your eldest sister is determined to be nothing more than a housewife and your younger sister is living with a group of frauds in a make-believe world. As for your brother . . .

"Read it till the end," Narpat said.

As for your brother he comes and leaves the house like a shadow. He seems to be waiting for my death but this old man is not going anywhere in a hurry.

I will end this letter by saying that I am in good health. Although on many days I do not eat, my mind and body are still strong. I will delay the start of the school construction until I hear from you.

Your one and only Pappy.

Jeeves was surprised by the letter's clarity.

"I want you to send this to Kala as soon as possible. I don't know her address. When she come back with her big degree, she will put everybody in their place. That bogus Sookdeo and all these neemakaram farmers. Your mammy was right about them." He smiled, and Jeeves noticed the gaps between his teeth. "She see things I wasn't able to spot. All along she used to say that the farmers was a bunch of rogues. She warn me that I was wasting time with them." He paused, then added, "But that was my duty. Is still my duty. You see, boy, without that vision, I would be no different from all of them." His voice had softened into an almost imperceptible gentleness. "Ever since I could remember . . . since the day my father die, I fighting. My father was a fighter too, but his battle get cut short." He looked at his son's bare chest and said, "This strength get pass from generation to generation." Jeeves wondered whether he was referring to him or to Kala. "This room too hot, boy. You should sleep with the louvers open." Jeeves stretched and opened the nearest louver. "The first battle was against my uncle, the second against my mother who just give up, the third against poverty, the fourth against these rich landowners and proprietors who didn't like the idea of a boy who had to drop out from school challenging them. That battle last for a long while. But the fifth battle was the most difficult." He paused, and Jeeves wondered whether he was about to mention his wife or his children. "This battle still going on. Is against ignorance and superstition and small-mindedness. Against weakness parading as strength. Against gossipy people who good at pulling down others because they incapable of doing anything themself. These people . . . believing in fables instead of what they see all around. Blaming everybody but themself. Freeing themself from action. Crying at the slightest problem, not out of grief but just to get sympathy. You didn't cry for your mammy funeral?"

It took a while before Jeeves realized a question had been posed.

"I can't remember."

"Why? Why you can't remember?" When his son did not reply, he added, "It don't matter. She gone now."

And Jeeves felt a whiff of tenderness, a shrill affection for his father that was like a burst of pain because it was so unexpected and because he knew it would not last. He remembered their first visit to the canefield. The old man placed both hands on his cane as if he were about to get up, but he remained in that position, staring at the wall or perhaps at the dresser Sushilla had bought. The dim light accentuated his profile, and Jeeves imagined he saw his father, in repose, not as a cantankerous, cruel old man but as a solitary warrior. Finally Narpat got up and walked out of the room.

During the following weeks, he visited everyone whom he had asked for help, and to each he revealed that the school would be built after all. The Manager watched his approach and fumbled for some quotation from *Open Spirit*, but Narpat was in an unusually ebullient mood.

Narpat's mood changed. He hobbled down the road each day, visiting villagers randomly. Salima grew worried and warned Huzaifa. At home Narpat now spoke regularly with Jeeves. At the end of each conversation he would ask if Kala had replied.

One morning he went outside to the backyard garden and, kneeling on the dirt, pulled out the dried weeds and molded the tomatoes and ochroes. He piled the trash in a heap and set about repairing the machan, now sagging from unwanted vines. "Allyou plants suffering since Mammy gone, not so? The parasites springing up on all sides and shutting off the light. I will put a stop to that." He hummed songs his wife had sung in the backyard. At the end of the day the garden was almost restored to its former state. While Jeeves was walking home, he noticed the fire at the side of the house. He quickened his stride and saw his father sitting on the tractor's step, staring at the fire. The first thing the old man asked was whether Jeeves had received a reply.

"No. Nothing today."

After a while his father said, "When you wait too long, nothing ever come back. I get the garden back in shape just in time. In a little while all the nice vegetables would have been gone."

"It look very clean."

"Nothing ever get accomplish without effort."

"Yes. I going inside now."

"Boy."

Jeeves stopped and turned around.

"How long it take a letter to reach America?"

"About a week, I think."

"And another week for a reply to get here. Today make it twelve days since I give you the letter." His voice lightened. "You remember when Mammy use to come to the backyard all the time?"

Because plants don't quarrel, Jeeves thought.

"Today I hear her humming a song over there. Listen. You could still hear her."

Jeeves heard the snap and crackle of twigs and the hollow puffs of bamboo exhaling. Then a thin, low sound. He looked at his father. The old man's eyes were closed, his head swaying slightly as he hummed. The ebbing fire coursed to an adjoining pile and burst once more to life, the flame waving like tattered flags. A frog leaped away from the heat, pausing as if in indecision, after each hop.

Narpat was still humming and swaying ever so slightly, as if in a trance. He seemed at peace. Jeeves walked quietly into the house. The following day there was another fire. "Why you burning all these books from Carnegie?" Jeeves asked him. He pulled out an old Hindi book, its pages curling from the heat.

"Hocus-pocus stories. They will reincarnate as better books." He grinned.

When his father limped to the house, Jeeves tried to rescue some of the books he had seen his father reading silently on the Pavilion. The old man returned with an assortment of papers stabbed onto a copper wire. He pulled out the assorted sheets and one by one threw his jottings and bills and clippings into the fire. "Getting rid of attachments," he told his astonished son. "Purifying myself."

"You shouldn't do that."

"Why?" The fire's reflection glinted in his eyes.

"Because"—Jeeves didn't know what to say—"because they were in the house when Mammy was still alive."

"They have no value again. They belong to a different stage."

Each night he asked about the letter, and when Jeeves shook his head, he grew silent for a few minutes before he provided some optimistic reason for the delay. Perhaps there was a postal strike in America. Maybe Kala was busy with her exams. The letter might have been lost in one of the chaotic local post offices. The reply, when it came, would put the entire village to shame. Adjustments to the construction would have to be made for lost time. The basic structure would be unchanged, though. One huge classroom, a room for stocks, a small office for Kala, and a big playing field for the girls to exercise. At the center of the field would be his wife's statue.

But as the weeks passed, some of his optimism faded, and he repeatedly asked his son about the location of the post office from which he had sent the letter, and if he was certain the correct postage had been affixed. One night he mentioned a nebulous conspiracy and threatened to go to the huge post office at San Fernando to register a complaint. He went first to the village postal agency, then to the Princes Town branch, and finally to the San Fernando center. At each of these places he demanded a list of all the incoming mails. No such records were kept, the officers explained. He accused them of secreting away letters from America that they assumed contained cash. The officer from the Princes Town branch, a man with long, oily hair and pockmarks on his sunken cheeks, grew nervous and pretended to read from a dusty folder. He shook his head. Nothing from America for the last month. Narpat threatened to sue. The officer, as if he had been through this before, said public officials couldn't be sued. You will have to bring up the government, he said. Them big pappy from Port of Spain, lawyers themselves. Narpat poked his cane through the aperture, startling the officer. Just wait and see, he shouted.

He knew he couldn't afford a lawyer, and he was averse to once more appealing for help. The notion of being enclosed by a selfish hostile world rose in him. Not only was everyone expecting him to fail, they were ac-

tively pursuing this goal. He searched for alternatives to help him build
his boarding school and came up with nothing. For the first time in his
life he allowed the possibility of failure. But failure was a reflection of
weakness; it was associated with a mind encumbered by superstition,
fear, and doubt. He had railed against this chaos for his entire life, had
been enraged by the stream of excuses for inaction, where suffering was
refined into a technique, poverty into a virtue, withdrawal into a gift. This
loathing turned on himself. He saw, as if for the first time, his gaunt,
wrinkled arms and his shrunken chest. He studied his broken leg and noticed how the muscles had atrophied, and the twist of the broken ankle.
A body like that was a receptacle for disaster, he thought. On his bed at
night he tried to still his breath and concentrated to pinpoint the precise
points of pain. He focused on the dull ache in his leg and tried to connect
it with the tension in his stomach and the pulsing at the back of his neck.
His blood he imagined to be thick, black, and lumpy. One night he awoke
with a thought desolate in his mind: it was time to put this body out of its
misery. He got up from his bed, shivering. He tried to ignore the thought,
but it grew stronger, like the pulsing, dull pain in his body. Arguments
presented themselves. Useless animals were put down. The old and infirm died. It was the way of the world. Then another thought, just as sudden but more seductive danced in his head: *We are made complete only
through death. All that happens before is just a preparation.* The evolution
from student to householder to hermit extended to another more significant phase. He wrested with this concept all night, but his mind failed
and retreated to the fables he had scorned. Kama the god of death, dark
and foreboding, appearing at the doorway. Shiva the destroyer, striding
multiple universes. Hell populated with horned demons. A boatman fer-
rying across the recently dead. Men reborn as useless butterflies. A simple syllable of regret offering redemption to a deathbed murderer. Wounded
spirits haunting familiar spots. The ghost of unbaptized babes wailing for
lost opportunities.

By morning, he was convinced his mind was going. He had limped to
the kitchen thrice searching for his wife. He'd heard the laughter of children and felt the weight of a baby on his shoulders. He'd dreamed rest-
lessly of his own father.

In the six months preceding his death, his father had passed through long periods when he no longer recognized his children, when he had forgotten his name, forgotten his canefield. His brother had seized the opportunity. House and property had been swiftly transferred. His family was reduced to tenants. The illness was sudden and devastating, but it might have been there unknown for years. Now there were names for these ailments. Alzheimer's. Dementia. Pick's disease. But Narpat had constructed defenses against this devastation. He had strengthened his mind, ruthlessly weeded out weaknesses. And he thought: *I have done all that is necessary. The fault cannot be mine.* So he banged his cane on the floor when he heard distant snatches of laughter and shouted angrily at the kitchen when he heard a familiar song. He sat on the Pavilion and, with his eyes fixed firmly on the table, delivered long lectures on treachery. Over and over the phrase came to him: *The fault cannot be mine, I have prepared myself.*

Jeeves noticed the old man's restlessness and the stream of inexplicable conversation. He had expected this, though. As always, his father's moments of tenderness were swallowed by frenzy. But he had not expected the hatred directed at the dead. He had not expected the self-mutilation. He spoke to Chandra and Sushilla of the bruised mouth, the battered leg, the lacerated wrists and, faced with familiar excuses, decided this time to act alone.

One evening a white van drew up. The old man stared at the attendant injecting the sedative into his arm as if this were another of his phantoms, but in a few minutes he slumped back onto the couch, his mouth open. He awoke in the hospital on a bed with dirty sheets. On an adjoining bed was another old man with huge eyes and a scar on his neck. There was a persistent cough from a bed by the shuttered window. Narpat smelled the wash of antiseptic and faintly of excrement and rose up in a rage. Death factory! Death factory! He screamed. A plump, surly nurse marched to him, and he pushed her away. He clawed at a male nurse who was trying to administer a sedative. Another nurse was summoned. When the sedation wore off, he stumbled groggily from his bed and, without his cane, fell on his face. The nurses ran to him, and he surprised them with his strength. At the end of the second day, the coughing at the window bed stopped. A sheet was placed over the body. A few hours later the corpse was removed. The following day during his afternoon visits, the doctor said in a bored voice, "Carry this one down to the morgue. It look like he die sometime this morning." He glanced at his watch. "Let's say at eleven forty-five."

Narpat gazed at his approach, and when the doctor leaned over his bed, he reached for his throat.

Jeeves was summoned to the hospital. He entered the ward and saw his father strapped down on the bed. A male nurse came to him. "This is your father?"

"Yes."

"Take him away. We can't do anything for him here." He released the leg straps. "He still halfway tranquilized." He unloosened the straps from the hands and chest. "You better carry him home fast." Narpat gazed insensately from the nurse to his son.

"Where is his cane?"

"We had to take it from him." The nurse groped at the top of a cupboard, retrieved the cane and placed it at the foot of the bed. Jeeves held his father's arms and gently pulled him to a sitting position. He placed one hand around the old man's chest and got him standing.

"They well beat him last night." Jeeves, unable to distinguish the words, turned. The man gazed with his big eyes at the boy. He placed his palm over the scar on his neck and wheezed. "They well beat him last night. Check his back."

"This is how you all treat old people?" He saw the other patients gazing at him and a nurse glancing up from a table. He was surprised at the anger in his voice. "By beating them? Blasted savages."

The nurse sucked her teeth and returned to her folder. An attendant walked stiffly to Jeeves. "What going on here? What is your problem? You think this is a damn charity we running here?"

With his free hand he collared the attendant and pulled him closer. "If anything at all . . ." He heard the attendant's surprised gag, his father's low breath, the hollow gasps bubbling from the hole in the patient's throat, and at the door, the male nurse screaming for help.

"Carry him home fast." Jeeves saw that the patient was crying. "Fast!" He released the attendant, who stumbled away, and he walked out of the hospital with Narpat leaning on him.

———

For two days Narpat lay on his bed, indifferent to the bowls of porridge and soup brought by his son. On the third day he limped to the toilet and tried to relieve himself. A few drops of urine the color of saffron trickled down. His face in the mirror seemed darker than usual, a dull, faded black. On the way back to the bedroom, he gazed at the rusty tint thrown by the evening sun on the curtain and the sofa. The pictures hung on the walls by his wife absorbed the amber and seemed aged and muddy. The remaining books looked like ash-covered dying embers.

He lay flat on the bed, the sheet up to his neck, and stared at the shadow falling on the house. He imagined he could smell the darkness— rotting fruits and dust and a cold, pungent aroma he could not recognize. A mango fell on the ground, and he jumped. Another fell, and he bolted upright, pulling the sheet around him and gazing at the doorway. He closed his eyes and counted. One. Two. Three. Four. Five. He reached seventy-four and opened his eyes and began counting once more.

When Jeeves arrived home, he was still sitting on the bed, clutching the sheet and counting.

"You sleeping?" the boy asked from the shadow.

"You come at last. I was waiting for you." His voice was cold and flat.

Jeeves entered the room, and in the gloom, his father stared at him in fear and hatred. "You didn't eat any of the porridge." The old man's eyes followed him around the room as he closed the louvers. "I will reheat it." When he returned, his father stiffened and recoiled from the spoon thrust between his lips. "Come on. Is just a few spoonfuls." The lips slackened a bit, and Jeeves fed him one spoon, then another. When the bowl was finished, the old man looked at his son. His lips, still slack, seemed to be grinning, but his eyes, alert as ever, were frightened and cal- culating, like an animal's.

In the morning when he heard the approaching footsteps, he closed his eyes and pretended he was asleep. He heard the bump of the bowl on the side table, then receding footsteps on the outside steps. He opened his eyes, brought the bowl to his lips, and slurped down the porridge.

When Jeeves arrived home, he was gone.

The boy checked the rooms, calling his father's name. He ran shout- ing to the backyard and, in a moment of panic, peered into the copper. He was still searching outside when Ray and Chandra brought him home. When he saw his son, Narpat struggled against the hands supporting him.

"Somebody see him walking pass Crappo Patch and bring him by us," Chandra said.

"You better keep this fella under lock and key." Ray leaned to Narpat. "What you was doing walking all alone in the night? You wanted a lil exercise?"

"Stop bothering him. You and all." She exhaled.

Narpat freed an arm and pointed to Jeeves. "Him!"

"What happen to him now?" Ray was speaking in a childlike voice.

"He want me dead."

"Stop talking nonsense, Pappy. He taking care of you."

"Poison. Poison." He began to struggle once more. "He want to burn down the house."

"Maybe allyou should keep him," Jeeves said.

"How we could keep him, Jeeves? Where we will put him? Ray mother using the spare room, and he have his house right here."

"You hear what he just say."

"Don't bother, boy. Is the sickness talking. He don't mean it."

"Keep him away from me," Narpat shrieked.

"Help Ray take him up the step." She stopped at the front step. "I make a promise."

When Jeeves tried to help, the old man began to scuffle. Jeeves stepped back and Ray took him to his room. Chandra was saying something, but Jeeves only heard the old man's shrieks.

During the following days, after he had placed the food on the side table, Jeeves knocked on the door to let his father know he was leaving for work. One night Bhola came to the cinema. "I hear you taking care of the old man all by yourself." He coughed, as if embarrassed. "Looking at you, I never woulda expect that." He paused, then said, "You working here long enough for a raise. What you think?"

"Is up to you."

"Boy, you just like your father and real different from him." He did not explain. "I think four dollars a day is a good raise.'

When he left, Dr. Who said, "You taking care of Jhanjhat? What wrong with him?"

"He a little sick."

"That is why you don't be watching all these chicks again? But I does see them checking you out all the time." He glanced at the boy in the gloom. "You does look a little like Amitabh Bachchan, you know." He fidgeted with his shirt. "Maybe is because you get so quiet. I can't remember when last I hear your voice." When Jeeves did not reply, he added, "It must be real hell taking care of that old man."

"Is a kinda promise." He hesitated. "A perfect pledge."

"Eh? What is that?"

Jeeves recalled his father's explanation about being prepared to die to protect something dear, but he knew he couldn't accept this. "Is something that fall on your lap. Nobody else could do it."

Dr. Who seemed satisfied. He said, "Is like the promise I make to beat my children every night." After a while he added, "Not much fellas would do what you doing."

THIRTY-EIGHT

When Narpat disappeared once more, Jeeves assumed he'd taken off for Chandra and that he'd soon be brought back. In the morning he saw the empty bed and imagined his sister had decided to accommodate him. He felt a wavering relief the entire day, but in the night he saw Huzaifa on the porch, waiting.

"I try to get him out. But he wouldn't listen." Huzaifa spoke in small, nibbling sentences. "I carry across two blanket and some food. Salima don't know. It have a bench inside. A table too. Table and bench."

Jeeves couldn't understand. "Where he is?"

"We build it together. I help out with all the plans. It real strong. Stronger than this house."

"The factory?"

"The tower. Is like a nice little house, when you think of it."

"He inside the tower?"

"Is what a true hermit will do." There was a trace of admiration in his voice.

Jeeves left him on the porch and ran toward the factory, slowly, then broke into a stride.

When he returned a little after midnight, Huzaifa was still on the porch. "I know he wouldn't leave. Is how a true hermit does operate. Salima will be mad like hell. I have to go now." Huzaifa sounded worried. "I think he will be all right. He have to protect the factory."

Jeeves left work early the next day for his sister's place. For once, she sounded concerned. She mentioned snakes and scorpions and sudden thunderstorms and the strength of the tower. "He there by himself." The statement was uttered blandly, and she grew silent, as if from this distressing thought, nothing further could be drawn. Then she talked of their mother. There were long contemplative pauses.

When Ray arrived home, he said, "Inside the windmill? *Qui pappa!* That man have real courage."

Chandra's mood changed. "What courage you talking about, Ray? You know how dangerous that place is?" Jeeves noticed she had slipped into her nasal half-complaining, half-provoking voice. "You and all."

Jeeves got up. "You hear from Kala?"

She glanced at her husband.

"Ay! Don't look at me. This is allyou family business."

"Is just a card," Chandra said.

"She mentioned the school?"

"Ray, bring the card for me."

He returned with the card. "Allyou sister real brave, boy. And she making headlines and thing in America."

"Oh gosh, Ray. You and all."

Jeeves took the card. His sister's face was imposed on the body of a woman poised above a huge waterfall. At the side of the image was the fake headline: Daredevil breaks record. Kala had scribbled just four lines. Exams are over. It was real hell. Using the break to travel. There's so much to see.

He returned the card to Chandra. "Tell Sushilla, when you see her, about Pappy."

"I hardly ever see her again, boy."

"I hear they chasing out all the animals from the forest with they chanting."

"Just what your father used to do all day in the gallery."

"Ay. He use to be writing books, girl."

She turned to Jeeves with a little tolerant smile. "Wait, boy. I going to pack some food for Pappy. I could use your icy-hot, Ray?"

"You mean the one you give me for my birthday. Bye-bye icy-hot."

"This Ray," she pouted as she went to the kitchen.

At home, Jeeves bundled up some sheets from the clothesline and went into his father's room for pajamas and shirts. The room was heavy with the smell of stale clothing. He pulled out shirts and pajamas and khaki trousers from a rack, and when he reached for a towel, he realized it would be useless. He retrieved it nevertheless and wondered how and where his father was relieving himself. He searched around for a box to pack the clothes, and beneath the bed he found a cardboard box stuffed with plans, some drawn on brown paper, others on the backs of calendars and on torn pieces of cardboard. He saw sketches of wheels and cylinders and baffling intersecting rectangles and triangles, the angles scratched out and adjusted. He saw the care his father had paid to the tower, drawn on several sheets until he had been satisfied. In the final version the blades had been sketched in, and a boxed inset rendered a diagram of the tower's interior with a long bench and a small table. Had he known? Jeeves wondered. He sheaved through other plans at the bottom of the box and was surprised at the meticulous planning for all the failed projects, even the revolving table, the clothesline, the swiveling stool, and the can opener. "You have to plan for everything in life," he had said years ago. "You have to be a futurist."

The last two plans were of the hot-water contraption and the carriage that had evolved into a stationary tricycle. He gazed at it for a while before he removed the sheets and pushed the lot beneath the mattress. As he was about to leave, he saw the old gas lamp sitting at the top of Carnegie. He stretched, got it down, and heard the tinkle of gas.

It would take him about an hour to get to the factory if he walked at a normal pace. His father's old scooter was lying against the tractor, and for a brief moment, he considered firing it up. But he had never driven it before, and he was not even sure he could get the engine running. When he arrived, it was quite dark, so he placed the box on the ground and lit the gas lamp. The dried wick burst into flames, spluttered, and died. He held it upside down until the wick was saturated and lit it once more. From inside the tower came a faint rustle, followed by a tap. "I bring some clothes and food for you," Jeeves shouted. "And the gas lamp."

For a minute or so, there was silence. Then three distinct taps. "Leave it outside."

"I could bring it in for you."

"Leave it outside."

A bat flapped out from a blade, and instinctively Jeeves ducked. "I will come tomorrow night at the same time. You want anything else?"

Jeeves didn't hear a sound.

Halfway on the return journey, he broke into a jog. He liked the slap of cool breeze against his face and the smell of hogplums and pawpaws and mangoes. His father had often said the night breeze strengthened and purified the body.

But the journey to the factory, burdened with food and clothes, was not so pleasant, and before each trip, he eyed the scooter with its convenient tray. One night he got on the saddle, started the engine, and revved the throttle. The next day he released the brakes slightly and lifted his feet from the ground. The scooter inched forward. After a few nights of this, he pointed the scooter to the road and slowly released the brakes. The scooter shot forward. Jeeves spun the brakes wildly and in his confusion also rotated the throttle on the other side of the handle. The scooter roared and pitched straight into the drain. He struggled from beneath its weight and pulled it upright.

"You have to learn to control both hands separately." Mr. Doon, on the way to the rumshop, offered. "It's the simplest thing to ride, but it takes some practice."

"You know how to operate it?" Jeeves was a bit embarrassed.

Mr. Doon emitted a brisk whinny. "Rode one for years, buddy. Belonged to a bikers' gang at university. High Hegels." He got on the saddle. "Semiautomatic. Piece of cake." Jeeves expected him to lurch into the drain too, but he brought it to a stop just in time. During the following nights, he taught Jeeves how to control the bike while at the same time chatting about his university days. "Had to drop out, though. The funds dried up. Harridans and termagants. A common story. Sought a rich old dowager in vain." The memories sparked some of his old enthusiasm for writing as well as his frustration. "This place drives you to the pubs, buddy. It's the only way to retain your sanity. An absentee society, my boy. Absent culture, absent responsibility, absent intelligence." His eyes glazed a bit. "The villager is a master of irrelevant gesture. So where do you leave for every night? I haven't seen you in any of the pubs."

"I take food to my father."

"Aah, yes," he said as if he understood.

"He's living in the tower."

"No kidding. Like Quasimodo. Yes, yes." After a while he said, "But these bitches will never believe any of it."

A few nights afterward Jeeves placed the food and clothes on the tray and set off. He drove slowly, and whenever he heard an approaching vehicle, he braked and drove on the grassy curb. The journey took twenty

minutes and on the following nights just fifteen. By then all the village
knew of Narpat's new madness. Jokes were made. The jokes led to gossip,
and from the gossip, speculation. Narpat was paying for his sins, they
said. No, no, he was fulfilling some pact. He had developed some horrible, disfiguring disease. He was hiding from his children. He was planning something big. Some of the villagers who had never seen the factory
swore they had heard strange noises in the tower. The more imaginative
described the sounds. Pops and crackles and muffled explosions. A few
mentioned conversations in unintelligible foreign languages.

Yet apart from Huzaifa, no one visited him. Some nights Jeeves would
see Huzaifa, his head bowed, walking briskly to his home, and he guessed
the other man was worrying about his Salima. Jeeves could not understand his father's connection with this strange small man. He knew that
Huzaifa sometimes brought food because he would see a container in his
hand. He never stopped to acknowledge Huzaifa because he was always
in a hurry and he guessed the man was rushing back to his wife. But one
night he slowed his scooter just before Huzaifa, who jumped back with a
little cry.

"Is me," Jeeves said.

Huzaifa held his bowl against his chest like a shield. "Who?"

"Narpat son."

"Is you who does be driving this unit every night? Where you get it
from? Is your father old bike? You have license for it?"

"No. It not licensed."

"I does license my Humber every year. You going to the factory? What
you have in the tray?"

"Food and clothes."

"I just leave a bowl of kidney beans. Take it from the pot when Salima
was in the back. Carry a few books too. Take it from the shelf when the
owner was in the back. Don't know if it have enough light in the tower.
Have to remember to bring a bottle of gas for the lamp." He tapped the
headlamp. "How this lamp so dim? You think a fuse blow? Or maybe a
wire leggo? You should get it fix. But these things complicated like hell. I
had a small radio that used to pick up cricket from Pakistan. It get destroyed." He said softly and with some pain, "One setta wire and guts inside. Never see anything like it."

Jeeves smiled at the rapid talk, but Huzaifa had given him an idea.

The following night he packed the old gramophone and the vinyl records in the tray and left it at the tower's entrance, beside the food. He recalled his father's annoyance at the music and didn't know what to expect, but the next night the gramophone and the records were gone.

Now he usually stopped to chat with Huzaifa for about five minutes during each trip. "We listen to some music this evening. Frighten all them bat like hell. They was flying 'round the place like they get mad."

"He ever come out from the tower?"

"The light." He grew worried. "I better go now. I tell Salima I visiting teacher Haroon. He have some sickness or the other. Doctor say is either heart or liver or kidney. Or lungs. Dentist fella want to cast him up."

Late in the night, during the occasional thunderstorm that rattled the roof, Jeeves awoke and thought of his father. And during these moments he imagined that someone of influence, like a police officer or a county councilor, had finally persuaded the old man to return. But he realized this was a vain hope: no one in authority would bother unless they were bribed or threatened. He knew too that if his father were eventually removed, it would be to the madhouse at St. Ann's, where he would be strapped down and beaten. Sometimes he imagined his father was listening to a record, singing and waving his hands while the rain thrashed the cane and the blades spun and spun. Maybe, he thought, the old man crawled out during the storm to wash his body. He pictured his father creeping out from the tower and standing naked as the rain drenched his body and the wind tossed his long hair and beard.

He tried not to think of his father when he was in the cinema, but often there were segments set in unfamiliar locales, scenes that bore no similarity to his own situation that either reminded him of his childhood or conveyed the vague hope his father would miraculously be healed and return home, a wiser and more compassionate man. For a number of days he was comforted by the idea that Sushilla—whom he considered the most useless of the children—might be activating some favorable karma.

One night he asked Huzaifa, "You believe in miracles?"

Huzaifa replied immediately, "Is why I still married."

"You think my father will get better?"

"Better than who? Is what he want."

"Living alone? Like a monkey in a cage? Coming out only in the night?"

"He was preparing for this all along. He protecting the factory."

"Protecting? From who?"

Huzaifa glanced around uneasily and whispered, "The Outsiders. Tate and Lyle. The Manager. All of them."

"How long you think he will manage like this?"

"He have a plan."

Jeeves thought of the box of plans he had pushed beneath the mattress. "What sort of plan?"

"Aah aah." He sped off, his head bowed.

When Jeeves arrived at the factory, he shouted to his father, "I find a old box of plans below the bed. I could bring it here for you if you like."

Silence.

"You want it? It have the plan for the tricycle that couldn't move." Jeeves heard a low gushing laugh, but it might have been the water gurgling from a nearby ravine. "And the design for the hot-water contraption."

"The design was faulty."

It took a while before Jeeves realized the old man had spoken to him. "But all the calculation was correct. All the angles and measurement. I look at all of those."

"One fault."

"What?"

"One fault could spoil everything."

"It don't matter. All these things build already."

Silence.

"They like records now. You might enjoy looking at them."

"Records have no use, Carea."

Because his father's voice sounded lighter than usual, Jeeves asked, "What you does be doing inside there?" He repeated the question.

From inside came the scratch of a song. As if the old man were trying to drown out his son's inquiries.

That night Jeeves dreamed of children dancing around a windmill as music floated from the whirring blades. The windmill, though, was at the top of a rolling hill surrounded not by cane but by meadow grass. The children linked hands and frolicked down the hill.

The following evening he carefully arranged the plans in a manila envelope. Perhaps they would remind his father of happier times the way, in the movies, some insignificant object created a flurry of memories in a senile old man or a grieving woman. He was surprised he had not thought of this before.

He left earlier than usual to solicit Huzaifa's opinion. He would be excited.

And Huzaifa *was* excited. He was running wildly, and when he saw the scooter's dim headlamp, he diverted to the center of the road and waved both hands like a traffic policeman. He was out of breath.

"Pappy?"

He placed a hand on his chest, doubled over, and coughed. "Fire. The canefield. Was running to get help. Couldn't manage by myself." In the distance was a very faint orange glow that tinged the topmost leaves of the immortelle so the leaves looked dried and papery. "Hurry, hurry."

He rode in the center of the road, the old scooter vibrating from the speed and the potholes. The yellow turned to orange. A bamboo exploded, and a shower of sparks cascaded in the air. He jumped off the scooter by the hogplum tree and left it on its side, the engine still running. The uncleared field, cluttered with withered stalks and dried grass, was an inferno. The flames shuddered and leaped from row to row. Burning flakes dropped from exploding bamboo onto the cane, igniting new sections. Fluttering crimson tassels rose into the night sky. Entire columns burst into flames simultaneously, creating a wall of drumming heat so suffocating that Jeeves had to cover his face. He gasped for air and swam through the waves of fire. The blades of the windmill were spinning slowly from the heat-generated wind. Bats, confused by the fusillades popping and shooting over the blades, were flying wildly above the tower. One dropped onto the ground. Another bumped against his head. He ducked and fell on the hot concrete. He stumbled up and braced against the doorway before he entered.

Huzaifa was waiting on the porch. "You have him?" He touched the old man's hand and sprang back. "Aah aah." Jeeves took his father inside and gently lowered him onto the couch. "He didn't get burnup. Was the smoke that get him. Just last night he tell me about a new plan."

Jeeves noticed Huzaifa's hand trembling as he gently touched Narpat's torn and blackened shirt. Huzaifa walked to the chair at the corner of the porch, where he had always sat while listening to Narpat. He began to cry.

Jeeves stood over his father for an hour or so. Someone walked up the front steps, entered the house, and stood behind him. Another came, gazed at the body, and went to Huzaifa. Jeeves heard other footsteps and whispered conversation. He went to his father's bedroom and retrieved from the old dresser one of his mother's embroidered handkerchiefs. He wiped away the ash from his father's face and arms.

By the early morning, a small crowd had gathered. Kumkaran said, "He was the last of the apostles." Janak said, "Agree or disagree with him, he always speak his mind." Premsingh said, "He was a fighter. Nobody else like him." The Manager wept openly. "Just last night I was talking to meself and I say, 'You know something, Manager? Something bad going to happen. I just know it. The goat gone and dead this very said morning.'"

Interspersed with the testimonies were whispers about the cause of the fire. The rotating blades had created a draft that had overturned the gas lamp. Narpat had set the fire himself. The Outsiders were involved. Some of the villagers glanced at the sobbing Manager and thought: *I wouldn't put it past that Sookdeo.*

Kala kept her vow and did not return for the funeral. Her only visit to Trinidad was four years after her father's death. She stayed at Chandra's house and was remote and distant throughout. She was noncommital during Ray's jokes about fixing up for America and during Chandra's nasal rejoinder, "You think the American government want a drunkard with a fat wife and four children." Chandra had resigned from the post office to tend to her stream of children. She had grown fatter and carried her weight like a much older woman, walking with measured slowness and breathing heavily. She complained ceaselessly about her husband leaving her for a more attractive woman.

During one of the couple's bantering arguments, Kala said, "I'd like to return this weekend."

"What happen, girl? Like this little house too small for you?"

"I tell you she shoulda stay in one of them fancy Hilton-schmilton hotel in Port of Spain."

His laughter drew out Radhica from her room. Her grandchildren shouted in taunting children's voices, "Draggy! Draggy!"

She pointed a wizened finger at Chandra. "You! You teach them to call me Draggy. We will see who will drag longer."

Ray said jovially, "You think you could get this excitement in Hilton-schmilton? Or in America?"

She returned to America without seeing Sushilla. She had displayed little interest when Chandra had mentioned that Sushilla's ashram had folded following an accusation against the guru by a plump middle-aged woman. Sushilla had said of the guru, "He working his own way toward salvation. It will just take a little longer." Her own path took her to a newly formed Christian evangelical sect that distributed pamphlets to unsuspecting country dwellers.

Jeeves saw Kala the night before she left. She was sitting on a wrought-iron chair beside a potted dracaena. He asked about her visit. She talked of North Carolina. He stared at the dracaena's red leaves hanging like lolling tongues. His mother had placed an almanac of a fearsome Hindu deity with her tongue hanging out at the side of Carnegie. His father had often commented on the almanac, "How you could love something that you fear," and Jeeves had agreed because the picture of the deity had deterred him from rifling through the books on Carnegie. He suspected that was his mother's motive.

Kala spoke of her job at the university, which took her into vast forests. She mentioned the trees there. Redwood. Fir. Pine. Jeeves remembered a card of many years past with a desolate snow-covered cottage. His sister grew silent as if she were thinking of these measureless forests.

Kala left on the first Saturday of her visit. The only taxi available at such short notice was Janak's. He was glad for the job because most of the time his Austin Cambridge was parked at the taxi stand in Princes Town, and it was only when the other cabs were filled that he would get a solitary passenger upon whom he would unfold all his morose views on the island's modernization. He would talk of the new wealth and the accompanying crime and mention Narpat's construction of the factory and the old village council meetings and the trip to Whitehall as the good old days. He clucked laconically whenever he passed an abandoned cane-field. Occasionally Huzaifa rode with him, and both men reminisced silently, shaking their heads and sighing. Although Huzaifa had retired from the bookstore, he escaped regularly to Princes Town with the excuse he was working on "a commission." He was as thrilled with the lie as he was by the other acts of mutiny he committed around the house. When his son, then his wife, joined a fundamentalist Muslim group, he had been overjoyed because it meant they would be away more often, but each week some new decree was insidiously leveled on the household by Salima. Huzaifa secretly broke all these rules and gradually he began to see himself as a saboteur. The word excited him. He encouraged his family to leave for a hajj to Mecca, hoping they would not return. With Janak, he spoke of building a rice mill and constructing a school for nonfundamentalist Muslim girls. He imagined the girls addressing him as "Teacherji" while he sipped Darjeeling tea from a fine teacup, as a bookworm and aristocrat would.

During the trip to the Piarco airport, Janak spoke with stiff affection of Narpat and the other old villagers who had passed away. Typically, disquiet displaced nostalgia as he compared the careening progress to a slowly spreading plague. But he must have been disturbed too by his passenger's silence or perhaps by the way she gazed out uninterestedly, her composure threatened neither by the massive new mansions reputedly built by drug lords nor by the settlements of flimsy cardboard and aluminum shacks. Soon after they passed the sugar mill at Usine, he decided to keep his views to himself. Her only words during the entire trip were spoken as they passed the upper-class enclave of Valsayn, with houses of eclectic and inventive architecture: "Imported slums."

The week after her departure Bhola came into the projection room where Jeeves was peering above the projector, streams of light reflected on his face. "I hear your sister come down. She visit?"

Jeeves noticed that even in the gloomy room, his uncle was wearing his dark glasses. "She was only here for a week."

"Prutti coming from the States for the Ramayana. She was here last year too." Ever since the initial diagnosis and the worsening of his diabetes, Bhola, on the advice of several pundits, had held annual Ramayanas and kathas. But he still drank heavily and oscillated between moments of curious religiosity and bouts of drunken vulgarity. He had prospered from the oil boom. He had bought the nearby cinema at Tramline street, which showed only Indian movies, and soon after, another truck. Dr. Who operated the other cinema, and Jeeves the original. Occasionally Bhola still spoke to Jeeves as to a young boy. He pinched his shoulders and whispered rude comments about Samdaye.

In the nights Jeeves still saw Mr. Doon floundering to his house. Success had not erased his general displeasure, and he frequently conveyed his frustration at teaching in the now-derelict school, to Jeeves. "Do you know what happened a few days ago, buddy? Some of the children fainted from the turpentine fumes, and now all the parents are saying the school is haunted. Bitches!" Jeeves remembered when oilsand had been layered over the schoolyard and he had walked home with globs of it on his shoes. He wondered whether Mr. Doon, in his perpetual alcoholic haze, recalled his early days, when he had regularly spouted poetry to the confused children; whether he recognized Danny from the short newspaper article that had mentioned his murder as one of three that day, the corpse, marked with cuts and stabs, found near a manhole. Did he make out Quashie in the local newscast, *Panorama*, wearing the uniform of the paramilitary outfit The Flying Squad, his arms loose, one foot before the other, standing before a dead drug runner or an arms cache? But Mr. Doon diverted frequently to Canada or mentioned his problems with his father-in-law, his wife, his sons, and the bookstores. Often he would splice in a quotation from his book, *The Dialogue of Doubt*.

His publishing success was quite unexpected, and he owed it to his wife's habit of rebuffing his drunken advances and his tipsy forays into the Brahmin's old stockroom. One night, he stumbled across the Brahmin's incomplete manuscript, *Interpreting the Signs: Conversations Between a Guru and an Acolyte*. If he had been sober, he would have thrown it away immediately, but drunkenness showed him its local potential. He followed the Brahmin's premise, but his writer's instinct seeped into the dialogue. He added flourishing descriptions and enterprising dialogue. For instance, he had the guru request of his acolyte: What do you see when you gaze at me? What are my physical attributes? And the acolyte painstakingly described all his features. The population lapped up the book; it had been an immediate best-seller. Domestic, religious, and medical problems were brought to him in the bars. The drunkards called him Dr. Doon.

The Manager demanded rent for the downstairs apartment. "Teach, is five years now you living in this nice apartment, and I never yet ask you for a rent. I know you had you dreamsanhopes, Teach, but now you gone and write this big best-seller, is only proper you pay a little rent. Just last night I was talking to meself, and I say, 'You know something, Manager? Is not *me* people will condemn but *he*.' Is only rightandproper."

Mr. Doon explained his difficulties in collecting royalties from the leeches who owned the bookstores. He mentally drafted his next book, *Dialogue with a Bloodsucking Bitch*. He threatened his wife with returning to Canada. She told him he'd better return to his poor old mother in Cocoyea. That drove him to an incoherent rage. Harridans and termagants, he screeched. He hated Cecilia Arjoonsingh, the woman who had moved into the Manager's house and who he suspected was really responsible for the rent issue. He listened to her nagging the Manager upstairs and noted his father-in-law's now-spotless clothing, his dyed hair, his clean shoes. He was satisfied by the Manager's harassed look, and he suspected he was missing the pleasures of his dirty, disorganized life. "The bitch sucking him out," he told Kamini. "Why you think she move in with him? Because of his sophistication and erudition? Is because the bitch noticed all the money he making from bribes and kickbacks."

"At least he is making money. Where all the money you make from writing that big book, you thief? Why you don't build your own house with it? Eh, Dr. Doon?"

To which he would scream, "You don't build anything on a boat. Why bother?"

Narpat's boarding school for girls was eventually built, but as in every instance of accomplishment on the island, progress was closely allied with treachery. The Manager had cut the ribbon and delivered a speech crafted by Kamini. He spoke of the difficulties he encountered and his own undying dedication to its construction. In reality, its construction had been easy. The property had gone to the government because Narpat— like his father—had not written a will. The Manager used his political contacts. The old factory walls were used. The roof was painted a bright red. The tower was expanded into a parlor. Iced drinks and lollipops and snow cones and pickled fruits were sold by Cecilia. For a while, the Manager contemplated constructing a statue of himself in the playground.

Jeeves had gone to the function, where he'd met Chandra and Sushilla. He had not seen his youngest sister for more than a year and was surprised at how much she had changed. The smile was still there, but she had given up the pretense that it reflected an inner peace; her face was thinner than he remembered, and her eyes, once so lively, seemed drained of life. Chandra, better dressed, was sweating and edgy. She daubed the folds beneath her neck with a handkerchief, leaving trails of powder. "You know what today is? Today make it exactly six years since Mammy pass away."

"Really?" Sushilla bent her head and stared at her old rubber slippers. When she looked up, she seemed satisfied, and Jeeves wondered at the connection that had momentarily satisfied his sister.

When Chandra began complaining about her children, Sushilla listened silently, her face frozen once more. Ray came up with two little girls. He greeted Jeeves and told his wife, "Keep these children with you. I going for a little spin down the road."

"Try not to smoke out the entire ganja field." Chandra began to comment on her girls' looks. They got their broad noses and small eyes from their father. Her voice held none of the old playfulness. She tugged her youngest daughter roughly. "Stop pushing out your lip like your grandmother." She complained about the heat and about her stomach. Jeeves felt the complaints were foils to Radhica's "rumatism."

The Manager's voice, over the loudspeaker, sounded strained and breathless. He quoted with long pauses from *Open Spirit* by Boros and mentioned his good fortune in securing Kevin Arjoonsingh as the principal of the girls' boarding school.

When Jeeves walked away, Chandra was complaining about her children and Sushilla was staring at her slippers. He walked past the colorfully dressed villagers until he caught the familiar fragrance of rotting hogplums. The root of the tree, exposed through steady erosion, wormed through scattered beds of tiny purple plants with nipple-shaped flowers. Epiphytes with variegated bulbous stalks clung to the scarred trunk and to the creased branches and the thick vines rooting between the purple plants. Peeping through the epiphytes were wild orchids with brilliant crimson and pink flowers. The pendulous nests of cornbirds swung from the topmost branches. And at the brink of the chattering crowd, Jeeves saw the scene first as a lingering movie shot, then as a postcard, and finally as a painting from his *West Indian Reader*. A title for the painting came to him: *Lovely Decay*.

The sugarcane field was now a tangle of spindly weeds and paragrass. Solitary, defiant tassels waved above the wild grasses in a few spots. Inside the tangle, Jeeves knew, were ravines with crystal-clear water and guppies flitting over mossy rocks. A cornbird flapped out from the immortelle.

The sails of the windmill were turning slowly. They were decorated with flowing crepe paper, which left the illusion of streaming, blurred shapes as they trailed and floated. Inside, Cecilia was selling snow cones and iced drinks from a cooler. Children squirmed and escaped from their parents. The Manager finally finished his speech. A record was being played. Closer, Jeeves heard the chink of coins. Each chink sounded like an interruption in the song, as if the needle had bumped over a scratch. He closed his eyes. *A fierce fire raging around him. Bats flapping crazily and dropping from the heat. Wild drifts of smoke blowing from every direction. An old man, his cane on the ground, hopping and dancing and losing his balance. Stumbling up, his arms stretched as if he were about to take flight. Choking out the words, "You come . . . you come for me," before he collapsed on the young man. The young man hoisting and cradling his father in his arms, surprised at the lightness of his body. Stumbling out into a sea of smoke. Closing his eyes and gauging the path from its pebbles and boulders. Guided too by the aroma of roasting hogplums. Running to his house. Dimly aware of shouted questions from neighbors. Laying his father's body on the couch. Gently closing his vacant eyes. Standing over the body with Huzaifa.*

"The bitches have already set up shop." Jeeves opened his eyes and saw Mr. Doon. "Boarding school for girls. What they should call it is money-making factory run by leeches." He glanced at Cecilia. "Bloody termagants."

"What is that?" Jeeves asked distractedly of the word used so often by Mr. Doon.

"You will find out as soon as you're married, buddy. Trust me."

EPILOGUE

Seven months after the function, Jeeves met the girl he was to eventually marry. Her name was Angela, and she had moved in with her aunt, a Portuguese shopkeeper in Princes Town, after the death of her mother. The girl was tall and slim, and Jeeves noticed how uncomfortable she seemed at the cash register, enclosed by a wire guard from the shoving, rummaging crowd in the store. It was this uneasiness that caught his attention. She had glanced at him too, standing apart from the shouting, and a few days later she had spotted him beneath Woolworth, again by himself. He came soon after to her aunt's store and pretended he was examining a dusty musical box that had lain on its shelf since the shop opened. When he brought the box to her, he avoided her eyes. His shyness made her mischievous. She had never spoken to the customers other than to explain the cost of some item. "I saw you the other day."

"Yes."

"Were you waiting for a taxi?"

"Not really."

"Not really? Do you live around here then?" She felt like giggling.

"In Lengua."

"Where's that?" Before he could answer, she added, "And you could look at me now."

He glanced up and met her smile. "A short distance away. Do you work here?" When he realized how silly his question was, he said, "I work at the cinema."

"Really?" She didn't know what else she could have said.

"Yes."

"What do you do there?"

A fat woman in a ruffled floral dress just behind Jeeves said loudly, "I thought I did come to a shop. I didn't know I did come to a lovers' lane."

The girl reddened. Jeeves collected his change. "You can come and see if you like."

Jeeves felt that every date would be their last because there was no common ground to keep them together, but soon they began meeting every night. Although she was not normally talkative, she spoke at length of her high school, St. Augustine Girls, about her father who had died when she was eight, and her mother, less than a year ago. When both parents were alive, the family had explored the bird trail at Mount St. Benedict's, and the rivers flowing from the mountain into the Caura valley, and the bird sanctuary at the Caroni swamp to which scarlet ibises and flamingoes migrated each year. And soon Jeeves saw these places with her. At Mount St. Benedict's, he saw the island falling away, the confusion from a distance confined to the squares of housing settlements and the circles of the canefields. He felt the cool mountain air on his face and the aroma of cinnamon from a secluded tea shop almost at the top of the mountain. At the Caura valley the only sounds were the creaking of bamboo gliding against one another and the trickle of water. Each sound echoed, the echoes softened by the hills and the tall trees and splintering into little gasps and gurgles. On the way back he gazed at the cocoa trees in the shade of the immortelle, and the plump christophene trailing up the bamboo. The gloomy bird sanctuary with its desolate mangrove and the shrill cry of birds seemed like a place from a movie, a place to which an old prospector might have retired.

Each of these places evoked some memory for Angela, but Jeeves, witnessing these spots for the first time, was astonished that in this island there could be areas of such perfect tranquility. One evening at the Caura valley, he told Angela, "A man could live here and be separate from—"

"The commess," she said lightly, having heard him use the word so often.

After a while he said, "A man and a woman."

When Jeeves told Bhola of his intended move to Arima, his uncle said, "Use to pass through there to the quarry with my truck. Boring little place. One setta church and river and thing. Old house too with them obzokee jalousie and them heavy window."

The house Jeeves rented from Angela's aunt and that he and Angela later purchased was a two-bedroom stone flat with a red corrugated-metal roof. On both sides of the driveway were dwarf palms with clusters of pale green nuts. At the base of the trees, wild anthuriums twisted into one another like bewildered birds. The house's interior was simple and uncluttered. Most of the furniture was wicker. On the window ledges were trinkets that Angela had brought from the store in Princes Town. The sides of the house were spotted with hydrangea bushes, and at the back, sloping up a hill, were coconut trees sheltering wispy heliconias with yellow yawing flowers. A rococo cast-iron bench faced the coconut trees. The couple spent two months painting and redecorating, and during that time Angela got a job at the Barclay's bank, and a short while later, Jeeves began working as a projector operator at Monarch cinema.

Alone in the dark projector room, smelling of overheated filaments and old plastic, Jeeves watched the beam, corrugated with smoke, streaming through the aperture, the light congealing on the mildewed white screen, the colors coalescing into vast landscapes with men and women fighting and making love and chasing some dream. Sometimes he recalled other stories, about dyed jackals, and families of foxes, and monkeys decorated with rubies and emeralds.

When he stepped into the house after work, he would smell the preserved guavas and plums that Angela had set in small decorative jars. About half an hour later Angela would look through the jalousie at her husband staring at the dim lights on the mountain, and after a few minutes she would dry her hands and join him. Once she had asked him what was so interesting about the view, and he told her instead a story about a man who had promised to protect the thing dearest to him.

"His wife?" Angela had asked.

A piece of land, he thought. But he could not tell her that.

Each evening they came to the bench—the Pavilion, Jeeves called it—with its view of the Northern Range in the distance. They would remain there until the night breeze grew too cold. Before they returned to the house, Angela would gently press him for a trip to Bucco Reef at Tobago or a gathering with her old friends. He would pause as if thinking seriously before he agreed. And she would smile and take his hands because, although she was still getting to know him, she realized that he always kept his word.

ACKNOWLEDGMENTS

I am grateful to my agent, Hilary McMahon, for her faith and encouragement. I am also grateful to my editors, Diane Martin of Knopf Canada and Ayesha Pande of Farrar, Straus and Giroux, for their guidance, patience, and instinct.

This book was made possible through the financial support of the Ontario Arts Council and the Canada Council for the Arts.